Staring at the Light

Also by Frances Fyfield

A Question of Guilt
Shadows on the Mirror
Trial by Fire
Deep Sleep
Shadow Play
Perfectly Pure and Good
A Clear Conscience
Without Consent
Blind Date

and writing as Frances Hegarty

The Playroom
Half Light
Let's Dance

Staring at The Light

 *Frances Fyfield* 

ALFRED A. KNOPF CANADA

PUBLISHED BY ALFRED A. KNOPF CANADA

 Published in Canada by Alfred A. Knopf Canada, a division of Random House of Canada Limited, Toronto, in 1999, and simultaneously in the United States by Penguin Putnam Inc., New York. Distributed by Random House of Canada Limited, Toronto.

Canadian Cataloguing in Publication Data

Fyfield, Frances
Staring at the light

ISBN 0-676-97244-6

I. Title.

PR6056.Y47S72 1999 823'.914 C99-931133-6

First Canadian Edition

Printed and bound in the United States of America

10 9 8 7 6 5 4 3 2 1

To Gill Coleridge and Esther Newberg,
with love and thanks.

ACKNOWLEDGMENTS

I could not have written this novel without assistance in the research. All those mentioned below had the grace to hide their incredulity at my ignorance and they combined to dispel the lingering myth in my own mind that those with a scientific bent might be *dull.* Particular thanks to Leslie Payne, BDS LDC DMCC, and to Janet Payne for allowing me to glimpse the sharp end of dental practice, and also for access to Leslie's unique library and network. If either of you should ever read this book, you will recognize some of the scenery. Thanks also to the memorably kind Elisabeth Allen, who set me on the right track, and to Dr. Norman Mills, who got to the root canal of the matter, gave me good ideas and provoked me to write this in the first place. Otherwise I could never have paid the fees. Thanks also to Howard Hersch and to Greg Woolgar, and finally to Peter Gurney, MBE, ex-Chief of the Metropolitan Bomb Disposal Squad, for the clarity of his explanations and the infectious quality of his laughter. Between you all, you manage to prove that there is more courage in so-called ordinary life than fiction could ever allow.

Staring at the Light

PROLOGUE

Guy Fawkes favoured gunpowder because that was what he knew. An artist, after his fashion.

It had been an exceptionally mild autumn after a wet summer. Winter was not quite real yet, although Sarah Fortune never did think it became quite real in the metropolis. They were all cocooned here, benefiting from body heat and the borrowed warmth of buildings. London was made for winter, became a garment all by itself.

Here and now, in one corner of it, comfort clothing was the order of the evening. Bonfire Night was hardly an occasion for style, especially since the entrances to the park were marked with notices exhorting crowds to beware of pickpockets who would take advantage of the dark and the distraction of lights. There were anoraks and wool jackets, and shoes dirty from muddy grass. A kindly mist had covered the day's preparations. The witnesses from the gracious crescent of late-Victorian houses had been unable to spy from the windows exactly what had been done out there to make the monster bonfire from dry, eco-friendly rubbish and set up the fireworks in the cold, all of it surrounded by sufficient mystery to cause anxiety. The mist, not quite a fog, had been enough to obscure it by daylight, and if it had continued, no one would have seen with quite the full splendour the extent of the council's generosity in the form of the annual firework display. This would have been a cheat.

The locals to the park scorned the event, complained and campaigned about it, and yet felt unable to resist. The crowds gathered. Gradually, the inhabitants of the crescent began to emerge. Their children insisted. Watching a bonfire from the front windows was not the same: you had to watch it with the crowd; feel it, fear it slightly; observe with watering eyes. The annual protests against the use of the park, the crowds, the racket, the drunken bums, the mini fairground and the thieves had given way first to grudging acceptance, then to excitement.

In the interests of the liberalism that persisted among the local worthies, there would be no ritualistic burning of an effigy of Guy Fawkes. The man had flair, but he had been found out. He had only tried to blow up Parliament, no more, no less—a perfectly respectable ambition after all: an almost unbroken succession of persons had been trying to do it by one means or another ever since, although none of them had been publicly eviscerated. Sissy Mallison, from number fifteen, told her daughter to stop moaning about the absence of a Guy Fawkes to throw on the fire. It was an emblem of hate, she said, perfectly barbaric; you would loathe it if you saw it. It is obscene to burn the effigy of a once live man and watch his limbs curl in the blaze; even dogs go mad and bark at such a thing.

I want one, said the child. We had one last year at Mary's house; it was great.

Mary was a little swine. Mary's family are a bunch of heathens, was all Sissy could say. Roman Catholics never burn Guy Fawkes: he was one of us. Out of spite, there had been a local movement, which Sissy declined to discuss, that perhaps there *should* be some sort of dummy to burn. Any unpopular figure would do. There seemed to be a strange sort of yearning for that sort of sacrifice. The child submitted to hat and scarf, whingeing.

There was an urge to feel the fire; it was imperative to stand near, or at the very least in sight of flushed faces. There was a general settling down after the first, paraffin-induced roar from the edifice of planks and branches. A *whoosh* fit to satisfy the soul of an arsonist, into which category Sarah Fortune put most children and many others of the population. A cheer, a few screams of delight and a few squawks of alarm, until it died down to a steady crackle. Then the fireworks began.

They sounded to William like a series of bizarre bodily functions but, then, William had always supposed he had little imagination, which, such as it was, extended over fifty-two years and tended towards the basic. He had been a mere youth when he had wanted to be a painter. If you closed your eyes, which was, of course, *not* the object of the exercise, all you could hear, he told an imaginary companion, was a series of dramatic burps and farts. A *pimph, a pamph, a tiddly pamph, a cushion creeper and a tear-arse.* A cracking groan of sound with the major rockets (rumoured to cost a hundred each: he was glad he did not live in this borough); a sigh of desperation, like a dyspeptic hiccup, when the multicoloured stars burst forth towards the end, falling to earth in a whine of relief. The colours blinded him, the fumes sickened him, so he concentrated on the sound. He had missed the person he had come to meet: he was always losing things.

Superficial observation revealed that some of the crowd were drunk, in contrast to the quiet and respectful parents, clutching children and instructing them in science. Then there were the semi-adult kids, and the self-grouping gangs of men and youths who formed their own momentum, chanting, *We WANT a guy, WE want a GUY*, or was it *WE WANT GUY*? William wasn't sure, and was equally unsure that it made any difference what the hell they wanted, apart from the sensation of power from making a noise.

The display ended with a setpiece of gigantic proportions. I wonder what *that* cost? he heard someone murmur, wondering to himself, mourning his own prosaic tendency even to think of what kind of a noise it would make, or if it would reveal a message in the sky. And, if so, what it would say. *Phoomphh, phoomph, woof, woof, wooof!* It filled the firmament with rebellious sound. *Pshaw, shaw*, screamed the lesser starbursts, which went on and on and on, *crick, crack, crick*, another and yet another, louder than the OOHS! and AAHS! below, before the last of it fell to earth. There was another sigh, almost of anger, as the light went out of the sky. While the sparks fell, he could see the crowd as a picture, all those faces, upward-turned and vulnerable with hope, still wanting more. Anticlimax; dull with wonder.

They seemed at first oblivious to the greatest sound of all. A huge

WHOOMPH. An air-sucking, ground-sucking *WHOOMPH,* which made him tremble. No one seemed to notice it. It was part of the spectacular effect, and it was only he who had been listening for sounds alone, keeping his eyes shut half the time.

And then, gradually, the crowd began to turn. Not the group who resumed the chant, *GUY, GUY, WE WANT GUY, WANNA GUY, WANNA GUY,* oblivious of anything but their own momentum, but the others, children first, readier to abandon one sensation for the next, little feet better able to feel the trembling of the earth. His section of the crowd, the one safely away from the heat of the fire, those who had most carefully chosen an avenue of escape, began to flutter and mutter and turn their collective head. He thought of a hydra, a single creature of many heads, turning simultaneously, uncertain of the direction to follow. Finally, there was selective comprehension.

The last house in the crescent, the biggest and the best, was collapsing in front of their eyes. The windows spat at them, pane by pane, a small distraction of smashing glass. As if by some magic trick, part of the roof crumbled out of sight. Like mother and child, locked in some ghastly embrace, the walls disappeared inside themselves with a shudder. There were no flames shouting for attention, simply an ominous, gut-churning rumble as debris fell. After the fireworks, it was curiously discreet. They were mesmerized, puzzled, as William was, but, all the same, he felt an obscure desire to cheer.

Some of those around him wanted to break ranks and run, but they waited, still unsure whether this was merely an extra spectacle. Others simply did not notice. Many people were transfixed in the act of chewing—bonfire toffee, hot dogs and beefburgers—while their pockets were picked. The crowd near the fire, kept back with increasing desperation by the guardians of the blaze (*We believe in safety first! Please stand back!*), still chanted, WE WANT GUY! The fire gave a ritual groan, settling itself with a sigh.

One section of the audience watched the house come down. There was a tendency to laugh, as if the whole thing were a pantomine, while a few began to move uneasily. William was with them, until he stopped and turned back towards the fire without the slightest knowledge why.

WE WANNA GUY! William closed his eyes, registered the pull in the opposite direction, shuffling movement on the periphery nearest the collapsing house; while, close to the fire, the chant went on. A central group of young men, disparate sizes and shapes, was hauling a carcass towards the blaze. A low-slung, dead-asleep body, peculiarly weightless, held between six sets of hands, swinging. William started towards it, yelling, *Noo*, no, no, screaming at the top volume of his lungs, listening to his steps and still screaming as he pushed through a crowd hell bent on the opposite direction. He was as heavy as the oldest, as inept as the suddenly screaming children; he was aware of the barking of dogs and he was too late. The band swung their figure, in a strangely disciplined fashion, on to the fire. *ONE, TWO, THREE! Yeah! Burn, you bugger, BURN!*

He shrieked. He pushed his way through, found himself yelling again without hearing an echo. And then standing there, a complete and helpless fool, as the thing landed on the embers of the fire. It curled into a phantom of itself. A corpse of packing material, foam and chips, dying painlessly in an instant of grotesque, twisted disfigurement. Those who had thrown it paused, the laughter and the chant quiet now. Someone tried to whip up fervour by a cheer, but that, too, died.

Then, across his line of vision, hurtling from the direction of the crescent, came a small, round figure, moving with a strange progress. A man, running with his hands above his head, holding a piece of paper, which he tore in half. The hands were gloved. The man ran all the way round the circumference of the fire. "Have it, Johnny!" he was shrieking. "Have it all!" His voice was high and feminine, muffled by the scarf round his face. The dummy curled and melted, intensifying the heat. Then the man stopped moving, his hands empty, still raised above his head. Turned and faced the fire. Ran towards it, howling.

William knew what the man was going to do; felt as if he had known as soon as he saw him. He was, obviously, going to throw himself on to the fire. It was a conclusion that followed a shameful thought, which had crossed his mind far earlier in the evening, an idle thought: what would he do if he was ever called upon to rescue someone who was burning? What would he do? Something or nothing? Would he take the ignoble course and stand back, because his own soft and flexible hands were far too precious to risk?

He watched with horror. There was nothing to be seen but the strange little man, vaguely familiar and silhouetted against the fire, as if everyone else had disappeared. The man was already exhausted by his own screaming: he shuffled towards the fire rather than sprinted. He was measuring the distance for a final leap into the flames, and all William could do was watch, paralysed. Until another figure entered, stage left, cannoning head-first into the running figure, butting him in the hip, bringing him down, clasping him round the middle, just as his extended hands reached the flames. Then there were two figures, locked in an unholy embrace, rolling together on the hot, ashy ground and snarling like fighting dogs.

Then others closed in on them. William heard only a shrill cry above the rest. He could not distinguish if it was anger or pain.

He felt sick in the knowledge that his hands were safe.

He walked two or three steps backwards, repelled, yet drawn. Turned away, finally. There was the ominous sound of sirens. The house at the end of the crescent was no longer a house.

Breeze blew the litter over the park among stampeding feet. When William looked for the very last time, the fire stood alone and deserted. The raised arm of the carcass waved a last valediction.

No harm done. A joke. But he thought he knew who they were, that grappling pair. Two people who had touched his life and threatened to engulf it, like the flames. He must be wrong: he was often slow to recognise faces, even those he knew best. A piece of torn paper teased at his feet. He picked it up idly, because he was tidy, read a line of clumsy writing.

> *OK, lover, I'll make you a deal. You've hidden her for three months, clever boy. Now how did you manage that? She'll change, you know; they all do. And your friends will change, because we have no real friends; we never did . . . Let's play the game for one more month . . . I can't go on for ever . . .*

He felt like an eavesdropper, even more than he had just felt like a voyeur. He dropped the torn sheet into a bin and went home.

PART ONE

1

There was never enough light in late November, not even in the morning. She lay, brownly naked, sprawled in a huge armchair upholstered three decades since in cherry cotton, now a dull colour of rust, rumpled and torn in places. She looked as if she had been flung into it by an almighty force, then shoved down and left, stunned and broken. Her buttocks were sunk into the cushion, one arm behind her head supporting a mass of red hair, which was pulled half over her face. A hand extended itself beyond the hair to clutch the back of the upholstery, the fingers plucking at the frayed fabric. It played on his conscience, this endless, distressful movement of her long fingers, as if she was copying him. He had been so busy with his fingers. Delving, stroking, stirring. They were fat, broad fingers, he had, poking out of swollen, ugly fists.

The breasts were smaller than he liked, rather languid things resting against her ribcage as she lay in the hair with her torso twisted, the legs splayed over the arm of the crooked chair, ankles close, feet arched. An auburn bush exposed. Her left hand lay above her cleft, as if to protect it. Too late: his eyes had seen, his fingers explored, greedy, greedy, greedy, and his hands were still steady. Not like hers. She was touching herself, almost absentmindedly, one finger twisting a small clump of that abundant pubic hair into a tight curl. He imagined the bush decked with ribbons. Apart from these minute movements of the hands, she was perfectly still. A woman satiated by every kind of abuse it was within his talent to inflict. Her mouth was slightly open. Breathing deeply, blowing away a wisp of her thick red hair.

He almost regretted what he had done to her. She looked so exquisitely helpless. So pliant, so biddable, so deliciously responsive to commands. Nothing about her was beyond imagination, and still her fingers kept moving piteously. She was *willing,* he told himself angrily; she asked for it. Look at the way she lay now. Wide open. Trusting. He was the mere beast to her beauty. She had *asked* for it.

It was a room that cried out for devotion and expertise to make it into something of habitable beauty, although that was a matter of indifference to him. The air was damply warm, condensation streaming down the ceiling windows, dripping now and then, somewhere. He wore gloves and a scarf. When the heat rose from him, the scarf began to smell like an old bandage, with overtones of turpentine, antiseptic and sweat. His nose was red, adding to the melancholy of his features. There was misty, diffused light; still the brightest light of the day. It was his torture chamber, decorated with his triumphs and disappointments.

He smiled now. His face rearranged itself from one set of folds into another, reminiscent of someone pulling up a set of ruched curtains to let in the sunlight. When he was serious he looked like an idiot, with a chin that seemed to reach his chest, but as soon as he grinned there was a massive rearrangement of everything: his furrowed forehead seemed to disappear into his hairline, his dark eyes were almost lost, and he seemed like a rumpled boy. The volume of hair made his head look overlarge for his thin shoulders. When he smiled, he looked perfectly, malevolently mad. Which, in his sober moments, in this room, with his bed in the corner, he knew he was. One had to be mad to inflict this abuse. He felt wretchedly older than his thirty-three years. Such cruelty pained him. At the least, the very least, he should have tried his hard-earned domesticity and offered her coffee. Dreadful coffee, but still a gesture towards hospitality.

"Are you cold?" he asked. "I mustn't let you get cold. Must I?"

"No. But I have to move. Dammit, I can't move."

But she did move, cautiously. Leaning forward, the torso twisting in a way that made him wince, she reached for a packet of cigarettes that lay in the ashtray on the footstool beside the chair. Lit one, inhaled and put it back in the ashtray. Then she stretched out one leg and clasped the toes, extended it fully, grasped the calf with both ankles and stretched the whole limb, still in the chair, until her foot was level with her ear.

"What do you mean, you can't move? What do you call *that?*"

"I mean I can't stand up. Until I've done this." She grasped the other leg, held it with both hands behind the knee, straightened it. There was a small *crick*. Then she swung her feet on to the floor, raised herself on tiptoe and stretched. Thinner than he liked. As unselfconscious as a cat.

The shifting of the tableau and the moving of the image saddened him. Sarah Fortune was the perfect model. No vanity. She was a perfect piece of design, and his fingers were tired with the painting of her.

"Let me see," she asked, moving towards him with the cigarette in hand.

"No!" He was shrill. "And don't come near me with that thing. It makes me want one, and I shouldn't."

"Pooh. I don't know why you think of it. You could do with a few more antiseptic cigarettes. Every single bloody thing you do is bad for your health. But I won't look if you don't want."

"Not yet, please. I'm ashamed of it."

He shielded the canvas with his body, not trusting her, quite, although in his way he trusted her absolutely. She had that effect: she was natural and warm and generous to a fault, but the habits of mistrust were so deeply ingrained in him that they had become the natural response. Just like his shuffling walk, like a man avoiding the middle of the pavement and clinging to doorways, always looking for shadow. She had long since supposed that he had always been a little like that. It was not merely a response to his current circumstances. He would always have looked far older than he was, even as a boy; over-matured and slightly shifty, even in his innocence. He was still innocent now or, more aptly, a man who had never mastered the social code that governed the rules, constantly, almost childishly, uncertain.

"Do you know," he said, with more than usual animation, "that you have one leg longer than the other? At least, you do in my version of you. I shall call it *Miss Sarah Fortune With Unequal Legs.*"

"No," Sarah said. "I never knew I had one leg longer than the other. But thank you for telling me. I shall have to amend the way I walk. Do you know what time it is? We're going to be late."

"Late? Does it matter?" Cannon had a limited view of what mattered.

She was pulling on her clothes, retrieving them from the three-legged chair over which they were draped, neatly, as if they were important, which, as she smoothed on the dark tights, fastened a bra of white lace, buttoned the tiny pearl-coloured buttons of her blouse, he had to suppose they were: they turned her into something else entirely. No suit of clothes had ever done that for him. He sat down, weak with fascination. *I used to be a tart,* she had told him, long since. *Still am, but more of a hobby.* Naked, he could imagine that; when she was clothed, he could not. A tart with a heart. Sarah Fortune seemed to know about love: she gave it briskly and unstintingly. But, judging from the state of her body, she was also familiar with brutality.

"I don't suppose it matters in the long run," she was saying, "about being late. But it does create a poor impression. And it's bad manners. Have you got any other clothes? Something cleaner?"

The question surprised him. It was totally irrelevant to anything in his mind. He was watching the slow transformation of naked girl into woman. She brushed her hair and tied it back, shrugged on the jacket of the suit, reached for her fawn raincoat and the tidy leather briefcase. A set of innocent-looking pearls gleamed round her neck. The small nuggets of gold in her ears had never come off. He plucked the single daisy from the milk bottle in which it resided and handed it to her, hoping to make amends for the lack of hospitality, which shamed him even here.

"Thank you. How kind. On second thought," she said, "you're best off to show yourself exactly as you are. Only you'd better wear the coat that smells of smoke. Then no one will want to come near you."

He smiled. Then the face fell back into its bloodhound folds. "Not many people *do* want to come near me," he said matter-of-factly.

She patted his shoulder, ruffled his hair and planted a kiss on his cheek. "Hardly surprising, is it?" she said. "You snarling the way you do. Come on, now." She paused. "I'm forgetting the most important thing of all. Have you still got his letter? The bits you have left?"

He nodded, plundered the pocket of the coat to pull out a charred half-sheet of paper, badly crumpled.

"You were crazy to tear it up," she said. "I'll keep it, shall I?"

"I'm crazy full stop."

"Does he mean what he says?"

"Yes. Even Johnny has rules. Even Johnny has to set limits."

The day outside was cold and raw. He pulled the odoriferous scarf round his face and shoved his hands inside his pockets. They throbbed and hurt, but the pain, the glorious pain of them, was a comfort. It meant that they were functioning. He followed her meekly as she clattered downstairs from the attic, swept into the road and hailed a taxi. The driver slowed and listened to her crisp instructions to take them to the Strand, wondering, as he pulled away, what such a woman was doing with such a man. Maybe even a man down on his luck could afford a hooker these days. The cab seemed to smell of smoke. Woodsmoke and paraffin, overlaid with soap, and the high-class tart threading a daisy through the top buttonhole of her coat as if the faded thing was made of gold.

"Hurry, Cannon, please hurry," she was saying, pushing him out first, proffering towards the cab driver a note that was far too much and a radiant smile that made him, sour though he was, smile back. "Stop *sulking*, Cannon. I tell you what," she continued, "*smile* at the buggers. Mesmerize them . . ."

Obediently Cannon sustained his smile as they sidled past Security, where Miss Sarah Fortune's evident familiarity shortened the process of bag-searching, to which she still submitted with a brief exchange of banter. She towed him through behind her, although their gaze followed him with jealous suspicion. Briefly. The High Courts of Justice were well accustomed to eccentrics and at least this one was wearing clothes. An unnecessary number of clothes.

It was important to be on time for Master Ralph, but also pointless because the appointment schedule never ran to order, usually erring on the side of lateness but very occasionally, the opposite. Sarah Fortune, solicitor of the Supreme Court in what her employers, Matthewson and Co., described as her spare time, knew these corridors well but, in common with half a million habitués, never quite conquered the unmasterable procedure. It was a place where unhelpfulness was an art form perfected into a refinement of itself. The Masters dealt with the dull preliminary business of civil litigation. Cannon was before the court to be reminded of his obligations and Sarah, who hated this establishment with as much hatred as she could muster, was determined to enjoy it for once. She was good at enjoyment.

Another surreptitious cigarette. The woman from the Crown Prosecution Service, who arrived to demand the immediate execution of the confiscation order against Walter James Smith, better known as Cannon, criminal manqué of this and larger parishes, was highly amenable; in other words, nice. A lame enough word, for a civil servant with a civic duty often executed, as Sarah knew, with a rigour bearing on the ruthless. *Nice,* in Sarah's courtroom vernacular, meant approachable, reasonable, articulate, lacking in messianic zeal as well as egotism, and having the perfectly reasonable attitude of wanting to get out of these Gothic halls as soon as possible. Sarah knew that half the art of all this ritualistic confrontation was common sense and the achievement of a dialogue with the opposition. Get it down to basics. The Crown wanted immediate possession of Cannon's house, and that was for starters. They wanted it on the basis that it was an asset accumulated from the proceeds of crime and that although Cannon had served his sentence for the crimes it was not the same thing as paying his debts.

Cannon took a seat on the uncomfortable bench. He did not look like a criminal as much as like an outmoded anarchist of a vaguely Middle European school. He was still smiling, content to sit with his arms crossed, hands still in gloves, surveying the scene. "Do you think," Helen West said to Sarah Fortune, each of them greeting the other with the kind of mutual recognition and liking it was natural to disguise from their clients, in case amity was seen as complicity, "that you could get him to stop doing that? I'm so afraid his face might get frozen, like a salesman."

"He does something with his jaw," Sarah muttered. "And he's very proud of his teeth. He can keep up that smile for hours. I can't control it."

"Oh, yes, you can. His coat smells. Did you arrange that, too?"

They were in a line for Master Ralph. Some litigants could spend a while in there, while others were spat out with all the ceremony of phlegm. Sarah did not want a conflict with Helen West, not when she held all the cards and a client who was unpunishable by law because he was, for the law's purposes only, as mad as a snake. Helen West was wincing, not paying attention to any kind of portentous news, feeling her jaw, pinching it with the spread fingers of her capable-looking right hand, as if pressure alone would stop it hurting. "Bloody tooth. Hurts like hell. Sorry."

"Nurofen?"

"I want my head cut off. I've had every damn thing done to this damn tooth. Still hurts. Look, give me a break. Just get him to sign over his house as part payment of his bloody debts. Then we'll all be happy. I don't understand why he delays."

"He wasn't living in it and it was never really his," Sarah murmured, rooting in her handbag for pills.

"Never *his*? Like he never made any money? Oh, yes? They all say that."

"He grew up in Belfast, you see. Making bombs was playtime . . . His brother—"

"Nobody's saying he's a terrorist. Simply a destructive exploiter of knowledge. What kind of excuse is that for selling the stuff? What does your client *want* out of life?"

"Babies. He's crazy for a baby. Got a good dentist, have you?"

"Not if you judge by this."

"Look; about the house . . ."

The queue before them seemed to dissolve. An angry posse marched out, arguing and blaming. Then they were in, Cannon hanging back like a tail and Helen West hissing, Why did you have to bring *him*? Does he ever stop smiling? and Sarah felt a moment of sincere regret.

Master Ralph was a disappointed man, who found the incessant struggle to administer decisions to the ignorant inside a room that resembled a dungeon with a high ceiling too much of a challenge, even before the realization that every person who came before him was less informed than he and always would be. Every legal *ingénue* went this route until they were old enough to send someone else, leaving him to witness an endless parade of inexperience, all wanting something they could not have. It was not the iron that had entered his soul, but rust.

"I appear for the Crown," said Helen West in her quiet and authoritative voice. "The Master is familiar with this case." Out of the corner of her eye, she had the vague impression that Sarah Fortune and plain Master Ralph had actually *winked* at one another. Master Ralph was suddenly uncharacteristically cheerful.

"Mr. Cannon has been concerned in the illegal manufacture of explosives. He has been convicted of unlicensed supply to the building trade and others, served a sentence, and all that is history. Since he profited from this, the Crown wants his money. You have all these facts, sir, from previous appearances. Mr. Cannon, otherwise known as Smith, was in business with his twin brother but, alas, they are not alike. Under the cover of his brother's respectable property development and building industry, *this* Mr. Smith diversified into the manufacture of explosives. He was an expert for hire to the worst end of the trade, because he *liked* it. He would have been an asset to the Army. He also used the legitimate business to capitalize himself with a property and, we suspect, valuable paintings, by effectively stealing from his brother's business. Mr. Smith, Cannon, considers himself an *artist*."

"He *is* an artist," Sarah mumbled. "A *framed* artist."

"Did my learned friend say something?"

"I heard nothing," Master Ralph said. "Go on, Miss West."

She went on, "The only asset we have been able to trace is his house in Langdale Crescent. We want that house. This hearing is purely about that house. The other money we must pursue as best we can. But Mr. Smith—Cannon—has agreed he owes us the house. *When* he finds the deeds and chooses to leave it." Here, Helen West gave a look of disapproval to Sarah Fortune. "Mr. Cannon has asked for an adjournment of the order. He is, of course, quite consistent in such a request. As he would be." She grimaced, a brief illumination of currently pale, beautiful features.

Sarah rose to her feet. Hers was an infectious grin. "On the contrary, sir, my client has seen the sweet light of reason. My client no longer wishes to adjourn the issue. The only reason he's delayed with the handing over of the deeds is because he could not find them. They were not in his hands. He did not *live* in the house. The Crown is welcome to the house. What's left of it." She sat.

The Master raised his hand for silence and began to examine the documents in front of him, the better, it seemed, to delay the disappearance of anyone who could formulate a sentence. He glanced up from time to time, enjoying the view.

"What do you mean," Helen muttered, "what's left of it?"

Silently, Sarah handed her a Polaroid photograph. Helen fumbled for her glasses. "That's *his* house?"

The photo showed a ruin, one quarter of a house clinging precariously to the end of a crescent. The most prominent feature was the stairwell, with a bath balanced on the top step. There was something so entirely ludicrous about it, like a surreal painting, that Helen began to laugh. Mirth inside the Master's room was as dangerous as laughter at a funeral. It became infectious, subversive, travelled round the body like a missile, rapidly out of control, ready to emerge as a noise more animal than human. Then both women were half double, making small weepy sounds, like puppies, and for some unfathomable reason, without even knowing the joke, Master Ralph joined in.

"Look," said Sarah Fortune, on the steps to the high court. "You can't go back to work like this. I know a fantastic dentist. If I phone him, he'll see you straight away, I'm sure he will."

"No, thank you. It's gone. Well, it's gone for now. I need a dentist who copes with hysteria. I'm terrified. As soon as pain goes, I find an excuse . . . And it's gone. Well, it's gone for now. Where is he, this dentist?"

Sarah jerked her head in Cannon's direction. "A dentist who can cope with Cannon can cope with anyone. Wimpole Street."

"Can't afford it."

"Oh, it's not too ruinous. Although it has to be said," Sarah added in confidential tones, "it *is* far cheaper if you sleep with him."

Helen was not entirely sure she had heard correctly: she was dizzy with the end of the pain. She took the offered card, watched Sarah Fortune summon her client with an imperious wave, received the last blessing of that wide, outrageous smile and realized, once they were out of sight, how she had failed to record details of W. J. Cannon's current address. Yes, he was an artist; she remembered that. An almost incredible combination, but at his trial he had sketched them all, capturing their likenesses with uncanny flair. A man transfixed between opposing urges to create and destroy; a thief who probably made explosives for other thieves, stole from a twin brother, and even the gaolers liked him. Married to a wife who was going to reform him, common enough mitigation, speciously received. They all said that. She remembered more. He had looked different then. There'd been a suicide attempt in prison, so why did he look so much better three months out from two years inside? She gazed after them. That was the difference. That smile. His teeth. She did not want to think about teeth and she did not want to go to the dentist. She would wait, like a fool, until the next time.

Cold outside. Warm within. A morning of contrasts. A garret; a courtroom; an office.

I am lord of all I survey, Ernest Matthewson told himself each morning when he passed the plaque bearing his name on the office wall, knowing each time he said it that it was a lie. He was merely an ageing senior partner in the monolith that had grown from the microcosm of his once modest legal practice and he did not really control anything. He could not control the staff or their relationships; he could no longer control the character of the clients, and he often reflected how the firm provided unique opportunities for the wrong people to meet each other in sometimes advantageous, sometimes poisonous ways. One tried to *choose* the clients, but he no longer knew who they were and could only remember the nastier ones between the many. Charles Tysall, who had stalked and hurt Sarah; Ernest would always feel guilty about that. John Smith, the builder without manners he had passed on to ambitious Andrew Mitchum; clients with nameless needs, not always legal. Useless clients, ungrateful clients and barking-mad clients, who seemed to suit Sarah.

"Are you back? Oh, there you are. Do sit down."

These days, Ernest Matthewson adopted an elaborate formality with Sarah Fortune. It had come upon him like a cloud, this awkwardness, and he could not shake it off, a mixture of artificial reserve replacing the easy friendship and slightly naughty camaraderie of old, which he missed but could not resume—as if someone had told him she was subject to fits and he was waiting all the time for one to happen. Or as if he knew how she knew his weaknesses and his vanities and he could not forgive either her tolerance or her affection which, once faced with his coldness, simply incorporated it and behaved with the same good nature. Sarah's a good woman, his wife said, again and again, a *good* woman with a big heart, and she only makes you feel guilty. Ernest was neither analytical nor introspective. Questioning his own motives was anathema. Ah, yes, the firm was a network all right, like an unruly family drawing to its bosom, via the children, a number of unsuitable friends. Sarah had once been more like a daughter during her year-long affair with his own son, Malcolm. Such hopes Mrs. Matthewson had had then, but Sarah was like a fish refusing to be caught and he was aware that he had been punishing her ever since.

Now, he simply told himself, this was the promiscuous gal who had thrown over his boy, thereby catapulting *his* wife into an orgy of recriminatory disappointment. As an excuse for a retreat into behaviour that would have suited someone interviewing an upstart applicant for the wrong job, it was adequate.

There was more to it than that, as they both knew. She was totally unfit for her purpose, for a start. She never had cared a toss about the practice of the law, although after her fashion she was genuinely good at it. Totally irresponsible in the commercial sense. Couldn't give a fuck, he growled (aware, even as he formulated the word, of Mrs. Matthewson's strictures about bad language). She was immune to lectures, annual reports, training courses on the equation of time spent per hour to cost, and all that invaluable kind of thing, and although he was not fond of modern management systems either, at least he had always had the knack of charging the client until the pips squeaked and making it look convincing. The endless committees that ruled the life of the firm never voted Miss Fortune into partnership, but whenever her severance was suggested there was always this strange reluctance to act on it. She filled a gap: she took on the duffers, the no-hope clients related to other clients; the ones who wanted a spot of divorce or litigation so that they could get on with the business of making money. Clients who had once been rich. The children of clients. Clients they were not supposed to turn away without taking the risk of losing other clients and appearing to have no soul. Nobody knew where she got her clients: she seemed to find them herself and they came by the back door. For absorbing the misfits, Sarah was allowed a generous enough salary, unless it was compared to the partnership Turks—and how Sarah Fortune, glamorous widow, justified her existence remained a mystery.

She had recovered completely from past traumas, he told himself. None of it was *his* fault. She was decorative—that much was universally conceded: small, slim, agile up those stairs, watchable, without being classically beautiful. All the men felt better for seeing her around. The women looked out to see what she was wearing today. Ernest's wife often asked him wistfully to report on it. He suspected they were still friends, talking about him behind his back, but he could not prove it, and it infuriated him. Women were the devil for secrets.

"Are you well?" he asked formally.

"Never better."

Court gear with a bit of pizzazz, he'd tell Mrs. Matthewson, the way he would tell her every single detail of his day, especially if she asked. He was observant about women's clothes. Not exactly a black suit, he would say, but a sort of soft charcoal, with a long loose jacket over a gored skirt, which swung round her ankles. Cream shirt . . . Why does she always have them buttoned so high up her neck? But an old thing, antique even, with tiny buttons matching the pearls. And a belt? Mrs. Matthewson would ask eagerly, waiting for Ernest to shut his eyes and remember. Ah, yes, grey again, but darker, velvet, I think. Broad belt: her waist is tiny.

She stood in front of his desk with her hands thrust into the pockets of the unstructured jacket, oblivious of his attempts to record the design. He would see it again, of course: she was artful with clothes (she was artful anyway); it would appear in several guises over trousers, over a short, straight skirt with a nice length of leg and, yes, he looked forward to that.

"Do sit down," he repeated, the sound of his parlourmaid voice making him cringe, but there was nothing he could do about it. He loved and missed her in a way that made anything else impossible; but, by God, for all sorts of reasons she would have made a terrible daughter-in-law: flouting the rules, both moral and social, was all very well, but not with one of his own.

She sat. Elegantly, of course, leaning back into the chair with her arm over the back, legs crossed under the fluid skirt, at ease, cigarette lit. Useless to remind her about the no-smoking zone. They had been that route before. Oh, Lord, he wished he was not fond of her. Sarah, for God's sake, help me out, was what he wanted to say. I'm a half-way redundant old man in a firm that has outgrown me and I need you to act as my protector, the way you do for everyone else.

"How did you get on with Cannon? Our artist?" he added sarcastically, suddenly remembering that obscure and disastrous client. Where *had* she got *him* from? God alone knew. *She* said *he* had seen the name of the firm on headed paper on a relative's desk and come along by chance because he knew no other lawyers, had been sent upstairs because he was scruffy. A feasible but unfortunate explanation. They did not normally deal with criminals, unless purely the white-collar kind.

"Oh, fine. Someone blew his house up."

"Oh." Sarah had this tendency to exaggerate; you couldn't believe a thing she said.

"And the opposition had toothache and the Master got the giggles," she added.

He was lost, so stuck to his own agenda, changing the subject, not daring to say, You know what you should do with Cannon? *Dump him.* Dump him like you dumped my son, only I don't understand why we all still love you. Instead, "Still househunting, are you?"

"Yes, of course."

"We've a new project," he announced briskly, after coughing and clearing his throat. "Every other leading London legal firm is doing it, so we have to do it too. Get an art collection."

As a change of topic, this took some beating. She shook her head to clear her face of incredulity. "This firm wants to collect *art*? For what?"

"Not wants, Sarah. Needs. Helps raise our profile in places where—"

"Rich corporations go in order to raise theirs," she finished for him crisply, rallying faster than a Centre Court tennis player.

He nodded. "Part of the image, you see. Doing our bit. We get a few dozen paintings, maybe the odd sculpture or two. Decorate the foyer. Place looks like an empty cricket pitch with walls, anyway. Then we put them on show, oh, wherever these things go on show. Our logo all over the place, of course. It was these Japanese chaps started, buying *Sunflowers*. Hopefully we make money on our investment at the end of the day. But we can't have things like that man with his dead sheep in tanks. None of the partners knows the first thing—and none of them has got time. So we thought . . . you."

She laughed. Another reason why they could never bring themselves to get rid of her. This easy, non-contemptuous laughter that embraced them all, without ever accepting the ethic of any one of them. A potential blackmailer, too, of course.

"Is there a theme to this collection?" she asked. "I am not, emphatically not, going out in search of stags at bay in Scottish Highlands. Or dogs on cushions."

Personally, Ernest liked the idea of anything featuring food, especially if it was going to include dead game ready for the pot, but he shook his head, then changed it to a nod. The worst was over. She had not said no, or told him he was being ridiculous.

"Investment pictures. Modern art, but not too obscure, right? Why don't you just go to one of the reputable dealers?" she asked.

"Bunch of charlatans. Take huge commissions. Besides, *you*'re artistic. Only another mug's game, isn't it? You just swot up on it and away you go. Why pay anyone else?" There was the implied suggestion that Sarah was already paid too much. A slight threat, *Do this, or else* . . . He nodded, agreeing with his own wisdom. Nodding had become habitual. He tried to make it look wise rather than foolish.

"What's the budget and the time-scale? Do I have complete freedom?" Now she was going too fast for him, as usual.

"Oh, a few weeks at least . . ."

"Yes. I'll do it. Three dozen. But I will, of course, need time out of the office. More than usual. I'll have to go to all the exhibitions, scout round dealers, that sort of thing. Time-consuming. Ernest darling, what ails you? Talk to me, please."

"The budget's generous, Sarah. We've to prove we aren't a bunch of Philistines. Get out of here, will you? Just go."

She went. Uncurled those slender limbs without a word, and went. It was only after the door began to close behind her that he remembered he had meant to enquire what else she had done with the morning. Without adding the question he never asked—namely, whose bed had she left before she began? Her own?

"Oh, Sarah, one more thing . . ."

"Yes?"

"You've got to get rid of that ridiculous Mr. Cannon. Where did you get him from anyway? We simply cannot subsidize our clients. We can't."

She paused delicately, hand on hip. "Oh, I don't think so, do you?

He's a very knowledgeable artist. He'll help with the collection. He'll be an unpaid consultant, and where do you ever find those?"

The door closed softly. Ernest remembered a stray piece of information. The child had grown up in a convent. She could be vigorously clumsy, noisy, ebullient, and yet oh-so-silent. Even when she had the last word. He put his head in his hands and groaned.

Miss Fortune climbed the stairs to her office, which was a very small place as befitted her almost itinerant status, and a pretty cluttered space in accordance with the way she was. The services of a secretary had been withdrawn. Yesterday's flowers still looked fresh, but the rug on the floor was crumpled, showing signs of intruders. People stole into Sarah's room, sometimes to weep, avoid the open-plan, or sleep off the hangover. Space was at a premium in Matthewson's firm, while privacy was even harder to find. Which, of course, made it all the more ridiculous that they should have such a large foyer as proof of prosperity. The shop-front, like a marbleized cave, long, narrow and high, a perfectly natural art gallery, the rest a custom-built warren. She sat, yawned and stretched. Got up, closed the window, prowled around the room, which took a matter of seconds. Felt, although she had only just come in, the same old claustrophobia and the desire to be anywhere else. Looked longingly at the envelope full of estate agents' particulars. Pulled a face at herself in the tiny mirror by the door. How the hell, she asked her reflection, did God and man between them ever make a lawyer out of you? Because if it wasn't by divine intervention, it was otherwise a miracle of misjudgement.

She smoothed out the charred fragment of letter given her by Cannon. He had told her what the rest of it contained; she had to take his word for it as she struggled to read the remainder.

> *. . . rotting away. I tell you what, if you can keep this up until Christmas, I promise I'll leave her alone. Promise. Let's see who finds who first, shall we? But you won't keep it up. You'll get careless. You'll realize what's* GOOD *for you . . .*

Cannon said he believed this promise, and she had to believe Cannon. Someone must. She yanked open the neck of the blouse. Fingered a small, white scar on her clavicle. There were others spread over her torso and arms and, just at that moment, she felt a strange pride. She *had* taken a look at Cannon's portrait, and he had not noticed the scars. No one did. She was proud of that. It was as though they had disappeared. Little white scars, pieces of history. The work of a *client.* One of Matthewson's *better* clients, which was why it was odd that he should be so fussy about the rest. It was not as if they were saints employed to deal with sinners.

Nothing mattered now, except loyalty.

The door opened and a young man sidled in. Sarah stifled a sigh. A reputation for a sympathetic ear and a room that doubled as a haven for frustrated smokers was not always an advantage, attracting as it did not only the gossipers, the jokers and the anxious, but also the others. There was no such thing as a legal firm consisting entirely of nice people; there were always the sedulous, the ambitious and the jealous. Andrew Mitchum entered the room as if he owned it, sat without invitation, lit his cigarette and looked round with lazy appreciation. He coveted this room.

"You'll never guess who I had dinner with at the weekend," he drawled.

"Jamie Lee Curtis?"

"Ugh! Darling, how could you? Why waste my time on trash like that? Prince William, more like. No, he's too young for money either. I only dine with clients."

"Who, then?" She was watching a grasping young man, verging on the theatrical in a less than attractive way, convinced he was God's gift to both sexes while clearly preferring his own. The stories of his conquests bored her, but she was not going to say so. Instead she smiled encouragingly.

"John Smith. Our mysterious Mr. Smith. He with all the houses. My God, you should see *his.* Vulgar, my dear, beyond belief."

She kept her face clear of all reaction but polite, impressed curiosity. "Oh, and what did he want? Another acquisition?"

Andrew Mitchum wagged his finger. "Secret," he said teasingly. "A little extracurricular activity is all. Wants me to do a bit of research for him." His eyes took in the pictures on the walls, yesterday's flowers, the heavy blue ashtray, with indiscreet approval. "I'm good at research," he added modestly. "I've found out quite a few things about *you,* for instance. Such an interesting life." He sat back and scrutinized her with frank, asexual curiosity, watching the anxiety flicker over her face to be replaced with an even wider smile.

"Not a lot to know, Andrew."

"No? I don't understand you. All you had to do was marry the boss's son and you would have been a partner. What stopped you? Ah, I know. A penchant for the wrong kind of man and entirely the wrong kind of client, I gather. You were the one Charles Tysall fell for, and when you wouldn't have him he beat you up, right? Tut, tut. No ambition. The man was as rich as Croesus."

"A long time ago, Andrew. Another country. And he's dead."

She was relieved that that was all he wanted to impart; equally relieved that he was so dismissive of her clients. She did not want him examining their identities and seeing any connection between her waifs and strays and his moneyed men; far better that he should be as contemptuous as he was. His ambition was not distracted by imagination. He fingered his immaculate tie, unembarrassed by the silence.

"So what *are* you doing for John Smith? Screwing him?"

"If only. The dinner was wonderful, but he doesn't seem interested in food."

If there were more to tell, he would tell it. He would not be able to resist. Ernest had hired this boy but, then, Ernest's judgement was not always sound.

"I suppose having been attacked yourself is what gives you sympathy with all your dozy victims?" he said, without really expecting a serious answer.

"No," she said, rising to open the window and wishing he would go. "Not always. Look, Andrew, take a tip. Do *not* take money from John Smith for this *research.* Everything you do for John Smith has to go through the firm's accounts. You might think Ernest's a woolly old buzzard, but if there's any hint you're raking in a personal cash profit you'll be out on your ear. *Finito.* End of career."

"Oh, ho, ho, occupying the moral high ground, are we? From what I hear, that's not like you, Sarah, really it isn't."

"Oh, yes, it is. Sometimes," she added demurely, smiling again to defuse the malice in his tone. "Are you staying for coffee or are you going out to make money?" She fumbled in the top drawer of her desk and handed him a red apple, slightly dusty. "Want one? They're good for you. The man on the corner . . ."

He looked at the mess of letters on her desk, mixed in with estate agents' particulars, the arm outstretched with the apple. "Eve offered Adam an *apple*, Miss F. I suppose some poor version of Adam offered the same sort of thing to you. Pity about you, Sarah. You could have had it all. What do you want?"

"A house with lots of white walls," she said, and sank her teeth in the fruit.

White. Should be the favourite colour of a dentist like me, William thought. But white, my boy, is a non-colour, a state of nothing, a mixer. White is never white: it is either white mixed with yellow or brown, or bloodstained pink; skin is never white, it is multicoloured; white is never pure, it is muddy or creamy or tinged with grey. Or, at least, it was when it came to teeth.

He paused, paintbrush in hand, about to advance on the last wall of the waiting room. What colour, then, if he was aspiring to match their teeth? Make them feel at home when they saw their own teeth in a monitor. For God's sake, paint the place white with a hint of apple green. He paused. Isabella, his ex-wife, would loathe this colour and the thought exhilarated him, although he still wanted her approval. Isabella, the stuff of dreams and nightmares, probably at this very minute examining some new abode with her new, second-hand lover. Isabella, met all those years before in the curtain-material department of John Lewis, he confused by choice, she revelling in it. Houseproud Isabella, to whom the pursuit of perfection indoors was a kind of holy grail. A frustrated designer, a design snob, but what a series of cocoons she had made for them. White shaded green? *Dated, yughh!*

There was one small alcove to go. He continued with the off-white apple green, humming . . . droning, since his voice could never hold a tune, any more than his hands could have played a fiddle, or done one of the many things he had once aspired to do. They were pretty hands, his mother had told him, the exact opposite to the way a surgeon's hands were supposed to be. Splayed, to be honest. Short-fingered with a broad span and no arthritis, every damn finger working with an individual dexterity, capable-looking hands. His were the elegant, long-fingered things of a woman whispering behind a fan. His hands, with a permanent tendency to irritation, fungus, fast-growing nails and a dislike of any chemical, were currently enclosed in gardening gloves with rubber gloves beneath, and it was quite insane for a Wimpole Street dentist, with a practice surely lucrative enough to get someone else to do it, to be painting his own public rooms. The private rooms, both above and below, were ignored; they were beyond aesthetic redemption anyway. Why, then, William, why? he droned. Because you're an ass; the prosperity is all on the surface and, let's face it, you have nothing active left to do when everyone has gone home. And you are fascinated by the technique of it . . . and, besides, everyone else makes such a devil of a mess.

The doors would have to remain wood-coloured doors. There were too many doors and too many locks. He liked the arrangement. Reception desk by outer door; short corridor to large waiting room; surgery off that, with another damn door opening to reveal not the immediacy of the surgical area and the chair but another little seating area for consultation to the left, out of sight of the door. A non-threatening view.

He tried to whistle. What emerged was a breathy, piping sound, unrecognizable as the tune that had been going round in his head all day. "All things bright and beautiful, All creatures great and small . . ." Such a well-known hymn, coming out of the blue to irritate. As far as his patients were concerned, all things bright and beautiful meant nothing more than teeth.

He finished and took the paintpots and the brushes into the bathroom, which was beyond the reception room and flanking the surgery. *Yes*, he had made it nice, this public part of the whole damn thing. What always amazed him was the way the patients always asked permission to use the lavatory when it was clearly marked, not in a dozen languages, perhaps, but quite evident for what it was, and the notion that he would want any of them sitting on his chair with a full bladder was so extraordinary that it made him shake his head. The bathroom, too, was filled with paintings. Perhaps that put them off; in which case, too bad. Pictures stayed.

On his way out of the bathroom, he detoured into the surgery. White upon white. There was something perfectly appalling about a surgery with no one in it, like a car park without cars. It had all the impersonality of a laboratory. The chair at lowered level, the machinery on a swing, far out of reach, his chair, with back-rest, crouching beside it, the footpad ready for his feet. No one there, and yet it all looked alive. Blue and white in here. Nothing superfluous. All of it chemically scrubbed. Cupboards full of equipment, as little on show as possible; no labels. Everything in sterile packages hidden from view, as much for the sake of hygiene as for fear of causing alarm. The place had been made to look like a high-tech kitchen display in a shop window, not exactly inviting, but efficient, at least, with the implied promise that there would never be any mess, spillages, stains, the distinctive burning smell of dentine dust, or failures.

William sat in his patients' chair. It was an eccentric habit of his to do this when the place was empty, and made his assistant feel uneasy if she caught him at it first thing in the morning, but he did it often enough. It was important, he told Tina, to keep on reminding himself of what the patient could see from this chair, and whether the view could be improved. There had been a series of soothing pictures on the far wall, limpid watercolour scenes featuring very blue water, until Tina had tartly reminded him that what the patient in the chair watched, as often as not, was the arc-light, until the name of the manufacturer, Siemens, was emblazoned on their eyeballs. She suggested, in her youthful and heartless fashion, that he put goggles on the patients and be done with it. Then they would see nothing and he would not have to bother about the view. No, he told her. That would only have the effect of refining their concentration on what was going on inside their mouths: they needed to see so they would *hear* less.

Tina had nodded; she had the benefit of perfect teeth, a child of the fluoride age. But at least, she added, if you put them in goggles, they won't have to see what they see almost as often as they see the light. Your face, looming over them in a mask. Was it such a bad face? he wondered. Nooo, she had said doubtfully, examining it with those cornflower-blue eyes of hers, which held not a moment of doubt. It isn't your face would frighten anyone. It's the height of you. I'd stay sat down, if I were you.

No respect, that girl. Beanpole, she called him—a slight improvement on the school name, which was Telegraph. Six feet and three inches was not such an unusual height, was it? Inconvenient for canoeing, horse-riding, bicycling, certain team games he had never liked anyway, and quite an advantage among school contemporaries who would otherwise have bullied him, although it imposed the necessity of owning up to any crime because he was always so visible. It had forced him to develop a slouching stoop, which even now he found difficult to correct; nothing more than a slightly lopsided air but, he thought, at fifty plus, he was used to it. Ah, he thought, oh, please, never let me see myself the way other people do. Let us all be spared that.

He was tired, but not tired enough. He supposed a good night's sleep in a dentist's chair was possible, although it was difficult to imagine anyone wanting to try it. People lay in it under sedation happily enough. It was an awful thought, that the only time patients looked serene was when they were deep asleep. Not anaesthetized, but slumbering without memory. It was then that they sometimes made pathetic efforts to co-operate and even to join in any conversation. It was then, instruments allowing, they muttered about their deepest preoccupations.

William left the chair rapidly, and hit his head lightly on the overhead gantry, which reminded him of one of his first mistakes in the early days of practice. "Right, you can get up now," he would command gaily, only to have the poor sap stand and hit the equipment, or trip over something else on their grateful way to the door. All exit and entrance paths must remain clear, even if they were not in a straight line, as his were not. If only the patients knew how much trouble he took, maybe they would loathe him less. No, they wouldn't.

He had moved to the bathroom. Green paint dripped beneath the tap. "All things bright and beautiful . . . all molars great and small." He felt the same thing when *he* went to the dentist. A defensive fear, as if the man *meant* him harm and was positively relishing the mere prospect of causing pain, giving him that wary handshake he might have afforded a self-confessed sadist, telling him immediately how much he hated being there, just in case the man did not know—the way his patients did to him *ad nauseam*. When the causing of pain was unavoidable, it drained him; on those rare occasions, it was excruciating. He dreaded it as much as the patient. It made him sleepless and hyperactive, like now, as he painted the walls green in the hope that it would never happen again. But it would. He could not wish pain on any living thing. Except *her*, except Isabella, and then it was not so much pain he wished but something else, which made him profoundly ashamed.

The whiteness of the room, contrasting with the black panes of the night, made him dizzy. It was a bad habit of the time of year to make the light so short and the nights so long. Christmas was beginning to look like a blot on the horizon.

The flash of the orange silk flowers in the waiting room reminded him. The flash of fireworks and red hair. William picked up the phone, dialled and, when she answered, felt a grin creeping across his face. "Sarah! Why aren't you here?"

"Because I'm here, silly. How are you?"

"A bit low. Nothing too bad. Half-way down the pit, or half-way up, whichever way you look at it."

"Half-way up, I would. Light at the top. Has that bitch been in again?"

"Nope. She's due tomorrow."

"Tell her to get lost."

"I can't. I just can't. You know I can't. Look, are you busy?"

"Never. Can you come over?"

"I thought you'd never ask. With my toothbrush?"

"Behave like a good boy. Yes."

"Fine. About half an hour? Look . . . It was you by that bonfire last week, wasn't it? You and Cannon?"

There was a long, unembarrassed pause. "What *bonfire*?"

And that, he supposed, would enter into the file of things they did not talk about.

"Lady in red," Sarah yelled along with the radio, turned high to give her the gist of the tune over the sound of the vacuum-cleaner while she improvised the words.

"You're so perfect *tonite* . . . forgive me please . . . you have no knees, but that's *all right* . . ." She gulped the first gulp of wine and grimaced as she put it down—there was something odd about the taste. Slowly, she took another glass and polished it with a paper towel. The music was nicely relentless. "Love the one you're with, love the one you're with," she hummed, then stared at the glass. Filthy.

If she were a good housekeeper, there would be no need for this occasional and frenetic activity. *If* she were the kind of person who could host a party without looking round in a panic for the exit . . . *if* she had enough sense of the future even to take the risk of keeping a cat, she would be calm and collected, as quiet a closer of doors as she was in public. She knew she would never be able to keep a cat: they would have too much in common. Malcolm Matthewson had told her that on the day they had parted. She remembered him with regret. But I would never be catty enough to use my flawed good looks as a passport to a new billet if

I was fed up with the old, would I? she hummed. That's the difference. I'd just go, starve or not. And who would take me in, covered in scars, like a feline with fleas, unsuitable for human devotion even if I were fun enough to stroke for a while? I did love you, Malcolm, but you didn't *like* me and, besides, I'm congenitally incapable of living happily in a pair. Leaves no room for other loyalties. *Love the one you're with.*

Find the life that suits. Like whoever you want.

Enough wine, as always, even if the glasses were dusty. There was rarely enough food. "*Yesterday!*" she bellowed to the music. "I don't believe . . ." She pounced. Yes! A result! Two pound coins under the overturned cushion even before she had thumped it. Life was rich. She was perfectly comfortable living alone with her inexplicable devotions and equally eccentric retinue of lovers. Liking was more important than loving. She seemed to have turned into a bit of a gipsy, encumbered with a small mortgage and very little else, her ambitions lessening with each succeeding year. She wanted the flat with the white walls and the freedom to be untidy in her life as well as in her own home. How else would she ever find the surprising coins behind the cushions and revel in the enjoyment of strangers?

Looking upon herself as an outsider, she decided she lived not only in an unconventional moral zone but also in a cultural vacuum. That much was clear from her taste in music. She scarcely knew Beethoven from Bach, and the omission had never yet cost her a sleepless night. She knew Thackeray from Trollope, since reading was a passion, and as for fine arts, she could certainly tell Rembrandt from Renoir and Degas from Van Gogh. He was the one who cut off his ear.

Her apartment was full of pictures. She would say, glibly, that this was another result of the vacuum of the soul or possibly the avoidance of any other decision about interior design, and because things hung on walls were less likely to get broken. The mirror had been an exception, and she did not think about the mirror.

Except sometimes. The old mirror had been smashed by Charles Tysall, a man in pursuit of perfection, disgusted to find it did not exist in her. He had broken the mirror into tiny pieces and forced her to lie among the shards. Life had begun after surviving that: she had never since experienced the luxury of hatred—not even for him when she encountered him again, pathetic creature he had been by then. Neither did she pursue perfection, but delighted in its non-existence. She was in love with flaws.

As it was, the two large rooms and the smaller bedroom had enough pictures to furnish a gallery, provided the owner had taste as varied as hers. Paintings were acquired with zest and compulsion, sometimes in unusual places, some thrust upon her in payment of a debt, some purchased out of pity; and on the basis of this highly random selection, which spread into her office, Ernest Matthewson had come to the conclusion that she was artistic. He should have known also that, although her eye was good, she never bought anything for investment and she was hardly discriminating about anything. Not a fussy person. Unlike the patient of William's who had brought them into contact in the first place. William, another back-door client, introduced on the recommendation of a friend and all because of a girl with porcelain veneers who was suing him because, infuriatingly, the veneered teeth glowed a different shade of white in certain nightclub lights. Sarah had settled that case fairly rapidly by the simple expedient of finding the plaintiff and getting her drunk enough to confess a life history of similar legal pursuits featuring plastic surgeons and hairdressers. Ruthless, perhaps, but vanity was not, in Sarah's view, a matter for litigation. It was a matter for you and your mirror. Meeting William had been timely. She hadn't had her teeth checked for years before that, and she *liked* William.

She crossed the living room to the open french windows, and looked out across the green from the tiny balcony. This was the best feature of the place she was seeking to leave—with a degree of regret, even though movement and upheaval came naturally. It was a nice flat, but it was not home; it never could be home after that broken mirror; she felt like an alien in it and the urge to find *home* had become a mission. You had to take a robust view of interior decoration when you had seen your walls spattered with your own blood; you covered the new paint with pictures to remind you of other vistas and other lives. Or you did if you were *frivolous*, she told herself, repeating one of Matthewson's favourite accusations, echoed by his son. *Deeply frivolous*, she told him. Dedicated to it; life is far too short to be taken seriously. All those pictures on the walls, though. When she took them down, the place would look as if someone had been round with a machine-gun.

The dark was soft and damp. Across the narrow stretch of grass, she could see and hear the noise of the road. A figure moved between the shrubs. She wanted to shout a warning. It was dangerous out there. So dangerous there was no longer any point in being afraid. Not for herself anyway. Not any more. She had become fearless ever since all her fears for herself had become transferable into fear for others. She owed Charles Tysall that liberation. He had thrown her a kind of death, but it was he who had died; she was alive.

"William," she called. "Don't just stand there. *Do* something. Come in from the cold."

He knew what he would find. Warmth. Pictures and a fire, handsome objects frayed at the edges as if they had all been rescued or recycled rather than purchased new. Always something broken, as if she could never quite preserve anything fragile in its entirety; always something so old it would no longer function without brute force. A lamp that required dismantling to change the bulb; a door with a non-turning handle in pieces; a tap in need of a washer. William was not sure if she failed to notice these things or attempted to mend and repair with such haphazard abandon that the task could never be complete. It was a contrast to all of the many abodes he had ever shared with Isabella; he was not entirely sure he liked it and he knew, with slight satisfaction, that Isabella would *hate* it. Things should *function*. Always assemble your tools before you start, he scolded. Make sure you have what you need. Look: it's easy. Do as I do. Before the patient arrives, I have a tray of equipment ready, sterilized and waiting. *You* don't have single tool that works.

A foolish little lecture, because he did not really want Sarah to be proficient in that way. There was nothing he liked better than fixing things and, in any event, his ability to do so was an essential part of their understated relationship. It was payment in kind for what she offered; so much so that, if there was absolutely nothing for him to do in her house, he felt profoundly disappointed. He owed her rather more than a discount on treatment and the proper instruction on the maintenance of her near-perfect teeth. He owed her stimulus, interest, sexual affection . . . a number of irreplaceable things that had enriched the latest months of his life. William disliked the sensation of being in debt, and it was one of many reasons why he always had to put his foot in it. Insist on redefining what they had, if not every time, often enough. Especially if there really was absolutely *nothing* to do to ease him through his first moments of awkwardness.

"You've got paint in your hair," she said crisply, as soon as she saw him at the door.

"I was painting the waiting room. I'm in excellent painting form. I could do the kitchen in, oh, under an hour . . . I could— "

"No," she said firmly. "Absolutely not."

"But it *needs* doing."

"That," she said flatly, "has nothing to do with anything. Sit down and have a drink, will you, please? And take off those gloves."

He looked down at his own long hands, saw them still encased in surgical gloves, made a strangled sound of agonized embarrassment, which emerged as a brief yelp. He clawed at the gloves, the wrong, cheaper kind which gave him an allergic reaction even if they did afford protection. They tore at the palm as he ripped them off and threw them away into the corner, where they lay curled on the carpet, looking almost alive. She would pick them up tomorrow, maybe.

"New dress code for travelling the underground, is it?" she teased him, pressing his hands round the bowl of a glass. There were faint bubbles in the wine. He stared at them, fascinated. "You must have looked a little . . . odd. Over-fastidious, perhaps."

The glass was emptied before he spoke. She had an amazing facility for silence: she seemed able to maintain either that or ceaseless chatter exactly as the mood demanded. Suddenly he felt a whole lot better, found himself smiling for no other reason than that image of himself, reading a newspaper on the train with those oh-so-obvious, not quite flesh-coloured rubber gloves, as if the print would contaminate him, and he could not bear the proximity of other kinds of dirt, humanity included, for that matter. He laughed because it might have been true.

"Must've thought I was the burglar. Ready to avoid fingerprints. Dressed to kill. Or one of those men who goes round poisoning rats. Something like that. Give me a hug, will you?"

She did. An almost all-encompassing hug, hands scratching the back of his neck the way he liked. They stayed like that for some time. He could feel the warmth of her enter his bones, struggled against it; failed. He tried to tell himself she was amoral, feckless, promiscuous, insincere on that account, untidy, dishonest, disloyal, insensitive, unkind, calculating, and knew, as he recited to himself this litany of adjectives, that he was really thinking of someone else entirely. Applying to Sarah those angry descriptions that best suited Isabella was hardly fair, although Sarah *was* amoral in a way he never cared to define and certainly untidy. She was also far more than a fair-weather friend, but still he had to ask.

"Are you *sure* there's nothing I can mend? Do you *like* me at all?"

"Oh dear," she said, removing herself from his lap and fetching the wine. "You *are* in a bad way."

"No worse than usual. Better for seeing you," he added, in an attempt at grace. She did not come to the surgery for treatment these days. She claimed to enjoy the ambience, which flattered him—although he doubted it was true—even though she had helped to create it. First, there were the additional pictures, which added something to the waiting areas; she inflamed his existing enthusiasms for collecting and made him bolder in his choices. Then there was the increased flow of patients. Sarah recommended him to everyone she knew, and Sarah knew a lot of people. Some of them were strange enough to have crawled out of very peculiar woodwork, but they were still people with teeth. And, one or two of them, people with whom he could empathize without quite understanding the process. Especially Cannon. Cannon was nicely mad; both he and Cannon had gremlins. How Sarah had organized an artist and convict into his surgery was another thing he could never quite fathom. Networking. One day his life had been normal; the next he found himself spirited into a prison to see a patient, then launched into bureaucratic obfuscation to get the patient treatment. A client in need, she had explained: Do this for me, William, *please*. You're the only dentist I know who's treated people like him before. He needs you. She wouldn't tell him much about Cannon, pleading professional confidence, but he never minded that. Cannon's treatment had been a triumph, and William was profoundly grateful for the pride it gave him. Oh, for another patient like Cannon. It might be enough to dispel the dreams of inadequacy.

"Still haunted, are we?" she asked gently, sitting away from him to light the cigarette, despite his disapproval. (They are *bad* for your teeth, Sarah darling. They inhibit the circulation and retard healing . . . accelerate periodontal disease . . . *bad* for you, wanting to say it, but admiring the precise way she smoked.)

"Yes," he said, sighing. "I couldn't bear another night of the same nightmares. But you told me *not* to mention her name."

She settled on to the floor by his feet and shook her head. "Nothing is absolutely forbidden, you know it isn't. Break me in gently. Tell me about the other nightmares first."

Tell me again, she might have said. William's nightmares were constants, variations on a few themes with different pictures. They were the result of the pursuit of perfection and an underlying guilty conscience that would not shift, and although the recitation of the dreams had lessened considerably in the time she had known him, they saddened and irritated her because William did not deserve such afflictions. No man of such conscientious kindness deserved them, and that was why she listened. He did not deserve to remain half in love with his shallow bitch of an ex-wife either. That was a private opinion.

"Well, take last night. I woke up convinced that the hall was full of brilliant paintings, and I'd painted them all. Although, of course, I hadn't, when I came to look at them, never could have, never shall."

She shrugged. "You can't paint pictures when you're obsessed with *technique*."

"Don't interrupt," he said crossly. "I don't *mind* about not being able to paint. I haven't minded for years. But there were three people in the hallway, looking at the paintings. They were sharpening their nails, ready to tear them to pieces and, after them, me." He gulped the wine too fast and felt the bubbles go up his nose. "There was that child, Adrian. You know the one I mean, the one I told you about?"

Yes, she knew.

"Pale and ill and coughing, like someone who's blocked off half a lung. That piece of amalgam I dropped down his throat locked inside his lung somewhere, and no one knowing why he was so ill. All skin and bone he was, but as for his sister, well . . ." He shuddered.

"She was the one where you *think* you took out the wrong teeth?"

"Yes." He patted her shoulder, grateful for her recall, as if she had never heard these nightmare stories before. "Overcrowded mouth. Had a lot of them at the time. Got the records muddled up. Didn't concentrate. Only realized what I'd done after she'd gone."

"*Might* have done."

"*Must* have done. Otherwise, why does she stand in the hallway in my dreams with two ugly incisors on either side of two huge gaps? Her smile was *obscene* and, really, she could have been so pretty. So beautiful. And, of course, you can guess who had brought them in to mash up the paintings and haunt me all over again? *I* couldn't trace those children, however hard I tried. But *her*. She could."

"Your ex-wife. Who else? No doubt she was looking perfectly wonderful."

"She was, actually. She always does."

"William, how can you be so helpless? Why do you allow her to tease you? I never heard anything so insane. Both of you. She wrecks your confidence and betrays you and comes back for treatment, and you *let* her. Why can't you say, '*Go away*'?"

"I don't *know*. Habit, I suppose. Perhaps I really enjoy the temptation to put the drill through the roof of her mouth. Perhaps I like to think of her nicely sedated while I sew her lips together. Stitch her tongue to her back teeth to stop her talking. Wouldn't do a great deal of harm."

Sarah rose with her usual grace. "I think," she said, "that even Isabella might notice something like that. I'm ordering pizza."

The nightmares always faded into nonsense as soon as he talked about them—another thing that shamed him. It seemed to mean they might have no significance at all because they were soluble in wine, digestible with food and they never survived time with Sarah. But the night had its own inexorable, bullying pace, taking him straight back into a broken sleep, even after pizza and too little lust. Far too tired for that, hugging instead, grateful for her body smelling of clean cotton, curled against his in a neat fit. Grateful for being accepted without demands or criticism, nothing but affection, which always felt exclusive at the time. That was what saved him from the trouble of having to think about love and all its strictures.

Of course he did not *love* Sarah Fortune; lover and friend was all. For William, love meant a grand passion, a gnawing of fingernails, intensity, anxiety and being connected at the hip; it was not supposed to be tranquil like this. This was a matter of mere liking and glorious convenience. Not the same thing at all.

And she thought, as she often did, about how the longing to protect other people had become so habitual that it was far more important than love. A mental check: everyone she cared about relatively safe for the moment. Aunt Pauline, Julie, Cannon, William. Falling into sleep, she wondered, briefly, what Cannon might be doing.

There was a rustling in the dark, in the back there, over by the wall where the nettles were thickest. Wet and dank, they had covered the sound of his fall, and now they whispered with life. Cannon half sat against a wall, which felt strangely warm against his jacket, watched the nettles with mild curiosity, content to wait until they settled. He was not afraid of the dark: he liked it. It was something he had tried to explain in paint, about how the night was never completely silent and the darkness never entirely impenetrable. Look, he mouthed, wagging a finger at the moon. Look at you, you old bugger, shining on. It was mirrored in the back window of the chapel, which held its own light, visible as he had clambered over the high wall and snagged his trousers on thorns. He was willing to take a bet that the noise in the nettles was some rat. Rat or snake, ferret or tiger, he didn't care. As long as it was not human. See? You can even read your watch by the light of the moon, my love. Why worry about the dark?

The clouds were moving across his vision, racing to catch up with the moon and wrap it round, pull it down and rein it in to serve some God his supper; a nice half melon of moon. Not a new moon, or Cannon would have paused, taken off his hat, bowed his head in the cold and made a solemn wish. Now that he was older and wiser, he would not waste the wish by using it to wish for three more wishes. One would do. It was time. He knew it was time without squinting at the watch: it was the slight shivering of his limbs, thin under all his garments, which made him realize. A numbness to go with the shaking; a fever that owed something to anxious delight. He swept softly through more of the undergrowth, feeling a tin can bend beneath his feet while the other boot scrunched on broken glass before he reached the door. Even as he reached it, it opened slightly, revealing a chink of subdued light. The iron latch made a sound like a small animal in pain. Dear Lord, Cannon thought, even a piece of metal resents us.

"Is it you?" He had meant to speak perfectly normally, but it was impossible. What he produced was a sibilant whisper, a sign of the fear he hardly felt, but which still infected him. It was only the dreadful fear of finding nothing behind that door.

"Of *c-c-c-c-course* it is. Qu-quick, come in." She copied the sibilance of his whisper: he felt it could have been heard a million miles away, as if she was shouting, but she never did shout. She looked too small to produce any great sound, apart from an uncertain stutter, and as he enveloped her in his great big woolly embrace, hugging the life out of her, he felt as if he could have wrapped her up and put her into one of the capacious pockets of his coat. She seemed to sense it, too, getting her small self inside the jacket so she could snuggle closer, struggling to put her arms round his middle, worm her way through all the layers into his heart. He touched her hair, level with his chest, amazed as ever by its softness; then he felt blindly with his stubby fingers for the sockets of her eyes; kissed them first, one by one, and only then her mouth. The skin around her eyes was dry, her mouth against his lips warm, and her hands, beneath the jumper, hotter than burning coal. He was twice her volume and he staggered beneath her impact. Only her nose was cold.

He knew this was the sacristy to the chapel, although he had never quite established where it was in relation to anything else, or whatever it was that lay beyond. This was the only entrance he knew, always approached at dark as if he was approaching a place of pilgrimage on his hands and knees. Cannon would not have minded the bare-footed progress of a pilgrim.

They moved from sacristy to chapel, through the rows of seats to the back where a small light illuminated a statue of monumental ugliness. A garishly coloured plaster saint with a chipped red robe, lovingly dusted along with the rubber plant on the table supporting both. Cannon was carrying her: he felt as if he was carrying every single thing that was precious in his own life inside his arms, but still he paused, his face puzzled as he looked at the statue that gave them light. There was a dragon curled at the feet of the saint, a harmless-looking thing in the act of being pierced by a spear through the mouth, wide open to welcome such intrusion. The dragon looked as if it were an invalid being offered soup, while the saint looked smug.

"Not his best side," she whispered into his ear. "And the dragon has lost its teeth."

"I'm a dragon," he growled, pulling her closer, listening to her gasp. "Only I found my teeth. Why did I waste all that time?"

"I don't know, I don't know, how should I know?" He could feel her laughter, along with her whisper, vibrate down the lengths of his arms and jolt his spine.

Her hands were finding his and he was trying to hide them beneath her skirt. Thick tights and skinny shanks: she could feel him through every centimetre of her skin. She felt the bandage. "Oh, Cannon, is it still sore?"

"Nothing, lovely, nothing. I don't know what came over me. Fireworks madden me. Won't happen again. Are you all right?"

She nodded against his chest. "Why did you d-d-do that, Cannon, *why*? Clumsy man. You need your hands. You don't need d-d-dying, not yet. Not a long while yet. And if you go alone, I swear to God I'll kill you. Honest I shall."

"It was a bad day," he whispered lamely. "And it was never *our* house. I wanted him to know what I thought of him. I wasn't living there. He left me a note. Telling me he'd get the house back for me if I'd come home. Don't let's talk about him." Then he stood with her still in his arms, that little strong scrap of her bound to him like a limpet as he bowed towards the altar and then sat down again. There was a smell of polish, which he rather liked.

Oh, to make love in a big, light room to the sound of the sea through a window. He had never envied anyone, but he did now. Never believed in a God either, but he did here, temporarily, in the hope of the fulfilment of his single wish. Listen to me, God, please. I shall obey every letter of the law, and if you let us free, I shall sacrifice whatever else I hold dear. Paint, canvas, fine wine, notoriety, curiosity and my few friends. You can have them all. Vanity and ambition are long since gone, so you can see I've made a start. *Free me from my brother; free Johnnyboy from me. And free me from the urge to destroy things.*

"How do they pray in here?" he asked into her ear. "Isn't it too cold to pray?"

She shook her head. Soft hair touched his face and made him want to moan with longing.

"They wear a lot of clothes. And it's only cold at night."

Cold, but not lonely; not with the statues and the altar light and the moon through the windows.

"Are they still kind to you?" he whispered urgently.

"Of c-c-course. And I'm busy."

That was a relief. Idleness had never suited her. She felt guilty if her hands were free of work. Born to it, took to it like a duck to water, proud of it. His wife, who should have been breeding babies by now—three already if she had not had to wait for him to grow up and free himself and watch him make a mess of it, a process begun as soon as he clapped eyes on her. Waited for his self-discovery, and then his discovery by the rest of the world, and now, still waiting for this long process of revenge to work its way out. Never, ever blaming him. There's no such thing as a future you haven't built with your own hands, she had told him with her sweet stutter, which was worse when she was cross. And I don't see how you can build one on destruction. You may have grown up with bombs and evil. You don't have to continue.

"We shouldn't have stolen from him, should we?"

It was kind of her to say "we," when all the decisions had been his, wrong decisions of course, however justifiable at the time. Stealing from Johnny because Johnny had never paid him and had told him to get rid of her. Knowing that even if Johnny had put one of the houses in his name, it didn't mean it was his. Futile to try to take something from Johnnyboy. Oh, yes, he'd stolen quite a bit and let Johnny frame him for more. He thought of the explosives made at Johnny's behest; shuddered; never, ever again. Thought of the picture he had bought to launder the money, and the fact that it was now all that was left, with his dwindling reserves of cash. Thought of Johnny's revenge, played out in this game.

"What's happening out there?" she asked.

They were warming each other: she pressed his hands between her thick-clad thighs. Her own palms were callused with work; he fancied he could feel them rubbing his back. Cannon coughed quietly, loud in the silence. "Not so much yet. I got rid of the house. We just have to wait and see. Until Christmas. He promised. He keeps to the rules as long as it's him who makes them."

"Why don't you just give him everything? Give him what he wants? Everything. Even the picture." It was a sad question, not really expecting an answer.

"You know why. Because it leaves nothing. He'd burn the picture. I couldn't bear it. And because it would never be enough. It's *me* he wants. Me, coming home."

"Yes, yes, I know. D-darling, I know."

Just as she knew why she was here. She was both his strength and the weak link in his fence against the enemy. His hidden weapon, his vulnerability. Because she knew, as well as Johnny knew, that Cannon would lose his mind if Johnny ever attacked her again. She was small, brown-haired, otherwise insignificant, except to him. And she knew there was no worse enemy than one related by blood; no worse adversary than a lover betrayed; and Johnnyboy Smith was both.

The tingling of blood was impervious to the chill. The embrace on the hard bench becoming frantic, his hand now beneath the two layers of sweater, cradling her breast, full and soft, large for her miniature person, perfect. Ah, he could paint a naked woman, but never desire any other than this. She had taken his scarf and wound it playfully around both their necks, binding them. The kiss was an endless kiss. There was nothing to say, everything to do.

"Cannon, we *c-can't.* We *can't.*"

"Yes, we can . . . Oh, I do love you. And the babies we'll have . . ."

"Oh, you and your babies," she said. "That's all you want from me."

"No. But we *must* have a baby," he said. "We *must.* I'd die for the chance and I'd die for you both." He wanted to climb inside her for safety; he wanted the baby to prove what he was.

The light was suddenly blinding: he felt he heard it rather than saw it, coming at him like a monster and assaulting his eyes. A torch shining straight at his face, catching his white skin and making it glow red. Then the beam played over the length of his body, with hers curled inside his coat, and dropped, modestly, to play around his feet. Instinctively, he curled his feet beneath the bench, clutched his wife closer and, for a moment, forgot to breathe until he heard her whimper. He clutched too tight for comfort. The light snapped off. There was movement away from them before the light clicked on again, illuminating the linoleum floor and another pair of feet that were clearly not his own. They were half covered by black cloth.

"No," said a voice, whispering like their own, but louder and far more precise. "No, you can't. I'm awfully sorry, but you just can't."

Cannon felt a jolt of sheer relief run through him like an electric shock. Julie shivered in embarrassment and a similar relief, struggling to sit upright, if not quite detach herself: she could not bear to do that.

"I'm sorry, Sister. We were c-c-c-c-carried away." Her small voice was apologetic.

The torch illuminated a pale hand, waving a gesture of dismissal. There was a flurry of shushing sound as the woman sat down beside them, arranging the folds of her robe with one hand and adjusting the rosary beads that hung from her waist. She must have held them as she moved, put them in a pocket. Such silent creatures they were, these nuns; only the beads gave away their presence with the polite clatter they made in movement, like a version of a motor horn. So silent, he wondered how they knew the presence of each other.

Sister Pauline was sighing gustily. "Oh, Lord. It wasn't apology I was wanting," she said. "It's I who feel I should do that. We aren't very hospitable at this hour of night, are we? But you can't take your clothes off in the house of God to make babies. Quite apart from anything else, you'll catch your death."

They were silent.

"Mind you," Sister Pauline continued, "I doubt if He would mind. If you've created man in your image and liking, you can hardly be surprised if he behaves in the way you designed him. I'm not attempting to speak up for God, you understand, only for the sisters in this order who would not like it at all. And they'd know, of course." She adjusted her robe. "Imelda can detect a fingerprint in here at fifty paces, let alone anything else. Although I suppose if she were to put sins in categories it would be the discovery of a cigarette end would really give her the vapours. I had a hard time with that, I can tell you."

Last week, a cigarette in here. Cannon shook his head. He had never been more ashamed of smoking in his life. If his presence in this place was going to be revealed by something so venal and stupid, he did not deserve the fulfilment of any wish.

"I imagine we all grade sin in accordance with our own understanding," Sister Pauline mused. "Imelda was probably tempted to smoke once. As for sex, I doubt it somehow. She grinds her teeth instead. And now, I suppose," Sister Pauline went on, "I'll have to pretend I made a bonfire in here. You must do something about that coat, Mr. Cannon. Get a new one from Oxfam. I don't know how your wife puts up with it." She sighed. "I knew I was right to choose God. He never snores either."

Julie giggled softly. "Oh, Sister . . ." Her voice trailed off into uncertainty. There was a tiny rattle of the rosary beads. Light from the window caught Pauline's features. A large hooked nose and a wide, mobile mouth, slightly sunken eyes with bushy grey brows, and a bony forehead. The contours of her face predominated over the detail.

Cannon thought how much he would like to paint that face, but this was not quite the time to suggest it. An idea formed. He could present himself as travelling artist, offer to paint the whole order one by one . . . No. He could do nothing that in any open sense connected him to this place because Johnny would find out but, all the same, he liked the idea of painting a face like this, so bereft of vanity that its owner would not even have been able to define what the word really meant. How old was she? Seventy? Difficult to tell: they were ageless.

"And now will you tell me, Mr. Cannon, how much longer is this charade going to go on? I think I know why you can't arrive by daylight like any other visitor. My niece told me, and I don't doubt her since she's not exactly subject to paranoia. I must say, a visit from you in the parlour would be nice. You could pose as Julie's long-lost suitor. The sisters would be totally delighted. They adore the very sniff of romance. But not, however, in the chapel."

The silence was companionable. Cannon bowed his head deeper into his chest. It was difficult to meet the intensity of Pauline's gaze and he was grateful for the gloom. Seen in sunlight, he imagined her eyes would have the effect of lasers and her voice, ascended from its current whispering murmur, would probably stop a herd of elephants with a single order. She would not need to fire a shot. Her teeth were very white, whiter even than his own.

"Only I know it's all very well for God to be relied on to provide," she said, "but the devil flourishes on ignorance. I, on the other hand, do not."

"It's better that way, Sister," Cannon muttered, and Julie nodded agreement.

"Oh, is it, I wonder? Or do you and my niece persist in the sweet belief that a nun cannot comprehend the wicked ways of the world without fainting from shock? You really should know better. And so should she."

Julie squeezed Cannon's arm, reminding him not to argue. "*I* don't think that, Sister."

The nun laughed softly, and leaned across Cannon to pat Julie's hand. "No, I shouldn't think you do."

Julie shook at the touch, remembering, as she always would, that it had been Pauline who had first seen her naked state when Sarah brought her here, her back scored as if she had been flogged through her torn clothes, ribs cracked from a kicking, the lacerated arm dragged across concrete, not an inch of her unbruised. She had mended quickly with tender, loving care; the eyes had lost the emptiness of terror, but if ever this child were to be tortured in any such fashion again Pauline doubted that she would survive it. It had crossed her mind to wonder why the torturers had not used a more subtle approach, if it was mere information they had wanted. Tricked her, persuaded her, fooled her, perhaps. Julie was disposed to see goodness even where it did not exist, Pauline thought, wryly, but she was not cunning. She might prove harder to conquer than subvert; persuasion or deceit might have been more effective. The sight of that skinny body, like a plucked chicken, covered with bruises, haunted her still. There was no other rhyme or reason for taking the child in, except that appalling need and the persuasive powers, as well as the purse, of a niece. And a very tall story about a psychopathic brother-in-law and a husband still in prison. An insistence on a ludicrous degree of secrecy.

Sister Pauline raised her eyes to the dim outlines of the crucifix on the wall to her right. Forgive me, Lord. If she asked them both to get down on their knees and beg for the same thing, they would do it only to please her and because, for that minute, they were in her power. Such power was corrupting: she doubted the Lord would approve, so she contented herself with a question. "Why, Mr. Cannon, did your brother go after her and not after *you?* Why are *you* free to roam the world at dead of night and Julie isn't? Why does he hurt her if it's you he hates? *Why?*"

Put like that, he wasn't sure, or at least not sure of an entirely correct answer, which he knew the question demanded, and he struggled with some approximation, unable to explain: *He doesn't think he hates me, he loves me.*

Intelligent he certainly was, Pauline surmised, but that was not the same thing as good with words. She stared ahead, composed, her hands in the long sleeves of her robe.

"Because my brother doesn't want to hurt me, on account of him being blood, and all," he said. "Inhibits him, see? Besides, he'd tried that before, tried it for years, and he knows what it does. He's beaten me more times than either of us could count. Makes me so dumb, like I've lost any command of my tongue first and my bowels next, and he's squeamish, see? He's not as squeamish with a woman, provided he doesn't have to look at her. He thinks women are the very devil . . . Easier to hurt me by hurting her, believe me. That's why we're both hiding, but not for much longer, and—"

"*Shhhhh!*" Pauline whispered. "Shuttit," she hissed, for emphasis. "*Lord help us.*" They sat in wordless silence, hearing nothing. But she had heard with those antennae that decoded convent sounds, nodded to herself in confirmation. "Quick, in here," the command reinforced with gestures that steered them back into the sacristy with a speed neither thought possible. Not a mutter from the beads. Cannon thanked his trainers for the lack of sound over the wood floor, Julie her slippers.

Pauline drew the door closed behind them with a soft click. No doors were ever slammed. She glided back to the place where they had all sat, spread her habit around her, knelt with her bony thumbs pressing into the side of her nose, wishing to God there was no lingering smell. Gradually, the sound became clearer. *Shuffle, shuffle, rattle, shuffle, shuffle, rattle,* rhythmic but slow, so slow, in fact, she was tired of waiting for the sound to take form, Oh, hurry up and get it over with, for God's sake, forming at her lips as she waited. Imelda moved like a snail, slowed by a sense of duty. Imelda woke in the night as a result of grinding her teeth; she wandered and she gossiped. Pauline saw her now as an elderly pig, hunting truffles. The thought was not charitable.

Why should a man want to destroy his brother? Pauline sighed, manufacturing out of it a massive yawn. *Or his brother's wife?* The corridor entrance to the chapel was by means of a swing door, supposed to be soundless in the interests of late-comers but it still made a wholesome creak.

Sister Imelda saw the empire and the sanctuary of *her* chapel arranged before her, with Pauline, sunk in an attitude of abject prayer, in the *wrong* bench, taking up plenty of space. Not that there wasn't space to spare, especially at midnight and beyond. Imelda hesitated for a moment, sniffed the air and moved forward, with her usual infuriating hesitations. Pauline was forbidding: although one could never fault her perfect manners, she was difficult to touch, even in the best interests of friendship. Pauline detested those she managed to intimidate; she had said so, and Imelda remembered that. She did not pause to consider her identification of the robed nun in the wrong pew. She knew who it was, and if ever interrogated about identification would be mystified by the questions. There were only three in the order who still wore the full robes, with the rosary; but, with or without them, they all knew one another by instinct.

"Sister? Are you all right?" Imelda sniffed again as she asked. Strange smell: foreign. Her sniff was loud.

I shall never understand, Pauline said to herself, why someone with such dreadful halitosis and a teeth-grinding habit can be so sensitive to smells. She sat upright with dramatic flurry, moaning and gripping the front of the pew with two surprisingly large fists, which glowed an unearthly yellow, like bleached bone. "Is that you, Imelda?" she asked faintly.

"Yes, of course." Imelda sniffed yet again.

"How nice. I came down to pray. Only I don't feel so well. Could you help me back to my room?"

"Oh, my dear, of course. Do you know, I thought I heard noise?"

Pauline accepted an arm, leant on it heavily and awkwardly, propelling Imelda towards the door.

"It is a sin, dear Lord, to take advantage of kindness," she murmured. "Really, it is. *I am so sick of kindness.*"

Back inside the sacristy, Cannon wanted to weep. "She humbles me," he said. "She protects you, exactly as she's been asked to do. She accepts. She doesn't insist on knowing why. How can she be like that?"

"Faith," Julie said. "It's called faith. Don't question it. But d-d-d-don't ask it to do the impossible. And please don't leave me with her much longer. I'm ch-ch-ch-ch-changing, Cannon, and I d-d-don't want to change. I love you."

Making love through all these clothes was a fine art, almost perfected and still imperfect, full of longing for nakedness and warmth and row, instead of mouths clamped shut against noise. "I adore you," he whispered. "I adore you." And then, as they rearranged themselves, he said, "I'm not a bad man, am I, Julie? Am I? Not any more. Would their God forgive me?"

She whispered, "You are not your brother, Cannon; you owe him nothing."

He kissed his wife's hand, passionately formal in his leavetaking. The skin was rough with housework.

Oh, yes, I do owe him.

Perhaps, he prayed, they had made a baby.

3

Nobody knew John Smith. Andrew Mitchum made a guess that no one could. Smith was a man of brief appearances, strong aversions and no loyalties.

Seven in the morning: bleak and cold outside, overheated indoors, and they seemed to be discussing the brotherhood of man.

"I am not my brother's keeper, sir."

It was disconcerting to be called "sir" by someone older. Andrew, a twenty-five-year-old solicitor flirting with dishonesty in this extra-curricular work, had never been called "sir" in his life and recognized this as more of a conversational tic than anything to do with respect for his opinion, but it was uncomfortable all the same, especially with someone not even a decade older bearing all the gravitas of middle age. "No," he said. "Of course not. Sir." It stuck in his throat to reply in kind and he realized, too late, that he might be mistaken for a mimic. There was no jauntiness or sense of irony in John Smith. This man had neither logic nor humour, which did not mean to say he lacked charisma; only that he looked as if he had never laughed, except as a private and derisive reaction to something horribly personal, which Andrew did not like to consider. Aside from that, he was attractive, if only as an acquired taste. A folded face was what he had, jowled and lined in a way that might make a sallow French film star attractive and a pale pink Anglo-Saxon resemble a certain kind of pedigree dog with a long tongue and plenty of spit. There was a faint scar leading from the left corner of his lip. Imagining John Smith in the privacy of his bedroom was not therapeutic; neither was it sufficient to stop Andrew Mitchum from being afraid. Or to prevent him from wondering how it was that a man as rich as this should have such terrible teeth. The better to eat one with. One ceased to notice, after a while. One never ceased to be surprised.

"What I fail to understand," he found himself saying, with deferential but genuine curiosity, "is why it matters."

"Why what matters?"

"Finding your twin brother. If you aren't his keeper. Sir."

"You miss the point entirely."

"Perhaps I do."

John Smith emerged from behind his desk and stood by the window with his back to Andrew, looking out and jingling coins in his pocket. The window overlooked a large garden, level at this height, with the branches of a horse-chestnut tree festooned with the tattered remnants of a few orange leaves. Andrew imagined the ground below littered with conkers. No one would collect them.

"If ever I leave this house," John Smith was saying to himself, "I'll leave it empty and let it *rot*."

This announcement was entirely irrelevant to any that had preceded it. Andrew allowed himself to be differently distracted. The house already seemed wasted. Nobody, surely, needed so much space or so much ornament. The curtains drawn away from the vast windows were as opulent as something borrowed from a theatre—the opening of them demanded an overture. The carpet yielded to every step: he felt as if he was walking across a sand dune inside a house unnaturally quiet. If the statue of a preying eagle, carved in silver and standing guard on the mantelpiece, were to fall from its prominent position to the floor, it would make no sound—and it would take a very long time indeed for this house to rot. As for the pictures on the walls . . . Andrew shuddered.

The paintings were all reproductions, highly coloured to the point of being inflammatory. Above the fireplace, cornered by the eagle, there was a battle scene, *The Charge of the Light Brigade* or something of the kind; men with muskets and red uniforms, many contorted in dramatic attitudes of death while non-specific Hottentots appeared to be on the winning side. On the opposite wall, in similar, massive scale, two battleships of 1914 vintage were engaged in furious combat on the high seas, one sinking in scorching water. They were vivid enough to make Andrew imagine explosions and screams, without being subtle enough to stir his emotions. The canvases were extraordinarily shiny. In the hallways were Andy Warhol-style posters, huge heads and one-dimensional faces heavily framed as if they were Victorian, looking odd against flock wallpaper and Edwardian picture rails. The whole house was a riot of garish acquisition.

"It would be perfectly easy to find your brother, even though he is . . . a trifle elusive. I *did* manage to get access to his prison records."

"Part of them," John Smith barked. "What did you do? Pose as his doctor? You found the fucking *dentist* they gave him. That's all."

Andrew had to concede that it was not a lot, just as much as he could achieve with the chance phone call of an amateur, but it did not explain why John Smith should go into such spasms at the mere mention of the word *dentist*. "The question is, why do you want him found?" he queried, opting for the holistic approach.

"He stole from me." It was a flat statement, without undue emphasis.

You have plenty left. The obvious remark was on the tip of his tongue, but Andrew refrained from making it. From lawyer to client—albeit one in strictly unofficial consultation, moonlighting and currying favour without the knowledge of his employers—that would have been impertinence, and John Smith, man of mystery, was a perfect client. A cow for the milking, with an undefined business that seemed to consist of acquiring and selling. Others collected newspapers, conglomerates, manufacturing plants, shops; John Smith, on a lesser scale, collected houses. Started life as a builder, Andrew recalled, not the first to reach such a pinnacle of reclusive respectability, which made it even odder that he should spend so many of his waking hours now thinking of nothing but his twin brother. He, Andrew, would never be like that. Once he was rich (a state of life devoutly to be wished, by any means whatever, and soon), he hoped he would abandon all resentments, relinquish all tedious family ties and realize when enough was enough.

Smith gestured to the wall above the fireplace. "All my life I tried to get Cannon to paint something like *that*," he said carefully. "But would he ever? Like shit he would. He wanted to paint tables and chairs and draw silly little patterns and *women*, for God's sake. Mind, he was good with a bomb, I'll grant him that."

"Good with a *what*?"

John Smith sat. "You heard me. A bomb. If you're going to build anything, you nearly always have to clear something away first. Trees, earth, another building. Besides, a small blast late at night can bring down the price of a house wonderfully. I've had a few bargains that way. Lord, we had such fun. Raised in Belfast, you see. Bombs are only toys, and boys are boys and they play with them. My daddy taught us how so we could wreck places and he could make money building them up again. Taught us everything, the bastard. You could always find a use for a bomb. Don't ask whose side we were on, I can't tell you. A shame you couldn't find his lovely wife."

John Smith was not a conversationalist. Andrew knew he was privileged. He remained silent. For a moment he had relaxed, but the creeping feeling of unease was back, like a breeze round the nape of his neck, making him feel as if someone else was in the room, the other persona of polite, respectable Mr. Smith, stalking behind him like a tiger. Andrew Mitchum told himself, with the wisdom of his over-qualified years, that Smith was *not* a gangster. But gay, for sure, in the current use of the word; not at all the same sort of thing as being festive, in the other sense. This was homosexual screaming for release, and then another appalling thought crossed Andrew's mind. Perhaps that was why John Smith wanted to find his brother. No, no, no. Incest had gone out with the Middle Ages.

"He stole from me," Smith repeated.

"Yes, he used the business to make things for other businesses. He siphoned off some money," Andrew said impatiently. This was old ground.

"*No. Love.* He stole *love*. As if it were simply a commodity. He stole *my love*." The shrill, unnaturally high voice rose to a shout.

"What will you do if you find his wife, *sir?*"

"Hurt her so much that this time she'll run. Thought I'd done the worst I could, but no. This time she'll really scream. He won't want her back. He'll come home to me. But I've only got a couple of weeks more.

I promised him, fool that I am. We always played games, but you have to have rules. Like a boxing match. She *stole* him. The *bitch*."

Suddenly Andrew craved to be beyond these doors in the street, jogging for a bus, home to his lover or back to his office. Out. Instead, politeness ruled hysteria, so instead of taking his leave he laughed nervously. The sound was subdued by the room. There was nobody else in this house, except the silent fat man, the house servant and factotum who opened the door. The one Andrew knew had been deputed to track down the dentist and find out, casually, what the damn dentist did with his weekends. Smith had mentioned that over dinner. *I want to get a look at him,* he kept on repeating, *measure him up, the cunt, see if he'll do, but I don't want him seeing me.* What strange and pointless preoccupations he had. This client was warped, but rich. Exceedingly rich. Too rich to be needing love. "Love? Oh dear, if that was all, everybody would be suing," Andrew spluttered. "For *love*? I mean, suing like mad."

Smith had opened one of the windows, which led on to a small balcony. "I bought him a house," Smith said, with a hint of sadness. There was never more than a hint of any emotion. Spread across the desk was a double-page article about someone who had won the lottery, and bought seven houses with the proceeds for members of his family. It was possible to imagine Smith doing that: there were houses enough, although only God could guess at his motives. It takes the average family man twenty-five years to pay for a house, Andrew thought, with contempt.

"I'm grateful," Smith was saying over his shoulder, "that you were able to get here so early in the morning. Even if there is so little to report."

Andrew shrugged modestly. "He's gone to ground. The wife entirely so. I, er, didn't tell a soul about my researches, like you said. Or this meeting," he added.

There was an approving nod.

"Do come and look at the view."

Mollified, Andrew approached. After all, they had *dined* together the week before. Hadn't that been some sort of overture? Smith, asking questions, eliciting hopes and fears, apparently confiding his own. Telling him about a deserting mammy and a builder daddy, who had sent him and his brother away to make good here when they were fifteen, and hadn't they just? Well, *he* had. Told him about the freakish brother who had somehow learned to paint, even when all they had been was a pair of urchins, abandoned by women, abandoned by everyone.

They stood together as the sun rose, slowly dispelling the mist. The view from here might be tremendous on a good summer day. It was an area of vast older houses: on his way down the long road, Andrew had passed a convent and two nursing homes, suitable uses, he thought, for houses of the size. He felt John Smith's massive hand, tracing with a gentle touch the cleft of his buttocks, under the flap of the jacket, one finger only along the smooth fabric of his new Marks & Spencer suit. Thrilled to the touch. Stared ahead, muscles tensed, not even suppressing the thought that this could be the way to *serious* money; a house, perhaps. The man had plenty of houses and he, Andrew, was a very handsome boy. Then John Smith put his right hand on to Andrew's left shoulder, turned him to face himself, the jowled face lit with a smile, the powerful body bent. "Andrew? You've been a great help, a real comfort to a fool like me. Really." The charm was sincere; felt like a breath of summer.

"Whatever you want, sir."

They seemed to have arrived at an embrace. John Smith was touching him with both hands, grasping for hold; Andrew suddenly floppy, preparing himself for his own reaction to a kiss . . . And then, in a shade of second, he went over the balcony, hoisted by his groin and his shoulder as if he were a lightweight. Two floors down, crashing softly through the branches of the tree, bouncing from each to each, clutching at twigs, first suspended by his jacket, then snarled by his tie, at once upside down, then scrabbling for purchase until he clung by his hands, more by luck than by judgement, oblivious to the scratches and the grazes, looking at the ground. The branch dipped; the buttons on his shirt ripped. He swung like an ape in a cage, a child at play the way Mother said, "*don't*," and finally plumped to earth on a damp, dark lawn, before he had time to scream. The seconds had felt like minutes. There was blood on his forehead, razor grazes on his hands, and nothing he saw fit to notice yet. The last drop had been a mere ten feet from the last, dipping branch. A game, that was all, with a tree especially designed to save him.

He told me too much. If I repeat it, he'll kill me.

The mist drifted back. He watched it in a peculiarly disinterested way, as he lay on his back, stunned by the sky and the omnipresence of the branches rustling angrily, as if scolding, shaking themselves in indignation.

He moved his limbs slowly, propped himself up on his elbows, had some dim, unpleasant memory of where he was. Including the realization that if John Smith thought this was a game he did not care about the consequences.

He shuffled forward until he was in a kneeling position. Felt the first surge of relief that he was whole, if not entire. Then saw the man looming above him.

"Don't *wink* at me, boy. Don't you *dare*. What do you think I am? Some *pansy?* Such lovely *teeth* you have, my boy, you useless little *cunt*. All the better for smiling with. Now, go and tell your boss how you were moonlighting. See how long you keep your job and how long it takes to buy your house. Greedy little faggot."

He saw the piece of wood in John Smith's hand, the size of a piece of fence, crashing into his face as he made to stand, his mouth open in a scream of protest. Felt three of his teeth crack, his jaw shudder. Rose to his feet with his hand clapped over his lips, backing away, choking the scream, hawking blood into the carpet of leaves and damp grass.

The fat man bowed and showed him to the gate of the garden, as if he had been an honoured guest.

No one was going to get close to John Smith.

Whistling on the walk to work; that was the way to do it. Planning as she went, but not a precise form of planning. Thinking with glee of the excuse Ernest had given her to bunk off work, wondering if he had realized it yet; contemplating the rest of the week and how to manage it. Go to see one of the lovers, the one she called Mole, pick up a tip or two on how to form an art collection: he would know, there was always someone who did. Look up where that exhibition was that showed them all; check on Cannon, and if he rang, as he often neglected to do, ask him to go with her. With all that, the done and the undone, the other clients with their divorces and problems, Sarah was glad to be alive.

She stopped by the fruit-and-flowers stall. Michaelmas daisies, shaggy and purple, or should it be three of the monstrous, drooping orange chrysanthemums, or no flowers at all but pounds of the cold russet apples for biting later? When in doubt buy both, and take a full five minutes in a talkative set-the-world-to-rights chat along with the purchase. Early yet. The reception hall was empty. She paused for a minute, picturing those barren walls alive with decoration and, as she envisaged some large canvas of huge colour and conspicuous obscenity fit to make the senior partner choke, she grinned to herself. Then she whistled up the endless stairs, proving she could whistle without breaking step or breath—it was the swimming that did it—kicked open the office door, which was scuffed from this daily attention because she always seemed to arrive with her arms full.

There was that peculiar smell, instantly recognizable only to those who knew it. Blood, unmasked by antiseptic. Andrew Mitchum sat in the chair facing the desk on which he was more accustomed to place his feet, stemming blood from his lips with a teacloth he had found, rocking back and forth, moaning incoherently, dabbing at the droplets on her desk, mixed blood and tears. There was a hideous sense of *déjà vu*. Her step arrested in horror, until the horror receded into a kind of weariness. He, too, had got up all these stairs; he wasn't dying, only bleeding. She should be used to this, seemed to attract it. Don't make a fuss. And don't run screaming for help without checking first. When she had been rescued after being attacked, it was the last thing she had wanted anyone to do, so she herself was not going to do it now. Touch him, tell him it's all right. Don't scream and dial 999 until she had found out what he needed. She should know by now that not every walking wounded wanted to go public. She dropped the burdens; the apples rolled across the floor while she pressed his shoulders lightly to quell the shaking. "There, there," she said. "Tch, tch, what have you been doing? And you such a handsome man, too."

He quivered. Gently, she prised the cloth from his fingers while his eyes remained fixed and wide, looking in terror for a verdict on the damage. Vanity mixed with fear, a sign of health. She remembered what she had done, looked for a mirror, wanting to know the worst.

"Seen worse," she commented. "You'll be as gorgeous as ever inside a week, I wouldn't wonder. Who did this, you daft bastard?"

Seen worse. Herself. Cannon's wife, Julie. She was trying to shake herself free of the purely personal remembrance of injury, the shame of it, the humiliation; trying to make him realize that it was temporary while already it must feel endless. Trying to refine her own memory of what it was she had needed then. Touch; reassurance; the apparition of despised common sense. A joke in bad taste.

"A man . . . I thought he fancied me . . . Didn't . . ."

"And what did he want? Sex? Something easy like that? You shouldn't be so desirable."

The nod was painful but clearly negative.

"Yesh. But he didn' wanna. I didn,' either. Hit on me . . . hit me . . ."

"Sure about that, are you?" she asked, chafing his hands, examining him. If she buttoned the blue serge of his jacket and wrapped him in her shawl, favoured today over the favourite coat, the blood on the shirt would not show sufficiently to shock. She could pass him off as a nose-bleed; she suspected that that was what he would want.

"Inna club . . . Nithe place . . . Nithe client . . ."

You made a pass at him, you little tart, she thought without saying it. Andrew was always making passes at clients with money. Oddly, the thought of ambition frustrated made her more sympathetic. The boy had had injury *and* rejection, not nice at all and not any easier to bear just because he was a creep. There were sounds downstairs, Matthewson's voice shouting an order, his first-thing-in-the-morning attempt to exert control. Andrew's eyes closed in a different kind of terror.

"You were moonlighting, weren't you?"

He raised a hand in acknowledgement. The shaking was slightly less.

"And you wouldn't want anyone to know that, would you?"

The hand moved.

"So I think we'll go out the back way, don't you?"

When Isabella came to William's surgery, she was treated like royalty, red-carpet service except that the front-hall carpet was claret-coloured already. The thought of her filled William's day with a shadow of grief.

"Mummy's got a bib on!"

"Yes, she has, hasn't she? Are you on any medication, Mrs. Oakley? Turn your head slightly to one side for me . . . Feeling OK, are we?"

William knew he should get out of the habit of asking more than one question at a time. Even during a check-up, which in this case was half designed as a pantomime exercise to teach the child to feel at ease. Mummy first, you next, the child a new patient, three years old, and William with no idea of what he would find—a mouthful of caries or nothing at all.

"I'm on the pill," she whispered, as if the information was classified or somehow embarrassing in front of the child. "Doth that coun?'" He was probing the gums, half of his mind elsewhere, with the muted sound of the radio, the joyful memory of the previous patient, the disturbed memory of the night before, while the other half registered what he did and heard. The surgery was blissfully quiet. He had taken in what she had said about the pill and shaken his head. Long may she remain on it: the previous pregnancy had wrought havoc with her teeth and he did not want his mending undone. Isabella and he . . . Would it have been different with children? No, she didn't want them; she wanted the perfect house; she would still be searching for it now.

"An X-ray this side, I think." Nor should he ever say *I think*: he must sound definite. "Bite down. Lovely. Thanks." He moved to the door, beckoning the child with him, stepped back after the button was pressed to remove the saliva-coated square and hand it on behind her head. Never pass anything across the patient's face, least of all a syringe: let it find its way into the mouth before they knew it was there. William's mind went back to the last patient. Such a nice man. Impervious to the whine of the drill, the hiss of the aspirator and the final ignominy of the impression. Lying there dreamily peaceful, with his mouth full of bright red gum, so gentle and vague and comfortable that he had had to be persuaded to bite. William wondered if he would insist upon crowned teeth at that age—such a nice old man. Probably not, but everyone was allowed their priorities. The rules in this practice were dictated entirely by what came through the door. William strove to see himself merely as an engineer and a pragmatist. It wasn't the demands that fascinated him: it was the challenge of technique.

The child clambered into the chair without a qualm and happily revealed a set of even milk teeth. Mother's dental history made her careful; she would be strict on his diet and do her damnedest to make Baby brush, although no one would save him from accidents; no one could.

"Very *good*," Mummy was crooning. William's mind wandered again. An unbusy morning, but he missed the hyperactivity of his former National Health practice, as well as the anonymity of sheer numbers. Conversation had been minimal in those days, the patients mainly stoic and silent. He did not miss the ignorant and terrified children who had to be anaesthetized to keep them still. That had been barbaric. What he resented now was the expectation from every one of his fee-payers that he should form some sort of personal relationship with each of them.

"Do you like sweeties?"

"Yeth."

Such beauty would not last. Better to eat the sweeties and never bother brushing at all.

"Do you mind if I take a photograph? I'll give you a copy. The teeth are so perfect."

"Course." The mother was pleased, as if he had complimented the child's brain. He could see it now: a photo of the child's teeth alongside one of his face in school cap. A photograph for the family records, alongside those of innocent, babyish nudity, produced some time to embarrass a girlfriend, a reminder of fluoride, genetic good fortune or sucrose-free babyhood. The child obliged for the camera, then waved from the door. William felt the vaguest stirring of affection, and then remembered the children of his nightmares: the one with the suffocating chest and the one with the missing teeth, the others crowding crooked into the gap.

His receptionist, a young Australian female of whom he was secretly afraid, sat at the outside desk engrossed in conversation with Tina and an ancient rep flourishing a fistful of brochures, who had failed to notice in the waste-bin the similar stack of adverts for new hygiene aids deposited there every morning. William hurried by, baring his own teeth in a semblance of a smile, carrying with him the wax mould from the old man's teeth, making a brief wave with it. There was a humming from the autoclave, which was sterilizing the implements.

Past the pictures in the corridor, the coffee machine in the immaculate waiting room, the silk flowers, the greenish carpet and the newly painted walls, through the door, past an old, decrepit dental chair he could not move, and down the stairs. Shabbier with each step, full of crap, the detritus of an old surgery, the residue of the last dentist and his father before him, neither of them, like William himself, ever quite able to throw away anything. There were oxygen supplies; there was the heart defibrillator he had never had to use. There was an outdated sterilizer, kettle-sized for small implements and awaiting repair, an old Hoover, ditto. Three cupboards, one with sundry dried and diet foods and the girls' supply of tea, coffee, sugar, snack soups, which they made down here; another with stocks of crystallized mouthwash, throatwash, plaster for making moulds, an old chair or two awaiting rescue, a blanket, looking worn in the light from the window leading on to the dim well of the basement. One of these days he would spring-clean in here. William liked making moulds for crowns. He found it restful.

He picked up a plastic bowl already scored with the remnants of the last mix, half filled it with water from the single cold tap, which dripped into a sink spattered with white. By the sink was the telltale sign of Tina's unwashed ashtray, also covered in white dust. He shook the powdered plaster into the bowl, small amounts at a time, swirled the water until all the powder was absorbed, stirred it, picked up the brush and quickly painted the plaster mix inside the impression left by the teeth. Such cunning contours they had, teeny little ridges, grooves and dents: the liquid was refined, but not enough to reach them all. He painted again, added more, wandered round, waiting for it to dry, sighed with sheer pleasure.

There were rows of models on the table: imprints of jaws with three teeth left; distorted jaws; facsimiles of huge mouths and others of adult mouths so small he could barely insert an instrument. He had once felt a vague envy of a veterinary surgeon invited to treat the totally articulated jaw of a rhino. The conversational requirements would be nil and the teeth accessible with a pickaxe handle; the dentist as carpenter. He came here to fiddle and to dream, to quell the dread of the next hello! and because it was archaic, the whole damn thing, far removed from the gleaming refinement upstairs. And also because it was quiet and draughty and full of souvenirs. He could shut the door on it. His own small flatlet was above the surgery. He liked the sense of occupying this extended fragment of a house but, best, he liked the self-contained peace down here.

Until he heard the feet on the stairs and Tina, yelling out of more than a need for attention, her shoes clattering on wood, her face flushed. "Jeez," she said. "Disgusting. Get outta here."

He didn't know if she meant the room or the situation downstairs.

"Got some bloke needs a hospital bleeding all over the furniture . . . and a friend."

"Drunk?"

"Hurt."

He was a privately paid dentist now, at the front of a big, protective house, only an entryphone to connect him to the street. He did not need to deal with the unruly, the occasional inebriate suddenly aware of pain in his mouth. His duty was to existing patients, not to the rest of the suffering public.

"Your other patient brought him. Sarah."

"Oh. Bring him through to the back."

"I can't stop them, can I?"

A strange procession came into view at the top of the stairs. The man of the pair sat abruptly in the old dental chair, obviously under the impression that this was the end of the road. He held a folded, blood-soaked tea-towel over his mouth.

Sarah Fortune was patting his shoulder, beaming anxiously at William. "Hallo," she said calmly, as if she had not seen him in a while and this was an everyday occurrence. "I found this in my office so I thought I'd better bring him here. He won't let go of me, anyhow." The young man was holding the cloth in one hand and using the other to clutch at Sarah's coat. His face was runnelled with tears. William put his palm to the boy's forehead. This *was* still a boy: William regarded thirty as the threshold of the martyrdoms of adulthood and anything below that as boyhood. His hands were ice-cool from the plaster; the skin of the boy's forehead searingly hot.

"He'll only say that he collided with a tree," Sarah said helpfully and incredulously. "Maybe a lovers' tiff. And he won't go to hospital."

Gently, William prised away the tea-cloth. It was decorated with yellow roses, now red. He murmured to the young man as if he were a child, "There there, there there," thinking, as he uncovered the teeth and curled back the blood-filled lower lip, to see the cut, that this was exactly the playground injury he might have expected to see in a child who had run hard and crashed into a wall; the sort of injury incurred when there was no time to flinch and exactly the kind his three-year-old patient might acquire soon.

"Accident and emergency," he said firmly.

"Neuuuuugh!" The boy began to thrash in the chair, turning his head back and forth, pulling on the coat he still held in his hand. At least he hadn't broken his jaw: it was only teeth and shock. Only.

They moved him to the surgery proper. William noticed the filthy mark of a bloody palm on the fresh paint of the walls *en route*. He sighed. "What's his name? What does he do?"

"Andrew. Not the most promising lawyer. Brawler, by the looks of things." She smoothed the lank hair away from Andrew's forehead, smiled at him reassuringly, the smile negating the lack of compliment in the softly spoken words. *She doesn't even like him*, William thought. *Why doesn't she ever walk away?*

"Look in his wallet. Any prescriptions, notes about medication, stuff like that?"

"Nope. Mid-twenties, belongs to a squash club. Fit as a flea. Gay. If you do the wrong thing, I'll make sure he doesn't sue you."

"Thanks a lot."

Don't pass the needle over the face. This one needed restraint, he did not belong here—and when William tried to get inside that mouth the boy vomited. One of those. Make him comfortable; sedate him; calm him. That will be all for now. A lot of fresh blood on the shirt . . . How had she got him here without stopping the traffic? He felt a guilty relief that he was still wearing gloves. He also felt a brief surge of irritation against Sarah Fortune—her, outside, making arrangements on *his* phone, doing it *again*. Creating mayhem. Bringing the unpredictable off the streets and into his life. How did she do it? Why? What had he done to deserve it, with his quiet life? The boy's eyes were wide with fright. William touched him gently. *There, there, there.*

William Dalrymple was afraid of the dentist himself. It gave him a terrible empathy, and *There, there, there,* was all he could ever say.

It was eleven in the morning. Sarah should be elsewhere, profitably—or at least accountably—employed. She did not want to think about what frightened version of the truth she had been told. *Don't tell anyone, don't tell, I'll lose my job . . . please.* If he did not tell her more, she was not going to insist as a condition of helping him. Help was not a conditional thing. She did not need to know which frustrated loner had punched Andrew in the mouth. It did not matter.

Sarah walked with the speed of a racer, crossing Oxford Street and diving into Bond Street, tripping past shops in her low-heeled shoes, not pausing to stare. Reaching the far end of galleries, arcades of pictures, thinking of Andrew and her own alibi. Outwardly cool, almost languid. *She had to account for this time.* Staring into windows, Agnew Galleries, Bond Street galleries. There was something alien and arrogant about the galleries in Bond Street and St James's, which defied the casual visitor to enter. Even from the outside evidence of heavy glass doors, security systems refined into elegance, the absence of prices, the hushed, church-like atmosphere, they seemed designed to intimidate all but the initiated, while inside there would be the supercilious glance of some slender gallery girl, designed to repel the provincial plod who did not belong. She could see herself wiping her shoes on the doormat as a preliminary to flight: this was not where she could come to shop for art. On the way back, she paused in front of a sober display of old-master flower paintings, glowing with priceless splendour, and thought she would prefer the flowers themselves. *Why does it have to be art, Ernest? Why can't we collect plants? Or rare vegetables?*

There was nothing in these streets of excellence that she wanted, and nothing she wanted anyone else to want. She had once thought there were things she *needed* in environs such as these, in the days when she had *yearned* for the beautiful clothes and the intoxicating power of money, just as Andrew Mitchum did now, so she should empathize, and she did. But there are no short-cuts, Andrew, there never are; and it's never enough, don't you know yet? John Smith can buy what he wants, and what has it done for him? Will you please *look* at the clients, Andrew, before you want what you think they have?

By the time she was half-way back to William's surgery, the swift walk had accelerated and the mind had gone back into overdrive. *Poor little boy.* Juddering and weeping in her room that morning, spitting out words, exhorting her to secrecy about nothing. Well, she excelled at secrecy. He was safe in that regard, and so, she thought with guilty relief, was Cannon.

There was a dress in a window, on a single elegantly stately mannequin. High neck, close-fitting sleeves, a moulded sheath of scarlet wool crêpe with a broad belt in the same colour. She stopped and stared. Gorgeous: dramatic, striking. Now *that* would perk up Master Ralph in the high-court gloom. She was almost in there, tearing it off the model to try it on, until she saw the reflection of her hair in the glass. Some women could get away with a mix of auburn and scarlet but she was probably not one of them. She moved on, thinking that she had left her yearning fingerprints and the slight blur from her nose on the window, and that it did indeed help to be frivolous. Better to be haunted by a dress than by blood.

When she returned, Andrew was in the back, dozing on the old dental chair, cleaner than he had been—and supplied with one of William's shirts, she noticed, with a flush of gratitude. National Health practice had made William difficult to surprise. The door to the surgery was closed; she could hear the drill. With a vacant grin that merely suggested forbearance, the receptionist saw them off the premises to a taxi. *Not much I could do, said William's note, except stabilize his condition. When is someone going to do that for you? Explanations, please, in unmarked envelope to my address.*

When she had delivered Andrew into the arms of his flatmate with a sheaf of prescriptions and instructions, she went back to work, armed with a set of spurious excuses for his absence (road accident) just as he had requested, plus another set for her own. She took the stairs two at a time, feeling only vaguely guilty about all the lies, thinking that the note she had left for William was a shade inadequate. *Thank you, dear. That's your good deed for the day. Now you can be horrible to Isabella.*

Isabella did not simply enter the surgery, she floated in like a dream, a star demanding modest acknowledgement, flashing a smile that was supposed to make them faint, and had roughly the desired effect. They became like hotel staff with a celebrity, *Let me take your coat, madam, please*, the faithful greeting a guru of no known faith. Her entrance was, in all senses, ridiculous, but charming since she never could or would forget a name. "Hallo, Tina, how nice you look. What a lovely day outside." Her musical voice flowed on with a stream of social burble punctuated by sallies of laughter. There was a cry of indignation when she saw the colour of the walls, but remarks on any changes over the last two months were not criticism as such, simply an implication of sartorial superiority. William's estranged wife always told them where she had come from, where she was going next, enveloped the girls in an infective intimacy that seemed to subsist between visits, until William appeared. In that few minutes' interval, she would have asked about his welfare, shared a sweet little joke or two at his expense, united them against him, made them wonder how he could live without her shrewd beauty, shake their heads at the very idea of this failed marriage, which could never have been, by any stretch of the imagination, the fault of Isabella. Nothing was ever Isabella's fault, and yet he could not prevent that treacherous leap of heart when he saw her, or that racing-pulse guilt, which was related to nothing he could define. Not jealousy and no longer quite the same as desire, but a feeling of powerlessness all the same. She reduced him to a state of juvenile dependency; he became a person, suddenly, with no real will of his own. A look from her had always been able to dictate his mood. Isabella had made him what he was, driven him on with a whip, revealed him as inadequate and dull. She was the princess: he the lucky courtier.

These kind of nerves, subtly different from any other kind, made him falsely jovial, shouting an avuncular hello!, accompanying it with a swift peck on the cheek, just to show how amicable, natural, friendly and civilized a relationship with one's ex-wife could be, three years down the line; everything still hunky-dory and bitterness a dirty word. Never a mention of how she had rendered him so completely . . . impotent, then and now; the very smell of her enough to make him shrivel with the shame of failure. At least she knew he was a good dentist; everyone said so.

He led her round the corner to the chair; she settled herself with the ease of familiarity and laced her fingers together over her flat stomach, her legs crossed at the ankle, while she winked at Tina to her left. William adjusted his mask, reached the light to the right angle.

"Do you *have* to wear that thing, darling? I'm not infectious, you know."

"Of course not, but I might be." He laughed immoderately.

Tina looked at him strangely. "Do you need me?"

"No." She left the room, slightly miffed. William hummed as he began to examine Isabella's teeth. It was the one point in time when the balance of power was reversed and he could feel this perverse, guilty enjoyment. In this context alone, she trusted him: she had given herself no choice and, in this moment, all her vanity was revealed. Her eyes stared upwards vacantly, the interlaced fingers were more tightly interwoven and one foot moved slightly, as if remembering a long-forgotten dance. He could see the lines around the eyes and the mouth, wonder at which stage in her life she would try plastic surgery. She wouldn't, because it hurt and because Isabella's mirror would always be allowed to tell her lies. She would not accept age: she would simply fail to see it. And on the back of that stray thought came another vexed question to self: How on earth could he be, or ever have been, in the control of a woman so utterly self-obsessed that she would deny any inconvenient fact? She could eradicate knowledge like killing weeds. She was superb for the lack of any self-critical faculty. She was monstrously stupid and he was still in awe of her.

"All right?"

A crinkling of the eyes and a very slight nod, managing even now that shade of amused contempt.

I could really hurt you, William thought grimly. I could say there were caries in this back tooth, inject you not near the nerve but into it; make you scream. Go through a vein, give you a lovely haematoma; invent a treatment; take out a tooth, try to leave half behind, abscess, swelling, pain and more pain. He could not have done it any more than he could have hit her. What he was doing was probably worse.

"We did X-rays last time, didn't we?"

"Yes," he said shortly.

"And everything's fine, I suppose?"

"Yes."

"Good."

"Do the gums ever bleed?"

"*My* gums? Bleed? Whatever for?"

They bled when he probed. Deep pockets round the upper palatal and lower lingual teeth, more than six millimetres, significant recession of the bone at the back. To admit to bleeding would be an admission of imperfection, another inconvenient fact: she would not believe the significance. *The whitest teeth are not necessarily the strongest.* She had teeth that gleamed white in her professionally bleached smile, her care going into what showed; the rest, to use a non-dental phrase, grimy, especially the distal and mesial surfaces. There was more time spent on the care of the face. He remembered the rigorous beauty routines before bed. Perfection was hard to achieve: there were priorities.

Just you wait, William told himself. Just you wait.

She could not be less than perfect and she would always be so stupid . . . and yet the profile, turned to him in a practised way, moved him unbearably. Vanity and ambition made her so vulnerable; criticism, however phrased, would make her shrill, and even the most conservative of constructive suggestions about any aspect of her appearance would make her flush with fury. *You must clean your teeth rigorously* would make her feel a slut. *You have subacute periodontal disease and, while plaque may be simply a feature of the mouth, to you it is fatal* would sound like yet another lecture. Why say it? She would not hear it. There was little joy in this dereliction of duty, although it also gave him a slight satisfaction.

"Issy, there's something . . ." He stopped, arrested by her expectant stare, her constant, amused waiting for the dreaded moment of some personal revelation, some statement of continued desire. He realized, as his voice trailed away, that he was standing with his feet turned inward, hands clasped, body bent into an anxious and graceless stance, reminiscent of himself at five years old, the little boy again, making a desperate plea for the lavatory.

"Yes?"

He shook his head.

"Must go, darling. Lovely to see you."

Her eyes began at his over-large feet, travelled the length of him, taking in the red hands, the mask, absentmindedly forgotten and pushed up off his face like a misplaced party hat, and she smiled her gentle forgiveness of all his ineptitude, using her eyes to hold him still for one long, pitying moment before she swept past on her way to the door in a trail of Givenchy. There was laughter from the other side of the door; a murmured instruction, *Keep him in order, won't you?* as if he was a prized, albeit delinquent, possession, loaned into the care of others until he was ready for collection at a later date.

William moved to the window so that he could see her cross the road, three flights down. A swirl of olive-green cashmere cape, a quick look at her watch, the hand raised for the taxi, the dull gleam of her dark blonde hair, and all of a sudden he was overtaken by a feeling of sheer malice so intense it shook him rigid. The *first* thing she would know would be loosening of the back teeth, due to perishing of the bone. Then one or two would fall out; then more. Her face would sink; her lips would turn inward; she would scream at her own reflection. Rant and rave. Remedial treatment would be slow, expensive, unguaranteed, with the alternative of dentures to clack while she ate her delicate food.

He wrote up her notes with a shaking hand. *Never make personal comments in patients' notes: all prejudice will turn upon you.* That did not exclude lies. "Patient urged to have X-ray to monitor progress. Offered hygienist. REFUSED." Revenge, if conscience allowed it and she continued to encourage it, might indeed be as sweet as the caramels she ate.

Tina sidled into the surgery and began the routine wipe-down clear-up routine between bums on the chair, her silence a mute expression of hostile curiosity. "You must still *like* each other," she ventured.

"I don't think that follows," William said dismissively. "I don't think it follows at all." He was remembering the dream and the size of his feet. Seeing Isabella coming in the door with the two children who were not theirs, leading her little beauty parade of all his failures, the boy with the collapsed lung and the girl with the fangs.

He would write her a letter about her periodontal disease: he would; he should. *You are like the poorest patient I ever had, Isabella; it is only here such ignorance lurks, but ignorance in your case is wilful. You never wanted to know.* And when the pen went to the paper, he would remember all she could have learned and all the times she had so obdurately refused to listen to anything that concerned him, and then he could not get over his unholy glee at the thought of Isabella and the shrinkage of the skull beneath her skin. May God forgive him.

He tore off his gloves, scrubbed his hands vigorously, letting the pain bite. Perhaps if she married she would release him from the spell. William stared at her open notes, flicked from them an imaginary speck of dust.

Notes. It was a myth that he knew all his current patients: it was a knack of reassurance that he could pretend that he did. There were few enough of his patients he knew, only some he remembered. The notes were impersonal: they rekindled memories of the teeth, not always of the face or the personality. He liked it that way. It was four in the afternoon, and the day, in his current state of emotional exhaustion, felt endless, as if it had never once been light, only as dark as it grew now. Rain drizzled against the window. One more to go. William saw the name on the page and began to smile. He looked at his notes about Cannon and blushed at the way he himself continued to ignore his own best advice about keeping them impersonal. "Nutty and delightful," he informed himself from his own prose, wondering at the same time if it was not a better description for chocolate. "Brave": not a description he often found occasion to use. "Surly today; painting well," would hardly give a clue to the man's dental problems, but he had still included it. In the box on the first page, where he invariably wrote the name of the person who had referred the patient to him, it simply said, "Gaol." William rushed out to the waiting room to embrace him. Cannon was one of his triumphs, one of his rare affections.

Cannon sat, huddled into his evil coat, staring at a painting on the opposite wall, wagging a finger at it, measuring it with his eye, giving it the thumbs-up sign, lost in a dialogue that meant nothing to anyone else. It was one of many indefinable reasons why William liked him: their gestures and their nervous habits could have been those of cousins. The *non sequiturs* of their conversations made illogical sense. Cannon talked to paintings as if they were alive: he began each conversation with whatever it was on the top of his mind, scooping it into words like froth.

"He's got the fucking hands all wrong," Cannon said, jabbing his finger at the portrait as though rebuking it to improve. It was a portrait of a benign old man. "God bless the poor bastard. At least I'm not alone. Every bastard does it. You can paint the tits and the hips, but the hands and the mouth—total balls-up."

He stood, level with William's chest, grasped his shoulders and gave him a big, smacking kiss on the chin. It was audible: Cannon could make a kiss echo from wall to wall and start a hundred rumours. The grin seemed to dislocate his jaw.

William found himself returning it. "Why the hell have you made an appointment? No need."

Cannon was pulling a parcel out of a rucksack that had seen better days. The parcel was wrapped in tissue, secured with inordinate amounts of string. "Needed to talk, that's all. Listen, I got business for you." His skin glowed clean; his coat smelled of earth and damp, a contrast to the pot-pourri, and William laughed for the first time in the day. After a time it felt like exercise, a relief for some hidden set of muscles, undetectable except through disuse. Cannon tore at the paper wrapping of his parcel. A painting.

"What business? I've got plenty. I don't need any more."

Cannon sat on the floor with his legs crossed, eyes on the painting propped against the sofa, mind in focus. "A tribe of nuns?" he asked. "Gave up with the dentist years ago, costs too much, and one of the poor creatures grinds her teeth. So much for God, eh? I'm paying. Didn't I say I'd see you right? And, while we're at it, can you keep this for me? Only I haven't got room for it at the minute."

A nude. William stared at it, transfixed. It brought light into the room. He stared at the painting and then at Cannon. There was a certain bond between one man and another if they had met behind prison walls, even if one was fresh from outside and the other a sulky, suspicious suicide-risk.

"You just look after this for me, will you? And you'll like the nuns, I promise. Oh, and when you phone up and offer your fantastic services, don't mention all that cosmetic stuff, will you? They won't want to know. And don't say I asked you. Say . . . say Sarah Fortune put you in touch. She knows them too. Not too soon for a drink, is it?"

William was never surprised about whom Sarah knew. After all, she had sent him to Cannon in prison and got Cannon round to him, just as she produced others of her peculiar clients to visit him in his more usual surroundings. By common consent, they went downstairs to the glory-hole. In his treatment Cannon had been allowed free range of the place, originally to keep him away from the staff and the respectable customers, then as a concession to a man who came with his own gaolers. Let him and his minds stretch their legs, fulfil their curiosity about how everything worked. Difficult to imagine Cannon being acquainted with nuns, but he looked like he needed charity. Faith and hope seemed in reasonable supply. William knew not to ask questions. The glory-hole suited them best. On the three occasions post-prison when he had come back, shyly, to chat, this was where they had sat.

A dentist, and an artist who had given up making bombs and buildings: the contrast delighted William. He had minimal knowledge of the man and how he lived now, and did not need to know. Cannon asked for nothing, even brought his own whisky.

"Christ, William," he remarked, looking round, admiring the mess. "This place is an arsenal, you know."

"I should tidy it up, I suppose."

"No, don't do that. I like it here."

William admired the smile he had made.

4

B*OOM, BOOM . . . CRASH. I'll blow your house down . . .*

I'm going to do it now, Little Red Riding Hood . . . You'll never get a penny from me . . .

She woke with a short scream of surprise from a mid-afternoon doze. Day-dreaming, slipping into torpor, and all the images converged, *crash.* A woman in an exquisite red dress was orchestrating the demolition of a house, chanting through buck teeth the complaint of the divorce client whose file was on the desk and whose bleated fury stared from the printed page. *He said he'd never give me a penny and he hasn't . . . Nothing's safe, not even houses . . .*

Sarah blinked and took a slug of cold tea, wishing it was gin, lit a cigarette, pushed away the deposition and retrieved the other papers, which had slid to the floor with the wakening *crash.* This was better. Given this kind of literature, she was anybody's. Art catalogues were the picture-book stuff of speculation, but the particulars offered by property agencies held another kind of magic. They were made for dreamers. They were read by Sarah Fortune with all the fervour of a person who believes that it is better to travel hopefully than to arrive.

I want to inspect unoccupied properties, she had told the agents. I need to view them empty, so that I can see the possibility of myself living inside them without having to speak to an existing occupant and I don't know what I want. Houses, apartments, whatever makes a home. Price range, madam? She shrugged her shoulders expansively. Depends on the house, the apartment, the street. They looked at her clothes and her air of confidence, sent her everything they had because she looked like a well-kept lady. There was the same assumption she had noticed before, namely that if a woman is well dressed she is automatically assumed to be intelligent, her mouth framed to speak perceptions beyond the normal range, as if a flair for visual self-enhancement were anything more than a knack. There were similar assumptions, she had thought, as she moved insouciantly from one prestigious property agency to the next, such as the idea that a painter with visual skills would be articulate, an actress interesting and a tart also a philosopher. Or that women were sisters under the skin.

She was on the second sheaf of particulars when the word "sister" came to mind, a memory purloined from the sheaf of glanced-at unanswered messages on her desk. Some were already redundant; half were asking her to account for her time, and Sarah rarely attempted the impossible. ". . . charming terraced house with small garden, lovingly maintained in quiet road . . ." No. ". . . small, second-floor apartment overlooking green sward, near tube, small balconies . . ." These could be the particulars of her own abode, reduced to a terse description and thus acquiring a kind of glamour, appearing to her own eyes exactly the kind of thing she was looking for. ". . . *living room, 12' × 12'; two bdrms, 12' × 10' and 8' × 10'; bthrm, 10' × 4'; ktchn, 6' × 8'; use of lge gdn . . .*": what an odd shape it sounded, so impossible to visualize. She turned to the next. The text was compulsive reading: "*Overlooks canal . . . huge recep! no mod cons! Ideal investment opportunity!*" And if it were, the market, with its best gambling instinct, would have absorbed it many months ago. Damp and empty, was what she read, and chewed her fingernails with a gentle, inquisitive motion as if they might provide interesting food. She had to be *here,* dropping tiny fragments of nail into the ashtray, rather than out there, on her way to the ideal investment opportunity, which was so ideal that no one wanted it, the very thought of the thing creating a surge of excitement. More than a dress; more than a coat; more than a painting. This was *real* shopping.

The phone rang. She could hear the background roar of traffic. Then a muted swearing; a muttering of formless, threatening syllables that sounded like obscenities—and might have been no more than the human sounds of a stranger struggling with a phone card in an unfamiliar place while besieged on the outside by aliens.

"For God's sake, is that you?"

"It is, it is. What's the matter?"

"You're always out, is the matter. I hate this phone card you gave us, is the matter. Can't hear myself speak either. Mother of God . . ."

"Where are you?"

"I'm stood with my head in a bubble in a place where a dog pees down the side of my habit and the world thinks I'm a freak. I need to see you. Soon."

"Yes. I think so too. I've got to look at a flat. Can you come? About six?"

A chuckle; the sound of a kick. "Tell me where. I'm a sucker for a house, as long as it's empty. I've got strips to tear off you. Things to ask. I'm out on errands."

Sarah looked round the office. *Everything you ever wanted.* She looked at the elegant frontage of the place advertised in the particulars as she recited the address. *Everything you never had.*

Why do you *need* it?"

They stood outside a grey terrace in the dark, Sister Pauline and her niece Sarah, waiting for the agent. Pauline had a box with her containing her errand, which was a duvet. "For Imelda," she explained, as if such a luxury required explanation. "We have to spoil her to stop her grinding her teeth." The girl from the agency had a cold: she was immune to Sarah's charm and jealous of her coat, and she was intimidated by the firm handshake of a nun with a face like a hatchet. She fumbled with keys and opened two doors leading into a raised ground-floor flat. From the windows at the front, the waters of Little Venice gleamed dully. The inner door was stiff, requiring a shove, first indication of the overpowering smell of damp. The girl shivered. "Why don't you go and sit in your nice warm car?" Pauline demanded.

"I shouldn't . . ."

"You should. We might be a while."

She went, ungratefully. What did it matter? Twelve times she'd shown this place; no one would buy before the spring.

"Why would you *need* it?" Pauline repeated. "All this space."

Sarah did not answer, drew her coat closer. The main room at the front was huge and echoey; the room behind half as large and darker. The walls were fifteen feet high with a cornice and a crumbling central rose from which there hung a solitary bulb, swaying in the draught from the door. Cold. There had been an ornate fireplace, untidily removed to leave a cavern in the wall and a black hearth. There were holes in the walls for the missing light fittings. The floor-covering was garish in the electric light, with big splodgy flowers. They moved through the wide hall into the kitchen. Grubby yellow units with gaping doors, gaps where the white goods might have stood. There were droppings in the corner; an acrid smell.

"It was burgled," Sarah told her aunt conversationally. "The agent told me. The owner can't be bothered to clean up or get it done, doesn't seem to care. Puts a jinx on it for buyers."

The air of neglect was almost palpable: they could taste it and breathe it. Anything that might have given life to the rooms was gone. The width of the house was narrow; it was deep from front to back, with the kitchen and bedroom facing on to a back garden area. The rear rooms were meanly proportioned for their height: even in daylight, they would be dim.

"I'd want to knock these walls down," Sarah said.

"You have a penchant for knocking down walls," Pauline replied equably. "Now, will you tell me why you've dragged me along to look at this dump? And tell me what's happening to Mr. Cannon. I don't care if that little girl out there perishes from frostbite. I'm not leaving this filthy place until I know . . . well . . . a lot more than I know now. Julie Smith's been with us three months. I'm not sick of hiding her, but I need to know how long."

Sarah found herself suddenly defensive about the flat, as if by having elected to view it at all she had acquired a stake in its reputation. "It's a *glorious* dump," she insisted. "Look at that front room. Give it money and care, it could be *magnificent.* I *love* faded grandeur. The bathroom's OK, and as for the back, well, you could hide in it. No one would know you were there."

"Ah," said Pauline. "I see. Distraction. Somewhere magnificent in which to hide. That's why you house-hunt. That's why you've been house-hunting for a year. You're a courtesan in pursuit of faded grandeur. Needing a new face some time soon. Or a new place to hold court. You can throw bread to ducks from the front. Or let them eat cake."

She swung her arms wide for warmth and folded them across her chest, tapped her feet against the cold of the kitchen floor; her long habit rustled and the beads rattled. Sarah took out her cigarettes, extracted one and proffered the packet in Pauline's direction. Pauline took one greedily; they lit up in silence. Sarah heard a sigh of satisfaction. "Go ahead and bribe me," Pauline said. "It's easy."

"I believe," Sarah said, in the tones of a tour guide explaining the finer points of the museum, "that this flat, as part of this house, is owned by one John Smith, Julie's brother-in-law. It has all the hallmarks of a Smith property. He buys them, sometimes lives in them, then moves on. Lets them to destructive tenants sometimes. He can't quite bear to let them go. What is *his* can't possibly belong to anyone else, or not for a long time. He doesn't have the same sentimentality about office blocks, so he has plenty to indulge his little hobby. He won't knowingly sell to a woman buyer, which restricts it a bit . . . and the price will be too high, which restricts it further. Smith puts them on the market and makes it impossible to sell. He'd rather let them rot."

Pauline was silent.

"He sells in the end. When he's besieged with offers and fed up with the game. When it's so decayed its own architect wouldn't know it."

"Sarah," Pauline said, "you are wasting my precious time. My God, it's so cold, I should wear this thing." She kicked the duvet box. "Here we are, looking at a place you're never intending to buy even if you could, and you're telling me facts—interesting facts, I grant you—which do not really help me. At all."

Sarah stubbed the box with her toe, pushed it to one side. There was a sale sticker; Pauline could scent a bargain from the other side of the street.

"They should," Sarah said. "Although I'd rather not be telling you. John Smith is Cannon's brother. Brother-in-law to Julie Cannon, who, I think, *you* have grown to like."

"I don't just like her," Pauline interrupted, "I love her. I care for her profoundly. A girl who drops out of school, chucked by family, and brings herself round from drugs . . . clever . . . decent . . ."

"I thought it might be useful for you to see a John Smith property," Sarah continued, "because it might give you some idea of his attitude to possessions. He can't relinquish or respect either people or things. This includes his brother as well as his properties. He wants his brother back, body and soul. Dangerous men don't understand their own motives."

They were surrounded in a grey cloud. The cold stuffiness made smoke linger in the air.

"So how comes it, niece, that *you* understand them? Are you so well versed in the mind of man you can decode it at a glance now you've slept with so many of them? Is that it?" She blew smoke into the air, the action somehow contemptuous, the words quiet. "You used to seek attention as a child, you know," Pauline continued. "Not that you got it the few times I saw you, for all your trying. Such a fine little storyteller, with just that *grain* of truth." She snapped her fingers to show how little. "Don't know why I chose to believe you now but, then, I suppose I live by faith. One way and another."

"You know what he can do. You didn't learn that from *me*."

"I know what *someone* can do. *Did* do. To Julie. She has this quality of goodness which is appallingly addictive. She shines." Pauline spun on her heel, gripping the beads of the rosary. The habits of silence were instinctive. It seemed wrong to make a noise here, even though she wanted to shout. "He whipped her," she said wonderingly. "You told me and I believe you because I saw the result. He got to her, a fat man, just before Cannon was due out of prison. He and another man brought her to a place like this, had her whipped and tortured for the sheer impertinence of being alive. Covered her face so he wouldn't have to see it. He thought she would run. She didn't. You found her. She told me she knew it was *him* because of his *teeth*, I ask you." She slapped her palm against the wall, which felt wet to the touch, withdrew it hurriedly. "I want to know *why* . . . and how *you* know *why*. And don't tell me," she went on furiously, "don't *dare* tell me that Cannon is an innocent just because his wife is so clearly that. Don't make him into a hero for me. I'll never believe you. You are such a *romantic*. Don't tell me that this villainous brother put him away into prison simply to detach his wife."

The cigarette in the other hand was finished. Pauline held the filter tip between her thumb and finger, looking at the dead end of it longingly. Sarah hesitated. An empty flat, with the promise of what it might become, seemed to make her want to slur and hurry the words. She and Pauline were sometimes awkward together in the manner of those who loved but would never understand one another.

"No. Not quite. John Smith masterminded a complex business, mainly legitimate, admirable even. Building, property development. The arrangement of explosives was a sideline. You wanted a building to come down before the bureaucrats told you to save it, they were your men. I don't know who they supplied—Cannon's too ashamed to say. There was certainly money in it. Then Cannon fell in love, married quick, became the total renegade in his brother's eyes. The illicit end of the business was discovered when Cannon wouldn't co-operate any more. He took the blame for it totally and went to prison for the best part of two years. Not before he'd pocketed a fair chunk of his brother's money. Hates explosives now, even fireworks make him crazy. He's a man of many talents."

"Could he bomb the bishop for us, do you think?"

"No. He has a mysterious affection for clerics. One of them married him to Julie, after all. He's grateful."

"I never know when you're exaggerating, niece, but you never fail to give me food for thought, and prayer. You're like a tabloid newspaper in that respect—I never quite know what to believe and I can never complete the crossword puzzle. Do they have anything else in common, these brothers? Any weaknesses, apart from lack of conscience?"

"Teeth."

Pauline ignored this as facetious. "We must go," she announced. "I, at least, must. You can sit here and dream if you want. I can't. I take your point. Your only real point. Only a devil would leave a flat to rot when a thousand other people *need* a room. He must be wicked. It doesn't follow he's a sadist."

"Cannon says he is. I have to believe Cannon. No one else *knows* John Smith."

Sarah waved from the front window to the girl in the car outside. Unsmiling, she came to the door, let them out, locked up and got back into her car again. They walked a way down the street, Sarah carrying the duvet box, crossed the road, rested against the railings and looked at the water of the canal. It looked like black jet in the lamplight.

"What a shame J. Smith owns that house," Sarah said. "I've always wanted to live by the water."

"How many places like this?"

"Oh, ten, fifteen, at any given time. All of them interesting." She lit another cigarette and did not offer the packet. "Ironic that Cannon, after destroying his own house, hides in a property belonging to his brother. Possibly the last place for his brother to look. Can't work in the long term. Smith is looking for his brother, but not very hard. The person he's really seeking is his brother's wife. He wants to cut her into little pieces and hang her out to dry. And then he thinks Cannon will come home to him again."

Pauline gripped the railing. "*Would* Cannon do that? Abandon her? Oh, for God's sake, I sound like a litany. *Why?*"

"I don't know. Cannon and John were everything to one another for most of their lives. I don't know what he'd do. But Cannon's wife is the biggest insult Johnnyboy has suffered in his whole existence. She's the one who took Cannon away. No question in *his* mind of Cannon going of his own accord. Anyway, it isn't a question of what Cannon would do—no one can predict that. It's what his brother *thinks* he would do."

"She might die if she lost him. She couldn't stand any more violence either," Pauline said. "She'd crack."

"Cannon thinks she would be destroyed if his brother found her. He's sure of it."

"Are *you* sure?"

Sarah hesitated. A car swung into the street, catching them in the headlights. A nun and a still young woman, staring at the water, the nun crossing herself, her head bowed. A tableau for the curious: a scene of conversion on a route to Damascus, perhaps; the older woman exhorting the younger to mend her ways. It could have been an argument about the box that stood between them.

Pauline shivered.

"I have to be sure. I can't take the risk of not believing. You'll keep her, won't you? Only until Christmas. A few more weeks. That's the deadline Johnny's set."

"Of course. Did you ever doubt it? Answer me two more questions. Now." She counted them on her fingers. "How do you have all this knowledge? Papers? What you lawyers call *hearsay*? Cannon? Pillow talk? And then why do you care?"

A duck swam on the dark water, a calm and lonely thing. Sarah began to explain, keeping her voice low in deference to its tranquil progress.

"I met Cannon when he turned up at the firm—he'd seen the name on one of John's letters and he was sent up to me as just another loser. I like him and I care because he and Julie exhibit a kind of love of which I would never be capable. I admire it beyond reason. I believe beyond reason. And what I know, yes, I've learned from pinching office files, listening to the gossips, and I've got a spy, my boss's wife, who tells me the real lowdown on clients because she gets the information he'd never share with me. Mrs. Matthewson and I are friends. *And* I've listened to Cannon, and *yes*, I believe, because somebody must. And *yes*, I've got close to an estate agent or two to get the gist of this property angle, but I might well have done that anyway. I like that sort of thing. Men are such fountains of knowledge."

Pauline picked up her box. "Julie reads all her spare time. She tries to improve her mind."

"Don't you *dare* to subvert her beliefs, will you?" Sarah shouted. "Don't make her question this love of hers. You'd do it, I know you would. Look after her, but leave her mind *alone*. She has more virtues than I, Sister. At least she endeavours to save herself. I'm beyond all that."

Pauline leaned forward and kissed her cheek, touched her face with the rough knuckle of one hand lightly. "Hush, niece. You've the most generous heart I know. I'm not criticizing. Do I ever?"

"Yes," said Sarah. "You do."

"Only when I'm tired. Imelda keeps me awake."

Sarah pecked her on the cheek. "Take her to a dentist. I'll find you one."

Pauline returned the kiss. "She wouldn't go any more than I would. I'd rather face the fiery flames of hell." It was cold. Pauline looked for something to say. "If the interrogators of the Inquisition had hired dentists as torturers, there'd be no martyrs to the faith. They'd have killed themselves first. Why didn't they think of it?" A bus drew into sight.

"There weren't any dentists."

"Don't be pedantic. And, if we really need one, God will provide. Yours would be far too expensive."

Know thine enemy. Always the way—they would part on a waspish note, Sarah Fortune and her dead mother's sister, leaving each other with love and a rising tide of sheer irritation. Blood, for ever coursing thicker than water; the presence of God in one life and the lack of it in the other stirring the brew. We are, Sarah Fortune told herself, the most worldly women of our acquaintance, and yet, and yet . . . she never accuses me and all the time I know she might. There was a resurgence of old longing for family love, to be accepted and *admired.* Pauline could never do either; the knowledge left Sarah bereft.

She walked down the wide street, looking into windows. I could live here, and my life would be different; I could live *there* and my life would be different again. I could have had a different husband, raised a cricket team and made them sandwiches; I could have been a nun. I have nice teeth and a body covered with scars, and I want for nothing but a new house and the fulfilment of some perverted, romantic urge. Don't tell me about hellfire, Aunt. I know. If I can't save myself, I'll save who I damn well can.

Good advice, even that held on the cusp of the tongue and only mentioned in prayers, had always been the worst as far as Sarah was concerned. Pauline always resurrected second-degree guilt. Sarah slammed the door inside her flat, changed her clothes, made her way back to the West End environs she had passed in the morning, toothbrush inside handbag. She was shyer of the bathrooms of her male acquaintance than she was of their bodies.

If in doubt, don't think, do. Look in shop windows and visit a lover. Do all of that which would make Pauline disapprove.

Wet pavements and a million cars; a loquacious taxi driver. The Bond Street lights beginning to suggest the promise of Christmas, a bedding-down into winter and serious spending. The taxi chugged in the traffic, slow enough to allow the gaze to travel across shop windows. Into St James's, with the beautifully tailored houses of dealers in art and gambling, so remote, so aloof, so arrogantly exclusive that she could see the temptation to destroy them as well as admire them. The taxi stopped. She walked through an arch into a courtyard, rang the bell on a heavy door, glanced at the window display. Inside were paintings of heroic significance. Oil-painted scenes of battles and oratory. Hunting scenes; portraits of glum dogs in packs; portraits of generals and elders of the parish; nothing suitable for a boudoir. And, beyond the paintings, a small dapper man, waiting to feel important. A nice, lonely man who liked living alone, but not all the time. Another lover and a fellow frivolous hedonist.

I like him, too, Sarah told herself, as she waited. I like all my friends and all my lovers. That's the problem. There is no rhyme or reason to my liking, no discrimination. It makes my knowledge of the world extremely eclectic. It hides the fact that my heart is cold.

"Hallo, Mr. Mole," Sarah said, when he came to the door. "Why do you always look so anxious?"

Drip . . . drip . . .

Late in the evening Cannon wanted to write furious letters, but he had never had much patience with words. Letters of love to Julie; begging letters to his brother, if he were not afraid of making even that contact. Johnny might regard a letter as part of the game; might use it as an excuse to renege on his promise.

There was a steady drip of water from the ceiling windows of his garret, which puzzled him since it was not raining. The roof seemed to store rainwater until long after the event, then release it into the room in minute quantities. The dripping was irregular, so that while at first he had steeled himself for the next *plop!* he was now content to ignore it as he might have done an irregular metronome guiding someone else's piano lesson. He put the battered armchair beneath the site of the drip, so that the sound changed from *plop* to *plip*, and was satisfied with that.

No light but inadequate electric light, and it was all his own fault. He had, after all, destroyed the house, which was theoretically his own but it had never been his house anyway. What Johnnyboy purchased never belonged to anyone but himself. The destruction was a gesture of contempt that Johnny, of all people, should have understood. What was he to do? Live in it and wait for the State to take it while waiting for Johnny to cease his own, incessant calls, in case he was there? That was his last piece of destruction, his very last, and now he was hiding for fear of Johnny's presence and Johnny's voice and what it might persuade him to do.

No light meant no colour except primary colour. Poster paint, powder paint, the sort they had used as kids for lack of anything else, aerosol cans far beyond the price of what they could afford. Johnnyboy got bored with it; he never did. From graffiti to oil paint on canvas, he was never bored. This was what he had always wanted to do. From a background such as theirs it was a miracle he had ever learned.

He had meant to work on the Sarah portrait, but the quality of light forbade serious endeavour. The colours would be all wrong; the result would be garish, the paint on the palette too strong for the daytime tones he had sketched. Such lovely skin, she had. He could not resist for a minute working on the skin, including those features lodged in his memory. Little white flakes on her breasts, like tiny soapflakes . . . there! Then he put more brown in the hair. The rich auburn hair with which she played had disturbed him; a little more brown made it less luminous. Stop: he would ruin it. It was artistically dishonest of him to try to turn the portrait of one woman into that of another simply because he wished the model had been his brown-haired wife.

He had caught the facial likeness, though. They were the same height, Julie and Sarah. Perhaps it was not a cheat to change the colour of the hair, provided he did not alter the distinctive shape of it, curling down to the shoulders. He wished Julie would grow her hair into the way it had been when she visited him in prison. She had laughed at the suggestion and said she would, when they were together in a setting where vanity could be indulged.

Oh, Johnnyboy, you fool. Johnnyboy had refused outright to meet Julie. Refused that privilege repeatedly, even turned his face away from the photographs Cannon had shoved into his hand, saying, Look, look, isn't she beautiful? They had fought when Johnnyboy had tried to tear them up, but it was useless fighting with Johnny. He won with contemptuous ease. Johnny had muscle, one of their many differences. They were no longer identical in feature and physique, not notably similar even, apart from a familial likeness only apparent when anyone saw them together. In the bed shared as children, and somehow never quite relinquished even after Johnny began to bugger him, Cannon had admired his brother's muscular development against his own skinny chest. It had not seemed an unnatural thing to do: he had massaged Johnny to order; made love to him to order; loved him, feared him, and then abandoned him. He stared at the gap on the wall where the painting of the woman had been, the one he had bought with Johnny's money. Johnny was the first lover.

Never easy to excise love, whatever kind. He knew only of this incestuous kind, and the love of Julie. One love did not replicate another: it simply predominated, so that the old one had to be hacked out of the system, the wound cauterized to prevent infection. Johnnyboy had not done that. Cannon thought he had, but at times it came back like a rogue virus, with symptoms of guilt, sentiment and a feeling of weakness so intense it immobilized him completely. *He was the first.* The love virus did this even after what Johnnyboy had done to Julie—returned, made him feel septic with it all over again. Brother; lover; twin; same flesh, same DNA. Oh, for a child. If they had a child, Johnny would know it was too late, and ever since he'd loved her he'd wanted her child. To be the father he had scarcely had. To prove himself.

Enough of that. In the absence of light sufficient to distinguish subtle colour, he would not paint, he would draw with a big fat brush dipped in vitriolic black ink. The head emerged as if it had grown from the stark white paper. Johnnyboy's smooth black hair, slicked back into control, like the rest of him; the frown-line between the bushy eyebrows he had once plucked, seeking that Valentino look in a broad face that would never allow it. One ear slightly larger than the other; the creases in the cheeks; the fold of flesh beneath the jaw that made him look as if the whole of his face was sinking; the scar to the left of the mouth.

Remembering, too, how Johnny had got that scar. So frightened of the lady dentist, they'd tried a general anaesthetic to deal with his teeth, with Cannon waiting for him in the outer room because he wouldn't have gone at all otherwise—any more than he could stay unconscious for more than a few minutes, whatever they did. But it had been long enough for the boiling-hot handpiece she had left hooked inside his lip to burn through the flesh, so that he woke screaming. Both of them staggering out of there, fighting like rats, two undersized urchins on the run. Back home to hugging in bed. She hadn't meant any harm, of course, but they blew down her door anyway. That was the day they became lovers: they owed her that. Even the first painful buggery had been provoked by pain.

Nobody knows you, Johnny, except me. Don't cry, please don't cry. He lit a cigarette. These were things he should tell Sarah. Make her understand that Johnny did keep his promises.

The talent of capturing likeness was a frightening gift. This was not Johnny now, but Johnny in a few years' time when the good looks would be gone, the apoplectic colour of his skin higher and the brown eyes ever more hooded. Finally the mouth, large and wide like Cannon's own, the only real point of resemblance, with fleshier lips drawn back into a rictus of a smile to show chipped, uneven teeth, stained dark. A shadowed face, hurt and lonely and cruel. Puzzled. Quickly, before any element of pity could enter the equation, Cannon inked in three of the teeth to make them blacker and added an additional crease to the forehead to indicate pain. He stood back from his handiwork. "I must remember what an *ugly* bastard you are," he muttered.

The *plip* of drops into the chair had ceased. Condensation, not rain, dripping from the skylight, rotting the beams. The light from the roof would be the only sign of his existence here, apart from his anonymous comings and goings in a street largely devoted to shops and offices. The end of both the dripping sound and the whisper of brushstrokes across the paper left a vacuum of silence. He stood and stretched; wished, for a fleeting moment, that he had Sarah Fortune's flexible limbs. Then froze.

There was someone downstairs.

Rotten steps led up to the attic, with a notice at the base of the steep, narrow flight informing the unwary of the fact. Sarah had secured this place, hadn't she? Made an offer subject to planning permission, written the necessary letters on headed paper to make her sex anonymous, secured a respite from further viewers; he forgot the details. She had spared him those.

But downstairs there were indeed the slight vibrations of movement. A trio of voices, climbing upwards. Cannon turned out the light and braced himself across the door. If anyone were to touch it, they would feel the warmth and know he was there. The drip from the skylight resumed with the resonance of a drumbeat.

There was no timbre of anxiety in the conversation he could hear from the room below, the words of which he could not decipher. He heard only the rhythm of it, the pauses and the hesitations. The high voice of a woman, announcing exclamations of surprise or disgust; the low voice of a man and the more youthful treble of a second male, murmuring apologies. They came out on to the landing. There was laughter, and one voice, the woman's, was incredulous. "Someone's actually offered to *buy?* Amazing."

"There's a large attic." The apologetic one with the servile voice. "Can you see? Don't . . ."

"More than I want." The woman again, her feet on the stairs, coming on regardless with a light, swift step, until she was on the other side of the door.

"*Don't.*" The apologetic voice was becoming shrill, "Don't go up there; the beams are rotten, it isn't safe, come *back.*"

Unlike his brother, Cannon had always admired the insatiable curiosity of women; he had always venerated women, even when he was preserved from them, but this particular example was one he automatically detested. The woman pushed at the door; he leaned the whole of his weight to the other side. "Locked," she said. The tread of the top stair creaked ominously.

"Come down," the man shouted again.

She ignored him, paused, and shoved.

Cannon could imagine her, palms pressed to the door, touching his own skin through the panel, their foreheads and mouths separated by the mere thickness of wood. He imagined himself knocking a little hole through, so she might catch sight of a single eye, see him poking something through into hers. For a moment, he could understand Johnny-boy's congenital, intense *hatred* of women. Thought again of making another hole and sticking his prick through it. That way, surely, she wouldn't come back. They were both evil thoughts, which shamed him into a blush even as he contemplated them. He suppressed a desire to giggle, stuffed his fingers into his mouth. They went away, the men rebuking the woman, who was angry with them both, and they with her. Raised voices floated down the stairs. "You will *insist* on seeing everything. When will you ever *listen*?"

"There was somebody there, I'm sure of it."

"That isn't possible. It's dangerous."

"I'll complain."

"No, get *him* to complain. There's no point in us complaining; don't want it anyway."

"*When will you evah lissen*," Cannon mimicked, "*you silly moo?*" opening the door a crack as the voices faded away. The woman had left a faint trace of perfume: she must have reeked of it—all the better to disguise the smells of human life, turpentine, paint, the harsh soap from his hands.

For a whole minute Cannon felt instantly jolly, until the life went out of him and he dropped into the damp armchair like a doll. He lolled in it and picked at the frayed upholstery on the arm. It begged to be picked at; no wonder Sarah did it. However could he go on living like this? He was better in prison—my God, there were aspects of it he had positively enjoyed. He entered one of those temporary phases when he told himself that Johnnyboy would get bored with the game, long before his own deadline for winning or losing it, just like he did with the houses he left to rot when they ceased to be fun.

Oh, Lord, they had had fun. What else was there to do but wait for the time to pass? Sell the picture and give him back the money? No. The baby would need it; Julie would need it. Nor could he *bear* to hand it over to that—that—*Philistine*.

Cannon looked at the face in his drawing and saw again that they no longer remotely resembled each other, but Johnnyboy had already entered the room. Johnnyboy had the cunning he had never inherited and, in the same breath, Cannon felt the familiarity of fear.

The people had been sent to tease. Johnnyboy had always been better at games, better at everything. Probably knew where his brother was, in the way he always seemed to know.

There was not really anywhere to hide. From a ghost. A legend he no longer quite knew. From his own heart and the lure of destruction. From his own nature. From a world where he still did not understand the rules.

5

T*oday I shall need an onion for the stew and another bottle of wine,* William wrote on the margin of a set of notes. *Other than that, life is dandy. Why did Cannon bring me that painting to look after? Why am I so surprised that someone likes me?*

Sarah, where are you? It's too late for shopping. Perhaps you're working. He *must* stop writing in the margin of notes, as if that were the only paper he had; but he was, after all, surrounded by them. They were always to hand. William perfected the notes he had scribbled during the day in the evening, late afternoon or early morning; sometimes, such as now, at dawn, as if the very labour of it might encourage the sun to rise and the dreams to end. The notes were a record of expertise, a database for his credibility; he pored over them, wondering how he could have done things better. He did not just *need* the respect of his professional peers: he craved it. His papers in the international journals provided something of the kind. He was always looking for something fresh to write, but apart from that he yearned to describe his profession as a series of refinements and surprises; otherwise it all became pointless. Technique could always be perfected. William knew that the pursuit of excellence and knowledge (how pompous that sounded) was the only thing that could give him dignity.

In the early days of semi-idealism he had not been like this. He thought now that his was a route for a frustrated artist, or mechanic, rather than a medical man; someone who might have been equally happy tinkering round with cars, fire engines, trains, cameras and the other kind of bridges. Painting had been a passion until he recognized his own lack of vision. He could never make himself concentrate on the whole, only the part. Writing things down wasn't bad, but despite strenuous efforts he was not unduly talented at that either. Like the painting, it was the details that bogged him down in pedantry while the concepts evaded him. So he had to be an excellent dentist. That was all he could do.

And yet he wanted to write about the individuals and how temperament was such a feature in treatment; the mystery of the human response, which varied as widely as the colour of their eyes. Maybe colour and physical type were the keys to it all. Perhaps the pain threshold was dictated by the thickness of the hair, while the size of the feet governed tolerance of anaesthesia—perhaps it was as simple as that. This was too large and wide a theme: he wanted something both factual and anthropological to enhance his self-esteem. All right, then: he wanted to write about how trauma changed attitude; still too fanciful and vague. What was required in his dull circles was articles on new techniques in root-canal therapy, implantology, rather than anything with a personal touch, but in this particular dawn he wanted to write about how a terrified patient became the opposite of his former self; changed from unwilling to willing, from afraid to positively enthusiastic. He wanted to write a paper about Cannon out of sheer affection for him.

This is achieved by extreme measures, William wrote on a fresh sheet of paper while glancing at the large bundle of Cannon's notes. *First, allow the patient to develop a truly terrible set of teeth which he comes to loathe. They have made him socially anathema; disfigured him. Then get fate to make them worse. Incarcerate the patient. By this time, he will no longer care and may become very co-operative indeed . . . Encourage a suicide attempt. This often leads prison authorities to allow special treatments not normally contemplated . . .*

He sat back in his chair and tried to reconstruct Cannon's history from his very clear memory of the remainder of Cannon's front teeth. Tetracycline was a useful antibiotic for adults, no longer given to children who had yet to develop their secondary teeth because of its pernicious side-effects. Cannon had been unable to remember why he had ingested so much of the stuff: both he and his brother were sickly, he said, not subject to the best of medical or parental care from a single father with other things on his mind. At that age tetracycline made the new teeth emerge a ghastly brown shade; healthy at heart, maybe, but uneven, misshapen, with the appearance of dirty decay. The larger the teeth, the less attractive. A tetracycline smile was not a pretty sight. And there had been delayed, inadequate treatment of caries, an impatient dentist, (I *bit* her, Cannon had said. I bit her so hard she refused to treat either of us again). Some phobias were more reasonable than others.

The other way of getting a patient to become co-operative is to ensure that a dental appointment is a high spot in an otherwise boring life. Ergo, it really does help if your patient is in prison at the time. His stomach rumbled. He moved into the kitchen, poured cereal, the bachelor's standby food, into a bowl and added milk. He waited for the flakes to become a soggy mess and ate absentmindedly. The stomach continued to growl.

It also helps if the patient regards sedation by Diconal as the best time he's had for ages. It is as well to prolong such treatment if you have any curiosity about the fellow at all. He may tell you things while under the influence which he might not otherwise reveal. Nor might you wish to know.

He knew what he might write next, if this mood of frivolity prevailed: a book of Diconal poetry, a slim volume admittedly, in which he would put into rhyme all those disjointed, sometimes revelatory things that people happened to say under the magical influence of deep sedation. Like that poor boy, Andrew, with his broken front teeth, two to be extracted, two to be saved and crowned. Tetracycline would not harm him; Diconal would obliterate any memory of what William had done, as well as any memory of what he had said. Not that Andrew's lisping, fretful replies could be said to be significant. He moaned about not wanting to lose his job.

Cannon, under sedation, was rather more amusing and infinitely varied. Cannon growled. He could not keep his hands still: they conducted an orchestra with minute movements, or made tiny little motions resembling an artist with a brush, which were, in their way, endearingly vulnerable. He repeated the name of Julie in a high, sing-song voice and the name of Johnnyboy in a low hum, apparently aping the music from the radio in the surgery. On the day William had asked, Do you have any children, Mr. Smith? he had moaned in his sleep about how he longed for a child and feared he could never achieve it. Then he sang that his twin brother wanted to kill his soul. When his mouth was not full, he chanted as if he was in the playground, something that sounded like a skipping rhyme. *Johnnyboy, Johnnyboy, dirty fangs, Johnnyboy, la, la, la.* He mimicked the radio.

William reminded himself to ask Cannon more about his next of kin and cursed himself for not having asked before. A *twin* brother. They might have the same teeth. There would not be too many left with the ugly distinction of brown tetracyline fangs. The very thought stunned him; he closed his eyes to savour it. He was tired; concentration, even in excitement, slipped. Sleep had been punctuated by the same old nightmares, the children, and Isabella's skull beneath her flawless skin. Isabella, rampaging through the waiting room with those two in tow, hacking to pieces the paintings on the walls. The recurrence of the image was so vivid, even now that he was awake and noisily ingesting his bowl of cereal, that William stumbled downstairs to check. He tripped on the bottom step, swore and catapulted himself into the room. All was safe, and there on the wall the picture Cannon had brought. To be apt, the third picture Cannon had brought.

There was only ever Johnny and me; everyone hated us. Afraid of our teeth.

Cannon had thought that he was paying for his extensive treatment of beautifully crowned front teeth by bringing along, every second visit, a sketch or a small watercolour, executed with cheap materials in prison. Cannon was not paying for it at all: sleight of hand with the forms, a conspiracy with a prison doctor, Sarah, and officials frightened into fits by the prospect of another suicide attempt. They had paid for it. All the same, it had had moved William that Cannon came armed with gifts; but, then, the attitude of the prison patients, the existence of whom Isabella so deplored, had always surprised him. Since his first practice, which had had a prison on the doorstep, he had always included prison patients and he had volunteered to continue at the same discounted rate long after Isabella had got him out of there. *Why?* she had shrieked. You could treat princesses and you treat *them. Why?* Because it was a chance to make a *difference.* And because they were churlish and pathetically grateful by turn.

Cannon had been practically dragged into the surgery, his guard agog at the poshness of it all and his charge gibbering with fear and white with pain; abscesses from broken, untreated teeth; suicide risk. William gave them both a large shot of whisky for starters. Promised Cannon he would not feel a thing and almost made him believe. Not quite. Until he became utterly passive.

The very first sketch Cannon had brought him was slightly macabre. William moved down the corridor towards the door to where it sheltered in a corner. It was a pencil sketch of his own hands, caught in the act of making busy explanations. They were sketched as if they had been held in front of Cannon's face, in front of Cannon's mesmerized, terrified eyes, watching every movement, as William, after stroking the jaw, rubbing the numbing ointment in the gum, talking incessantly while he worked, getting the needle in there while Cannon was still hypnotized by fear and the constant stream of words. Cannon, sweating with relief, when William said, We are going to do nothing today, but you see, you had an injection without realizing, didn't you? Then explaining, with dramatic use of hands, pointing, illustrating, finger-wagging, cupping, expansive, what he was going to have to do after the massive dose of antibiotics had worked. You'll feel better tomorrow after they begin to take effect, and next time we'll put you to sleep, promise—the hands folded at last in an attitude of prayer alongside his face. William was accustomed to using his hands to explain; the language of gesture was less specific than words, suited him better.

And the patient had recorded exactly what he had seen in movement, and made it still. Cannon captured William's elegant hands, palms outwards, fingers fully spanned like birds in flight, anatomically correct, unmistakably his own hands down to the last crease, but looking as if they were born to bless, caress and heal. The sketch of the hands thrilled him still, made him proud. *You gotta take care of those hands,* Cannon had said. William wanted to go back to sleep. He did not want to write or to think. The light crept through his windows and revealed the clean paint, and the extra-clean mark where yesterday's boy had steadied himself against the wall. William's stomach continued to grumble. The milk had been too cold. It did not seem much to complain about.

Seven thirty and the phone buzzed. He ignored it, listened from a distance as the message recited briefly the services he could offer, implants, cosmetics, enamel facing, crowns and a whole new life, addressing the unwary in cheerful tones he scarcely recognized as his own before inviting them to leave a message saying they were going to cancel. Or whatever they were going to say at this godforsaken hour of day when the light still awaited arrival. He waited to hear if it were Sarah—she owed him explanations—but it was a man, pleading a business meeting. William did not have the faintest idea who it was. Identification of this voice required consultation of the damn notes. Maybe one of those who promised to return but never did. He moved on, tummy growling, vaguely upset, to look at the second of Cannon's drawings and the third. In his dreams, these were the first the children destroyed: his hands.

The second hung in pride of place in the bathroom, in case it should otherwise cause offence. It was of a slim, heavy-breasted girl-child perched on the end of a high bed without frills. She sat on the very edge, supported by her arms, looking at her feet, which were both just on the ground. One foot was raised from the heel, for particular inspection of the toes; she was nervous but amused, eyes fixated by the foot rather than by the audience. The room had all the appearance of an institution, a hospital ward or a lecture theatre of the old sort, bare, apart from the lights in metal shades hanging above her and the surgical green of the walls behind. Her skin was dark, the sheet, covering the bed on which she sat, white. She was an object for inspection rather than seduction. William could imagine students standing in front of her in a circle outside the picture, waiting for a description of her history, her times, her disease, while she, quite simply, waited on life to continue.

The phone burred again. By this time he was in the waiting room with the fancy sofas and the coffee machine, and the message was muted. He was looking at Cannon's glorious loan of yesterday. Then found he could not look at it. Hurried upstairs to the flatlet where he lived in his miniature space, so that Isabella could live in relative splendour with some rich paramour, whose name by choice he could not remember, for as long as she kept her nerve and her face. And her teeth. *Her teeth.*

He brushed his own. Rigorous attention to detail; like hell. Should have given her disclosing fluid, make her teeth brilliant blue to show where the plaque lingered, tell her a thing or two, get the message across. Those teeth had bitten him, more than once, in a playful bite on the shoulder which hurt like a series of minor pinpricks. Isabella nibbling and saying, *More . . . But . . . when are you going to earn more money, William? We need more.*

He left the dental floss and the whitening toothpaste, the scolding in his ears, and belted downstairs through the foyer, into the street and the café down the road, where he sat and consumed a cappuccino with sugar and a Danish pastry. Sticky on his tongue, fresh as the day, souvenirs of it lodged in the precious spaces between his back teeth. Then he went back to face the morning and Cannon's loaned painting.

The sun streamed through the window, the sky was pink with promise, and William wanted to yell with delight. The painting was exquisite and he had the fascinating prospect of another paper to write. Twins and their teeth.

The flat where Sarah had stayed the night with the man she nicknamed Mr. Mole, was small and potentially neat, like the dwelling of one who might have preferred to live, like his fictional counterpart, underneath the riverbank. The potential for neatness lay in Mole's insistence on the numerous fitted cupboards to maximize space, the state-of-the-art kitchen in miniature and the stark, military nature of his furniture. There were campaign chairs, which could be folded away, a chest that doubled as a table, an expandable suitcase, which could be used as either a wardrobe or a seat. He was as fully equipped to embark on a major expedition at any given time as a nineteenth-century general. The man called Mole woke from a deep and dreamless sleep to find that his place was full of foreign noises. Splashing from the bathroom, which was so close the sound could not be avoided, the flushing of the lavatory and the sound of low, musical singing. It disoriented him for a full minute until he opened his eyes.

Sarah's clothes, visible but hardly colourful, hanging not in a cupboard but on the door, the way she did. Sarah's melodious voice over the rushing of precious hot water and the indentation of her head on his pillow. A different smell to the room. They had talked too much, and he had eaten and drunk too much, was the problem. Had he or hadn't he? It would clearly be far too insulting to ask. The progress of the day would clarify memory which, so far, extended only to that of an extraordinarily pleasant, over-indulgent evening.

She had set out cups in the kitchen, pulled out two stools from under the counter, cleared space for them both adjacent to the coffee machine, which dripped, to order, sternly calling him to attention. It was still the middle of the night, as far as he was concerned: Mole's business rarely began before the end of the morning. Her preparations alarmed him, since it looked as if the scene was set for serious conversation of the life-threatening sort. Maybe she wanted to talk about *life*, their life, and how it should be further intertwined. Oh, no. He sat heavily and watched the coffee jug fill.

Supposing she wanted to discuss *them*? Supposing she wanted to move in with him? She always said how much she loved the place. They were fond of one another; comfortable together once a week or so, and she was used to the making of unilateral decisions. Perhaps this was it: the table was laid for the making of lifestyle commitments. He braced himself against the counter and counted to fifty, slowly. That was usually the length of time it took her to dress. The speed of it always amazed him, in the same way the clothes did. There would be a simple subtraction of a belt or piece of jewellery, and the more festive creature of the night before would emerge soberly clad and ready for work. The kitchen was so small she had to sidle into it and sit carefully, which she did with the maximum of grace. Hangovers appeared an unknown quantity in her life, but not, unfortunately, in his. She was picking a bad moment to tell him how much she loved him.

"Now, listen, Mole," she said. "Answer me this one. It's extremely important. Supposing you have a *person* . . ."

"Yes?" he said, holding his breath. "This *person* . . . ?"

She poured the coffee and he waited, tremulously.

"Supposing a *person* has a budget to buy paintings for a corporation. You know, a showy-offy collection to impress people without losing any money at the same time. Now, where would this *person* start?"

He was nonplussed, but rallied quickly. "This *person* could have all my stock for a start. I can't wait to get rid of it."

"Thank you for that, but no. I think the subject matter has to be . . . rather more domestic, if you see what I mean. Suitable for a very broad base of taste or non-taste. You see, the corporation doesn't know what it wants. It thinks it does, but it doesn't."

"And what about the *person* in charge of the collecting? What does *she* want?"

Sarah sipped the coffee as if it was the only coffee she would ever drink, savouring it for a lifetime. "The *person* wants an excuse to display the work of unknown, or virtually unknown, unfashionable artists who could do with a chance. Not money, necessarily; the encouragement of being seen. Let the rich actually feed the poor, in other words. The other instinct of this *person* is to trash the whole thing. Get them a collection which is comic, or laughable. A mimic of pretension."

"Then it really would be state-of-the-art," Mole said, relieved and thoroughly warmed to the topic. "What's required is a *theme*. Then you can get away with *anything*. And you must go to the big exhibition on Saturday. A must. Has everything."

"A theme?"

"Oh, whatever you like. Historical. Geographic. The sky, sunsets, sunrises, the sea, English landscape, Africa. Or you could make it conceptual. Poetry in motion, love and war, men at work, women at work, the movement of the seasons, friendship. Captivity . . ."

"Captivity," Sarah echoed. "'Stone walls do not a prison make, Nor iron bars a cage'."

"Exactly," Mole said. He was looking round himself at the smallness of his kitchen and, at one remove, the dimensions of his really rather satisfying life. Sarah was on her feet, planting a kiss on the top of his head, the whole of her a sudden flurry of movement.

"Thank you," she was saying. "Where's my coat?"

A green coat, to go with a sanguine temperament that did not believe in bad luck and always brought the opposite. He watched it whisk away past the paintings of battles, gathering dust on the hem as it went into the sunshine it seemed to have evoked. The careless, almost joyful slam of the door and the sight of her striding through the courtyard, fixing her in his mind. Mole was not sure if he should feel irritation or sheer relief.

Instead, on the whole, he felt absurdly disappointed.

Racing down Piccadilly for the bus that would take her back to the prison of work, Sarah remembered Sister Pauline's slower steps and all her many admonitions. My darling Pauline, she told herself, you should not worry about my morals. Men who really want *good* women will always find them; and, as for sexual licence in the current men of my acquaintance, they are almost invariably too tired.

I must account for my time, my time, my time . . . I need my job. Everyone on this bus needed their job. *I was out doing research for the art collection* . . . Oh, what an excuse Matthewson had given her. *Don't forget the exhibition. Take Cannon. Put it on the time sheet.*

Accountability simply requires inventive words on paper to explain the hours spent. The bus rolled through London, half full of people who still looked surprised by sleep. Sarah loved the winter in these early stages when the cold was a stimulant, the sunshine a catalyst and there was an explosion of seasonal hats and scarves, far more effective than the Christmas decorations. The bus was so much more convivial than the underground: chat was allowed although by no means mandatory, and there was always the view. She sat upstairs towards the front, wondered why she ever bothered with the lonely back seats of taxis. Central London: last night's playground, full of those plodding and rushing to work, drawing them in like a vacuum cleaner only to spit them out again in the evening. The bus snarled at the traffic in Holborn, where the tall buildings of the city began to close in, blocking the sun. Top-deck people were reactive to the weather, kings and queens of the road for twenty minutes at a time, able to peer into office windows with a degree of impertinence they might never have exhibited to their suburban neighbours; it gave her the urge to pull faces. There was a young man with beautiful coiffed dark hair sitting immediately in front of her, staring ahead, his shoulders hunched in misery, his newspaper ignored. Sarah wanted to touch his hair, to see if it was real and as soft as it looked, tell him how nice it was and somehow convey the fact that the day could not possibly be as bad as he seemed to anticipate. He reminded her of Malcolm Matthewson, the most consistent of the lovers. Today would be a good day; she had decided it. There was nothing simplistic about the Fortune philosophy, such as it was. It was the very cutting edge of pragmatism.

That was it, the right phrase: *cutting edge; state of the art; interface.* She began to rehearse the outline of the initial report on her ill-chosen task of amassing paintings with the firm's money. *Consultants suggest that the cutting edge of art-investment theory indicates that the collection should have thematic unity, each work to interface with another to create organic harmony* . . . That should do it. Keep them at bay for a while. There were other things to do: look at houses; keep Cannon on cue until Christmas; keep Julie hidden; keep all the secrets and hope he was right.

I must account for my time. But there was no Matthewson lurking inside his door, waiting for her explanation. No bloodstained, weeping boy in her office either, explaining his hurt and the need for silence, because he, too, needed his job. The door was closed, the route to non-accountability clear, but she paused to listen. There was a murmuring of voices, an undertone of irritation in the blurred words, until she heard Ernest raise his. Far too early for Ernest to do this: bad for his ulcer. "I am only a consultant," he was saying, portentously and conveniently loud for an eavesdropper. Big talk: that should get them on the run; that was really talking dirty and laying down the law. She supposed she had better explain the nature of the *consultant* in her consultancy document on the collection; listened a while to pick up a useful phrase. And then, still at the foot of the stairs, still listening, wondering if more of the estate agents' particulars had arrived, she felt a tremor of hesitation and a desire to run away. An appalling sense of responsibility, which was tantamount to terror. She ran up the stairs and slammed the door.

Johnnyboy Smith was in that room, talking with Cannon's distinctive voice. *Don't go near him,* Cannon said. *Don't ever let him see you.*

"I don't care a shit about fucking consultants, if you'll pardon my French," John Smith was saying to Ernest Matthewson in a pleasant brogue, which did not make him easier on the eye. All jowls and hair from four feet away. He wore a highly coloured Hermès tie, predominantly red, which looked, around that pink neck, like a cheap ribbon wound round a birthday cake, with the obvious difference that Johnny-boy would never be sweet to eat, what with that broad, short body and the way he muttered to hide his vowels, or maybe his teeth. Wait till he told Mrs. Matthewson about those teeth.

"I know all about this *consultant* stuff," Mr. Smith was saying. "You *consultants* only use broad brushstrokes, right? The . . . the minutiae are left to others. I mean, the fucking details." Ernest could only nod.

"I hate lawyers," Smith said, without any degree of real recrimination. "MPs, they're all lawyers. Guy Fawkes had it right. And what's a lawyer anyway? Just a man who oils wheels so the wheels can turn round. So what's a *consultant* wheel-oiler?"

"I take an overview of what your requirements are," Ernest said, looking earnest and bending forward to lessen the distance between him and this menace while in fact he wanted to increase it. "In the absence of your designated lawyer, for some time, I gather, following his car accident . . ."

"His *what?* Oh, I see, yeah."

The accent was false: Ernest knew it, but could not pinpoint it, and continued earnestly, looking at the eyes of the man rather than his teeth, ". . . then I shall isolate one or two people who can replicate what your own designated lawyer did." There was a hollow laugh. "I've looked at the files. My word, what a lot of them, ha ha! Property slow-moving, eh? Well, well, well, winter's here. Personally, speaking as a *consultant*, mind, I think you could maximize your investment and avoid tax rather better than you do, which means specialist skills which we can easily provide . . ."

J. Smith took advantage of Ernest's confidential stance and leaned forward himself, so their noses almost touched. Ernest remembered, just in time, not to recoil from that mouth.

And later, after he had gone, Ernest wondered what all the fuss had been about. The man was only a client; a good client admittedly, but not the best or the most powerful; there was no need for anyone to kiss his feet. God help anyone who had to kiss any other part of his anatomy, Ernest muttered fastidiously. More tales from the battle-front to tell Mrs. Matthewson, though. What he could not understand was why everyone was so afraid of the man. There was nothing fearsome about him at all. Watching him making his flat-footed way out of the room was not like watching a warrior of the commercial world. It was like watching a sad clown. He wanted Sarah to see it, called for her, but she did not answer the phone. He wanted to gossip, but it would have to wait until he got home. Darling, he would tell his wife, such *breath*, such *teeth*. A *peasant*. You should have seen him.

It was not the power of rendering the patient so helpless and speechless—with the rubberized insertion that isolated the tooth and covered the throat to protect them from the debris and the accidental swallowing of one of the tiny brushes he used to dig out the pulp—that made William take a secret pleasure in root-canal work. The patients hated it, and he sincerely, if sometimes irritably, regretted that, but it had the sole purpose of relieving pain, permanently, and it was the cleverness of the instruments and their current variety, the prospect of surprise and the tension it generated in himself that kept him going. Locate the canal; establish the working length. Enlarge it gently to the point where the file starts to bind. Straight files used in a large to small sequence with a reaming motion, the rotary action preparing the canal into a round cross-section in this anterior tooth; the minimum of pressure. Watch out for danger zones, weakness in the cavity, weakness in the instruments. Remove the pulp with infinite care, an ultra-precise form of spring-cleaning, leaving nothing behind to infect, working slowly, mostly by hand and wishing, for once, they were smaller. Avoid the nightmare of a broken instrument, lodged in the dentine and impossible to remove; the discovery of an extra canal, a canal so twisted in shape it made the original estimate of the treatment time entirely false and the patient would begin to fret. The omnipresence of grave discomfort, the dentist's most euphemistic word, made speed imperative, while the precision required dictated the exact opposite.

There should not be such satisfaction in rendering a tooth dead while keeping a patient sentient throughout, but there was. William preferred them awake in the interests of greater co-operation. And if he regarded it selfishly, the level of relief was so much more palpable if the patient had known what was going on. It was a horrible fact that their consciousness refined his own concentration and improved his technique. He was actually pleased with himself.

The perfection of the notes would have to wait. There was an arrangement to see Sarah. He did not want to tell her about Cannon's painting: he was shy of it and did not quite know what to do about it apart from admire, and wonder, as he had all day, about the motives. It was Sarah who was so clever on the human motive; he, who was so dense, wanted to work it out for himself.

It was she who had brought Cannon into his life, but that did not mean that she owned every aspect of the relationship that followed, nor any more of himself than he chose to give. Where was *she* when she did not see him once a week, more or less? He did not ask, he guessed. He referred his own dilemmas to her and told her stories; revelled in her intelligent interest. He wondered if he bored her, and decided he did not. It was a strange middle ground of intimacy, which was close enough for the exquisite comfort it provided, with no merging of identity. It was, he realized with a shock, the only relationship he had ever had with a woman that was based on mutual respect.

Would it be different if I were more curious? he asked himself. Would it? If I *loved* her? If she really trusted me and I really trusted her? Is *love* the same thing as this big gulp of infuriating pleasure when I see her coming towards me? I must work on technique for living. There's something I'm doing wrong.

Let's walk somewhere, he had said. They met between their two places of work at Hyde Park Corner and walked the well-lit circle of the park, popular on the evening of a dry, bright day: joggers, cyclists, a floodlit football game, walkers and strolling lovers. At Speakers' Corner, a lonely figure stood on a box and shouted global warnings at passers-by, convinced of some major truth, blind to the fact that he had missed the meeting of true minds.

"A consultant," William murmured. "He reminds me of mine, at dental school."

"What *is* a consultant, William?"

"Ah," he said, tucking her arm through the crook of his own. "I can tell you a story about that."

"How was the darling Isabella?"

"Fine. I did *not* succumb to any temptation to torture her. In case you wondered."

They strolled arm in arm. She adapted her pace to his long-legged stride; he slowed down. The lights of the park glowed yellow. There was frost in the air. "I have an aunt," she said, "who says she won't go to a dentist before hell freezes over, because she thinks dentists are torturers at heart. Perfectly placed to be sadists for hire. She has the theory that if half the martyrs to the Catholic faith had been faced with a professional dentist-torturer they would have denied God soonest. She thinks you could all have alternative careers. Hirelings to the secret services of brutal dictators. And there you were, contemplating torture, exactly proving her point."

A jogger dressed in red huffed into view and swerved to avoid them. A puff of his breath lingered in the air.

William laughed, took her seriously. He took most things seriously. "Does she mean someone like me would have been *useful* in the Inquisition, depending on which side you were on? What a ghoulish imagination she has. A dentist would *not* be a natural for the job of torturer. We're descended from *barbers,* for God's sake. We wouldn't be natural for it because we like to *mend* things; that's what we're here for. Second nature, professional pride, call it what you like. You *can't* destroy without wanting to mend. The dentist would be *useless*, tell her. He'd be looking at what he could *mend* after the event. He'd be putting on a show, you know, lots of blood and stuff, but everything capable of restitution. The mouth's good for that. Has this extraordinary capacity to heal."

Another jogger, this time in sinister black, overtook them silently from behind on winged feet, padding towards nowhere.

"So exactly what would you do? Tell me and I'll tell her. She used to tell me dreadful tales of decapitated saints to make my skin crawl. I could get my own back."

"Oh, same things I've thought of doing to Isabella and never would. Open the gums, stitch them back. Drill where it did least damage. Let the burr catch inside the cheek. It would all mend. I could drill a hole—"

"I think I'd prefer the story about the consultant. I like stories better than facts."

He grinned, tucked her arm more closely against his own. The lights of Knightsbridge loomed ahead like a fairy palace.

"The consultant . . . Well, once upon a time there was a town where they had a problem with cats. The feline population had grown out of control, largely due to the sexual activity of one great big bold tomcat with great energy and irresistible appeal to the female of the species."

"A serial seducer."

"Possibly. Anyway, the parish councillors hunted down the tomcat, emasculated it rather than killing it and let it go. The cat population dropped dramatically and everyone congratulated themselves. Then, suddenly, it went up, ten times worse than before, kittens everywhere, stopping the traffic. None of the kittens looked like the old tom. The councillors met and decided, nevertheless, that they hadn't done the job properly with the old devil tomcat, so off they went to hunt it *again.*"

"And?"

"They found it, finally. In the graveyard, sitting on a tombstone, surrounded by other, younger tomcats, telling them what to do. Now that, dear Sarah, is a *consultant.*"

She laughed, and felt warm, let him carry her with the tide of people towards the other side.

I'm a consultant, she thought, the cat on a gravestone, trying to conduct the offstage orchestra, with no skills at all. Trying to give something from an old, cold heart. Trying to act on faith, without quite knowing what I should believe, with not much time before Christmas.

Trying not to fail anyone.

I think I *shall* go and try on that red dress after all.

PART TWO

6

It was always a mistake to base anything on a lie. Pauline knew this better than most. If lies were necessary, and *oh, yes, they are*, it was always better to construct the thing so that it was as close as possible to the truth, leaving the least scope for embellishment. A lie was a living thing, demanding growth: it could develop like a vine with tendrils to throttle itself; it could be a little creature growing into a monster. Like the kitten they were watching, it could trip over its own legs.

Pauline sat with Julie in the convent kitchen, a place of utilitarian warmth and ugliness. Like the rest of the building, a devotion to cleanliness outstripped aesthetic consideration without any sign of contest between the two. The radiators against the walls kept up a steady rhythm of protest: a moaning, keening sound that reminded Pauline for all the world of a high wind through an ill-fitting window and gave the impression that they were secluded on a mountain-top—which, in one fanciful sense, they were—without a view. The only thing that was beautiful as well as dangerous was the kitten that played at their feet.

Named Felicity, without anyone having the skill or inclination to ascertain its sex, the kitten gambolled on the lino tiles with no better sense than an eye for movement and a suicidal instinct towards warmth. There was an industrial-sized gas cooker, which excited curiosity and a turn of unsteady speed in the animal: it seemed to want nothing more than to get inside the lower oven designed for other things than the cooking of cats. Barred from this compulsion by an old firescreen, which Julie had found, the kitten had crawled up the inside of Pauline's leg, beginning at the ankle, mounting via cotton stocking and habit, to be rescued via a hole in the capacious pocket at the hip. Pauline had held it by the scruff of the neck, shaken it and stuffed it in the opposite pocket, which did not have a hole. "And now," she announced, as they bared their teeth at one another, "I'm going to sit on you."

That, too, was a lie. In a different degree from the lie of pleading poverty, which had led to the second-rate service of the central heating, which had led to the noise. Or from the lie that had got her into the kitchen and Sister Imelda out of it, credited not only to Imelda's influenza but also to Pauline's as yet undetected enthusiasm for cooking. Or from the original lie that they were, all twenty-five of them, so democratic that they should all take turns at the stove, since all women can cook, a resolution which, for a while, had brought about results so unspeakable that there had been a universal weight-gain attributable to desperate reachings for bread and chocolate. After that there was bland food, prepared with meticulous lack of imagination by five of them in turn, until the arrival of Julie and her subsequent gravitation after a fortnight from sick-bed to kitchen; but then, she too, had arrived on the tide of a lie.

The radiators moaned like a theme for *Wuthering Heights*, and the kitten played with a ball of wool. There were members of this community who could knit for England. All of them were retired from active life; some of them were poorly. They liked nothing better than outings to Westminster Cathedral. It was no place for a girl who was scarcely out of her third decade.

It had been a lie to introduce Julie to the sisters as some kind of refugee, recuperating from the ailment of a violent family but bankrolled by an uncle who paid for her keep, just as it had been a lie to present her with the impeccable credentials of a believer. The poor child did not quite know how to behave at mass, although she had learned, and her earlier fumblings with genuflections had been put down to a certain stiffness in the limbs. The fact that she could cook made up for many of the lies surrounding her. The sisters were incessantly curious, as inquisitive as sparrows and readier than hawks to dissect the origins of their guest and gossip about it to their many outside contacts, but discretion was maintained by that strange, instinctive consensus they were able to reach without discussion. The way to the suspicious heart was through the stomach. So much for spirituality, Pauline thought. The kitten pounced on the wool. Julie was scooping out the insides of baked potatoes, a staple of the convent diet. Never before had they been served with crisp skins and a filling flavoured with cheese and chives.

"Why on *earth*, child, do you love that man?" Pauline demanded.

There was an eloquent shrug. "B-b-because I *do*, I suppose. D-d-does there have to be a reason?"

"Yes."

"I shall have to think of one, won't I, then?" She laughed. Post-laughter, the stutter improved.

"'How do I love thee? Let me count the ways—'" Pauline quoted.

"Oh, the *ways*," Julie interrupted. "The *ways* depend upon the means. I can love him here by praying for him. Or pretending to pray," she added, with an apologetic nod. "That doesn't have much to do with the reasons, though, does it? Here, Kitty, don't be such a fool. Drink the milk—it's good for you." She pushed a saucer across the floor towards the kitten, who ignored it in favour of the wool ball, which Pauline threw for it again and again.

"There's a good *reason* for loving a kitten," she said drily. "It's a piece of perfection. Beautiful without making any effort. No one could say that about your husband."

Julie seemed to consider that. The radiators whined. Never once had Julie whined. Not a single hint of it. In fact, she seemed in some perverse way to consider herself lucky.

"Loving the kitten has nothing to d-d-d-do with its looks," Julie protested. "I love that thing because it came from the gutter, like me. Rescued, wasn't it?"

Pauline was not about to dispel that myth. The kitten had been all that was left to the aged convent cat, deceased in the aftermath of a misguided pregnancy. After a dozen confinements, it should have known better. Pauline thought she would never understand the female sex.

"I can't tell you the reasons for loving Cannon," Julie went on, "because I don't rightly know. Because he rescued *me* from what I might have been. And because I could actually make a difference to *him.*" Her hands paused about her work for a second. Her constant industry added to her popularity. "Can you imagine it? A man who would *let* you love him. Gives you a life, and says, 'It's all yours now, tell me what to do.'" She was cutting the chives, the knife slicing neatly and quietly. "A man who'll *let* you reinvent your life and his. Wants to marry you the week after you've met, so sure is he. Abandons all his ties to be with you. Oh, no, Sister, you don't let go of a man like that."

Pauline paused to wonder if her niece Sarah had ever found a man like that. If she had, she was perfectly capable of throwing him back into the gutter.

"My man Cannon was an unwritten page," Julie said, "all talent and nerves and energy and fear, and I don't know what. And if I was abused as a child, which I was, mind, I'd got nothing on him. He was his brother's creature, in every sense. Oh, he had money, if he asked, but he didn't know the value of anything. How could he? He'd been kept in darkness. A man of thirty, as ignorant as a child. You think I'm an innocent, Sister, but I'm the worldly one. The stronger one. Or at least," she added sadly, "I was. I'm not so strong now."

She picked up the kitten, tickled its ears and put it down. When it grew up, it was likely to be a very ugly cat indeed.

"He hardly knew the difference between right and wrong. A moral vacuum. All that misplaced talent. The oddest mix I ever saw, tearing himself to bits. I wasn't a good person, I was sliding into nothing. He *makes* me something. I made him want to live. We'd disintegrate without each other. I *need* him, he *needs* me. Although . . ." she hesitated ". . . he needs a child as *well* as me. He needs a child because it's the only way he can really begin again." She laughed unsteadily. Her stutter had quite gone. "So it isn't just my life in the balance, it's his. I'm sorry, Sister. You and your niece seem to have taken responsibility for both of us. I hope you don't enjoy power."

"No," said Pauline insincerely. "No, I don't think I do."

"Nor I," Julie said. "But I had it and I have it still, although how it ever makes a person proud I can't imagine. It makes me weak with the thought of it, the *need* of him, the gift he gives me, the *amount* he needs me."

"You could despise a man for need like that," Pauline said carefully, smothering her words as she bent to pick up the kitten, which squirmed in her lap and covered the black cloth of her habit with fine white hairs. She could swear it had a squint. She stroked the cat because she wanted to hug Julie. Julie had turned her attention now to the making of pastry and, despite her general indifference to food, Pauline found herself curious about the next meal, as well as the items Julie might ask her to fetch from the shops next time. She would miss this industrious mind.

"Despise him? Oh, no. Oh, *yes*, perhaps if he was *weak* in himself, but he isn't. Oh, Lord, how c-c-c-can I explain it?" A level of agitation brought back the stutter. "I know . . . I want you to know, but you can't, can you?" She paused. "Th-th-th-think of what it would be like, Sister, if you met someone lost to the devil and they saw your *God*, saw another life, a p-p-perfectly marvellous life on the other side of the clouds, and they rushed, *rushed* to embrace it. Full of joy. And they were *determined* to embrace it, and you'd been the one who'd made them want it, and then—and then out came the claws to drag them back, beat their bones and make them bow to the devil again, all for someone else's vanity. Wouldn't *that* break your heart? Oh, tell me it would. Tell me it would matter. Tell me you wouldn't rather go to hell yourself first."

Pauline nodded.

"A *g-g-good* man, I mean. It would have to be a good man. A good man corrupted, not a bad man or a lazy one. One with a talent to give to *your* God. Have you seen his paintings?"

"No."

She was lifting the flour, rubbing the fat between her fingers with gentle ferocity.

"Sarah has. Perhaps that's why she never needed explanations. My husband sees things no one else can." The bowl bounced against the surface of the table. The kitten slept. "Am I making sense to you?" Julie demanded.

"Yes." There was a vision, for a moment, of Sarah, her niece, embracing not her style of life, which she would not wish upon anyone, but the power of her faith. Sarah with *belief*; what a leader she could be. Julie's analogies made profound and perfect sense. They were inspired. The child had a chance. And there was she thinking that any woman who waited on a man, as well as waited for him in the face of patent unreliability, must be a fool. The bowl thumped. The whining of the radiators rose to a shriller whine. *Yeeeeeh*, followed by *uuuuuhmmm.*

"I would want to die if I lost a soul in torment," Pauline said, inadequately. Julie kneaded the mix. The soon-to-be-ugly cat slept. The kitchen was warm. She had made Julie angry, and she felt perversely pleased about that.

"And, of course, there's another thing in this *love* business. That p-p-peculiar thing. Wanting to *fuck* him all the time. All the time. Wake up to it, go to sleep to it. *All the time.* Him, too. Like wanting to feed. *All* the time. Being hungry to get him inside me, him and his babies. All the time."

Pauline nodded, without any meeting of the eyes. She wanted to pretend she was not shocked, but she was. It seemed slightly out of context somehow. "Cannon's brother," she began tentatively, willing to take advantage, test Sarah's version of things and change the subject, "what's *wrong* with him?"

"I'm guessing," Julie said. "Guessing on what I'm told, but it has to be true because Cannon doesn't know how to invent things. You won't like it."

"There's a lot about men I don't like," Pauline said severely, "which does not mean I have to be spared it."

"They grew up with bombs," Julie said, "the pair of them. Daddy an amateur terrorist in the Belfast back-streets. An opportunist in a senseless war, making his sons the same. They grew up learning to destroy things and the dad making money out of building them again. They were children who threw stones at anything and anyone, and not a breath of religion in them; it had nothing to do with that. Escaped off over here in their teens to make good and get out of it." She laughed nervously. "I try to picture it. Little Cannon, throwing stones at the bomb-disposal man who might save his street from falling down. Then his dad would build it up. What chance of a moral code in that? And the trouble is, it must have been *fun*. You can see that, can't you? Running, chasing, hiding, breaking things, *blowing things up* . . . all *fun* when you're a kid. And noise, all that lovely noise."

"But it might leave you with a great big lump of hatred," Pauline interrupted. "No enemies, just hate, sloshing round inside you, nowhere to go . . ." She realized she was holding the kitten down rather too hard. It squirmed.

Julie shook her head. "Unless you have an alternating love of harmony and, by some miracle, Cannon does. Thank God for the teacher at school who made him want to paint. The only class he went to. They played truant for the rest."

Pauline wondered briefly what it would be like to *want* to push the kitten inside the bottom oven, close the door, listen to it scrabble and scream to get out as the heat rose, confining it to hell. She shook herself. Her fingers teased the softness of the stumpy little tail protectively.

"I can't believe in a soul incapable of redemption. I *cannot* believe that."

Silence.

"You stole from him, didn't you? It *can't* simply be pride. You must have done *something* extra. *Did* you?" More silence. "*Did you?* What did you steal?"

Julie was putting the pastry in the fridge, moving awkwardly, the answer a shake of the head. She was embarrassed, tight-lipped.

"What does he look like?"

Julie grabbed the sleeping kitten from Pauline's lap and held it against her own face. Her hair had been cropped like theirs; now it grew. Her eyes were wet. "I don't know. How would I know? I've never seen his face. Only a glimpse of his mouth. He had the fat man put a pillow-case over my head so I could breathe but he couldn't *see* me. Then he . . . Then they hit me." She raised a stubborn face shiny with tears. "I don't *know* him, but I know it *was* him. No one knows him except Cannon."

The swimming-cap made her look like a nun. A yellow rubber cap, beneath which Sarah's red curls lay squashed against her head, uncomfortable and tight, until she began to swim and forgot everything other than movement. She hated the cap because it was a rule of this club, all rules were anathema, and she did not much like swimming either but she needed her health, something to complete the vicious circle of wine and cigarettes and all the rest, and this was one way to do it. The costume and the cap were all there was to carry; there was no timetable to maintain and the activity was mindless. Up and down, down and up, like a mechanically propelled toy, counting the lengths and often wanting it to end, enjoyable for the sensation of virtue afterwards and the water itself. A slab of blue for the carving, her body making the wave, the feeling of weightlessness, the rasp of her own breath and the sight of the far end coming closer. Turn, push off, turn; sound and reality distorted.

Hockney's blue pools; Californian blue water and a sun-filled sky; blocks of blue in those pictures that suggested languor and health. The theme for the picture collection could be the hypnotic effect of water: no one quite immune to it; drawn like lemmings to the invitation and the threat. Sarah tried to think of the sea, floated on her back and tried to imagine the screech of gulls and the sound of waves. The water of the pool, conveniently close to the office, currently empty except for herself, lapped against the edge with the more prosaic sound of a domestic bath, and the view of the ceiling showed not sky but white plaster, peeling in places from the damp. It was a place beset by rules: caps, single-sex swimming sessions, a club run by a martinet, who ignored a falling membership in the interests of a regime. Sarah floated and wondered how long it would last. A man stood by the entrance to the changing rooms, his arms folded as he surveyed the scene. He tapped his watch and pointed at her. *Five minutes,* he mouthed. She nodded, understanding. Men only in five minutes. She lingered, wallowing in Saturday-morning privacy. On a weekday morning it was like a scene from the sinking of the *Titanic.*

As long as she was weightless in the water, the burdens of the mind became weightless, too. As if, mid-length of the blue pool, they carried themselves alongside rather than within. Threats became mere imaginings, obligations mere bagatelles, time immaterial in the face of the current challenge. *Five more lengths; just five and you're finished. Go on, you can do it.*

Another man came out of the changing area. Saw her swimming towards him, the emerald green of her swimsuit and her disfiguring cap stark against the water. He stopped, changed direction, spat on the tiles and went back in the direction he had come from. Sarah hauled herself out of the water. Ah, John Smith, oh, for a better look at you. You are shy of the public eye.

Cannon had told her that John Smith came here because of the rules. He did not like to swim in the same water as a female, in case, by chance, she touched him. As if the contact with a woman's skin would bring out a rash. What ailed the man? And what ailed her, that she should want to get closer?

Arrogance. Some dim dream that once John Smith was seen, smiled at, spoken to, he would assume some other, manageable personality, like other men, reveal his secrets, if not his desires, prove amenable to reasonable suggestions. Arrogant to assume any such thing, especially of a man who spat at the sight of a woman in *his* stretch of water. As if he owned it. She ran for the changing room before the martinet came out to shout. A gob of spittle lay shining on the tiles. The air outside the water was as cold as spite. *Mens sana in corpore sano.*

Sticky damp skin refused to dry after the shower, no time left; the cloying warmth of the changing room, the whiff of chlorine in the hair. The pulling on of clothes that twisted and restricted after the cool freedom of the water; the sight of dead-looking skin on her hands. There were no easier ways of trimming bodily excess and driving those scars back under the skin.

Dressed, warm but shivery, she went up to the gallery and watched him swim. Two of them: the fat minder, carving through the water with an easy breaststroke so fast and powerful the water purred in his wake; the man himself, slow and clumsy, waddling in the water with a slow, ungainly crawl of maximum effort and minimum result, rolling around like a loose barrel with kicking legs; a little laughable, maybe. The man Matthewson had described to his wife as a clown, and Mrs. Matthewson had described to her, looked clownish in the water, with his trunks ballooning behind him. The little white whale no one would want to preserve. Who could be afraid of a man like that?

It was the second time she had spied on him here, the first with an impression endorsed by her own particular spy. She wished she had not done it. The sight, and the opinion, was making Cannon's version of a *bête noire* difficult to believe. Sarah counted on her fingers. Cannon,

Julie, herself: they could all be wrong. It could all be an innocent lie. Or a real lie. Maybe that was why Cannon had said, Don't go near him.

Saturday morning and the City was deserted. Sarah hurried in the cold, which stung the damp hair on the back of her neck, rammed the hat down harder. She passed the policeman at his outpost on the corner, standing in his little box and rubbing his gloved hands. They had stood there day and night since the last of the City bombs—the City's ring of steel against the antics of terrorists. Cannon might have become one of these, but Cannon was cured of his amorality. She was the one who had graced him with total belief. She must continue in faith until the Christmas deadline. But somehow she was beginning to doubt. It was difficult to believe in a devil moulded out of hearsay. The lawyer in her rebelled at it.

Cannon woke because of the cold. Blue patch of skylight, cold feet the death of sleep. Heater, socks, stumble back to bed, looking at the light. "That patch of blue the prisoner calls the sky," something forming in his mind. Supposing he looked up at the skylight and saw someone trying to get in? Not trying to get *out,* as he often envisaged, engineering in his mind a series of ropes and pulleys, Heath Robinson style, but trying to get *in.* There was a construction of a canvas forming in his mind: a figure reclining across the skylight, languid and naked in the cold. If there was anyone up there, all he would do was invite them down.

It was the second week of December, light was precious; in a minute it would bloom and he could paint in it. He fell asleep instead, dreaming of the freedom of Christmas. Johnnyboy had promised.

Woke to the rattling of the door, the skylight patch now a rectangle of grey, the heater burning his feet, disoriented, but not alarmed. He was not in this camp bed, he was in prison; half alive to the sound of shouts and the pounding of feet. Lying in a bunk with his life seeping away, from four o'clock in the morning when he had first started to cut his wrist with the sharpened prong of his belt, to the sound of the man in the bunk below, snoring. Two hours, three, before anyone would notice; easier because the pain in his teeth persisted until he caused a competing pain. He remembered looking at the anatomy of his wrist with mild curiosity in the dim light. There was always light outside the cell: they were never left in the dark. Such a treasure trove of veins and sinews beneath that pallid skin. Scratching at it with the buckle sharpened against the wall, he had felt like primitive man in search of an instrument, angry with the sheer effort of it, digging into his own disobedient flesh, but at least he bled. Knew enough to clench and unclench his fists to increase the flow, the man below still snoring and enough blood to *drip, drip, drip*. Cold feet, pain and shame, and still not enough to take away the toothache. He had raved about the toothache later; long after he dozed and listened to the *drip, drip, drip*, as if the toothache had been the reason—as if it ever could be: he had lived with toothache most of his life. One pain did not take away another. All he had done was damage.

The rattle at the door was louder. Voices in memory. *Let's have you, you daft bastard. What you done?* The sound before that of the suicide squad, running towards the cell in a clatter of boots, ready to drag him back into life for trying to outwit the system. Like an army, pushing everything out of the way, tramping towards him with practised panic, fear and fury echoing in their voices. *What you done, old man, what you done?*

"My teeth hurt," he'd said; the last thing on his mind. Bonfire Night, it had been; a few weeks after he got there. Fireworks in the sky, visible from little windows, driving him mad.

Most people talked such *shit*, Cannon concluded, relying not on contempt, which he did not feel, but on his own experience of doing exactly that under stress. He had blamed the toothache, which had nothing to do with it; it was feeling useless and desperate, and wondering what the hell his brother was doing on the outside, that had had everything to do with it . . . and wanting to make love to her and cherish her, *all* the time, and not wanting her to die, or to live without him either. If *he* himself was out of the way, *she* would be left alone.

There were qualities of sound, he had decided in prison, that presented themselves in ways that only the subconscious could judge. He was alarmed by the rattling of the door now, not frightened. The sound of the suicide squad, boots on concrete, fireworks: *they* were frightening; this was not. Prison senses had refined him, or perhaps these were senses he had already had. The instinctive knowledge of the dangerous sound; the isolation of the opposite. No one had rattled the door in quite such a fashion before, but he knew it was unthreatening. Cannon came into the full realization of his senses with a groan. He had missed the best of the light, and that was the worst start to a day.

He knew who it was before he removed the chair; regarded her with a wariness and a feeling suspended between gratitude, mystification, irritation and a kind of awe tinged with affection. Quite simply, he wanted to be in a position to return favours he did not understand. Sarah looked like a drowned rat. He left her at the door and hurried across to the painting, standing face out against the wall, and turned it the other way round. He did not wish her to see herself naked with the scars he had given her. Or to let her know he had forgotten their appointment the way he sometimes forgot the promised daily phone call.

Sarah had none of the timidity of a trespasser: she walked round every place as if it was her own, politely enough but still as if she might have command of it, like the captain of a ship, respectful of privacy while knowing all the time she could invade any part of it. She sat. "God help me, Cannon, you gave me a fright. Are you awake yet?"

He *knew* she would try not to end his sentences for him as he felt around for the words; she would wait, half knowing what he wanted to say before he said it, dying to articulate it clearer and quicker than he could.

"I owe a lot to the suicide squad, let me tell you," was all he said.

"Why's that, Cannon?" She knew the answer—she had been part of the equation—but she was always trying to make him talk, about anything and everything. Practice for the outside, fear that the isolations of his life would make him even less confident, he guessed, and wondered, for the fourteenth time of asking, why she should care so much and how long she would go on believing everything he told her. It was a question he never dared ask.

"Because they stopped me. I seem to have this instinct for self-destruction, don't I? And if I hadn't been a suicide risk, I wouldn't have been allowed to get my teeth fixed. Prisoners only get stuff like that if they scare people. And if there's someone on the outside like your William. He must have fudged the books. He's nice, your William, isn't he? Why don't you love him?"

"Well, he isn't *my* William. And I do love him, for what it's worth, but he doesn't want to be loved. He wants to be approved of. Do you want to do more of the portrait? You said you did on the phone yesterday. That's why I'm here. Then we're going to the exhibition. Remember?"

He shook his head, glanced towards the covered easel. It was an old stand for an archery target, broken when he had found it. "No, not the portrait, if you don't mind. The light's bad. Anyway, I want to think about it for a few days. Let it mellow, if you see what I mean."

"Let *me* mellow, you mean." She grinned at him. It was infectious: he found himself grinning back, despite his low spirits. She prowled round the room, not consciously checking for changes but noticing everything just the same. Flakes of wood had fallen from the beams and been swept to one side. It was tidier than before, as if he was packing to leave, precious few possessions since the only things Cannon semed to cherish were his paints and his brushes even if they stopped him travelling light. Not that there were many paints: too many tubes were only confusing, he said. She stopped. "What have you done with it, Cannon?"

"What?"

"You know what. The Bonnard sketch."

There was a particular blank space on an otherwise blank wall, marked by a nail. The space had been wiped clear of dust, showing a cleaner surface and smear marks. Cannon shook his head slowly, like a donkey trying to distract flies around the eyes, sat down on his bed and motioned her towards the cherry armchair. "I'm allowed to make decisions, you know," he said resentfully.

"Of course you are. Everything is your decision. But what have you done with it?"

He stared at the ceiling, hands clasped behind his head, as if the sight of the ominous stains would give him inspiration. Sometimes it did. "I took it somewhere safer. It isn't safe here. People have been round. I'm sure *he* sent them. I took it to William's surgery."

"Does William know what it is?"

"No, but he knows it's beautiful. He'll look after it."

"Cannon, people are in and out of there all the time."

"So? People don't go to the dentist to examine the paintings on his walls, do they? They can scarcely *think* by the time they get there. They sit, frozen, with a magazine, pretending to read it, that's what they do.

And, when you come to think of it, it has to be the last place Johnnyboy would go. A dentist? Never in a million years. But he might come here. I feel it. He'll sense where I am, in time. Johnny has his own satellite."

It was a long, infuriating speech for Cannon. "Does it work the other way round?" she asked, trying to keep sarcasm out of her voice. "Can *you* picture where *he* is? Because it would be bloody useful if you could." He treated the question with the utmost seriousness.

"In a vague kind of way, yes. But there's nothing special about that. I know his regime and his habits, you see. I lived with him every day of my life until four years ago. He won't alter, you see. He can't. So I never know, if I close my eyes and see him in places where I expect to see him, that it's because I already know where he'll be. He was swimming this morning, wasn't he? There's nothing . . . what's the word? . . . telepathic about that. He always does on a Saturday. Same place, where he can have the pool to himself."

"He looked ridiculous," Sarah said shortly. "About as frightening as a sick porpoise. Cannon, are you sure?"

"Have I ever told you a lie?"

She looked at him closely. He could look quite guilelessly stupid. The smile revealed the magnificent evenness of his crowned teeth. William's work. William had altered Cannon's life far more radically than she ever could. "No. I'm not sure you have the knack with lies."

"Doesn't make me honest either. Julie says I'm a moral vacuum."

But not a liar or a thief. Sarah was prowling again. She picked up the Johnnyboy sketch, bold lines, hangdog features, black teeth. She scrutinized it. The teeth, which were like bars in the middle of the face, turned the expression into a snarl far removed from Cannon's deliberately vacuous smile, and she frowned at the depiction. "This is what you think, you see," she said finally. "Your version, without him standing in front of you." She put the sketch down. "He *swims* like a sad bulldog. Cannon, why are we doing all this? All this running and hiding for *this*? He *looks* like a sad bulldog. He *swims* like a sad bulldog. My boss's wife says he talks rubbish."

"That's only a photo," Cannon said.

"What do you mean, only a photo?"

"Stupid!" he shouted, advancing like an avenging angel, taking the sketch, tearing it in pieces with his big hands. The rapid movement was so violent and sudden in itself that she might have been afraid, but she had never been afraid of Cannon. The hands were large enough to encircle her throat and throttle her; they were ludicrously large hands and, like his head, capable of independent movement, as if not connected by the same driving force of a common brain—even his fingers seemed to waggle free from each other. But nothing of his bizarre flurries of movement came to anything until he painted, leaning his whole body into it, unselfconscious, like the conductor of an orchestra, sublimely concentrated. She waved him away. Patted the air with the palm of her hand, dismissing his extremes, inviting him to sit but feeling impertinent for all that. They were both trespassers in this house.

"You don't understand. A proper portrait of a man takes time. It has time in the fabric, time in the paint. Time to watch the changes. That's a snapshot. Of one moment in time when I *thought* I could see him, did—do. I loved him, you see. I love him still. I couldn't even sketch him without *feeling* for him. What have I got, poor bastard? EVERYTHING. *Teeth.* A wife who *loves* me. A talent. And what has he got? *Nothing.*"

He sprang to his feet, lit with his own rage, precise with it, suddenly delicate in purposeful movement. He clipped a sheet of paper to the hardboard on the easel, flurried around for a pen, drew in a few strokes. Took it away and drew another on a fresh sheet, another, another. It was so frenetic she could scarcely look. Sheets of drawing paper scattered the floor with the ink drying. His brother; his brother; his brother, drawn without love in a series of cartoons that made him wink, grin all over his evil teeth, frown for a moment, distend his rubber lips, crease his brow, purse his mouth into a wavy line, look kindly, look like a savage, look like a photofit, a convict, a mad saint. It did not help. In the last he looked like a hungry ghost with nothing to feed his jowls. At the last there was love in the portrait. Her throat was sore and her mouth was dry. Cannon had begun to cough; the kind of polite cough that hurt but sounded as if it was designed to interrupt a conversation, with no other purpose, turning into a spasm of dry coughing, even as he worked. "See?" he kept saying. "See? See?"

She saw nothing, apart from the spaniel eyes in the sketches and Cannon's perception that no man was evil incarnate. She had never met a man who was; not even Charles Tysall, who had tortured her and given her the scars. Evil, to her mind, was a quality more shocking for rarity. She did not believe in the devil. She looked at the several depictions of the face and could only see, in her mind's eye, the clumsy body beneath it, barrelling its way across water with all that pathetic effort, afraid of witnesses. The sad clown.

"I'll paint you a proper portrait from these," Cannon was muttering. "I'll do it after dark. He never liked bright light much." Suddenly he laughed, sat down abruptly. "We used to go out after dark, you know, so no one could see our teeth and laugh at us. We never saw the light."

"What are we going to do, Cannon?" she asked.

He liked the *we*, although he resented it. "I don't rightly know. Wait, until the time limit. Believe him. Watch out for him. Guard everything. Until he accepts the fucking rules he set and finally *accepts*, I'm not coming back. *Can't* come back." Then, more to himself, he added, "Oh, *God*, give us a child."

"Is that what he wants, the resumption of a love affair?"

Love affairs were ten a penny to her, not to him. It was his turn to prowl, picking up his coat, putting it down uncertainly, arranging the tubes of paint in neat rows. "Yes, he wants that, and a new game. A nice fat explosion. He probably wants to blow up the Houses of Parliament with me to help. He always said Guy Fawkes was a fool for getting it wrong. Odd, isn't it? That's the only piece of history he ever remembered from school. *When* we went to school, him to history and me to the art class. I went to that. Teacher took me home and tutored me. Johnnyboy didn't like that, *nooo*, not at *all*. Beat the shit out of me for a while, then got bored with the effort. There's always hope. He always gives up in the end."

"Perhaps if you gave him the painting?" she suggested quietly.

"No," he said emphatically. "No, I can't do that."

"It's the proceeds of crime, Cannon. Money you took from him."

"It's the proceeds of *work*," Cannon shouted. "*My* work. Johnnyboy wouldn't recognize something like that if you shoved it up his nose. Money I took to turn it into something beautiful *he* would never buy. What would he want it *for?* He'd burn it or let it rot. Like his houses."

Nobody knows him but me.

She got up and rammed the hat back on her head. He liked the hat.

It made her anonymous and less intimidating, a softer version of herself. Someone perfectly willing to play the fool.

"Right," she said, saluting. "I shall continue to assume your paranoia is entirely correct. You'll need a new place to stay. I'll work on it. What else does your brother do with his Saturday?"

He could not understand any more why Johnnyboy so hated women. They were the only people who ever believed a thing he said. "He stays at home. Sport on telly, all day. Racing, football, rugger, anything. Saturday's a stay-at-home day. Too many women about. Mind, he likes the boxing best."

"Ritualized conflict," Sarah murmured. "While you and I go shopping for *art*."

"Do we?" Cannon said dubiously.

"Yes. Today you're a consultant."

It ebbed and swayed, this almost friendship. They could be silent companions or deeply suspicious. He could move from intense curiosity about her to indifference, to introspective silence, then shout a remark apropos of nothing, without minding if she responded. She found it restful to be with someone who had no recognizable code of behaviour: it entailed a certain kind of freedom in her own. Belief in Cannon was an act of faith.

Today he had all the suppressed excitement of a child taken on an outing: talkative, with thoughts flying into questions half forgotten before they came out of his mouth, interrupted as they drove with snatches of whistled song. That was what had drawn her in the first place: the ludicrous smile, the profound capacity for happiness, however temporary; the lack of reserve when he forgot his own predicaments. The ability to lose himself in the moment. He made her fiercely protective.

"How much does lovely William know about me?" he asked suddenly, watching her manoeuvring the car, badly, into a space. Cannon could not drive: it was a mystery to him. The engine and the vehicle itself filled him with alarm.

"Nothing. Next to nothing," said Sarah. "The bare minimum. Unless you told him anything."

"*Me?*" Cannon replied, watching her turn off the ignition as if it were a piece of magic. "*Me?* We don't talk about anything. Nothing personal anyway. It wouldn't be fair. *Nothing.* 'S why I like him. Accepts you without asking. We talk about everything and nothing, like we do."

"That's all right, then," said Sarah, and felt a stab of guilt so sharp it was like a stitch in the side. "I've asked him to come along too, but I doubt he will. Says he's too busy."

"Too fucking shy," Cannon said. "Adores you, can't admit it."

Then, as an afterthought, as they climbed the steps, another question: "How did you make the house fall down, Cannon? They say it was a gas explosion."

He nodded. "It was. But that's all right, isn't it? I paid the bill first."

"You promised Julie you'd never do anything like that again."

"Never. Never, ever, ever. But," he grinned, "it was *fun*."

"Yes," she said, thinking of some of the ugly houses she had seen in her search for a new home. "Yes. I can see that."

7

As they mounted the steps to the exhibition centre, Sarah knew that this might have been a mistake, one of those occasions when instinct clearly foretold embarrassment and was wilfully ignored. Cannon did not like crowds: he looked at the populace pouring through the doors and surrendering bags for inspection as if they were rabid. He shuddered when anyone brushed against him, refused to part with his coat, placed the entrance ticket between his teeth while he decided what to do with it, settled finally on top pocket, right.

A vast hall was thronged with separate stands, five corporate art collections immediately opposite the entrance and, on a separate floor, sixty screened stalls run by dealers, and a balcony above with more. The big works were in the middle; the smaller round the sides. Paintings large and small, sculptures dotted like mushrooms.

"Take note," Sarah said, *sotto voce*. "This is where people come to *buy*. The biggest show of contemporary art. Next year you will be *exhibited*, but today *you* are a *consultant*. A *diplomat*. You tell me what's rubbish and what isn't."

Saturday-morning hunters and spenders, full of goodwill and ready to be delighted. People with houses and eyes, eschewing the delights of do-it-yourself for the joy of looking at paintings. The presence of so many about the purpose seemed cause for celebration rather than for distress, and she tried to tell Cannon that—for the brief moment he listened. Isn't it wonderful that so many people want to *see* paintings? Not *wall-paper.* Paintings and drawings. You are my judge, she told him. Tell me what I should notice, tell me what has talent, I don't know. There was a hubbub of sound, a draught of heat, the scent of excitement finely tuned, the smell of perfume in a crowded train.

Cannon was immune, unbendable to the will of another. She had learned how a certain crispness of voice and a *rat tat tat* direction got his attention, as long as it sounded like an order, while persuasion, the method she always preferred, was more difficult to achieve. He nodded distantly, as if they were a pair sent to reconnoitre foreign territory with instructions to obey nothing but remote signals, and even then at his own discretion. He walked around with his hands clasped behind his back, the better to control the twitching of his fingers.

The corporate collections tended towards the large canvas of abstract art; paintings with titles suggesting serious concepts, such as *Life, Waste, Chaos.* Rather gloomy and colourless things, she thought; things with bubbling surfaces, cauldrons of paint, or a few spare lines occupying a vast tract of frozen wall. Cannon had to touch, jump from space to space as if he was avoiding the cracks in the pavement. He wanted to stroke the paint and work out through his fingertips how it had reached the surface; he wanted to poke at the canvas, lift the frame and stare at the back to see what had been used. Fashionably suited exhibitors hovered with unctuous politeness. In the corporate collections there was nothing for sale but reputation, while outside that the customer was God with a credit card, greeted with overpowering charm. Sarah loved a market red in tooth and claw but dressed in cultured clothes. She stared at buyers; he at the merchandise. William should have come: he liked a zoo.

It was a market ablaze with enterprise, promise and false promise. *I have been in places like this,* he whispered in her ear. *Don't condescend to me.* He had sat in places like this, he told her, and also the more permanent public places, national galleries where they let you sit and copy, see what other painters had done and struggle with the likeness until it emerged like the birth of an animal out of long, painful and envious perusal. He had lurked in these vaulted rooms, and then on building sites, watching figures at work; figures at night, hurrying past lit windows in a street, the movement of limbs he yearned to capture and never, to his own mind, did, quite. *But I know what I have to do . . . I know how each and every attempt should have the single purpose of capturing a moment of reality or perish.* He murmured into her ear, like a lover, full of indignation about the prospect of betrayal, the whispers louder and louder, the fury in him rising fit to bellow. She ran to catch him.

"Crap," he screamed. They were facing a large canvas across which there danced something that resembled a bright blue eel. On a white background, it had a single, malevolent eye, directed towards the frame it determined to escape; its back was decorated with minuscule lettering among the blue; a splodge elongated into a creature.

"Shhh," she said. "Shhhhh."

"That's what it says," Cannon announced indignantly, touching the lettering with a grubby forefinger. She had never seen him with clean hands; imagined he had been born with hands as stained as his teeth had been, and the darkness of his skin contrasted nicely with the white background of the eel. "*Crap*," he repeated, tracing the lettering. "*Crap, crap, CRAP!*"

"Be quiet," she hissed, secretly enjoying the row he made.

"Pretentious *crap!*" he insisted loudly. "Now where's the bloody truth in that? A poster not a *painting*. It says *nothing*. He's *crapped* on his own canvas. Does he know how much *paints cost*?" Spoken while he turned and hissed at the skinny girl with the suit and the bony knees and the winning smile. "*Judas!*" he yelled at her, stabbing the canvas again until the white paint bore the imprint of his stubby forefinger. "*Judas! Thirty pieces of silver for this SHIT!*" And then, suddenly, he was all charm again, hands in pockets, grinning widely, teeth first.

"These critics," Sarah added, smiling into the eyes of the girl and taking Cannon by the arm to give an impression of safety. "So *passionate*, you know. You'd think he was a *consultant*." She tried to blame the increasing discomfort of the heat. They moved on, arm held inside quivering arm, hotter and hotter as they progressed. It was becoming unbearable. "One day that person might be your dealer," she said reasonably. But he was gone, far gone; looking at a patch of blue, twenty feet away, anger forgotten, drawn to it like hunger to food; standing there, rationing a moment of bliss, postponing the possibility of disappointment; relishing the delight; dancing, twisting his hands, the whole of him in movement.

"Oh, bless him. *Bless him,*" he was murmuring. "Look at that fucking *blue*. He lives in there. Ohh, isn't that beautiful? Buy it, Sarah. Buy it."

She was only conscious of the heat, rising like a tide, stultifying, claustrophobic, and the painting being a very small thing. Cliffs and an Adriatic sea, caught in some miracle of early evening, outlines blurred, the scale announced by a single, vague figure in the water, colours as intense as jewels. He bared his teeth at it, ready to consume it whole, swallow it. She watched; she was born to watch; and, all the same, they were shouting at each other.

"It's a lot of money, Cannon. I haven't got it."

"Give it to him, Sarah. *Give it.*"

"I can't."

It was so hot; hot and humid. The painting mesmerized. Sweat trickled down the back of her neck. The hour had passed in minutes. She glanced at his flushed face and then at the faces of others. There was something unnatural in this stultifying heat; something far more artificial than mere excitement. A girl fainted; the public address system crackled; an apologetic voice boomed over the heads. "So sorry, ladies and gentlemen, the heating and air-conditioning have broken down. For your own comfort, would you kindly leave the building by the nearest exit while we fix it?" No urgency, but a command, nevertheless, creating an uncertain swell of movement, orderly but resentful. Accompanied children and bored companions sighed with relief; in the slow surge towards a side door, Sarah lost Cannon and did not mind. The cold outside was sweet relief.

She watched; always second nature to watch, while the tall and the small and the beautiful and the plain gathered in the side-road and waited in groups, and she thought, with a touch of resignation, that Cannon's presence always had an uncanny knack of shifting crowds. The Tannoy had announced free drinks on their return within the hour; an optimistic promise, perhaps, but the mood was resigned, although those who had surrendered coats huddled and grumbled more than the others and Sarah was glad now to have kept her own.

A favourite coat, full-frocked, voluminous and definitely green, the warmth appreciated even as the perspiration on her skin dried inside it, and she scanned the stragglers still emerging from the building. Cannon was one of the last, his face a picture of injured innocence, his arms folded crossly across his chest; a man aggrieved to have paid for a ticket only to be expelled. He shuffled towards her, her red hair drawing him like a beacon, his steps quicker and quicker until they collided and, to her amazement, he kissed her mouth, hard.

"I might have been followed," he hissed. "Here, take this," removing the object inside his arms and thrusting it into the open folds of her coat. Surprise made her obey. She found herself clutching the thing, hands already familiar with the sharp corners of a frame. Cannon swung his arms in exaggerated fashion, reached into his pocket for a cigarette, which he lit flamboyantly and held triumphantly, as if for an audience. *Look, I'm clean.* Sarah's only desire was to run, far and fast, while he smiled his vacuous smile into her white face. "You've gone pale," he said. "It's not so bad, is it, being kissed, is it? You could get used to it."

She remembered to saunter rather than run. Down the road, around the corner, past the main entrance to the centre where the crowds were thickest, strolling nonchalantly, waiting for a heavy hand on her shoulder, moving on automatic pilot, and once the safety of the car was in sight, turning on him and screaming, "You stole it . . . you *stole* that painting. Are you mad? Haven't you learned anything?"

"Be careful," he said. "You might scratch it."

"*Scratch* it?" she yelled. "You're worried about *scratching* it? What about *stealing* it?"

He hung his head without obvious repentance. "But you liked it, Sarah. I know you did. It was the best thing I'd seen. You wanted it and I owe you, so I got it. Don't you like it?"

The grinding gears of the car signalled her reply. They shot out of the space like a bullet and, for a moment, he seemed satisfyingly frightened. She drove as if trying to forge a path through a desert in a tank; he clutched his seat-belt with white knuckles.

"Moral vacuum," Sarah muttered. "Moral slut. Don't you *think*?

What about the artist who painted this picture? What about getting *caught*? Don't you *think*?"

"I did think," he protested. "I thought when the loudspeaker spoke. It inspired me." He tapped his fingers on his knees. "I thought, wait a minute, this is a right mess, and the dealers will be able to claim any losses from the organizers because it would be their fault, because of the air-conditioning, and there'll be insurance policies and such, and no one will really lose. Not really." And he smiled again, smugly satisfied with his own logic.

She braked sharply; his forehead touched the windscreen with an audible tap. "I shall have to take it back," Sarah said. "I'll work out a way to take it back." And then, as the distance grew between herself and the scene of the theft, wondered whether she would. Or whether the company she kept, the life she led and the lies she told had entered her very soul.

She could not drive back. She drove on.

William supposed he had turned up to this exhibition so late because he had dithered about going at all. Sarah had asked him to go, but perhaps not quite warmly enough and she hadn't been specific about the time. He had once tried to count the hours he had devoted to indecision and found the total depressing. On the other hand, there were days when his failure to commit himself to any plan led him simply to wander about, to do things he had never intended by sheer accident and thus let his eyes light upon treasures. He had woken thinking about the paper on twins waiting to be researched, but Saturday was the wrong day for it. Instead, he had stood by his window, with his tea in hand, watching a fat man walking up and down the street, pausing and moving on, as if he was walking a dog, as indecisive as William himself felt. He drank more tea and passed the time. The seventh day of the week was a playground, a day for pleasures, a day for children, and he always felt out of sorts in it, as if he should be having fun instead of wishing there was work to fill an inconvenient gap. So finally he went to the exhibition, wishing he had not wasted the morning and the chance of company.

He hesitated on the steps, slightly disconcerted by the presence of crowds and, as he moved forward, the strange feeling of recognition he had for the fat man standing to the side of the entrance and talking into a mobile phone, looking oddly like the man he had seen in the street. But there were many fat men, and his memory for faces was poor. Fat men or thin were not excluded from looking at paintings.

There was envy as well as pleasure in seeing the work of professional painters succeeding where he had failed, but it was an old disappointment by now and it was the positive element of the envy and curiosity that had made him the haphazard collector he was. He had collected paintings and drawings ever since he had known he would never be able to make them, and he supposed, as he mounted the steps to the exhibition, that what he collected revealed what he was like, in the way books on shelves were supposed to reveal their owners. William shook his head and climbed two more steps, struck by the implications of this. By their possessions, thus shall you know them. He looked at the people, trying to guess from the colour of a coat what the preferred taste of that person would be.

He knew absolutely nothing about fashion in art. He knew, sometimes, what he liked, and on rarer times what he liked to do. Potter. And he knew, just as he entered the heat of the hall, that he had come to look for something yellow. He also knew a minute of sheer contentment. Two hours before closing simply to *look*. It was the collector's version of complete happiness, and he could not imagine how he had ever considered resisting it.

A collector is a person who refuses to engage fully with human life. Sarah had said that, teasing him, explaining herself. William shrugged. He did not care.

Excuse me, excuse me . . .

All the way round was littered with *excuse mes*. He was aware at one point of being jostled, heard a rough voice, somehow distinct from the babble, whispering impatiently, *I just want to look, just a look*, as if something was preventing him. He did not know why all this was quite such a pleasure, apart from the general politeness of the crowd, but he loved harmony in beautiful things; the search for both dignified his life, and he supposed it did the same for others, or why were they here in pursuit of it? Oddly, his pleasure in the occasion was not diminished by all the examples of disharmony and, to his own conservative, pre-modern taste, downright ugliness: the contrast between what he had expected and what he found amused him.

Chaos, Waste, why bring them into your house when you spent your whole life keeping them out? And even here, there was no getting away from teeth. William found himself facing a six foot by six foot depiction of a gaping mouth with Andy Warhol-style Marilyn Monroe lips painted in primary colours and opened wide in a scream. The tongue lay flat and inert; the tonsils were huge. The head of a youth with a woman's lips. I'd have 'em out if I were you, he told the Mouth silently, feeling lonely in the making of this facile observation. He need not have been alone in this crowd: Sarah had said *come with us,* and he had dithered. It was the curse of inertia fed by shyness, the constant ambivalence of wanting company and yet wanting to avoid it. Sarah would have made him laugh at these obscene red lips. A child stood next to him, rapt with attention. William glanced at him. Froze.

This boy-child was so like the one of his dreams. Ash-blond hair, falling in a straight cut across his forehead; too young to be captivated by merely visual, immovable things, but significant in his fidgeting concentration, his mouth slightly open. Night after night William dreamed of a boy like this, as thin and pale and beautiful, but when William dreamed of him his dreams envisaged a sickly waif, a boy coughing his heart out from some undiagnosed blockage of the bronchial tubes. No strenuous games for this child, but quiet rooms and coughing fits and anxious parents making him petulant. The child seemed to notice he was being observed, turned on William and grinned with an unselfconscious confidence.

"This mouth hasn't got any fillings, has it?" he remarked. "And that can't be right, can it?"

William relaxed and actually laughed, louder than the remark demanded. Of course this was not the child of his nightmares: *that* child would be a teenager now and his sister a young adult, while this precocious boy would still have some of his deciduous teeth and pink cheeks to redeem his pallor. He was simply another blond child, out of context in his surroundings. Relief from his own ridiculous imaginings made William laugh again. "Why should she have fillings and who says it's a she? They could be white fillings."

The boy considered this. He had a look of intelligence, almost cunning. William found his interest fascinating. "Well, she's quite old, isn't she? Like my mum. She should have fillings."

"No, not necessarily so. But there's nothing realistic about her, is there?" William went on, conceding the boy's opinion as to the sex of the mouth only for the sake of conversation. "Nothing about the mouth, anyway. Whoever painted this didn't know much about teeth. She's got too many of them, for a start. Thirty-six, not thirty-two. And look at that widgy little tongue—it isn't even alive. How many teeth have you got?"

"I *had* twenty. I lost some. I'm getting new ones."

"Well, they started to grow as soon as you were born, so you can't stop 'em." He judged the boy to be about ten, canines and premolars erupting gently in his mouth even as he spoke. The boy stood with his own tongue protruding, curled it over his top teeth and ran it round the edges, as if counting his incisors, a task quickly relinquished. "My tongue usually feels too big," he volunteered.

"Tongues do," William said. "And they won't do what they're told. Have you noticed? You can tell your tongue to stay still, and it might for a second, but it's got so many things to do your brain can't control it. It won't be ordered; it has to be automatic, disobedient if it wants. After all, it's got to move around about a litre of spit every day. *This* tongue looks like a piece of dry bacon. Got no life at all."

The boy giggled. "It doesn't look as if it would hurt if she bit it, and it does hurt when you do that, doesn't it?"

"Oh, yes, but not for very long because it gets better very quickly. Everything in your mouth does, because it has such a good blood supply. It's made to heal super quick. You could stick a pin right through your tongue and be better next day."

"Yughh," said the boy, his tongue unconsciously licking his pink lips, his eyes still on the painting. "Are you a dentist, or what?"

"Yes."

"Gross," said the boy, and turned away, bumping into a large adult who stood close behind him, listening. William was unsure whether this remark was an indictment of the painting or of his role in life, but he hoped it was the painting. He watched the child rejoin parents, felt himself blush under their suspicious glance, and felt absurdly cheered by his small encounter. Like a child himself, he pulled a face at the painting of the Mouth and then continued to amble from stand to stand. The child seemed to have given him an excuse to behave badly. The delivering of a little lecture always relieved him and made him feel superior, as if he had done a good deed, and it was always pleasant to be critical of a ridiculously misleading representation.

But the point of a painting, he told himself, was not to be studiedly realistic. He loathed the kind that aped photography or the precision of the architect, because that was not honest: it was not what the eye saw. When you look at a face, Cannon had said, standing in front of the pictures in his waiting room—the existence of which had been the first stage in his trust of the dentist—you don't see every detail. You see the strongest lines. You record the strongest impressions first, the same way you do when you look at anything. And when you describe one person, or one scene, to another, you will be selective in what you say because you cannot hope to be complete; you can only give your own version. That's what I try to do; if I can get one off-centre moment of truth, one strong impression, that is all I can do.

Whereas I, William thought, as he wandered round, would become obsessed with the perfection of my technique: I could not allow myself spontaneity; I have had it trained out of me. I would buy the highest-quality materials, measure my brushstrokes to the millimetre, try to be comprehensive, record what I *ought* to see and miss the point entirely. I would be like the fussier patient, convinced that the world could see the black spot on a back tooth when she smiled, or the slight crookedness of her left incisor, instead of which no one would notice at all. *Stand three feet back from the mirror*: that *is what people see; rarely more than that.* No one studies your face the way you do your own. Only a lover.

"Excuse me, how much is that?" It irritated him when the prices were not clearly displayed and he had to ask, introducing a certain coyness into the whole exchange. He was aware of someone watching him from behind, probably sizing him up for financial worth, making him feel awkward. Not that he had come here intending to buy; he had come to browse because it was a Saturday—but he wanted to know, all the same. There was nothing here that had quite moved the cockles of his heart yet, but he faced a piece of prettiness, three russet apples in a bowl, looking ripe and ready to eat; a cheerful work of art for a kitchen wall.

"Eight hundred pounds." No, he would buy a supply of apples. He moved on, warm, surrounded by enthusiasm, content to look, but dizzy with looking, then backtracked to see what he might have missed. An argument at a stall: someone returning for a painting that had been stolen; raised voices. Disharmony; ugliness. It drove him back round the hall; back to the Mouth, out of sheer curiosity to see if someone had actually purchased it, and out of perverse fascination to see if anyone would love what he had detested.

Someone did. A red sticker in the corner of its garish pink frame; a gallery girl self-importantly writing out an address on the back of a cheque; a man standing by, shuffling on a coat and ready to leave, until he turned back to survey the painting one more time, and grinned. For the second time in the afternoon, William thought his heart would stop.

The man who stood with his eyes fixed on the Teeth was very still. He seemed so rooted to the ground on large feet that he could have been one of the sculptures: no one stood so still with a smile on the face; a smile meant some sort of animation; William thought he might have touched and prodded him without any response. He was not a large man, smaller in stature than the picture, and the top of his head was only level with William's shoulder, but there was a quality of massiveness about him as if his bones were heavy. Both feet pointed forward with military precision; the features were dark and harshly handsome, marred by the smile: full lips drawn back revealing brown, uneven teeth.

The teeth marred the face worse than a scar. They marred it for a stranger—a friend would cease to comment, the brown teeth would be accepted as part of the whole—and on first sight, even to William's experienced eyes, they made the man look like an imbecile. A cretin with dirty habits, the discoloration suggesting without subtlety that the rest of him was unclean, even though the skin of his jaw hung soft and shiny from shaving, the shirt was immaculate pink and the hair shone black with health. Efforts were made to compensate for these teeth; the neatness was vulgar and aggressive. The impression of the man would be entirely different if only his mouth was shut. William closed his eyes briefly, waited for the other impression to emerge. It would not. He felt a wave of violent pity, mixed with intense excitement, like someone coming home. The face meant little to him; only a pleasurable recognition of someone sweetly familiar, confused by lack of identification and almost greeted without thinking. It was the teeth that made him want to say, *Excuse me . . .* Tetracycline-damaged teeth, the very image of Cannon's before treatment. A vision of a man out of prison, smiling at him fearfully.

They were crowded together in the small space of the exhibitor's stand; too small for a painting that belonged on larger walls. William did not pause to wonder why a man with such frightful teeth should want to buy a dreadful picture designed to shock with its totally awful and misleading delineation of perfect dentine in a ludicrously overcrowded mouth; he thought of that later, and instead, in that second, found himself looking round in expectation of the blond boy, who somehow belonged in this scene. That was his only hesitation. Apart from patting the pockets of his jacket to find where he kept his business cards. The man had turned his back again, consulted a watch, business done, anxious to be gone, unconscious of William or anyone else.

There was nothing William could say, or think to say, even though his curiosity was overpowering. He skipped to the front of the solid body to find the man still smiling and staring in a fixed basilisk stare towards the dreadfully perfect, plumped-up lips of the Marilyn Monroe tooth model. What *could* he say now? Can I look at your teeth? My word, what interesting choppers! Where did you get them? All sorts of inanities bubbled up from his throat, and instead he bowed from his great height, unable to resist a second look, and proffered his card. It was something he did when he was too shy to announce his own name.

There was no movement. William could feel his own blush rise across his face like the warm lick of heat from an oven. The eyes moved. They looked like the liquid eyes of a puppy. Cannon's eyes, but alive with surprise and a furious fear.

William was still holding out the card as the man backed away. The white rectangle looked as pathetic as a stale sandwich; he could feel the man's shock and outrage, but he could not withdraw his hand. He had to stoop to be level with the man's face. Then a blow landed on the left side of his jaw, deflected by the slight embarrassed turning of his head, but still a memorable blow. He fell to his knees, felt his hands clutch the serge of trousers, feel the twin pillars of a pair of legs. The blow paralysed; he remained in his attitude of prayer; the legs removed themselves and the mist cleared. Some semblance of dignity made him adjust to sit back on his buttocks, cross his own long legs in front and prop his elbows on his knees with his head held between his hands. This way he was abject without being servile. The voices around him seemed to come from another country; a foreign sound which, after a full and endless half minute, he recognized as whispering laughter.

He came round into fuller consciousness with a growing sensation of pain without damage. Looked up, to find someone stepping over his knees with the careful respect owed to a drunk in a place where he might be sick. There he was, with his head propped in his hands, in artistic reverence.

The man and the painting had gone. In the middle of the crowd, William was left entirely alone to his eccentric appreciation of the subtle implications of an artfully contrived blank white wall.

Sarah propped the picture against the mantelpiece. It seemed to bring light into the room, carried within itself the promise of happiness, captured the feeling of sun on the skin, the first pleasurable sip of perfect evening. She could see herself on the balcony overlooking the ocean, alone and yet complete in a minute of sensual perfection. Then, looking closer, she identified with the figure in the sea, swimming around endlessly without purpose or direction, lost in the moment. She shivered, as if some creature had walked across her grave. The bottle of wine was half empty. The wine alone could not conjure up the smells and scents of the scene in the stolen picture; only colour could do that.

Alone on Saturday night, but there was never anything maudlin about such a regular occasion, except when she sat as she sat now and contemplated the new depths of corruption that had made her collude in theft. *I didn't have any choice.* Oh, yes, heard that one before. There was always a choice in someone stealing a painting. This one already felt like a necessity of life; if she moved it, it would leave a space. But a painting was not edible: no one actually starved for lack of paper and canvas; there was *no* excuse. No, she told herself, I had no choice because if I had taken it back immediately it would be obvious that Cannon had stolen it and Cannon's low profile was a bit of a priority. She recognized, as she formulated these words to an audience, that this was specious rubbish. She was inventive enough to have taken the painting back after she had got rid of Cannon, explaining away the theft as a piece of mentally defective delinquency by a friend driven mad by the heat. They wouldn't have cared—they wouldn't care if she did it tomorrow, but she knew she wasn't going to do it tomorrow either. It was already too late.

Why was she keeping it, then? Because it had been stolen for *her?* As if Cannon were flattering her with his boldness, earning his spurs and presenting them to a favoured lady? *Crap*. Yes, there was an element of flattery in his having stolen the painting for her rather than himself, but it was also, in its way, deeply insulting. The presumption that she *would* be flattered rather than shocked to receive a stolen gift she would never be able to show; the presumption that this was commonplace and therefore perfectly fine; the presumption of corruption. *It's not so bad being kissed; you might get used to it.* She felt a prickle on her skin that she wanted to scratch. I am hardly one for such moral dilemmas, she told herself. I sleep with two or three different men in any given week; they give me things and provide me with information; I give them affection and I don't think that makes me corrupt in the way *this* does.

The mirror in the hall was dusty; it was always dusty and she never knew why. Dust comes from skin, someone had told her; whenever you move, you shed and create it, then wipe it away. She stroked words in the dust. CORRUPT. Then she wrote DUPED and ended the D with a scrawl.

Sarah Fortune regarded Saturday night as sacrosanct, by accident and by design. Saturday night alone was a sort of statement about how she lived, breathed, plotted, planned and survived with more than a modicum of laughter. Saturday night was reassessment time, Sunday committed to glorious indolence before the circus began all over again. Until, that was, this extra element intruded. *Corruption.* She wiped the mirror clean with the sleeve of her sweater.

She had believed in Cannon; she had turned her life into a series of wheels for Cannon; she had championed him, defended him and given him her faith. Why? Because there was no one else; because he had talent; because he and his wife were worth it, according to her own code. She made her own evaluations carefully and did not doubt them. Between them that pair had an enormous capacity for happiness and fulfilment. She did not care if he made fortunes for thieves and dishonest builders; she did not care what he had done in the past, which made it entirely inconsistent that she should feel such revulsion for the act of theft that had implicated her now.

"What a *selective* conscience you have," she murmured.

She turned the painting so that it faced the wall and could no longer seduce her, but hiding such a beautiful thing felt like another sin. In her kitchen, Sarah shoved the cork back into the neck of the half-empty wine bottle with unnecessary force. The bottle slipped from her grasp and fell. No satisfying sound, merely a timid thud and the wine seeping away across the floorboards. A bloody waste, like all this bloody effort. What she saw in her mirror was a bit-player in some melodrama that no one but a dreamer would believe. She opened another bottle of wine and looked for something to do. If Cannon's imprisonment and the wife he had met on the first stop of his road to total reformation had failed to cure him of casual dishonesty, as they patently had, then why should she place any belief in him at all? Wasn't a thief also a liar?

She wanted more than anything to turn back the clock on the day that had passed to the evening that had preceded it, when she could still hold on to belief in Cannon, and all he had told her about his brother, as an obstinate act of faith, before he had shown he could not be cured of dishonesty. Before she had seen that ridiculous, harmless body barrelling through swimming-pool water. Before she had listened to the last bulletin from Ernest Matthewson's wife, relating Ernest's impression that John Smith was a *clown*. That was where the rot had set in.

She moved round her own abode, restless, the whole state of her a travesty of Saturday-night calm, peering into rooms as if she was a stranger, the pictures on the walls mocking her. There was no real reason to move house, except for the memories and the way that movement always granted the illusion of freedom, as if a fresh start wiped clean a scratched slate and got the blood and tears off the walls. She opened the balcony windows; the air bit nicely cold.

Cannon stood below, poised to throw a pebble against the glass, a method of gaining attention he seemed to prefer to ringing the bell. Perhaps another part of his fantasy life. She was coldly, furiously angry, ready to spit, but then when she opened the door, she saw him slumped and his face bloated with tears. He made no effort to cross the threshold. He had forgotten his coat and his teeth chattered with cold.

"I'm sorry," he said. "I'm sorry, sorry, *sorry*. It was an *awful* thing to do. Not just awful, stupid. Insulting. Sometimes I just don't know better. I can't stop. I don't *know* until afterwards. Can you see that? *Can* you? I'm so sorry."

"Sorry for what?" she spat. "Stealing? Or lying?"

She stared at him, the anger melting even as she struggled to retain it. She had never been able to harness anger to good effect: it always failed to have enough force and she could never make it last quite long enough to stop it feeling ridiculous, even by dwelling on it.

"I'm sorry," he wept. "You rescue me from prison and from fire . . . You believe me and what do I do for you? Steal. I've never stolen anything except from him, and that was *mine*. And I don't know how to lie. I just don't *think*."

She saw him then as she had seen him first: a confused and clever child. Julie had seen the child in him. He stumbled into her perfunctory, motherly embrace and she led him inside. The phone rang. Cannon squatted in front of the fire, the reflection of the gas flames glowing against his wet face; she watched as she answered.

"Sarah?" William sounded more distant and hesitant even than usual. "Sarah, could I see you? I could get a taxi . . ."

No. She did not want these two under her roof at the same time; it was too much. She did not want William to see the stolen painting. She did not want William receiving any explanations whatsoever: what he did not know would not harm him. She did not want him to know she had become a thief.

"Could it wait, love? Tomorrow, if you like."

Cannon coughed; a prolonged, hacking cough, a development of the dry spasm of the morning. He needed the warmth of the fire. Her mind moved on to think about food, shelter, warmth. She had an hour to get food into him: he would never stay longer than that.

Johnny would know. He would find you.

"Oh, yes, it can wait." There was disappointment in William's voice; it irritated her. *I suppose you had another bad dream*, was on the tip of her tongue until she remembered, with difficulty, how much she liked him. She liked them all; it was the hazard of her life to like the rejects no one else even noticed. My God, they did not know what they were missing.

"Tomorrow, then?"

"I'll see," he said, and put the phone down sharply. Slowly, less abruptly, she did the same.

8

Isabella Dalrymple woke with a Sunday-morning headache and the memory of snoring during the night. She was cold because the man on the other side of the bed was warm, with the whole of the double duvet wrapped around his ample body. Not simply draped, but inextricably linked with his limbs and jammed under his chin, thoroughly, if unconsciously, appropriated. Until she recognized that fact, and the futility of any attempt to get it back without waking him, she had been unsure of where she was; there had been half a minute of disorientation and a sense of another place and more forgiving time.

In the years of her marriage William had been an agitated sleeper, who moved and muttered and sometimes spoke aloud, but he was more likely to relinquish the duvet and wake cold himself than he was to take it. Isabella thought of William with regret, tinged at the corners with a nasty little shadow of conscience that hung over her eyes, like something minute stuck to an eyelash. There was no longer any point in staying in bed.

In the scale of marital misdemeanours recounted by contemporaries, William had done nothing *wrong*; no infidelities, no serious addictions, if the dentistry itself were discounted, no unpleasant self-indulgences otherwise, no obnoxious personal habits, no outstanding social gaffes. It was just that he had done nothing right either; he had simply ceased to be an asset. All he had done for his wife was do everything she asked him to do. In retrospect, an obedient husband who pandered to the ambitions of a wife without ever sharing them was the worst kind of partner. She had moulded him and schooled him, organized him and ordered him until he was a nothing more than slightly afraid of her shadow, and all she could remember now was how he had never once stolen the duvet.

With a backward glance at the sleeping form of William's far richer, more colourful replacement, Isabella took to the bathroom. For every morning of her marriage to William, she had presented him with a flawless face over his breakfast tea, a time-consuming challenge that should have commanded appreciation and was now such an ingrained habit that she had made herself regard it as a virtue. This is the face he will remember when he goes to work. Avoid having children if at all possible: it wrecks everything.

Everything had proved capable of wrecking itself by the slow, disintegrating process of her own disappointment and contempt, and this was what she had now. A richer, shorter partner with a far finer apartment and a far more interesting clientele of friends, plus a shared interest in bigger and better. Isabella tested the water in the shower with a delicate hand. It was too hot. She felt lethargic: the prospect of the hour-long ritual of hairwash, hairdry, *maquillage,* the selection of clothes, all seemed incredibly arduous, and that was the real cause of the malaise. *If* she had still been with William, none of this would be mandatory. He wouldn't have noticed; hadn't noticed for years. She had—as she still did—bled William dry in maintenance costs to sustain a face, a style of life and a wardrobe that meant absolutely nothing to him. Which meant she had taken away *nothing.*

Life seemed suddenly to be one long series of clichés lived out against a backdrop of hope. She brushed her teeth cursorily. Life with William meant that everything about teeth bored her; her own had never been any trouble; everyone else made such a fuss. The rest of her year seemed to unfold in an endless succession of doing exactly this. She raised her upper lip in front of the mirror, the better to remove a speck, saw blood on her gums and had a sudden vision of a face without teeth. No, no, her teeth were excellent and permanent—William said so, didn't he? But if they were not, who would love her then?

He would.

The bathroom wallpaper was richly decorated with birds of paradise, which made her want to screech in tune. The world divided, he had told her once, between those who loved wallpaper and those who detested it. She was cross and tired and could remember nothing that had given her any pleasure in the last week. Except, of course, the comforting thought that, in a similar fashion to the planned stripping down of the paper in here, her own life could be altered. Nothing was permanent about the way one lived, and whenever she wanted, she could go back to the husband who did not snore.

Mrs. Matthewson, loyal spouse to Ernest and equally loyal friend to the few she otherwise loved, laid the table for the ritual family lunch in a dining room of many colours: creamy yellow walls, vibrant swagged curtains festooned with brilliant blue hummingbirds, whose motif had been repeated throughout the house ever since a holiday in the West Indies. The house, which was large and solid as befitted Ernest himself, bore tribute to that vacation.

She always left the laying of the table until last, waiting until she was sure everyone was in attendance. There was nothing more insulting than a fully laid table displayed as an accusation of parental incompetence on the many occasions when her son had failed to turn up. The provision of food was one secret of marital stability—it had been sufficient to keep Ernest more or less in control—but it was not enough to ensure the consistent attendance of an emancipated son. With girlfriend, a pallid little thing with a pretty enough face mostly subsumed into overlarge spectacles and an adoring smile for her affianced. Mrs. Matthewson never ceased to marvel at what a good-looking, personable man her son had become. The revolutionizing of his body from the grossly fat boy she had nurtured to the streamlined and athletic male he was now had been his own work; the acquisition of social graces and, at long last, an appreciation of his parents had been the work of Sarah Fortune. Mrs. Matthewson approved violently of Sarah; she resisted the impulse to give the new girlfriend the napkin with the stain, just as she would try to avoid the temptation to pour gravy all over her skirt. Such activities would be childish and counterproductive, and would not achieve her heart's desire, which was to have cataclysmic Sarah Fortune, her *friend*, back in the family fold. Forgiveness of her son for the monumental carelessness of losing her was beyond Mrs. Matthewson, even though she privately, if not publicly, agreed with Ernest that a marriage would have been a disaster.

They sat. Malcolm and his father talked about the law, as lawyers do. A careful listener, and Mrs. Matthewson was certainly that, would recognize that this apparently intellectual exchange was no more than pure gossip, not about the law itself but the personalities in it, who was earning what with whom, which dog was eating which, and how they were managing to digest. Malcolm had become boringly ambitious. *Sarah would not have let you do that,* Mrs. Matthewson muttered to herself over the grapefruit segments, turning her face and a saccharine sweet smile to the newest replacement.

This girl was not stupid; a businessperson, with hungry eyes. Malcolm would never go for anyone stupid, not after Sarah, but he would, quite unconsciously, choose something more amenable, a little less *vivid.* Mrs. Matthewson watched the eyes, enlarged behind the specs, straying away from her own. Tricky; scenting an enemy; she was not going to engage in girl-talk with Darling's plump, middle-aged mummy, was she? She was going to cosy up to the men and refuse to be excluded.

"How's Sarah?" Mrs. Matthewson asked Ernest pointedly, ignoring his wince.

"Oh, very well, blooming. God alone knows what she does. As I was saying . . ."

"When are you going to make her a partner?"

"Yes, Dad, when are you?" Malcolm, amused, was not letting him get away with it, or his mother either; Ernest was glaring, finally giving in. It was no good resisting once it was started: when they were together, the three of them, they wanted to talk about her.

"Still giving her the no-hope clients?" Malcolm asked.

"She finds them of her own accord. She seems to have an aversion to clients who either make money or have it. She *loves* awkwardness," Ernest protested defensively.

"I wonder why." Malcolm's eyes were on his mother, who lowered her gaze towards her food. The girlfriend ate doggedly.

"We've one awkward client she won't go near. We've tried him with everyone. No one lasts. Now, if she'd deal with John Smith and make him happy, the partnership would love her, but she won't. I don't understand her sometimes."

All the time. Mrs. Matthewson shifted uncomfortably, and began to clear the plates. The new girlfriend was supposed to say, "Let me help." She didn't.

Malcolm adopted his dry cross-examining voice. "Not berthing her alongside the dangerous ones again, are you, Dad? Leaving our Sarah to handle the psychotics? You know what happens when you do that. If he's half-way mad already, she'll make him madder. Why don't you give her a decent client for a change?" His voice had risen. The girlfriend smiled into an empty face.

"She doesn't *want* decent clients," Ernest shouted. "She wants eccentrics. Like she wanted you."

This time the silence was longer.

"Do you like your beef rare or medium?" Mrs. Matthewson asked the girl.

"Rare, please," the girl said.

"What a shame," Mrs. Matthewson said, carving the burnt piece off the end of the roast and putting it on a cold plate. "Tell Malcolm about this John Smith, Ernest, do. What does he look like? So *interesting*."

And then, much later, she would tell Sarah. All the gossipy pickings from the rich man's table, in case, woman to woman, they were useful.

They finished the last of the overdone beef, followed it with ice-cream, and then said grace. The offer of alcohol had been made, but it was a token offer. Imelda had announced it as a challenge immediately after Sarah came into the refectory and remembered to stand for the prayer preceding food. "Would you have some wine, Sarah? We've plenty," she yelled, as a Christmas-present bottle was brandished like a club for the juggling. The parish priest followed its progress with a longing glance; the others with mild curiosity. Sarah could see herself sipping a single glass, for ever in debt for this special treat while they followed her consumption of it with their eyes, concerned for her soul in case she asked for a second. Only the one bottle between the thirty here present, as if a drop of the stuff would intoxicate instead of reawaken a growling need. Sarah refused politely, and prepared to drown the food in water, remembering to ask for more in order to flatter the cook. Not Julie; not today, although they wished it was. Your day of rest, dear. Let us bugger the beef.

"I wish they wouldn't," Julie whispered to Sarah, on her left.

"Wouldn't what?"

"Buy beef at all." She had caught from them a certain Irish intonation, a rhythm of speech alien to Pauline's crystal tones, which showed she did not spend most of her time in Pauline's company. Sarah waited for a topical reminder of beef-related disease while she and Julie ate the meat with equal feigned enthusiasm.

There was a buzz of voices in the convent dining room, none of them raised, all animated, argumentative even, discussing the day's news, the week's news, each speaker with a separate ailment that was never discussed in public except in an earnest invitation to make a joke of it. They were all slightly disabled, by age at least. They had faces without lines, bent bodies; they were old without protest; a dying breed, who knew they were unbanishable. Oh, for a life of virtue, free from acquisitive needs, never even *wanting* to house-hunt and full of appreciation for burnt beef. Sarah had learned her manners at this kind of table; she had a certain gratitude about eating, whatever it was.

"Once a month, child, you eat with us. You don't eat enough. Look at the size of you." Not once a complaint, or a curiosity for the outside world. Plenty to talk about, especially the prospect of the Cardinal's Advent sermons in the cathedral; they all went, even most of the walking wounded. What happened here was the will of God, illness included. That, and that alone, was what Sarah abhorred rather than admired. This dependence on the will of another, either divine or sent by the National Health Service, each couched in inefficacy and mystery. She loved their capacity for acceptance, but she could not revere it. God was a perverse old man to be indulged, with a passing resemblance to Ernest Matthewson, in her view. Deities and more temporal authorities begged and deserved the challenge of sheer bloody-minded disobedience.

There was a garden of a kind, which spouted rather than grew, the better for that on a good summer day, not now. These retired sisters had been too much in the world and moved about too much to find time to cultivate a garden. They were neat and tidy without being versed in domesticity or horticulture. The front garden doubled as a car park, the garden element revived from time to time with indoor potted plants and gifts and surviving shrubs, unlike the back area, which no one noticed until the nettles reached the height of the dustbins. The heart of the convent was the chapel, where each item was polished and revered, each statue and seat, shining with the touch of a hundred loving hands.

In the watery sunshine of the afternoon, Sarah noticed that Pauline looked frail, her skin like parchment and her movements less than brisk. It was only after dark, in electric light, that her deep-set eyes looked powerful; for the moment, although she was the strongest of her contemporaries, she looked an old woman. Until she spoke, and all the authority returned.

"I'm grateful to you, Sarah," she was saying gruffly.

"Why?" The statement was surprising. Pauline gave thanks for the existence of this niece in her own prayers, but never in public. She accepted Sarah's donations as no more than the convent's due; took it as conscience money from a heathen. She never gave thanks for charity, but if it was offered she never missed the chance.

"For your dentist friend, of course. A Christian, for sure. He phoned me to say he was willing to treat any nun virtually for free. We have to pay for materials only, now isn't that nice? He seemed to know all about Imelda, can't think how. Is he a Catholic?"

Julie was looking straight ahead, transfixed by the bare branches of a shrub, conspicuously innocent.

"Hm. I would say his religious orientation is not decided yet," Sarah said carefully, hiding her surprise in the palm of her hand and feeling vaguely outmanoeuvred. "He may want you entirely for research. The effect of diet on teeth, or something of the kind. After all, few people have a diet which is easier to predict. But I should take the offer. He's a very good dentist and a kind man, even though he sometimes doesn't realize it himself. Probably ripe for conversion, too."

"Of course we take up the offer—we take up *any* offer like that. I don't care about his motives. Sister Dominic went the same day he phoned—she raves about him."

"Everyone does, apart from his wife," Sarah said.

"No man is a hero to his butler," Pauline said inconsequentially, and rose from the bench where all three had sat. "Have a word with me before you go, will you, Sarah? I'll leave you in peace with your cigarettes. I can't bear to watch."

Julie and Sarah sat in companionable silence, Julie with a piece of mending in her lap. It was a cotton traycloth with embroidery and a frayed hem; it kept her hands busy. Sarah employed hers in the lighting of a cigarette. Each to her own. The sunlight caught Julie's growing brown hair and made it gleam against her bare face. In the warm light of a mild afternoon she looked almost saintly.

"Cooking and now mending?" Sarah enquired. "Do you also pray? Give you a habit and a rosary and you'd become one of them. Do you think it would suit you?"

"No." She let the mending fall, as if it embarrassed her. "No," she repeated. "But it has its virtues." Her face lit with an impish smile, dispelling the illusion of saintliness. Saints were not renowned for humour, or maybe their jokes were never recorded. "Obedience to divine will," she said. "The belief that all sufferings are temporary and have a purpose. I could do with a bit of that, although I might prefer a belief that everything was *preordained.* I should love to be able to offer up pain in the belief that it altered the sentence of some soul in purgatory. Turn it into something useful. That would be nice. And I'd like to be able to pray for the baby Cannon wants so much." The mending remained untended.

"Some of it must rub off, you know," she continued, with the same, hesitant thoughtfulness. "Even though I don't believe it. Because here I am, sewing and cooking, keeping myself busy to avoid going mad. I don't do it for praise or the greater glory of God, and I know that really I'm a prisoner, but I don't feel like a prisoner."

"It's your decision. You can leave whenever you want."

Julie shook her head vigorously. "No, I can't. Where would I go, except to Cannon? And if I went to Cannon, John would find us. You know what I think?" The mending had fallen on the ground and Julie did not bother to retrieve it. "I think John could find Cannon whenever he wants, whatever Cannon does. Not that he's watching him, but he follows him with his mind. He goes to the places Cannon goes to . . . He *imagines* where he is. Do you know this already? Has he told you?"

"Something similar. I don't believe in telepathy. No evidence, you see. If John Smith knows where his brother is, it's because he's sent someone to look. Or gone himself." Sarah felt guilty. Day by day, her belief in the ultimate wickedness and the almost supernatural powers of Johnnyboy Smith had been gently eroding.

"Johnny can't imagine *my* whereabouts because he has no link into my mind the way he does to Cannon's. But he would know immediately if I went to Cannon. Then he would come and destroy me." Julie stood, folded her arms across her chest and walked the few paces the garden allowed. She spoke with quiet certainty. "He'd do it out of revenge for me stealing Cannon away, as he sees it, or simply out of hatred and loss. Can you imagine hating anyone so much?"

Sarah paused. "No. Hatred is quite alien to me. So is revenge. If someone hurts me, steals from me, I keep out of their way. Take another path."

"But you might not if the *person* who was stolen was the only person you had ever loved. The only person you were *capable* of loving. The person who made you complete, allowed you to function. You would hate the thief who blinded you, wouldn't you? The one who cut off your right arm and took it away?"

"I might," Sarah conceded. "I just doubt if I could sustain it—not sustain it and carry it forward into some act of malice, such as bashing them over the head with a teapot. They say anyone could kill. I don't believe I could. I might wish someone dead, but that's totally different. That's only wishing."

She thought of her long-dead husband; the one she had loved with youthful optimism. Wanting him dead when she knew his unfaithfulness; not wanting it at all when it happened. Pauline had helped, then. Said it was God's will, not her own. In the end only God dictated birth and death. She thought of wanting Charles Tysall's death and not being able to hasten it or even wanting it.

It was growing cold, the December sun sinking in the sky, turning Julie's soft hair into a halo, somehow ignoring her own.

"Well, the game's nearly over. Two more weeks. We've got to believe that. Don't let Cannon boss you around. Do you want a baby as much as him?"

"I want what he wants. It would be the ultimate message for Johnny, wouldn't it? And, besides, I've always been afraid that if I didn't conceive Cannon would leave me. I'm not enough all by myself. No one is. There has to be something more important than either of you."

"Nonsense." Sarah did not believe her. Cannon had fascinated her from the first meeting; obligation and fierce defensiveness had grown from that and, at the beginning, his wife was only his wife; a once-clever school dropout who had lost a decade to drugs, pulling herself half-way out when Cannon met her, and now the wife of dreams. Sarah had never before seen such unconditional, determined love. She did not judge or measure it, simply felt the peculiar strength of it; it infected her and almost made her ashamed. She watched him blossom in Julie's presence; shrivel in prison without her. There was a magic in her potency: she made the unlovable lovable; she was the guardian angel, who chased away the demons. She remembered Julie's instructions and her terror. *Take me away—somewhere secret. Take me away . . . don't tell him.*

Who did this to you?

His brother—take me away. Hide me—he's coming back.

She had believed then in the evil of John Smith, although she could not encompass the reasons. Looking at Julie now, diminished by the attentions of this monster but restored to health, she found the belief slipping away, like adolescent faith. She remembered the incredulity of the police. *What? She* thinks *she knows who it is? Why would this man do such a thing?* She tried to summon up the hatred she had felt then and found she could not. The monster had no shape. But Cannon lived. Cannon and the bogeyman he might have invented to scare them all.

The Christian Sabbath was a bad day for reflection.

William was not going to phone Sarah. He was not going to be dependent on anyone who was so independent of him. He was not going to become introspective either. He was going to go for a walk, like other people did, mull over the week, pretend he was purposeful. Think on his feet, in case it made it easier.

He did not love her, never pretended he did. He simply thought of her a lot. He found it difficult to make his own kind of romantic image out of someone who was, however desirable, so generous with sexual favours and yet so self-contained. He was in the street outside on a dying afternoon, making himself walk away instead of walking towards her, ringing on the doorbell and saying, Yesterday I was punched in the face and it hurts, it jolly well hurts, and you were busy, with a man who coughs.

He touched the railings outside his premises. Sharp spikes on the top, if he reached to touch them, firm iron railings beneath. He paused, grabbed two of the railings and shook them. They made the slightest movement and all he felt was the sensation of flaking paint against the palms of his hands. The railings outside his building were a series of twins, bent at differing angles, nodding towards one another, identical but separate.

William felt a touch lopsided, because of the bruise to his face, and a trifle brave, because he did not really care about the bruise and was faintly proud about the means by which he had acquired it. He *hit* me, he repeated to himself wonderingly. Now, why did he do that? I have never in my life done anything which would justify a gratuitous blow, so why did he hit me? Perhaps that's what's wrong with me; I've never been important enough to hit. Isabella probably wanted to hit me all the time. His shoes were heavy, striking the pavement hard, *click, clack;* he could not dawdle. That man did not like you: you made reference to his *teeth* by staring at them and you almost accused him of having a *brother*; you might have offended him. As someone who by dint of his trade invaded the privacy of others all the time, William was philosophical about it. Every day of his working life he committed some kind of assault or was forced into statements that might cause offence. Passing the other set of railings, three doors down, he remembered the Arab princess who had arrived with her retinue and departed in disgust as soon as her translator informed her that all her teeth needed was cleaning. *Swish.* Down the stairs like a rush of curtains, flurrying with outrage.

He walked, expecting any minute that someone would come out from behind these serried sets of railings and hit him again. He felt like a bouncy rubber ball. A touch of violence had enlivened him; made him excitable. What made a man violent? William was not sure, but felt he ought to understand it; he had the feeling that Sarah would understand it completely. He had often wondered about the scars on her body; little white marks that in no way diminished her attraction, on her back, her chest, her arms. Flying glass from a car crash, she had explained, and he had not questioned: she was sensitive on the point. Scars on her *back*, from a car crash, teeny little scars rather than lacerations? He doubted it, but it was really none of his business. He would not ask a patient, How did you get that wart on your finger? and he really did not know how to ask intimate questions of a lover. He did not have a great deal of practice.

His hands were cold from his daft, unconscious touching of the railings, something he did whenever he left the building, greeting them, checking up on the continuity of his life. As long as the railings remained where they were, his life would remain as stable as it was. The railings belonged to another era; their variety amazed him. There were tall railings and short railings, railings with sharp, pointed, fleur-de-lis tops; there were sooty black railings tapering to elegant points, guarding the basements he passed, all built to repel rioters and prevent them climbing through the windows and now incorporated as part of the fabric. Dug up in the First World War to provide metal for armaments, replaced because they belonged. They comforted him, these railings. A burglar, breaking into his premises in a misguided search for drugs, had once snagged his shirt on the way out and there had been small compensation in that.

He walked briskly, making himself look at things. Perhaps he liked the railings so much because they were at eye-level, saved him looking up and noticing anything else, such as the sky and the enormity of his surroundings. Wide streets, lined with red-brick buildings, severely beautiful, designed for a stylish life. This is where Edwardian heroines might have alighted from carriages, tripped up steps to the wide front doors, rung the bell, or sent the footman to give a card, where Elizabeth Barrett was At Home to Mr. Browning in a first-floor living room, the better to command a view of the street, houses fit for the distinguished to receive suitors and accommodate servants in basement and attic. He could see them now, polishing the brass bells and whitening the steps.

No shops were allowed in Wimpole Street and Harley Street, only these gracious frontages to suites of offices and medical practices. The same sort of people came to these streets now, for different purposes, deposited from chauffeur-driven cars and taxis to pay munificent bills for private health to charlatans, profiteers and a host of decent and honourable practitioners. William supposed there was not a street in central London that did not have that kind of mix, whatever the trade.

It was Sarah, really, who had made him interested in people, the view from the window rather than the view with his back to it; Sarah who had instilled this habit of walking. She was easy to please, he found on their first acquaintance—"Come on, let's walk, discuss your case, have something to eat, oh, *look at that*." She had never wanted courtship, only communication. She seemed so honest, so open.

He crossed the road and smiled vaguely at the cyclist he had not seen, the collision averted. A scowl was returned.

But there was, of course, this strict economy with the truth in all their dealings; a mutual, unspoken agreement not to go beyond the confines of what was volunteered. Thus he did not ask her about the scars, and she refused the details of what Cannon had done; he did not go behind the scenes of what she told him. It was similar with Cannon himself: mutual affection of a surprising kind, which did not yet permit an exchange of confidences. William was worried that he should inspire such reserve in his few friends—maybe he was not trustworthy—but he knew more about Cannon, he felt, than anyone, because Cannon had mumbled and chattered in his Diconal dreams. *Johnnyboy, Johnnyboy, dirty fangs, Johnnyboy.*

The streets were wonderfully quiet on Sundays. Cars passing *en route* to somewhere else, stopping dutifully at lights with none of the weekday impatience; empty parking bays, allowing him to see the buildings and delight in them. Turning a corner into Marylebone High Street, the wind caught his face and the bruise stung. He felt an enormous affection for his own environment and, thinking of Cannon, a surge of excitement. Ahead of him, two Arab men walked arm in arm.

He had always wanted a brother, had created, as a child, an imaginary companion to offset his own single-child status. When that companion died of natural causes, although William had created an elaborate accident on a mountainside to explain his absence, he had mourned him. Cannon had an estranged brother; that much William knew. It was not beyond the bounds of possibility that this man with the similar teeth and oh-so-similar eyes was *that* brother. Maybe, he, William, could engineer a reunion? Rubbish, but he liked the idea, and it would be a fitting addendum to his paper on the teeth of twins; a double whammy; the coup of a lifetime. A service to humanity, better than merely professional, and it would make his paper remembered. As well as make him proud. He was wistful at the mere thought.

He could go back to the exhibition and find out who had bought the Mouth. Or wait. Or tell himself, as he turned back for home, suddenly reluctant to reach it, that it was sheer imagination that had led him to yesterday's assumption that the man who had hit him was Cannon's twin. William stopped, and stared at a massive front door of mahogany, polished to such a shine that he could see in it a blurred reflection of himself. Vainly he struggled to recall the features of the man who had hit him, but the face itself blurred into a strange photofit. All he could remember was the teeth. He reached his own front door, looked at it as if it had nothing to do with him, realizing at the same time how he had forgotten that part of the reason for the walk had been to buy milk and eggs. His cold, soft, well-tended hands were uncomfortably free. There were some things that were bound to be forgotten: toilet rolls, letters, the most tedious of necessities.

What was *wrong* with phoning Sarah? Why did he so often cut off his nose to spite his face? Because of the other men, who left him free of any obligation for her? He didn't care about that, most of the time. He hated admitting need, that was all; told himself, as he noticed how the door seemed oddly askew, that he was becoming old and strange.

The keypad worked, the big front door opening with surprising speed when it was usually slow, buzzing at him like an angry bee. He did not think of it at the time as he mounted the stairs to his third floor. He thought, That foyer might once have been a ballroom before they put in a lift. I wonder who danced there? And the same feeling of mild euphoria made him add, Bugger the eggs and milk, bugger everybody. I'll have beans and toast for supper and a bottle of wine.

It was deserted at the weekend. Five specialist dental suites and a penthouse suite above his own. Quiet as the proverbial grave. Thick carpets, which Isabella had chosen and the communal expense of which he heartily resented, muffling his steps to his own front door. Sarah also forgets the eggs and the milk.

The door to his suite was open, which did not particularly surprise him. William automatically assumed that any omission was due to his own negligence; he tended to apologize as soon as he opened his mouth. It was the presence of his dental records, released from their cabinet and spread, systematically, over the floor, that made him realize that this was not his fault any more than it was accidental. A large man sat on the floor by his records, leafing through them with every appearance of disinterest. He was expressionless, like a Buddha, grossly fat and unperturbed. William had a confused memory of a similar figure patrolling the street the morning before, the one who looked as if he had lost his dog.

It was so much warmer here than outside that his eyes began to water and the bruise to throb. He nodded at the man on the floor, as if to a casual acquaintance whose name he could not recall. He had the strange feeling of returning to an appointment he could not remember having made: the man looked as if he belonged, as of right. The nod was returned. William had a sudden vision of officialdom. VAT men? The Dental Practice Board investigating a complaint? On a Sunday? It all seemed extremely silent and legitimate. He walked into his surgery, heart thudding.

There was the man with the legs like pillars and his back turned, his arms folded and his head dipped in enquiry, nodding in deference towards the drill equipment, hoisted safely out of reach on the gantry, and then, as William watched, sitting awkwardly in the dental chair, still with his arms folded, his eyes fixed on the light. Adjusting himself for comfort, finding none, slipping on the seat. The features of the man suddenly made sense. Without thinking, William approached, flicked the switch for the overhead light marked Siemens and put his foot on the pedal to recline the chair. He moved round to Tina's side and turned on the aspirator. *Slugggh*, the head of the thing sucking at nothing, *slugghh*. Where there had been silence, there was racket. The man lay, his eyes blinded by the light, his lips in a rictus smile, his limbs stiff with terror. All he did was remove his hands from his armpits and put them over his ears, as if aping the monkey who hears no evil. He made a small sound, a hiss; then the prominent red lips, which had been parted, were clamped shut, forming a wide, red line splitting the jowls of his face. William stood over him. There was no time for fear; he was simply very angry.

"What can I do for you?" he said. He moved the drill gantry so that it hung between them, in front of the man's eyes. "If I drilled your teeth without water coolant," he said conversationally, "I could make them white hot. What the hell do you want?"

The man did not speak. William's anger became tremulous. "What do you *want*?" he repeated, moving closer. And then, in a voice that sounded petulant to his own ears, "Why did you *hit* me?"

The eyes opened wide and stared at the light, blinked and remained fixed. A large hand shot from the torso and grabbed William by the balls through his trousers. The hand gripped; William gave a sharp yelp. The grip lessened, but remained. He looked down at the brown paw clutching his groin and grabbed at the wrist. The bone felt like the indestructible iron of the railings outside. The man blinked again and, for the first time, diverted his glance to William's face, twisted his grip, then relaxed it. Then he smiled. "This is just to make sure," he said softly, "that we don't hurt *one another*."

They remained like that, William and he, staring at each other, William with watering eyes, mesmerized by brown teeth. Then the hand dropped away. The relief was enormous. As if in response to some command not actually made, William pressed the foot pedal bringing the chair upright. Almost a normal chair. The man sighed, pushed the offending hand into the pocket of his trousers and flourished from it William's card. "You gave me this," he said. The voice was extremely soft. "You *insisted*," he added, as if that were more than sufficient to justify forced entry and trespass. The argument seemed completely compelling. William felt at a loss—again, that strange sense that the visitor was here as of right, his presence inevitable, even familiar, and that it was he who was owed an apology. He found it difficult to take his eyes from the flash of the brown teeth, almost urged to touch them. He could do so much for these teeth; he could redeem a thousand wrongs by treating these teeth. The man got off the chair and began to prowl, his hands locked behind his back in a mute promise of no further intimidation. William could do nothing but continue to stare at him, scarcely aware of the third man, who made slight paper-shuffling noises from behind.

"How did you get in?" William asked stupidly. It was irrelevant how they had got in: the only fact that mattered was their presence—the *man's* presence. The other, somehow, counted for nothing. There was no reply. The man seemed totally absorbed in his own curiosity. He paused in his perambulations, looked at the battery of equipment on the dentist's side of the chair, equipment more cumbersome than that on the nursing side. A deep shudder shook his frame; his body trembled with profound revulsion. It reminded William of a dog shaking water from its coat.

"So, Mr. Dentist," said the soft voice, "you think you could do something about my fangs? I've got as far as your door how many times? Five? Six? Never made it inside until now. And I didn't need your card. Some little boy of a lawyer told me all about you. If you treat the crap inside prison, like he said, you ain't too proud to treat me." He retracted his upper lip, let the top teeth pin down the lower lip, the better to expose them. It was an almost comical snarl, like a child competing with another in pulling faces.

That's what you might have done as a child; made people laugh at you.

There was a photocopier in the other room by the reception desk. William heard the sound of its operation and, for a moment, his sensation of panic returned with a different focus. The *records*. They were inefficiently banked on computer; he was not particularly computer-literate and it was still those pieces of paper that mattered. Without records, he would be lost. The practice would be lost. So would his academic career.

He closed his eyes to blank out the thought. Concentrated on his own voice. "Yes. I could do something about your teeth. Veneers . . . crowns, all sort of things . . ." He faltered. "*Yes*, I could do wonders with those teeth. I've got all the relevant experience."

"Would it hurt?"

William shook his head, without sufficient conviction. "Totally pain-free dentistry is a modern myth," he said earnestly. "No pain as such, or never for long. The analgesics are highly effective, although people vary in response. But it would be . . ." he struggled for the right euphemism ". . . *uncomfortable*, at times."

"I need fillings, too. I don't want metal in my mouth. Poisonous."

"Amalgam isn't poisonous. You don't have to have it. Resin for the cavities."

"But you could cause *exquisite* pain," the man stated, emphasizing the word, gesturing to the drill. "You could *disfigure* me." The pause was poignant, as if both recognized that disfigurement of the man was already achieved.

"Your brother had no pain."

"You're quite wrong about that. I have no brother. I don't know why you think so."

William turned his head and, for one horrified moment, thought he saw tears in the other man's eyes. "There's always the potential for pain," William said. "I've devoted my life to avoiding it."

"Where do you keep the stuff? I'd need to know you had plenty."

William opened a drawer. "Plenty for daily purposes. I keep the minimum, order what I need. You could be sedated."

"No. I need to know what's happening."

It was a surreal conversation, he thought. He felt as if he were being interviewed, his premises viewed not from the point of examining his credentials but with some other agenda in mind. The man continued to pull faces, looking clownish, as if the working of his jaws and eyebrows were essential to the process of thought.

"Perfect," he said. "Let me ask you something, Mr. Dentist, before I make an appointment. A test, if you don't mind. What, in your life, do you hold dearest? Or, should I say, *whom*?"

The question was oddly shocking. The photocopier made its familiar noise. William tried to remember the order in which he stored the dental records, what they said, apart from the charts of teeth. They were stored in sequence, the most recent patients to the front, the bulkier records to the back of each alphabetical index. What privacy was being invaded? No layperson could read a dental chart. He remembered how he recalled names and addresses with a note of who had referred the patient to him, so that he could remember to ask after a patient's referring friend and thus make it seem as if he remembered who they were. Part of the personal touch he had to rehearse. *What* did *he hold dearest, or whom?* At the moment, his records. The man waited for an answer. It tripped, stutteringly, off William's tongue. "The pursuit of perfection. Professional *pride*. Technique." He held out his hands in front of himself, making a plea for the records. His hands were shaking. "And *these*, I suppose."

The man nodded. "You'll give me an afternoon this week, perhaps. Before Christmas. We'll fix it. I don't want anyone else here, do you understand? I don't want anyone watching me."

"There are rules—' William began.

"And rules," the man murmured.

He was moving towards the door, William following. He saw, to his relief, that the records were neatly reassembled, sitting on the reception desk. A briefcase stood by the door. What the other man had copied, he had no idea. It was what he was leaving behind that mattered. Suddenly everything was polite. Their method of entry was a mystery.

The man stopped and stared at Cannon's drawing of William's hands. He stared for a long time. Then he turned and held out his own. It seemed necessary to reciprocate, like civilized beings at the end of a normal, mutually beneficial meeting. The man wrapped William's knuckle in both of his own and crushed it. Then he lifted the hand to his own mouth and bit it. William could feel the movement of bone, jarring pain, felt as if the hand would crumble into sharp splinters. This time he screamed long and loud. The hand was released. The scream echoed into the empty hallway, continued as the door closed.

William put the hand across his mouth, moved his fingers and felt his jaw. He leaned against the door frame and looked at what he could see. Everything as normal, nothing disturbed, as if they had never been there. All the paintings still in place. The mark of an emerging bruise on his own skin.

9

The phone rang into the heavy silence and William looked at it as if it were alien. He listened to the message and heard the receiver replaced after the bleep. Slowly he flexed the fingers of his right hand, then cupped it in his left to control the tremor. Poor hand, mottled in colour, intact, the same as ever. It was a playground trick to compress the knuckle like that and make the victim scream. The body was shy of injury to the hand. A circle of purple toothmarks rose in the fleshy part between thumb and forefinger.

A series of possible and logical actions paraded themselves in the forefront of his mind without prompting him to any movement. He felt sick with a corrosive shame; paralysed by the conviction that he had invited the intrusion, played with this fire and solicited the burning. It made him responsible; he felt like a girl, guilty after the rape because she had been the first to smile and get into his car. This is your fault, William. Then, panic, mollified in part by the presence of bruises without blood; a mental check of the last tetanus jab; all immunizations in place as they always were. No bite more poisonous than a human bite.

To test the workings of his right hand, he pressed out 1471 on the phone, using three fingers and thumb. *You were called today at . . .* The number was Isabella's. She did this sometimes, never speaking or leaving a message, and he never knew if he was supposed to have known and phoned her back, whether she was lonely, whether she simply wanted a few seconds of his pre-recorded voice to prove he was still alive and earning money. He would have liked, for a moment, a touch of her unsympathetic certainty; he could ask her for help.

But he did not want *help:* he wanted redemption. He was too ashamed for help to be appropriate. Seeking help from Isabella, showing her the pathetic bruise to his face and the non-existent damage to his hand, which had made him scream like a baby, would only be tantamount to inviting contempt, while seeking help from Sarah would involve facing the briskness and wisdom of her sympathy along with an offer of strong drink. He decided on strong drink alone. *He* had got himself into this; *he* would get himself out.

William went to his kitchen and made tea with elaborate care. One Earl Grey tea-bag, indecision about whether to have lemon or milk, until he remembered there was no milk, the sharp scent of the tea a restorative. A sip of that, a slug of brandy into a glass, sipped and then gulped, which made him cough. Then he collected the bundle of notes from the desk and went backstage. He felt like a reviled actor, slinking into the wings.

The room that comforted in its mess. The reminder of the good old days of dentures and National Health practice; dangerous anaesthetics for children; no time for mere technique. Dentures and moulds on surfaces, looking as if they waited for a mouth. No one had come down here: he would have been able to tell by the disturbance of the white dust. He went back for the second glass of brandy and collected the bottle. He got ice from the fridge, noticed evidence of Tina's current passion for lemons, added a slice. The first drink had gone straight to his head. Somewhere in here was the first impression he had ever made of Cannon's teeth. He began to search feverishly, faster and faster, increasing the mess and the sense of hopelessness as he went, and all the time the bruises on the back of his hand faded indiscriminately until only the most prominent, left by the top canines, remained. He stopped the frantic searching; there would be nothing to compare but, all the same, he could swear that those teeth and the teeth that had made the impression would be almost identical.

There was no telephone here, deliberately, a decision made on grounds of economy, and a state of affairs preserved because he liked it. He wiped a surface clean with his sleeve, blew at the dust, and separated the notes into two piles. They were heavy; he found himself panting, with a vague inclination to cry, which, once recognized, made him cross. Oh, for heaven's sake, William, what happened after all? Nothing. A shock, easily treated with sugared tea, more brandy.

He made himself concentrate on the notes. They would be out of order; it might take hours to sort them and there would be patients arriving tomorrow. The thought of that made him tremble; the mere idea of ever again facing a patient without reading the notes first made him nauseous. That was what he had done with the girl-child who inhabited his dreams along with her brother; the one from whom he was sure he had removed the wrong teeth. He looked at the names on the first three folders: none of them meant anything. Without their notes they were strangers, although, if he looked at the chart, memory stirred in the way it might for a fingerprint expert recognizing a familiar set of whorls. The impression left by a bite was similarly unique. He almost wanted the bruises to reappear, to evidence their own origins. It had been a nip; the man had not wanted to *eat* his hand any more than he had wanted to eat from it.

William thought of another version of the same scene: the man's teeth snapping shut on his hand, not with the nip of a puppy but the bite of a Rottweiler, jaws locked, teeth grinding on sinew, remaining like that until prised apart or the hand torn away. The notes were not hopelessly muddled, and it might have been himself who had muddled them more by carrying them downstairs and dropping a few of the folders on the way—no way to treat treasured things, how could he be so clumsy? The mere touch of the folders reassured him, but what might have been taken out? From cursory examination it seemed that nothing was missing from the first few he examined. Gradually he relaxed and slowed down. He isolated the Ms; they were all together, like a family. Ah, Mrs. Macdonald, he remembered her from her chart, a lady with fine yellow teeth like a horse and a kindred liking for sugar lumps. Mr. Murray, a faceless memory with a highly successful bridge between molar and premolar of which William had been proud. Miss Motcomb, a child of the fluoride age, free of dental caries. He looked for the single folder on Andrew Mitchum, Sarah's emergency treatment, and could not find it. This was faintly disturbing, but since he doubted that patient would ever return he put second thoughts into the realm of non-being, calmer now. Sister Dominic's were gone, with the notation of Cannon's introduction to the sisters. *Cannon's friends,* he had written on the front, with a reminder to keep them all together. That did not matter either: he would remember Dominic's filling. What mattered was that there would be notes for tomorrow's patients: Tina would be able to find them before anyone arrived. The relief was profound. He sorted through until he found the folder that related to Cannon, filed under that name in the Cs without fuss. The name Smith was added in brackets; there was no address other than the prison, and Cannon's prisoner number was all that appeared. William sat back, sipped the brandy and read, slowly and thoughtfully, the coded record of what he had done with Cannon and in which order over nine months. A good job, was what—but, then, the raw material had been so much better than he could have hoped. Diseased teeth, but strong and recoverable; not a suggestion of degenerating bone or receding gums; an extraordinary case of underlying health.

He remembered Cannon trembling in the chair. Remembered the man downstairs, with his shudder of revulsion, the aggression, the bravado, which were surely the symptoms of fear. He looked again at the notes and felt satisfaction. A *good job;* he was *good* at this; in fact, he was *excellent.* He drummed his fingers on the dusty surface; the pain had gone.

Now, if these two were twins, there was every chance that the mouths would be similar, but professional instinct was telling William that *this* man would not have the same underlying strength. There was a lividity about him that suggested otherwise; blood pressure, lines to the face that suggested familiarity with chronic pain. And Cannon, virtually under orders and removed from prison for the purpose of mending his teeth, had had nothing to lose and something to gain from a glimpse of the outside world. Cannon had been curious; Cannon had been allowed to explore; Cannon had sat happily in *this* room. And Cannon had a capacity to trust: he *wanted* to believe and he *wanted* renewed teeth, he had said, because it would so delight his wife. Lord, he'd forgotten that Cannon had a wife. There was nothing about the state of his clothes to suggest it.

Would this man have the same to lose or gain, and did he have an ounce of faith? William doubted it. Would he stand a dozen or more long afternoons devoted to crowns and veneers? Would he submit quietly to the needle or the offer of Diconal oblivion? William doubted that, too. Would he be able to accept that some of his treatment would be experimental, at least a case of trial and error, and not everything would work first time? Probably not. William would not be able to treat this man in the same way as his brother, but all he knew at this point was that he desperately wanted to try. He craved the challenge of finding the *best* methods and achieving the *best* results, making a real difference to the man's appearance and attitudes, lifting a lifetime's curse by reversing a now rare condition, the way he had with Cannon, and against that desire the blow to the face and the pain to the hand became, if not forgotten, at least irrelevant.

He moved, restless, slightly drunk and becoming more so; he had consumed little food that day, and it was getting dark. He found the darkness a relief. He picked up one of the moulds on the table, counted the teeth. Twenty-eight in this particular head. What if he were simply to remove the disfiguring teeth and create a denture? The creature would endure this better, perhaps; the result would still change his appearance dramatically. William had a fondness for dentures. His National Health practice had featured them strongly, for reasons of budget rather than of fashion, and, ah, Isabella had been right to tread on his principles and insist he migrate to private practice, for the chance to do better, without restrictions . . . *she had been right,* without knowing why: dentures slipped, they broke; the mouth changed around them, for all that they served well. There had been dentures brought back for repair that looked as if they had been run over by a train; he remembered the dentures that had been chewed by a mimicking child, dentures chewed by a dog with similar ideas. Suddenly he began to giggle, holding his sides at the thought of a dog running away with a set of teeth, giving them to a bitch by way of courtship—*Here, have these; my master clearly thinks they're delicious.*

William told himself he was probably losing his mind and the loss would not make a difference. He laughed until tears rolled down his cheeks and he felt exhausted and sober. He rolled back towards the kitchen in search of more drink, dabbed at his face with a paper towel. It took some time to adjust to dentures: would the man be patient with something short of pain? Then he rolled into his surgery and sat on the patients' chair. Looked suspiciously to his left, expecting the man to be there, a substantial ghost, standing where he had seen him, with tears in his eyes, provoked by the denial of the existence of a brother.

Only a man then, not a savage beast. Only a man, like himself. And William wished, far and above everything else, for the chance to deal with those teeth, and then write it down for the world to know what *he* had done, and what could be learned from twins.

Write it down. Make a list of everything you want. Then look at the list and work out which of those things is less important. Specify at those things until you realize they are not very important at all and can, therefore, be removed from the list. Thus, make the list smaller. Sarah crossed out the word "garden."

She sat by the fire with another set of estate agents' particulars, saved as a treat, like a favourite book, to be consumed or dismissed at leisure. This is the stuff of which dreams are made. *I tell you, Sarah, you are never satisfied. If you ever get to heaven you'll say your wings are damp and the harp is out of tune.* Pauline's voice, not accusing, but puzzled about the nature of restlessness.

She had to think about houses. She had to retreat into this kind of dreaming because if she did not she would think about Cannon and Julie all day and all night. And when they were safe, she would have no life left. She had to think about new homes because it was the best antidote to nagging doubt, and the vision of Julie Smith with her inscrutable face and slightly swollen belly. Concentrate.

The next flat, when she found it, would be minimalist in style, unlike this one, an overcrowded tribute to the acquisitive habits of recent years. There was this passion for mismatched chairs, which was a particular nuisance: they crept in and out of corners, always making room for another one with a kind of courtesy. There was an additional sofa, purchased purely for the colour of its sun-faded cover, sitting ill at ease with the custom-built, like a poor relation. There was a dining-room table, which dominated its own room, acquired for the splendour of its legs but redundant because she had lost the knack of entertaining. The next flat would have none of those things; these items would have to be found suitable homes, like well-behaved orphans. She was going to have bare wooden floors and walls full of paintings; only the paintings were lifelong friends.

There had been a psychiatrist lover in here once or twice, who considered that her collection of paintings showed signs of paranoid kleptomania and subversive tendency. There's no *theme* to them, he repeated; they say *nothing* about you at all; they have nothing in common with each other or with you. Definitely like friends, then. It had seemed to disturb him; it didn't disturb her. It was not a *collection*. It would seem odder by far to have things distinguished by uniformity, a series of landscapes, for instance, or a series of interiors or abstracts, instead of a jumble nudging each other for space in their diverse frames. The psychiatrist did not seem to notice that there were more portraits than anything else; he might have analysed something sinister in that. Are you lonely, Sarah? Do you have need of inanimate, undemanding company? Do you seek solace in the form of these expressive faces on the wall? Do you *talk* to them?

Only sometimes. She looked at her own list and looked at the particulars.

Was Cannon making it all up, or was he exaggerating? There was one agent, more amenable than the rest, who seemed to understand that she wanted only as much space as she could get, with the maximum of light, the greatest height of wall, to accommodate the lifelong friends and the added company they were bound to attract. If the friendly estate agent found it odd that she demanded to know, in each case, the identity and address of the vendor of the places he described, he did not say so. None of this current bundle of properties was owned by John Smith; none looked quite right, there were none of his ruined homes; but those she had seen of his were always *right*. Despite their ruinous state, she had liked them all, felt that tug of excitement which suggested, *I could live here, I could fall in love with this.* Could a man with a taste for houses really be such a horror? He, too, liked big, tall walls and ceilings half a mile off the floor. It might not be enough to make the man virtuous, but it did make him sympathetic.

Have nothing to do with him; if you see him, don't let him see you. No, I cannot ever stay in your flat; he will know where I am.

She had obeyed, with the obedience of faith, and yet what nonsense it was. John Smith swam like a porpoise and collected houses the way she collected paintings, with a purpose so random it did not bear analysis. What was wrong with communicating with him? Especially after a long conversation with Mrs. Matthewson. What strange things they discussed over their Sunday lunches, to be sure. She pushed aside the particulars with their seductive photographs, drew a line through her list and began to draft a note on the same page. Stopped, fetched the fragment of the letter Cannon had given her on the way to the high court on a day that now seemed a long time ago. She would write to John Smith with a dual purpose. Purpose number one, to disobey orders and attempt to meet him on some sort of common ground. Purpose number two, the shameful one, to see from his reply if the writing was the same. She disliked this belated urge to cross-check, but she was sick of being reliant on third-party information. Maybe she wasn't such a bad lawyer after all.

"*. . . if you keep this up until Christmas, I'll leave her alone. Promise . . . But you won't keep it up. You'll get careless. You'll realize what's good for you . . .*"

A clumsy, trustworthy hand. An entirely illogical promise. He might succumb to the plea of ghastly flattery, like any other man.

> Dear Mr. Smith,
>
> Please forgive me for troubling you and do not consider you are obliged to reply.
>
> I am a respected member of staff with your legal firm of Matthewson and Co. We are seeking to create a subdivision devoted to the sale and conversion of prestigious metropolitan properties for purely domestic use by overseas clients. (We already have a commercial division, as you know.) With this in mind, I am writing to enquire if you, as a valued client,

would consider reviewing the way your domestic properties are handled in the marketplace, and give me your comments as to how this might be done better. This would assist us greatly in the creation of a service-oriented, experienced team, dedicated to the service of clients in this area.

Yours, etc., S. Fortune.

If he replied, he might suggest the meeting. *If* he replied by hand and the writing wasn't the same, she was in dead trouble.

It was so difficult to believe in a mythical beast. All her own ghosts were creatures of her own creation, solidly founded on real human counterparts. She prowled round the paintings. There was nothing of her own that she regarded as an example of excellence, except the stolen one, which would never be quite hers. All the rest had been chosen because she could see they were somehow flawed. Ah, yes, they were friends all right. No one, at the end of the day, owns anything, and it was probably unwise to trust the bright ideas formed with a bottle of wine at the elbow. Ghosts, mythical monsters and enemies were all scaled down to the size of a glass.

The armchair over there was too heavy, reminiscent of the parlour of her convent school where she had sat among uncomfortable chairs, waiting for the Reverend Mother to tell her the bad news of her imminent expulsion—for precocity and subversion, for telling other girls the facts of life, for introducing Tampax and raising a petition about the food. She remembered that parlour for a burning sense of injustice and the ice of the atmosphere, marking the onset of scepticism. She got up, stretched, yawned.

The next flat was definitely going to be minimalist. Just like the next life.

They sat in the parlour, Julie and Cannon, like a pair of awkward guests, each on the edge of a hard chair, knees touching. It was at the front of the convent, adjacent to the main street door, accessed from the body of the building by a gloomy corridor and another locked door. The nuns were passionate about locks, Pauline explained; passionate without being logical, since they always seemed to assume that intruders came from the front rather than behind and they left God himself to take care of the chapel. The existence of locks was the insecurity of women dwelling alone, but still at odds with the vow of personal property. Each owned minor personal possessions in their rooms, no more, but the locked front door, the locked porch, the third lock on the door connecting corridor with residence were by now established precautions, Pauline said, because, once known, the existence of a convent drew the drunk and the lame and the abusive. Led by pragmatism, the sisters took the view that discretion was the better part of valour when it came to charity demanded after dark at an inner-city door. The truly needy would come back in the morning.

Which all contributed to Pauline's idea that the parlour should be Julie and Cannon's trysting place after conventional bedtime, provided they did not linger long or deface the carpet and Julie removed all traces of their presence afterwards. Besides, Pauline had added tartly, this is where we entertain the *priests*. The smell of a cigarette would not be amiss over the other smell of polish, surely. And the other condition was that should any sister descend upon them, armed with a weapon, they would not retaliate in unseemly fashion and Julie alone would explain, taking responsibility for either her own truths or her own lies.

Cannon was uncomfortable. The parlour was a sizeable room. He was used to small spaces; he enjoyed the sense of confinement provided by walls he could touch; he hated double-glazing and the consequent lingering of smells; he liked draughts; he was not at home in rooms big enough for the swinging of cats. The only purpose of space was to provide light; this room was large with small windows. The whole damn building was back to front, built north to south, with no regard to the direction of the sun, and even the chapel, the one room that could maximize it, ruined itself by the barrier of the sacristy and the presence of thick stained-glass windows. They seemed to try to make all their public rooms as ugly as the chapel, he complained, although that was not the real complaint. In here, even Julie was a stranger, sitting prim and proper, although their knees touched. There was greater intimacy in the chapel, disdaining God and the presence of plaster saints.

"Hallo there," Julie said.

Ever since he had divorced himself from his brother's life and his brother's daily speech, Cannon was easily discomfited by a new environment. There were new nuances to the way he spoke now, but he did not expect his nearest and dearest to have learned a new vocabulary too. Or familiarity with new rooms and ways of being. Sitting opposite him, Julie was suddenly refined, with her skirt pulled down over her knees and a faint southern-Irish lilt somehow caught in her voice as if by accident. They could speak in normal tones and pitch in here, but he missed the urgency of their whispers.

"Lord, what a clutter," he was saying, shivering slightly. He looked around himself. He expected the door to open at any minute and a nun to come crashing in with a trayful of tea. Not that he would have objected to such sustenance to augment the half-bottle in his pocket; nor could the nun have objected to the sublime modesty of their positions, sitting so primly and overdressed. The chapel and the parlour were equally chilly, but it seemed intrusive to turn on the electric fire and Julie did not suggest it. The overhead lights were bare and bright, provided by a miniature chandelier with five shiny bulbs, enough to make the contours of their faces hard. She looked yellow in this light; he felt red. The mirror over the mantelpiece made him look flushed and poorly. He always smiled into mirrors, the better to see his teeth. "It isn't so much a clutter," he said, nodding at the furniture, "as a muddle. They've tried to cater for all occasions and ended up catering for none. They just don't know how to create comfort, do they?"

She giggled softly, but pulled the skirt further over her knees, a trifle defensive. The nuns were her saviours and her hosts: she did not like to hear criticism of them. She was coming to adopt their tastes and their economies with the same ease as her unconscious mimicry of their soft voices. "Oh, I don't know," she said vaguely. "It's a room with a dozen purposes. They entertain relatives in here, for tea and coffee, then there's priests and guests, not very many, then there's meetings . . . They let people use it for meetings, so it needs to be big enough for that."

"All these bloody *chairs*," Cannon muttered, sinking out of his own velour moquette of drab green, so that he sat on the floor with his back against it. That was better: now he was level with Julie's knees rather than with the rest of the room. It was easier to ignore what he could never fail to notice: the garish religious pictures on the walls, the forest of armchairs, the monumental sideboard, which looked as if it should have contained a battery of wines and spirits. It had all the equipment for a riotous party, except the ambience. Perhaps if they turned out the lights and danced to the bar of the fire, but they were sombre and inhibited.

"They'll have Christmas decorations in here next week," she said wistfully.

"Jesus," Cannon said. "That'll really make it perfect."

"Oh, *stoppit*, will you? What does it matter what the room looks like? They do their best. Why should they have *style*, even if they could agree what *style* was, especially since they don't care anyway? Stop carping."

He touched her knee. "I'm sorry," he said, formally and insincerely. "It's just that when I see you in a room I keep seeing you somewhere else entirely. Somewhere where I'd like you to be. A cottage in the country, with a garden for the baby."

"And roses round the door?" she finished for him, a note of irony in her voice, then sat back in her chair, refusing to join him on the floor. She laced her fingers together in her lap. "Sarah said she once wanted a cottage like that. With a cat. Then she realized she would hate it. All that silence, all those dead leaves, no cars, no shops. How would you live in the country? You're a town animal, through and through. The last time you saw a cow was from the window of a train."

"Well, we'd have to learn, wouldn't we? You can learn anything . . ."

"No, you can't. If Sarah reckoned she couldn't, nor could we. Sarah's more adaptable. Now, there's a woman with style." There was an element of jealousy, Cannon realized with a start of surprise. He touched her again, tentatively. There was no response. "I wonder if I'll be here for the New Year," she went on, "admiring the decorations. Paper chains, tinsel and a crib. Maybe it would be easier if I took to the faith. Swore myself to poverty and chastity. Learned to accept divine will . . . Gave up hoping for anything different. After all, it doesn't matter what you believe as long as you believe something."

"Look, love, it'll soon be over. Christmas. You've forgotten. All over by Christmas."

"Will it? Will it ever?"

He was silent, gripped with a sense of dread so acute it seemed to retard breathing. He looked up at her beseechingly, but in this light she looked distant and almost cruel. Immobile, like the statues in the chapel; a woman in the act of becoming an effigy. Angry with him, unable out of long habit to say so. Somehow on the verge of giving up. Something to do with all those books she now read. Challenging him.

"Can I smoke in here?" he asked.

She shrugged. "Yes. Can't do it any further harm, can it?"

He lit the cigarette, watched it burn, and after three greedy inhalations tapped the ash into the palm of his hand. There were no ashtrays; it was unthinkable to put the debris in one of three wastepaper bins. They were too clean. He blamed the room for this feeling of alienation. Another fear prevailed. Perhaps Julie and he would never survive in a so-called normal world; perhaps the intensity of the love would wither if it were not clandestine, the way it had always been. Love on the run, first from Johnny's fury and refusal to meet, then the flurry of hiding from the police, love on bail, love on remand, love from the distance of prison, love like this, after he came out. Love within the framework of something forbidden, defined by Johnny's contemptuous disbelief in it. Love in a battlefield. She was sick of it; she was changing, *just like Johnny said she would.* Put her in a room with real chairs, make their contact as normal as possible, and there seemed so little to say; there was no common life between them, nothing to create intimacy, and if she was looking for *something* in which to believe it meant she no longer believed in him. Nor, perhaps, in Johnnyboy either.

"Is that what you want to do?" he said roughly. "Stay here? Give up? Let me go? Opt for a quiet life? Oh, I'm sure Pauline would love to have you. Free labour and good food for ever. A halo at the end. Good luck to you." He tapped the last of the ash into his hand, held the remnants of the cigarette between thumb and finger, watching it die. The room was quiet, apart from the ticking of the clock, the item he loathed most of all. It began to chime midnight, with small, undignified sounds. It looked as if it had been given as a prize for twenty-five years' faithful service and a pension. She leaned forward and touched his hair; he shook his head angrily. She rubbed her eyes, pressed them shut with her fingers, then blinked to dispel the tears. They ran through her fingers on to her wrists. He noticed the red of her hands against the white of her face.

He knelt at her feet, leaning into her knees; he reached for her face and brushed at her tears, but she still held her fists pressed into her eyes. He buried his head in her lap and, smelling the animal smell of her, slid his hands beneath the skirt and stroked her thighs. She stiffened; the tears continued; she removed her hands to press against his, stop him. "Don't," she said. "Don't. Please don't." He remained as he was, gazing at her.

What was it light did to a face? Or was it the blurring of tears, his and hers? She was no longer harsh in feature, but childish in distress, sexless, vulnerable, hurt, small, furious. "Don't," she repeated. "Don't you dare." Then softened it by adding, "Please," fiddling in her pocket for a handkerchief, wiping her eyes and blowing her nose. He watched all this closely. Puzzled, severely alarmed. There was something so unfamiliar about her. The stutter had gone.

"They're brave, these nuns," she muttered. "Some of them suffered more than you and I put together, see? Don't criticize their *style*. Or not in front of me. They're the closest thing to family I ever had. Do you wonder I should think to stay? It's so frightening outside, so n-n-n-nice within." A deep breath. "So j-j-j-just so . . . Oh, shit."

He was ashamed of himself for welcoming the return of the stutter. Maybe he had never wanted her to be free of it, in case she should find it easy to outstrip his use of words; it was the stutter that had drawn him in the first place. Him and the builders, sitting in a caff, with them mimicking her behind her back until he intervened. Watched her smile into his eyes looking only at his eyes, nothing else.

She took a deep breath. "I'm not going to cry any more," she stated, "but I've come to love these nuns. We've something in common. Their life is controlled absolutely by belief in God, mine by belief in you. It's only natural that belief should suffer from doubt from time to time, isn't it? You gave up on your brother; you might give up on me. And the longer I stay here, the less use I'll be on the outside. I can't go out because you tell me I shouldn't. Soon it might be because I *can't*. And all the time Johnnyboy gets smaller and smaller in my mind. *Was* it him who hurt me? He stood in the dark and watched, and the fat man hit me.

I've tried to put it right out of mind . . . I don't know who was giving the orders."

"He wouldn't touch you. He'd always get someone else to do it."

"Why?"

"Because he never could bear to touch a woman."

She was suddenly completely still. "Ah," she said, after a long pause. "I thought desire and hatred overcame such things."

"Not in his case," Cannon said, suddenly exhausted. How many times and in how many ways would he have to explain to women what Johnnyboy was like? He did not have the words or the energy and, God knows, he had tried. Yesterday, to Sarah; a dozen times to Sarah, innumerable times to Julie, and they had believed him with wide eyes and open mouths at first, willing to accept what he said. Shock was the great aid to belief. Julie believed because she had suffered at Johnny's orders; how could she be incredulous now? A calm life away from him was lulling her into a sense of safety, that was all, the image of John Smith fading like the memory of a violent film developing into a series of cartoons.

"No, Cannon, you're wrong," she said, reading the expression on his face. "I'm not *less* afraid, I'm more afraid. It makes me weaker, not stronger, staying here. I'm preserved—like—like a jelly!" She laughed. "They like jelly, the sisters, they like childish food." She stroked his forehead. "I don't have to make decisions. I grow weaker rather than stronger, and that's what makes me afraid. Not being any use to you. And if he *did* find me here, threatened me, threatened any of *them*, then I'd have to run, Cannon, I'd have to run. Far away and not come back."

She had been so ashamed of her injuries, as if she had inflicted them herself. He had wanted her to forget them; now he wanted her to remember. The clock ticked past the quarter hour loudly. There was absolutely nothing to say and it was time to go. The rain lashed against the door as she let him out, and she made to pull him back, but he kissed her quickly and pushed her back inside. The light of the street outside made him nervous and he hurried away. Ran down the road until the convent was out of sight, then huddled in a doorway, lit another cigarette. Why should anyone believe him simply because he told the truth? Because he told it incompletely, that was why. Was selective with what he told, for fear of giving offence. Never told Julie, never told Sarah what Johnnyboy said when he went to see him, after prison, long, long before the letter. *You've got to leave her. You don't belong with her; you belong with me; we've got things to do. You wait and see; you'll come back. What? She was scarcely hurt at all. She asked for it. Let's see if she'll wait for you. I'll test her for you. The worst pain, I'll find it.*

The worst pain was loss. That was the very worst he could envisage. Loss of her; loss of hope. The worst pain for Julie would be loss of him. Johnny would know that; *he* feared the rot of his loneliness more than anything else. He knew exactly what he was doing in the waiting game: waiting for love to rot. Christmas was too far.

Cannon did not want to go home. There was no such thing. Home had always been a house owned by Johnnyboy; he had not progressed by a single step in all these years. He had regressed, because now he lived in one of Johnny's houses as a trespasser, waiting for discovery. Cold and wet as he was, he could not bear the thought of the drip through the ceiling, the damp heat, the sense of imprisonment. Where, then? Who were his friends? Sarah, William, scarcely any other who did not belong also to Johnny, and few enough, always, of these. He would have turned back to the convent, climbed the back wall, huddled in the familiar yard, if only to be close, but he had a superstitious dread of that. The longer he stayed in the vicinity, the sooner Johnnyboy would sense where he was. And the same would apply to Sarah. He was bad news to women. He began to walk.

On the main road, he saw the lights of the night bus, X12, Charing Cross, by the long route, offering for two pounds half an hour of warmth and oblivion and, for the price of the whisky in his pocket, a borrowed blanket with the homeless. It passed down the Edgware Road and into Oxford Street, a short walk from William's. He thought of William's basement room. The messy room with the teeth where he had been allowed to go to keep him out of the way of the real clients. William would never know; it was not for William to know. He could get in easy. Lie down somewhere; that old chair, maybe. Think of his precious painting upstairs. Bonnard, sketching his wife with love for the umpteenth time. A study for a painting rather than a painting, but fresh and lovely. Yes, he could think of that. And it would be nice to sleep in the home of someone who did not even know that Johnnyboy existed. Be a guest of someone who still had faith in him.

The rain dripped through the ceiling, unnoticed. The door of the attic swung open to the push of a hand. There was no sound but that of the *plip, plip, plop* through the skylight and the sound of laboured breath. Too many stairs. Ah, a room bought with an artist in mind, for the promise of light. Steps across the floor, a body stooping to retrieve the scattered drawings. Ink depictions of a face; the hand holding them shaking. Looking at the features, the jowls, the malevolence, the age and the black teeth, snarling; the angry face; the face full of need. The lonely face; the hateful face, captured by someone who would not, could not, look at it without looking away. Finally, the face drawn with an element of affection.

He still loves me.

He tore up the black and white sketches, thoroughly and systematically, and placed them in a pile.

The steps moved, the hands took the canvas from where it stood against the wall, placed it on the easel. Noted the abundant hair, more red than brown in this light. He could not remember her being described as red-haired; frowned. He had never looked at her before now. Glanced, looked away . . . hadn't got close, couldn't bear it. Looked again. Noted the full mouth and the long, slender legs with the prominent muscles in the calves. Athletic legs; a figure of strength. Examined with distaste the slightness of the breasts lying nonchalantly on the ribcage, the hand lying across the bush protectively. He wanted to slash the picture, pierce it at that point, extend the wide mouth, half open to show the white teeth, but it was only with the tip of a knife he wanted to touch; no closer. He bent, looked, memorized each detail of the face, the colour of the eyes, the way the hair swept back from the forehead, the small nuggets of gold in the ears. Traced the shape of the ears and the brows; moved his glance down, frowned at the pale flecks of paint around the neck, on the upper arms, the shoulders. Little scars, superimposed on the paint, added as a kind of signature, like tiny hallmarks. These distinguished her.

The man went back to the wall and looked through the other canvases. Scenes, interiors, playgrounds full of children. No other women. A dozen sketches of the same woman.

This, then, was the one. The one whose face he had always refused to see.

He took her off the easel and put her back against the wall. Closed the door softly behind him.

10

You have to live; whatever else you have in mind, you have to live. *Always eat when you are hungry; always drink when you are dry; always scratch when you are itchy; don't stop breathing or you'll die.*

Hardly a profound philosophy, but perfectly good enough. Cannon had not phoned. The year would soon be reaching its shortest day. Another foggy, early Tuesday morning, and this was it. *Two bdrms; bath, wc, lge living room; no stairs. Convenient for transport.* Convenient for everything, as if that made all the difference. A place to put a car three streets distant, but the car didn't matter. Sarah hated her car: it distorted her view of the city; there was no one to talk to in the car. This flat was walking distance from all that mattered. A mansion block, second floor; shabby without real decay; homely. An acquired taste, she was told. Someone had died in it recently.

She knew it was home as soon as she turned the corner. A little worn; a little scarred; just like herself. Following the agent inside, Sarah saluted the late occupant with a surreptitious sign of the Cross and a hidden bow to her memory. The dead warranted respect and she needed the blessing.

The place had the stamp of an elderly occupant who had been less than mobile. There was a high armchair by a fireplace in the huge living room, next to a table, flanked by a sewing box and a footstool, facing a television, a self-contained island of furniture in an otherwise empty space. There was a radio on the table. Between this assembly, suitable for long sitting with everything to hand, there was a well-worn path across the floor to the kitchen, which was small to the point of miniature, with old-fashioned appliances and open shelves within easy reach. There was a cooker of ancient but efficient vintage, an antique fridge and every indication that the occupant saw no necessity to change anything. No aspirations to anything other than adequacy and established routine; comfort without frills, nothing that required complex instructions. Someone had been here who cooked the same things, in the same way, every day; Sarah felt a profound affinity with her.

"Of course, you'd need to gut this and start again," the agent was saying, as they peered into the bathroom. Old bath, stained and clean, disused; newish shower shoved in the corner; hardly enough space to turn round. A bedroom with a large, low bed, depressed on one side nearest the door. A lady who had learned to economize with furniture as well as with movement; she had dispensed with obstacles and would have walked through her flat in a series of the shortest routes in a rigorous but dignified routine that sustained and allowed her independence. They went back to the living room. There were two large windows, a high ceiling with a flaking cornice decorated with grapes and tastefully tinged with smoky yellow; pale, unadorned walls. The sense of empathy was as powerful as a sweet smell. The air was clean and fragrantly dry. Happiness beckoned.

"What the family should do is get some money together, do it up and *then* sell it. They'd make so much more, but they haven't time, and it's chicken and egg—they don't have money until they sell . . ."

"Who lives either side?"

"Old block for old people. They're mostly deaf. I'm not sure anyone else even knows she's died."

I know. The light streaming through the south-facing windows turned the old carpet to full, faded gold. The empty walls were an open invitation. Shall I die here? Sarah thought. I may die friendless, but I do want to *live* here. *Now.* This minute. Perhaps I have never wanted anything quite so much in all my life. She sat in the old lady's armchair and asked again for her blessing. She looked at the wall above the fire and imagined the favourite ornament she might have seen.

An empty flat; deaf neighbours. Cannon could live here until Christmas, if she could get him in. She put to the back of her mind the fact that Cannon had not phoned.

"I want to buy it *now*," she said to Matthewson, standing in his office with arms crossed, a strange attitude he thought, in someone who had come to ask for advice. She should have been humbler. "How do I secure it? How do I make them take it off the market?" She was so fierce he almost wanted to laugh. He had rarely seen her so passionate, although when she was he scarcely listened, because it was always about some hopeless cause of a person and she had the loser's habit of defending the indefensible.

"Throw money at them. It usually helps. Most vendors find it irresistible," he barked.

"Why can't I exchange contracts *today*?" For God's sake, she had never even mastered the finer points of conveyancing, such as delay, prudence, patience, *caveat emptor* and the essential rule of let the buyer beware.

"You *could*, if you were sillier than I thought. You can make a contract on the back of an envelope, if you want. I agree to buy 1 Acacia Avenue for X pounds sterling, and he, she or it agrees to sell, signed by both. Perfectly valid, and perfectly senseless, of course. You could be sold a wreck with a motorway through it . . . pub next door . . . service charges. Those places have monstrous service charges. A survey, of course—got to check the roof and the drains. All that. Weeks. Get someone in the firm to do it. Usual discount, of course."

"I don't care about the roof and the drains. I want to buy it *now*." She sounded like a child demanding to be taken to a party.

He shrugged. She was behaving like the most intractable kind of client who would not listen. "There's one small point," he murmured, relishing the fact that she had asked his opinion. "I don't like to mention it, but have you got the money?"

She glared at him.

"Have you sold *your* flat?" he persisted.

"Almost."

"Ah." That was news. Mrs. Matthewson would want to hear about that. He sensed that Mrs. Matthewson would feel a vague sense of unease if she did not know where Sarah was. So would his wretched son.

"Money?" he said again.

"Enough."

"Well, give it to them," he shouted. "Give them a thousand to take it off the market and promise exchange and completion within a month. Only *don't* sign a contract. Please."

"Not even on the back of an envelope?" She was smiling now, somehow comforted by the yelling. How is it, he would ask Mrs. Matthewson, that she takes her reassurance in such strange ways? The mere fact that Ernest had failed to say *Don't do it at any price* was enough to provide some kind of moral support for impetuosity—but, then, he had liked the sound of the address. Montague Mansions, Marylebone. Faded grandeur, but still grandeur: Mrs. Matthewson would approve of an easy walk to Selfridges.

"It's very convenient for my dentist," Sarah said.

The cigarette was back in hand, sure sign of defiance, tension or relaxation, he wasn't sure, only that it was indicative of something alien. The sight of it infuriated him all over again. "I don't *care* who it's near. Unless *it's* a client. You've *work* to do. As well as the art collection."

"Ah, that. Don't worry about *that*." Beaming at him, as if a hundred-thousand-pound budget was nothing. The insouciance turned charm into anger.

"But I do worry about *that*. I want a report. You're a *consultant* in this regard, don't forget. Trusted for expertise. You have to take it seriously. As long as you aren't subverting any of the damned art budget on the deposit for your own bloody house."

The silence was palpable, thick and sticky; a boundary crossed. He had gone too far. There were innumerable times when he had accused her of white lies, evasions, abrogations of responsibility, general moral perfidy, but he had never suggested she could be tempted by theft. It was the lawyer's cardinal sin: they could lie to a client in this culture, lie to each other, but never steal. She may have once left priceless title deeds in a taxi, billed for a fraction of the proper price, given glib and erroneous versions of the law, seduced the male clients as well as their opponents, commandeered the irrational devotion of others, but stealing was another kind of sin. He was ashamed of his own tongue; kept his head bowed and wondered what to say next in the face of her righteous fury, but when the silence continued and he was brave enough to look up she was blushing. An alarming sight against the red hair; he doubted he had seen such a phenomenon before; it was almost as frightening as seeing her cry.

"There's no apartment worth that much," she said. The door closed quietly.

Convenient for my dentist. Certainly the flat would be convenient. Half of her male acquaintance lived within striding distance. There was Mole, a short walk in the other direction; the estate agent, closer; the judge; then Master Ralph of the high court and his service apartment occupied Tuesday through Thursday; one or two more, past and semi-present, a couple of ghosts, but convenience did not dictate the choice, never had, any more than any of the nice men who wanted her near and also wanted her far. Except William. William mattered. William would like it; she and William liked the same things. She wanted to show it to him, tell him how she had fallen in love with that old lady's chair, the dimensions of the room in which she sat, the things she might have seen and the things she had left. Tell him about how she had forgotten minimalism and about that last tribute to posterity which she had found in the bathroom cupboard when no one else was looking. The old darling's dentures, looking for company.

William found that he took pleasure in the day's work, as if his fleeting acquaintance with violence the weekend before and the prospect of a stunning new client had acted as a stimulant to energize his eyes and ears, and make him notice things he otherwise ignored. It was the energy of complete distraction; the power, suddenly, to acquire extra vision; he recognized it as mild neurosis. He seemed immune even to irritation. There were dentists of another kind than himself, to whom the human contact was all and the surgery simply a means to it; perhaps he was becoming such a dentist, whose pleasure was all in the kinship with the patient. He was jovial, complimented Tina on a new shade of hair, and then said he preferred the old in case the remark smacked of sexual innuendo, but she seemed to consider any compliment at all a step in the right direction. He wanted to thank her for tidying the glory-hole, something he had noticed mid-morning when he went down there and found it cleaner than he remembered, but instead he debated with her how they should deal with the man in the waiting room who was likely to slide out of the chair at the touch of the needle. It was always the big men who fainted. There had never been a heart-attack yet; the fainters came round; the allergic survived; and this bright morning he was actually noticing the contrast of patients. Miss Mallerson, a busy barrister, flying in to discuss a variety of cosmetic treatment to augment her powerful teeth, demanding grave explanation for the sixth time of the various improving treatments she would never find time to complete. Then the dignified alcoholic restaurateur of uncertain years, as passively proofed against life first thing in the morning as he was late at night, deceptive in his calm, frenetic with misery when anaesthetic, retarded by wine, took longer to work and his raddled face, at the end, looked the same way it had at the start. *When* Mr. John Smith came in for surgery, *when*, not *if*, he must ask what he did for a living because it was relvant to the drugs. Was he a boozer? Did he work with tar? Did he smoke?

He felt like the Mad Hatter in *Alice in Wonderland*. Do you know why the hatter was mad? he asked Tina. Because of the mercury he used in the making of hats, ha-ha. We don't use mercury amalgams so much in teeth any more, but they are useful. Californians want them out, you know, quite the worst thing to do, destabilizes the stuff, and it wasn't the solid form of mercury but the vapour that made the hatter mad. Mid-afternoon, she gazed at him sternly.

"You'd better behave. Say your prayers. There's a nun in the waiting room. Two of them."

The second nun had a severe face and pale blue eyes fit to scan far horizons; the first looked as if she could not speak and required guidance to cross a road. They both sat bolt upright, suspicious of the luxury. The elder admired Cannon's loaned sketch, enjoying the view of a naked woman stepping out of her bath. The other had turned her back on it.

"Ah," said Pauline. "Look who's here, Imelda. The inquisitor's apprentice." She stabbed a finger in the direction of her companion. "This one grinds her teeth. What are you going to do about it?"

Several hours later, when Sarah sat opposite him, he found himself examining her face for familial resemblance to her aunt. It was there, in the brilliant, watchful eyes and the strong chin. Hers, too, might be a gaunt face in her older years. An over-strong face, softened by the cloud of hair. Something had happened to William. Ever since Saturday he had not been able to stop looking at faces. In three days the bruise on his own had faded away to nothing. If Sarah had a child, it would look like her; she should have a child for that reason alone, even if the child looked as she did this evening. Jubilant, secretive, worried.

"I met your aunt," he announced. "We had an extraordinary conversation."

"Yes," said Sarah drily, the dryness hiding the pride, the surprise and the repeated sense of being outmanoeuvred. "She's unique and amazing. Should my ears have been burning?"

He hesitated. "Yes. Yes. She's enormously proud of you."

"Well, strike me down, Lord. First I knew."

He touched her hand, found himself looking at her as if he had never seen her before. Yes, she was definitely worried as well as happy and, in the same way he had been throughout the day, he was talkative to the point of giddiness. Various subjects would remain on the incommunicable list, Cannon's twin for a start, but how beautiful she was; what a series of colours. Pauline's eyes had faded with age; those of her niece were intensely blue, full of welcome mischief, and her mouth soft and desirable. If there had not been so much to say, he would simply have sat and stared at her.

"Your aunt refused a free check-up. She said she would save it for her martyrdom."

"I think I told you before," Sarah said, "my aunt used to tell me tales of the martyrs. She considered the best way to get children interested in the faith, was blood and guts. Mention of martyrs was probably her opening gambit. She never really stops." She sipped her wine. "Anyway, you look remarkably cheerful on it. I was worried about you at the weekend. Cannon was shivering in front of my fire when you phoned on Saturday."

"Oh, was he?" He had forgotten about that and it was no longer important, that brief moment of jealousy, followed now by a moment of relief. Cannon could linger in Sarah's house for as long as he liked since he was not a lover, and he did not want to discuss Cannon or have her discuss him either, not when he had such delicate plans for his long-lost brother, although, at the moment, on the third glass of wine, they seemed the stuff of sheer imagination. Cannon and Cannon's brother: that was his challenge; his only. Besides, the man had not yet made an appointment. The fingerprints on his glass seemed to proliferate.

Do you like me? Your aunt liked me.

"She asked me to Sunday lunch," he said.

For all of the familiar ease, there was something troubling about this conversation. Sarah could feel all the strings controlling her very secret life becoming entangled. There was Cannon, the loose Cannon, bringing the poisoned chalice of his friendship to William, giving him to guard a golden sketch of a painting that would not gladden William's heart if he knew either the value or the history. Cannon made people keep secrets: he was a manipulator, bringing the nuns to William's door, making all these friendships and connections into spider threads, lacing them together in a web, with a predator at the centre, waiting patiently. She felt the same chill of fear she had felt when she had known that John Smith was on the other side of Matthewson's door; an unaccountable, unquantifiable fear; a kind of toothache.

Perhaps she should explain; tell the story as she knew it right from the start; tell him how Cannon was the harbinger of bad news unless he was also an absolute liar. Tell him . . . but telling him would surely dent the shell of his innocence. She had no business sharing her responsibilities; he had not volunteered for that. So she lit the sixth cigarette and watched him watching. Regarded the frank gaze of admiration in his eyes. Almost love. She did not want to relinquish that; not yet, if ever at all. He was quite odd enough for her to love.

"Did you buy anything at the exhibition?" he asked, jumping topics with accustomed ease.

"No." Another stab of conscience; a vision of that stolen canvas; a reminder that she could lose that look of liking so easily.

"Nor I," William said cheerfully. "I didn't join you, but at least I went. Thought it was a load of rubbish, mainly." They were both being evasive and finding it all too easy.

"Any more bad dreams?"

"I think they're being temporarily displaced by new challenges. Shall we eat? I've been talking too much. I don't listen to *you*."

The bubble of her news had been blown away and no longer seemed as important. "I've fallen in love," she said, watching his face fall, enjoying the expression. "With an apartment. The person who lived in it left her dentures behind. Do you think I'll need them?"

She looked at him smiling at her, and felt unaccountably lonely. Felt, in the pit of her stomach, the same airtight bubble of despair. Ah, William, I cannot trust you to *like* me. Nor anyone else either. I must put my trust into bricks and mortar. There was nothing else to trust. And, as if he knew about the slippage of faith, Cannon had not phoned again today.

Cannon had no illusions about the durability of bricks and cement. A home was not a castle. No Belfast boy growing up in the seventies could ever think that. Stones and wood became fragments, like bones; a home was a flimsy thing, flung down on to the ground out of spite, out of a liking for the insurance money, or for an unscrupulous builder like Daddy to have the chance to put it up again. The bomb was simply another form of blackmail, like a threatening letter, easily deployed.

Cannon wanted his wife and child to have a home with thick walls and a serious front door to foster the sensation of safety, but he himself had no such illusions of permanence. He knew how soon a building could be destroyed if no one watched. That rumble of destruction, that cycle of wanton damage and noisy renewal was the music of his childhood. All he really cared about in a room was the quality of light. Or its absence. Whether it had pictures on the walls. Otherwise it would all come to dust. The interior was not important unless it surprised him somehow into noticing, and it had to be beautiful or outstandingly ugly to do that—like the convent or the prison at one extreme, but all the same he liked it here. William's ambience; the smell of him, perhaps. It was a very strange sensation for Cannon to have friends. He wondered if he would ever quite get used to it. Being around William's things gave him a quiet, intense pleasure, which was nevertheless tinged with the guilt of trespass. He tried to tell himself that if he had asked William for a billet for this second night, William would have said yes, but he knew that this avoided the issue because he had not asked for fear of a no, and a no would have prejudiced something as precious as it was fragile. Cannon had scant talent for friendship. Johnnyboy had seen to that. *When me and Julie have a house, William, will you come and see us? Julie would like you. I like you. Be god-daddy to a baby, will you?*

Besides, he had always liked mess, the stage in the construction of a thing, painting, building, when it was a mess. That was when it was full of promise, long before the disappointment was clear in the vast difference between what was envisaged and what finally emerged. Mess was the thing he liked in here, even though he had tidied a little. William would not notice, surely: the room seemed so little used. William told him so, all that long time ago when he had let Cannon explore. A glory-hole. Dentists are hoarders: they throw away nothing except ideas.

He felt guiltier, too, watching William go out in the evening dark before he himself got in. Guilty about relying on the fact that, although William had a nice eye for a painting, he was not really an observant man, let alone streetwise. He simply did not *expect* violation, as Cannon did, all the time. He didn't see life as a series of booby-traps. There were sets of teeth, mounted on a card, like buttons. He found those in a cupboard, grey with dust. There were the dental moulds on the table, looking as if they kept one another company. Yes, he liked it here. He could sleep in this battered chair, eat his sandwich in peace, drink water from the tap, look around and feel peculiarly safe, and if his hands itched with the idleness he would sit on them. Enforced contemplation. Use the nail-file left by Tina to file his nails. Nothing wrong with doing nothing until the early hours of the morning, although it seemed a long time in prospect. After an hour, the guilt got to him again: he had only wanted a sympathetic, private place to do nothing but *think*, but his dedication to furious thought about what he should do next, other than play out the waiting game, was simply creating confusion. Feeling guiltier still, he began to wander.

That William was out for the evening and the night was something of which he was fairly certain. He had not looked like a man popping out on an errand: he had looked like someone washed and dressed, carrying a bag, locking up with care. Dear William. Cannon found there was no toothbrush in the bathroom, the old rogue, out for the duration. His kitchen was empty of food; if he had to eat, he would not be eating here. Cannon's deductions made him feel cunning and, at the same time, treacherous. Privacy was not something he had ever been able to value much, but he knew that other people did.

A small, neat bedsitting room William had, featureless in style. A functional kitchen, again with no other mark of individuality apart from the colour of it, as if he saved his efforts for the bits of his domain other people saw. Or as if he was on the brink of moving on and did not care. All that mattered here were the waiting room, the entrance hall, which was the first thing they saw, and the surgery, where they would recline in various states of anxiety until they got up, looking at nothing except the light. He remembered looking at the light until his eyes closed; remembered William's kindly face even better and his hands most of all. You could judge a man by his hands. He drifted into the waiting room, noticing how the blinds were drawn, another sign of William's absence for the evening, a fact to be celebrated and also deplored. Cannon half wished he would come back through the door, whistling. He decided he could risk raising the blind.

The glow from outside lit the picture in the centre of the wall—as if it needed light, containing so much of its own. The painting he had loaned was its own complete world. There was Bonnard, not quite at his best, sketching his wife as she got out of the bath, the way he had sketched her a hundred times, beautifully fleshed but delicate. Fastidious in her toilet, pink and gold in skin, captured in the glow of his constant fascination, the little brown dog in the corner. A deliciously clean, gorgeously familiar body, totally unselfconscious either of the gaze or the desire of a husband, the gloss of familiarity suggesting *husband*, rather than mere lover, content to be exactly as she was. To Cannon, it told the whole story of a life he himself wanted to live. Painting his wife, again and again and again, making love in the bright light of the day with every brushstroke. Feeling the weight of her arm round his neck, the touch of her breast on his bare arm. Julie in sunlight for ever.

They had seen it together. *Could you ever love me like that?* she had asked. As if she could not know that he already did.

He lowered his gaze, and wanted to weep. Johnnyboy could never even look at a picture like this; it had been bought with Johnnyboy's money and it could never, ever be returned. Johnnyboy would slice it into ribbons rather than own it. It represented connubial happiness; a vignette of fulfilment. Johnny would not want to know about Bonnard's life.

He moved to the other side of the room, viewing from a distance, aching with longing, suddenly tired. He did not want the chair in the basement room; he wanted a bed and the luxury of dreaming his way into oblivion. A state of nothing in which he would wake in a sun-filled room with her by his side; watch her go to her bath and know she would come back. Let him know before she left the house.

A bed. A bath. But he could not sleep on William's bed or use William's bath, not without asking. He could use the basement room, because it seemed to him that such a room belonged to nobody and everybody. The sight of the clean coverlet on William's modest bed made him feel ever more the intruder; he stared at it, saying to himself, *I am sick of always being in a place where I must not leave traces. Sick of it. Sick of reliance on kindness.*

Madame Bonnard might not have been kind for all he knew, but she was *there.* Go, get out, *go.* Out through the basement window. No. He felt safe here. He had felt peculiarly safe here from the very first visit. Dear William had no idea what he had done, overturning the fears of a lifetime. Dear William had no idea of what he was like. He did make a person feel safe. Although not safe enough to take the liberty of sleeping in his bed without prior permission. Not when he was contaminating his life enough already.

William would not miss a piece of stale cheese from the kitchen fridge. No one downstairs would miss one of those six lemons past their sell-by date. And he *would*, one day, share a little of Bonnard's experience. He *would* leave his mark on the world without his mark being some destroyed building in a street, looking like a gap in a row of front teeth and an invitation to misery first, and the profit of a stranger second. There was a taste of salt on his tongue from the cheese, which stuck to his teeth. Leave no traces, sit on the stairs. He had washed in the junk room in cold water, still felt dirty. Finished chewing. Stopped with a terrible, weary sense of fear, mouth open.

Nobody hears what goes on in your mouth except you, William said. What is loud to you and visible to you is inaudible and invisible to anyone else, unless you happen to grind your teeth, a sound with a certain resonance. He loved to lecture, did William. Cannon was on the last set of the stairs, which turned a corner into the waiting room, part of which he could see. He was absolutely sure he had never turned on a light—who needed a light to look at the Bonnard painting? There was one now. Cannon detested any kind of God, but he thought of the nuns and prayed. You bastard, God, will you ever give me a night's sleep? Will you ever give me a moment's grace of feeling safe? I sold explosives to thieves; I was never big-time enough for terrorists; please, God, don't stop my heart, not yet, please. I am safe here. We only have to get to Christmas. Johnny would never ever be here. He could never even look at my wife's face. He would never come inside the premises of a fucking dentist. Tell me I'm wrong.

And yet there he was, crossing Cannon's line of vision, in front of the painting, which he ignored, confident here as if he had been invited, so oddly at home that the first thing Cannon felt was a spurt of jealousy. This is *my* place, *mine. I* found it, and there was a sense of *déjà vu* in that. How many dens, how many hiding-places had Johnny uncovered when they were kids? How many caches of paint and paper had he ruined before he gave up? Beyond count, and here he was again, doing the same. Johnny was talking to himself, suited and spurred with shiny shoes, as if for an appointment, convincingly debonair, fooling himself. Oh, how the devil did anyone with Cannon's use of words ever begin to explain the chameleon existence of Johnnyboy, when nobody else in the world had ever known him, ever been *close* to knowing him? Hirelings, paid and fired. These days, he was like a potentate with a series of speechless eunuchs who never lasted long. He looked so lonely down there that Cannon wanted to leap off the step and touch him, hug him, but he was paralysed. The first touch would never be the last; touch him, and his own soul and his own hope were as dead in the water as floating fish. No one would ever know. If he killed him now . . . if he killed him now . . . if he killed him now. He sat instead, the salt on his tongue, his mouth slack, watching, listening.

Johnnyboy, in his suit, was trying to read, trying to check from the notes in his hand. There was another presence, out of sight, calling back, a fucking eunuch fatty—they were always like that, big, sexless, brain-dead.

"Look . . . there's another one . . . "'C's friends,"' it says. He doesn't have any friends. She must be with his friends. There's no one else. Why couldn't that little bastard Andrew have got this far? Pay people, they focking let you down. Do it yourself. Only way. Christ, will you look at that rubbish on the wall? Sort of shit *he*'d want to paint . . ."

Cannon smiled. He did not know why he smiled. Once, they had only smiled for each other. Now the very intonation of that hectoring voice made him smile out of sheer recognition, bite back the desire to answer. He bit his knuckle instead. The figure moved out of sight; not far, three steps at most, the voice fading.

"Writes messages to himself, this fella, only in pencil, on his focking notes. Tells you who knows who and where they live . . ."

A distant voice, murmuring, indecipherable, discontented. Johnnyboy had filled his small horizon with similarly servile voices, muttering now, "Nuns, focking Sisters of Mercy."

The door clicked shut. He was not the only one who knew his way out as well as his way in. They were gone and he was here. Shivering.

Wanting to blow up this place now Johnny had been in it. Make it disappear.

"Can I ask you something, Sarah?"

"Anything. Shhhh, you're shivering. Here . . ." She held his arm across her body, his hand to her breast, her body nestled into him. She had pulled her hair beneath her head, so that his chin could rest on her shoulder in the crook of her neck, and that, to William, was the sweetest piece of generosity. She made room for him; accommodated her small self against his length, made herself fit. Made herself belong, without making any demands. Was this a kind of kindness, he wondered, technique, or the sensitivity engendered by serious affection? Was it simply a question of practice?

"Have you ever posed for Cannon?" He moved his hand and stroked the curve of her hip. Soft, the bone firm beneath.

She moved, closer into him, covered his hand with her own. "Yes. It was rather uncomfortable." She shook slightly with remembered laughter. "Cannon doesn't go in for creature comforts. And it wasn't me he wanted to paint, it was his wife."

"Tell me about his wife . . . his brother." The body, relaxed after love, tensed. William regretted that. He adored her like this, as floppy as a soft toy, sleepy, close.

"No, my love, I won't. Let him tell you himself if he wants. It's a long story, which he can tell but I can't tell for him."

"All right." The warmth he had lost padding to and from the bathroom was fully restored. He remembered the curve of her back as he had got back into her bed; the way she moved her hair to make a resting-place for his chin.

"Besides," she said sleepily, "that wasn't what you wanted to ask, was it?"

"No. Not quite. Am I a *good* lover, Sarah?"

She could have laughed at such a question at this stage in their knowledge of one another. How long was it? Two years, on his reckoning, since his first sight of her in that small office of hers, less than that since they had become lovers, almost imperceptibly. A drink at her place, several; a casual invitation, why don't you stay? A scene repeated more times than he could count. Understated passion, remarkably satisfying, marked by a gratitude on his part that denied the asking of any upsetting questions. What a fool he was to ask such a question now, but it was suddenly important to know that he did, actually, please her. He rewarded her; he paid any debt he might have by fixing things; he took on her acquaintance as patients; he tried to keep things equal; but did he delight her, as she delighted him?

She stirred in his arms, raised his hand to her lips, brushed his fingers against them. His right hand, the one John Smith had bitten. Suddenly he wanted to pull it away, retreat to his native state where all questions were superfluous except those justifying purely factual answers without opinions attached. Back to his own world, where the biggest mystery of the day was why, without scientific explanation, a solution of hydrogen peroxide could stop bleeding. It took an effort to repeat his question.

"Am I?"

"As a matter of fact, you are. Do you think I *pretend*?"

"Well, *no*. Perhaps I just needed to know in words."

She was wider awake now, turning with a *phumph* in the bed so that she faced him and held him by the hair. He thought for a minute she was going to grab him by the ears and beat his head against the pillow. The curtains were never closed in Sarah's room; she said she was afraid of the dark. Ambient London light through the window showed only the hollows of her face. She kissed his nose, then his mouth. He wanted her to say something more.

"William, I'd like to kill that wife of yours for what she did to you. You're a marvellous lover. You've got the heart for it. Makes you good at whatever you do . . . let it take you over. Makes you a good dentist and, yes, a good and generous lover. Will that do?"

Not entirely, but he nodded. There was something else he wanted to know and wanted to hear, but for the moment, in a state of contentment, he could not remember what it was.

Do you love me? Do I love you?

11

No. He had not seen Johnny, or heard his voice. There was nothing to indicate the presence of anyone else. The two men he had heard, the one he had seen, were figments of his imagination. They were nothing of substance; Sarah was right to suspect the soundness of his mind. Cannon blinked. He was stiff, as if he had sat still for a long time, fallen asleep without knowing and woken cramped and uncomfortable. He was not entirely sure of where he was, leaned forward and put his head in his hands.

There was no way Johnnyboy would ever come to a dentist. No way. Nothing in their subliminal understanding of one another would make him cross that barrier. The sheer smell of the place would make him sick, the way he had been sick the first time they put him in the chair and held him in it. Projectile vomit as soon as the probe hit his teeth. A grunt of disgust; the lady dentist wanting to hit him, except she didn't want to get so close. The twin, Cannon, watching from a corner. Johnnyboy refused to cross the portals without him. Johnny would never, ever go to a dentist, not if the pain killed him first. He'd had two of his teeth pulled by a barber later, and that was all. So it was a dream, then.

Cannon could still feel the taste of salt in his mouth; looked through his hands into the waiting room, comforting himself. Better to be losing his mind.

Then he noticed how the light was on down there. He had not put on the light. He could see what he wanted to see without that; he had merely pulled up the blind. And then he heard the voice, echoing through his head with its resonance of disgust. *That's the kind of shit my brother would paint.*

If only he could paint with Bonnard's joy. *If only* . . . How fucking ironic that Johnnyboy, who could not recognize talent, could not recognize what his brother had done with his stolen money. The desire to scream with outrage roused Cannon into the present. Of course it was Johnny, standing there, defacing the painting by the mere looking at it; there was something unique and corrosive about Johnny's capacity for disgust. The repercussions of what he had seen and heard intruded like a bad headache. This was what he, Cannon, had done, in return for William's great contribution to his life and William's tentative friendship. He had brought Johnny inside the door in his wake, like a wave of disease. A confident Johnny, too, who did not give a damn about who saw him.

Jesus, God, do something.

He ran down the last of the stairs, snapped off the light, stumbled further down into the safety of the basement, pulled the door, as if it was a shield. It was stiff and warped; it would not shut. It seemed so typical of William that the door would not shut—there was no need to *close* it because William had nothing to hide. And not a single clue how to protect himself either. Such a calm, skilled man; professional in his own field, devoid of any of the black arts he would need against Johnny if Johnny had singled him out for attention. *Why?* William didn't have so much as a stick, let alone a knife or a gun, in the same way that he had nothing to bar his doors. William could not hurt a fly, and now here he was, caught by a spider. *Why*, and what *did* he have to keep Johnny out?

You could only threaten Johnnyboy, not persuade him. What did William possess for that? A useless, gentle temperament was what. Cannon prowled in an agony of self-recrimination so intense it burned. He was disastrous to the people who liked him; he should not be alive; he was a walking piece of damage.

His eye lit on the detritus in the room. Bottles, jars, old packets spilling out of shelves with an air of abandonment. Cannon stopped and stared. Ah, Christ. Save me from my promises. Jesus save me, even though I don't believe. Hydrogen peroxide, somewhere; he'd seen it. What did William say it was used for? William and his lectures. Stopped bleeding; no one quite knew why. And over there, that old-fashioned disinfectant, in packets. Mix crystals with water, clean the lav. And over there, more of this redundant stuff. And, over here, potassium permanganate in disguised form, crystals again, the sort of thing he had found in his gran's cupboard before she, too, died; he remembered her creating out of it a dark purply-greenish mouth-gargle—*This'll set you right.*

He groaned, and he wept a little and brushed away the tears. There was the makings of destruction in here and the same old urge to use them. Some of the things he had played with as a child, bless him. Making big *bangs* out of household stuff, the way they made them now out of fertilizer and shit and subversive handbooks, and he had made them out of nothing without even knowing the names; just knowing what worked. High explosive, bigger, faster bangs and greater risk to health; low explosive, less dramatic and in the end more fun for a kid. He allowed himself a moment of moral superiority: it was so easy to make a bomb now—all you had to do was steal the stuff, no art to it, no art at all; no guesswork. Probably no fear either of the kind that now drove him mad even at the sound of fireworks. Never, ever again would he do such a thing. Johnny had made him go on doing it: it was him who had the knack, not Johnny; him who had the knack with everything except the orders.

Never again. I shall never again destroy anything, or make anything that can destroy, he had promised his wife, who had made him repeat it—as a Catholic repeats *Kyrie eleison, Lord have mercy*—until the promise was etched into his brain, made him forget that it had been *fun.* Wicked fun, she said, and all the more wicked because you never saw the result. You ran away before you saw the cost of it or you sold it to someone else and didn't see. We didn't *kill* anyone, he'd protested. How did you know? How many lives did you ruin? All promises were made to be amended, because Johnnyboy was on the threshold; Johnnyboy knew nothing of reason or art or anything, any more than dear William knew how to stop him coming back.

Listen, William. You've got to be on the right side of the door yelling to him that if he comes any further forward you'll blow the door into his head; he understands that. Tell him you've got a nice piece of high explosive.

He began to assemble things, like a cook in readiness for a feast. He poured the disinfectant crystals on to a cleanish part of the stone floor, ground them beneath the heel of his boot. He took the torch out of his pocket, flicked it on and off. There were batteries around here somewhere, bound to be, or he'd bring one. Johnny won't be back tonight; doesn't need to be; something planned. OK. Squeeze the juice from the lemon left in the fridge; improvise; put the mix of the crystal powder and the peroxide solution and the lemon juice into this bowl, cool to near freezing, maybe outside the window—God, it was cold out there. Leave it a few hours. Use the torch: break the glass on the bulb, give it that little bit of intense heat from the naked filament—better still, cross the wires from the flex of that old Hoover . . . Take it away, Joe. Tell *him* what you've got in here . . . Tell him to take his gorilla home, or else.

Cannon stopped and looked at the muddy mix in the shallow plastic bowl. Yes, Sarah was right. He had lost command of his brain. *Next task, tell the darling fool how to detonate the thing, point it, keep his distance.* Poke it towards the door like some fucking lion-tamer in a fucking circus. Oh, yeah. Easy-peasy.

The light that filtered through into the basement was changing slowly but perceptibly. Winter dawn, heralding itself two hours before the real event; a witching hour, and if he were Dracula he would begin to think of going home. Oh, yeah. Dear William would blow himself into smithereens before he could detonate or control a homemade bomb, although he might be fascinated by what was in it. He might be able to do amazing things to teeth with all his know-how, but he would be just as likely to drink this mix as use it. He'd be the same if you gave him a gun: he'd only want to take it apart. Give the bugger a knife, he'd cut bread with it and give you a slice. Cannon was monstrously tired and appallingly sad. He stared at the contents of the bowl as if it were urine in a potty. What a waste of effort, born of a fevered mind. What was he to do? Surreptitiously explain to William, say, Here's a bit of useful knowledge for you, just in case of—*what?*

He moved towards the ancient fridge with the tread of the defeated on a long march to nowhere, holding the bowl, not sure what to do. It was all absolutely useless. After all, he was not good at anything, directionless without Johnny.

Finally, he flushed it down the sink. He picked up the lemon he had squeezed, bit into it and chewed. There was still salt in his mouth.

Then he tidied all trace of his presence from the basement room. Stuffed his possessions into his pockets and squeezed himself out of the window. The cold of the railings bit into his hands. The daylight held no promise. There was nothing to do but wait. As the light reached the room outside the surgery, the answer-machine clicked and whirred. *Please speak after the tone.* A quiet, apologetic voice hesitated before speech.

Julie preferred the convent chapel when it was lit by the moon and a couple of candles, or when it was illuminated by electric light in the evening, not the way it was now, merely dim, the windows aching to admit the purer light that the heavy coloured glass denied. None of the sisters could bring themselves to use electricity for a task, when daylight would suffice, even if the light was scarcely as adequate as it was in here. Their sense of economy often outweighed convenience, but it was invariable. A room so dim mid-morning oppressed her. After dark, it mattered less. She was grateful for the winter and the dearth of daylight glimpsed through windows, because it was the light that reminded her she was in prison.

"Help me," she murmured.

A place of enlightenment, in one sense, but still a prison for over three months now, although she had hardly noticed the first weeks. An existence so artificial it was ludicrous. She was trying, before God, to continue to see the sense of it; not that she believed in God. Life was far too random a matter and people far too various to have either one Creator or one Controller, surely, but she did believe in saints, and that was a kind of concession. If Cannon had opened her eyes to visual beauty in his critical fashion, making her notice and admire, then this place made her at least acknowledge the existence of the kind of soul that needed no such stimulus.

They needed symbols, these women, ritual and statues to give form to belief and turn the ephemeral into the real. My, she was learning such long words from Pauline and her books. Three hours' reading a day and it had become curiously addictive. You'll go back into the world a heathen, Pauline had said cheerfully, but a bit more literate than many. She would certainly not go back the same, but then she had not been quite the person they thought when she first came in. She was already altered.

Julie had brought the kitten into the chapel with her for the daily cleaning, not an invitation of which Imelda would approve but a venial sin rather than a mortal one. The kitten was company; it skidded on the high polish of the floor and attempted to suffocate itself inside a duster, but she could scold it in her normal voice. "You stupid little beast, you! Behave or I'll strangle you with a sodding rosary and then which direction would you go? Heaven or hell?" The kitten was also something to hold; light, warm, soft and resentful, a poor substitute for human skin. "You gorgeous little sod," she said admiringly.

Imelda was suffering from the aftermath of dental treatment and was behaving like a tragedy queen, resting. She kept going on about the marvels of the dentist's waiting room; beautiful curtains seemed to be the stuff of her day-dreams. Julie tried not to envy her the joys of her excursion, only because although there were moments when she herself would have risked fire and injury simply to be *out* of here, if only for an hour, there were others when she was peculiarly reluctant to go. She smothered the jealousy with the realization that she could not possibly envy anyone a visit to the dentist, because such a thing terrified her, even the smell made her tremble. Cannon had been stoic in the face of it; she admired that, especially since she had not actually noticed his appalling teeth when they met, only ever his eyes. At the moment, she envied his comparative freedom.

The kitten made play with her ankle; its claws were sharper as it matured. "Sod off!"

She was dusting the statue of St George, flicking at it with absent-minded violence. The tip of the spear poised to enter the dragon's mouth snapped off and fell to the floor with a *clunk*. The kitten pounced on it. "Hell and fucking damnation . . ." Julie suffered a moment of panic, feeling shifty and sacrilegious. Then, in a gesture that surprised her with its swift spontaneity, she found she had made the sign of the Cross over her own body, touched first her forehead, then her breast, then each shoulder, left to right, just as *they* did two dozen times a day, not only in prayer, with grace before and after meals, in here, anywhere, but at moments of stress and impatience, a calming gesture, but also one of warning, an admonition. She was horrified to catch herself in such an act: she had already assumed the seductive rhythm of their quiet speech; now she was assuming the movements of their hands. Next she would be wearing their talismans and soon there would be nothing left of her original self.

"I'd rather go to hell," she said out loud. Jumped as a hand fell on her shoulder.

"Would you really? I'm sure not—whatever the alternative you were hoping to avoid. Hell's for eternity, a difficult concept I find."

"An eternity of having your teeth filled," Julie said lightly, thinking of Imelda, who had been the sole topic of conversation last evening, and hoping that Pauline had not heard her swearing, mild though it had been. Or seen her making the sign of the Cross; she was even more afraid of that. A vain hope for this gaunt gentlewoman of silent footsteps: Pauline missed nothing. Julie adored her, but the intense affection was tinged with a fear that went slightly beyond profound respect. Pauline had more than a touch of ruthlessness.

"And, yes, I did see you making the sign of the Cross, child. What a curious thing to do when all you had done to precede it was snap St George's perfectly dreadful spear. Don't worry, my dearest, don't worry. It really doesn't mean that God has *got* you, like St George supposedly *got* the dragon. Not that George was really after the dragon. He was only after the maiden, after all. Most men's ambitions centre on the carnal, in the end." She tapped the dragon's nose. "They have to be the way they are for the furtherance of the species. It afflicts them all the time, even when they do it with each other into old, old age without any discernible result. And they know, of course, by another version of the same instinct, that the women will look after the progeny long after they've gone on to plant some more. So don't trouble your head about St George's spear. He only wanted to get the dragon out of the way. A rolling-pin would have done." She touched the broken spearpoint with her foot. The kitten skittered away.

"Why did I make the sign of the Cross?" Julie asked, ashamed of the aggression in her voice.

"Oh, Lord, for the same reason you wave *thank you* at someone on a zebra crossing for failing to run you over. An automatic reaction against a repetition of danger or embarrassment. Really, it doesn't matter."

The St George of the statue had rosy cupid-bow lips, pursed in concentration. No primal scream forming through open jaws. The dragon looked like a larger version of the kitten, rolling on its back; not much of a contest, for all of its feigned agony, pathetic beast.

"But what if God had got me?"

Pauline sat in a flurry of sudden consternation, settled herself. "What if? I'd be delighted if He answered my prayers, but the occurrence of that isn't frequent so I'd also be surprised. *What if?* would be entirely for you to discover. It wouldn't prevent you from loving your husband, if that's what frightens you about it. Indeed, if you saw him as an instrument of God as well as a mere man, it would make you love him more. Is that what you mean?"

Julie shook her head.

Pauline went on, "If this casual invocation of the Holy Trinity meant a realization that no human love is complete, totally fulfilling and providing all the answers, you'll merely have taken a step forward. Several steps. It may make you judge him differently. Sceptically. Want something more reliable to love. Not *instead of,* as well as. You wouldn't believe the flexibility of religious belief. If it does damn-all else, it puts things into perspective . . ."

"*Stoppit!*" Julie yelled, holding her hands over her ears. And then, more quietly, "Stoppit. Stop *it. Stop doubt.* Stoppit." She hesitated; she hurt. Old bruises came to life. She wanted to shout, "I'm *pregnant.*" "Why is it that I could live by myself for two whole years when Cannon was in prison and never waver in the way I felt about him? Never waver in my complete conviction about whatever he said, never *doubt?* What are you doing to me?"

"I? Nothing. God might be working on you. There might always have been the need for another kind of faith. You've never been among religious people before, have you?"

"*Contented* people," Julie murmured. "Contented with a fraction of what I hope for. No, I've never dwelt with people who are content."

"Well, don't let the appearances fool you. Why do you think Imelda grinds her teeth? We can't all be free of doubt."

"What? Not even you?"

"Especially not me. But this has nothing at all to do with me. And it wasn't the same, being utterly faithful to Cannon when he was in prison and you weren't. Now the position's reversed and it surely gives rise to resentment, doesn't it? After all, it might be all his fault. Or his *fantasy*. But your injuries were real, child. Entirely real."

Julie turned on her with quiet fury. "Yes, they were, weren't they? Only I'm no longer sure who it was inflicted them. A man who refused point-blank to look at me, couldn't bear to see me. Put a pillow-case over my head so he didn't have to. Got someone else to hit me. It *must* be his brother—oh, God, I *hope* it was his brother. There was nothing I would not do to keep Cannon. *Nothing.*" She smiled uncertainly. "Maybe it was all simply an act of God, bringing me here."

Pauline laughed shortly, the sound of it loud in the chapel. Her reverence for the place was casual. "God moves in mysterious ways, but they aren't usually quite so convoluted." She touched Julie lightly on the shoulder, brushed her hair back behind one ear. It was as if she knew how much Julie longed to be touched, even as innocently as this. "Would you like to *try* to pray?" Pauline asked. "It's easy, really. All you have to do is just imagine God the Father does exist and chat to him. That's all there is to it, really. You don't have to praise him, you can complain to him if you like. I would, if I were you." She bent down and picked the tip of St George's spear off the floor. "A bit of Elastoplast, I think," she said.

"I'm hungry," Julie said. "Ravenous for food. Help me."

Sarah sat and looked at the mess on top of the desk. She had put all the estate agents' bumph into the bin, thought of the new flat and quietly applauded. Yes! Thought of William and smiled. Thought of Cannon and frowned. Enough was enough. In between everything else she had found a new place for him to squat: *her* new flat with the deaf neighbours. Throw money at the problem, Ernest had said, and she had. An immediate rental agreement, pending exchange of contracts, expensive but worth it. Cannon and Julie were going to bankrupt her, but that did not come into the equation.

There were more art catalogues and a letter.

> Dear Mr. Fortune,
>
> I have got your letter of today about "domestic properties," "specialized services" and all that stuff. I don't find much wrong with estate agents, personally. At least they tell you what's going on. This is just another way for you lot to squeeze more money, right? On account of foreigners who want flats having more dosh.
>
> So, I'll think about answering your questions, shall I?
>
> Mind, I don't see why I should advise you lot anything. I pay you lot plenty enough already and I don't go much on lawyers. I think you're a load of tosspots, reely.
>
> John Smith

She agreed with the last sentiment, albeit with reservations. She could quite understand why any member of the paying public might consider a lawyer no more than a highly trained thief extracting money from grief and necessity, a servant with an exaggerated sense of self-importance, not in the other guise, as protector, which was the way she saw it. Someone who led others through the minefield of highly regulated contemporary life, stuck with them and brought them through to the other side. That was what she did, when allowed.

So, Mr. Smith, I may have you on a hook. I may get to have a proper look at you at last. What will you think of me? Shall I be able to make human contact with you or will you spit? The writing was similar to what she had seen; similar, but not identical. The spelling was different and the result inconclusive.

The mirror faced her on one turn of her restless pacing. Window open for forbidden cigarette smoke. No, there was no way she could make herself look like a boy, but she could probably make herself look less like a woman. Scrape back the hair, omit the makeup, try to look pale and uninteresting; add specs. She rather liked the idea of disguise. It was only an extension of daily life to assume the colours of her surrounding company, not for camouflage but to make them feel at ease. An actress, playing a number of parts.

Cannon. Who still had not phoned. If Cannon was telling the truth when he said there was no answer to the terrible threat of Johnnyboy until Johnnyboy was tired of the game, then she would have to find the solution for him. Blackmail of the kind Cannon had forbidden. After all, at one remove she knew quite a lot about John Smith's business. The countdown to Christmas was short, but it was still too long, even if John Smith *had* promised. She had the sense of time running out, even before Pauline phoned. The office this morning was hot and stuffy.

"Where have you been?" The mere sound of that authoritarian voice sparked the guilt that had lain pretending to be dormant. Pauline reminded her how little of her own life she seemed to possess, but it seemed wrong to complain about that. She shut her eyes and tried to recall the moment when she had seen the new flat; a moment of unalloyed, undistracted happiness. As if it was ever going to be hers.

"I've been nowhere, Auntie." Pauline hated being called Auntie. "I've been busy doing nothing. As always. You know how it is."

There was the sound of heavy breathing. Sarah doubted she was using the convent phone, sited in the hall next to the dining room—not for confidential conversations and sparingly used as necessity demanded. Sarah had offered to buy them a fax and met a barrage of puzzled faces. Why would we need it?

"How soon can you come and see Julie? How *soon*?" She was whispering urgently, sounding childish, as if enjoying the conspiracy, relishing the keeping of secrets. No wonder it had been easy to persuade her into such discretion: she was a closet spy.

Sarah glanced at the letter from John Smith, ending with his illiterate signature. *Ridiculous* secrecy: the man could not even spell. He was a clown who swam like a piece of cork on legs, and she herself was delaying because she was no longer able to believe that any of this had been necessary.

"Why should I?" A weary question, sounding grudging. Julie was her responsibility was why, just as Cannon was. She had made them thus. Was it laziness and wanting her own life back that made her resentful? But she loved them both, Pauline and William, too. It was just that none of them seemed to be aware of it. "Oh, I don't mean *why*, I mean why now? It's only a few days since . . ." She was sounding apologetic, and cross for feeling it. Why could she never do *enough?*

"Well, if you came today, most of them are out. The sermon in the Cathedral . . ."

"*Why?*"

"Look, things move fast with the human soul," Pauline hissed. "It doesn't stay consistent. I'm worried about her. Cannon's missing two nights. They argued. She's getting frightened. She's also getting addicted to this way of life. Thinks it's easier than coming out. She's starting to *pray.*"

"That's your fault," Sarah said, icily calm in her anger. "*Your* fault. You can't leave well alone."

The breathing became heavier, indignant. "Do you think I want a *convert* at any price? Well, I don't. I don't want someone I can mould into belief simply because they're weakened, impressionable and fearful. Especially someone who feels they're being abandoned. Not much of a gift to God, is it?"

"I can't make her happier. Cannon's the only one who can do that."

There was a snort of derision, an unspoken curse. *Men.* "I wasn't suggesting you could, but you could alleviate this sense of abandonment. Come and talk to her. Make plans for her. Cannon's not communicating. Tell her there's an end to this charade. Give her *some* version of what might happen. Tell her he'll do anything for her. As she would for him. *Anything.*"

Sarah was silent. Pauline had always asked the impossible.

"She's afraid of the frailty of love." And Pauline added, saving the best until last, "I've a feeling she might be pregnant."

Perhaps it was something he had done or said; perhaps it was the imminence of Christmas, and a time when his clients consulted their budgets and decided their teeth could wait in the interests of other, less important and purely seasonal spending, but business was not brisk, William decided. This did not worry him unduly: money had never worried him much, apart from a vague discomfort about the fact that perhaps it should—in the way that a new suit or a different piece of wallpaper should excite him and didn't quite. In fact, anything that had to be *shopped* for, money included, was always a trifle disappointing. He surprised himself by thinking that what he really appreciated in life were the surprises: the events, the gifts, the people wished upon him unexpectedly before he had a chance to head them off. Sarah; Cannon; a truly unusual set of teeth presenting themselves for his inspection; the challenge of John Smith. The surprise to the eye or the emotions of something exquisite or hideous. He was not sure whether John Smith was a real person or an event. Whatever he was, there was something stupendous about his arrival. He was a gift without wrapping.

Early in the morning William was home, Sarah and he embarking in their always separate directions. Wouldn't have to be so early if she moved into that flat she'd described. He liked the idea of her living nearer; definitely liked it, a lot, so much so that he wished he could remember the address she'd told him before he'd been distracted, wished he had told her about John Smith, but on the whole was pleased he had not. She was so damned helpful. He wanted to deal with John Smith by himself; create an achievement all by himself, alone and unaided. I'm not such a klutz, am I? I can make a real difference to two lives. And I'm a good lover; *me*. She had said so.

What he liked about John Smith's teeth, and by the same token what he had liked about Cannon's, was the fact that they were so much *worse* than what he normally saw and they belonged to rather unreasonable people. The rest of his patients were *so* reasonable, so prosperous, so educated about the state of their fangs that they arrived at the first sign of trouble and did what they were told, boringly, so predictably cooperative they scarcely needed him at all.

By eight o'clock the wintry sun began to creep into the corners of the room. There had been a touch of frost as he had walked down the road and the railings flanking the door felt frozen to the touch. Shop windows, black, and what would he buy her for Christmas? A rubbish van was collecting black sacks left on the pavement; there was something positive about the place looking cleaner even as he watched.

One of the blinds was up. William frowned. He could not remember leaving it like that and he was precise about such things. He pulled up the blind that was down, releasing a shaft of sunlight. It fell on Cannon's painting, and he stood before it, lost. A woman in her bathroom, drying herself. Ready for her *toilette,* a dress strewn over a chair, the only furniture in a simple room with painted stone walls, a rough-tiled floor against which the nude had guarded her feet with bright-coloured slippers. A small selection of glass jars on a shelf, backdrop to her ease; she would not hurry for anyone; there was no preening in the pose, no apparent knowledge of the observer. Had he, William, ever regarded Isabella with such frank admiration, been allowed to gaze at her in this way? No; he could not remember it; nor, he imagined, could she. He could only recall the degree of lust, which did not comprehend details, and could not have stood back to observe her. Did not look, only wanted to grasp. He could also recall that the details of her *toilette* were always secret: he would glimpse her going into the bathroom, glance at her during her cursory scrubbing of teeth, but by and large Isabella never stayed *au naturel.* She emerged from behind closed doors fully armoured for the day. It was the finished product she presented for admiration, never the body, as if she had hated it.

William felt a great stab of pity for her, and shame for himself. How little they had known each other. How intimately, by comparison, he knew Sarah, who would sit joyfully naked for all the world to see and not care what it thought. She was the one happier without the clothes and the accoutrements, a creature requiring no second skin. He must ask Cannon about the painting. Why did he never *ask* things? In his heart of hearts, he did not want to know it was stolen.

Into the surgery, and yes, on this blithe, refreshed morning, holding on to his high spirits of the day before, he was proud of the place, too. *Clever* design, William. *No* immediate view of the chair, another little space to sit and talk about it, a corner to turn and a feeling of space. He had hated tiny surgeries. They got in everyone's face. There was no painting or piece of distraction facing the chair. How long since he had decided on that? When Tina had said there was no need, or because he had realized that, whatever he put there, it would have to be something *he* liked and it followed from that that someone else might dislike it. The wall in here looked bare. Fussily, busily, getting himself in motion for the day, William proceeded into the hallway and removed Cannon's drawing of his hands, placed it on the empty hook opposite the chair. Surely no one could take exception to that. Then he washed his hands carefully, reminding himself of how precious they were. Humming, he admired the order of all he surveyed and pressed the answer-machine button for messages. A sibilant voice, oddly without resonance, hesitant, instantly familiar.

Tomorrow afternoon, Mr. Dentist. The whole afternoon. And no one else there, you get me? No one but you, or I'll go as soon as I arrive, and you'll miss out on all that cash. But I can't have anyone watching, can I? Smith.

The words themselves were hectoring, but the tone ingratiating, almost pleading, as if attempting an apology.

Click. Beeeeeep. The sunshine seemed to depart from the room. William slumped. Examined his hand for the disappeared mark of a bite. Didn't the man realize it would all take so much longer without a nurse to record and assist? But then again, how would he know? Sarah would say, Do not do this. You have an awkward patient with high expectations; you *never* see such a patient alone, especially females. What defence could you offer if he sued? What protection would you have?

I don't care. I want to.

He looked in the appointments book. It was so much easier than the screen. Five for tomorrow afternoon, the names as meaningless as usual without the notes, all short appointments, no one booked for more than half an hour. No sedation, no anaesthetist to inconvenience, all capable of cancellation; nothing major. How *dare* the man give such short notice? Why the hell should he cancel? He hated to cancel, it was unfair and irresponsible, but he knew as he reached for the phone, formulating excuses and unaccustomed lies, that that was exactly what he was going to do. Tell them to come back next week or the one after; they were a biddable lot; so *good;* so respectful. Tina would be delighted with an afternoon off. Everybody would be happy.

And yet, when he looked at his hands, they were shaking. Long, elegant fingers, shaking like twigs in a breeze. Not nearly as confident as the hands Cannon drew. He was not used to telling lies. His fingertips tingled and grew pink. Sometimes he thought his whole life was his hands.

Cannon had not phoned, had not phoned . . . had not phoned. The realization repeated itself like a litany. He had rejected the idea of a mobile phone—typical Cannon, rejecting anything that made life simpler. Addicted to complications. And fantasies. He must be sulking in response to the increased scepticism that had come to surround him. Cultivating other credulous friends. Doing something to upset his wife. Making a mess as usual. The bright daylight outside made her angry. She had promised to find him the new place to live; she had fulfilled the promise; and still no phone call. What the hell did he think he was doing?

The small space of her office had the effect of multiplying the anxiety she had tidied away; she felt she wanted to push the walls aside. Maybe the daft bastard had gone on a bender, that was all. Not an entirely unknown phenomenon in Cannon's unpredictable life.

Lunch-time, at last an excuse to exit. Running downstairs, carefully past Matthewson's door, avoiding him, too, in case of question—*I must account for my time*—the green wool coat flowing out behind, such was the speed of her. A pause in the vast reception area with all its empty walls; a nod and a grin to the woman behind the desk. Out into the sunny street with an arm already raised for the taxi. Yes, Cannon was going to bankrupt her. Traffic made her snarl. The taxi-driver wanted to discuss it, as if it was news, but found her aloof and discouraging.

She had never come to the attic in the middle of the day. More often, it had been in the earlier hours of morning, or long after the afternoon dark had taken command. The street was busier than she remembered: she felt conspicuous and told herself she was not. She was an office worker, like all of these coming out into the cold to find sandwiches and dream of going home soon. No one would notice her entering the only domestic residence in the street, that empty place no one cared for. It was not her, it was Cannon who would look out of place here, but no more so than the man on the corner selling the *Big Issue*. If anything, he was smarter than Cannon. She unlocked the door and went in.

The chill was ominous; she could sense from the first floor that he was not there. "Cannon?" The sound of her voice was muffled by dust and the creak of the floorboards. Polish these, mend that, it could be a lovely house, she told herself, as she forced herself onwards and upwards. It was only an empty house with a harmless squatter; the worst that could happen was discovery. I am John Smith's lawyer, she would say haughtily. He gave me the key. Take me to your master.

"Cannon?"

The door to the attic at the last set of creaking steps gave easily as she pushed. The emptiness inside was a relief. Half-way up, the vision that had haunted her all morning since Pauline phoned had increased in intensity, become sharper, so that she almost expected to see it. Cannon, dead or dying in here, giving up on his allies because he could sense they were giving up on him. Cannon, lying on the cherry-red sofa, beginning to stink, victim to his despair; the artist artistically disposed in death in his garret, an image he might like. Another image had clashed with the first: she had seen herself coming up here to find there was no roof, that he had blown it all away, leaving nothing but sky and dust. The last thought occurred too late for her to guard against it as she closed the door behind her. He may have booby-trapped the place. Even if he had sworn on his solemn oath never to play with fire, he might have done that. He was mad enough. He kept his cash between the first beam and the roof. The beam sagged dangerously.

There was nothing. A stale smell of nothing, not the sharp smell of turpentine she associated with this place. He had not been messing about with paint in the last day or more. There was none of his leftover heat; no sign of activity. As tidy, in preparation for imminent movement, as she remembered it from last time.

There was the single difference that all the sketches of Johnnyboy's face had been torn. Ripped across and thrown in a heap, showing signs of systematic, rather than furious, destruction. That was Cannon all over, destroying what he had done, always at war between the making of something and its breaking down. So he had at least been back, then. There was a half-eaten sandwich on a chair. Cannon lived on sandwiches and yet he loved good food.

It struck her with a terrible conviction that no one with Cannon's love of light would ever consent to live like this unless they believed it was entirely necessary. Whatever the real nature of the threat posed by his brother, it was certainly real to him. Utterly real, for him to confine his free spirit into this and insist on separation from his wife. She had not done him justice. But he had done some sort of justice to her. Her portrait rested against the easel, turned towards the light from the window in the roof. He had done further work on it, lovingly, it seemed. Toned down the colour of the hair, and then added more of the red. He had caught the likeness in the body and the face; captured something essential in the attitude of careless abandon. It was a sensual portrait, which was not, at the same time, sexual. Not like the Bonnard, which was both. She wondered if he was pleased with it. Moved closer, admiring her mirror image rather than herself.

We form our impression of a face from a distance of three feet, at least, William said. It was only a painting that allowed the impertinence of closer scrutiny, touching, squinting, looking for flaws in the skin. He had found hers, the tiny scars on the breasts, slightly whiter marks against sallow skin, not disfiguring but oddly enhancing, like freckles on a sunny face. And she had thought he would not notice.

"Cannon, where are you?"

A pigeon cooed and tapped on the fanlight, startling her, making her want to run. But she did not run. She found a pencil and wrote a message, "Darling, where are you? Phone me," and then ran downstairs and into the street, locking the door behind her as if it were her own house.

12

I must account for my time; I must account for my time.

She sat at her desk, facing the screen, typing with disinterested fury. The law required such a vast number of words. There is *real* life, Cannon, real work: look at it. If I keep on skiving like this, they'll all lose patience. I won't be able to help anyone else because I won't have a job and I won't have money and I shall never be able to pay for the flat. There are other clients, Cannon, you aren't the only one.

Where did a man go all day? Where did he disappear?

The afternoon seemed endless, anxiety, as well as anger, extending each minute into an hour. Where would he go with his depressive nature, his capacity for intense joys and miseries? She remembered him running towards that fire, saw it mirrored in the screen; remembered that he had a valuable life but a frail one, and why, oh, why, had she ever taken on the burden of it to neglect it now?

Thinking: trying to remember anything relevant about him, affection sneaking back and catching her unawares. Cannon was at his most unpredictable when he had done something of which he was ashamed; what *might* he have done this time? Unless that fanciful ogre, his brother, had found him and spirited him away. What *did* Cannon do with his day?

You can sit as long as you like in the galleries. They're half full of weirdos like me. Some of them with sketch-pads, some of them just sitting. It's the best thing about London. That's where you learn.

And which one do you like best, Cannon?

Oh, I circle around. I always come back to portraits. I like the living dead.

This time, leaving the office, she remembered not to run, to look calm and casual as if slipping out to a meeting, even remembered to invent one and write it into the open diary on her desk. Matthewson sometimes snuck up here to see who was hiding. *Research into art collection; portraits.* He might not believe it, but it was a record all the same and almost true.

Believe in your instincts. The brightness of the day had faded mid-afternoon, and the city began to prepare itself for dark. A pavement artist outside the National Portrait Gallery began to clear away his chalks, regarding his depiction on the stones without sentiment, indifferent to its imminent destruction, counting the takings.

She moved through the vaulted rooms of the gallery quietly, feeling foolish and conspicuous. The few guards were yawning towards the end of the working day. What a job; what sublime boredom. The thought of that made her quicken her step, moving from one incurious gaze to the next, wondering what they would do if she was a thief strong enough to snatch one of these heavy frames and run with it. Surely portraits were too personal for thieves. As if anything were too personal for thieves. She found him finally, sitting, head propped on his hands, staring at a portrait of a bearded Victorian premier surrounded by his family, and the relief at the sight of him cancelled out the irritation. She sat. If Cannon was remotely surprised to find her there, there was no indication: it was as if they had met an hour before and met again by prearrangement. She thought, wryly, that his erratic faith in telepathy must have extended itself beyond its application to his brother, making him assume the same quality in her.

"Sometimes," he said, by way of introduction, waving at the noble lord, "it does one good to look at a thoroughly second-rate piece of work.

Which this is. This painter was doing what he was told, as if someone had said to him you can paint it any colour you like as long as it's blue. It makes me feel better. If I spent all my time looking at artists with vision who paint like I want to paint, like Bonnard, it would make me feel hopeless. I'd want to go back and white out everything I'd done."

"Or tear up your drawings," she suggested.

He shook his head in unfeigned surprise, shocked at the suggestion. "Oh, no, I never do that. I'm never angry enough to do that. Put them out of the way for a while. Then use the other side of the paper. Paper costs money. Where have you been?"

"Come on out, Cannon. We can't talk in here. They'll think we're plotting a robbery."

He followed her, shuffled level with her down the road, into Trafalgar Square. There was the dull roar of traffic, muffled into background noise by the well of the square itself and the sound of the fountains. Nelson, on his column, towered above them. There was a dilatory shifting of people, meeting, greeting, crossing; movement towards buses, trains, entertainment, home. He seemed unnaturally calm for a man who hated crowds, but the space was large enough to absorb them, no one came close enough to push or to touch.

"Never mind where I've been," Sarah said, pulling her coat around her against the cold of the bench, trying to avoid pigeon-shit. There was an enormous Christmas tree in the centre of the square. Another year gone. "You didn't phone. I'm sick of you. We're all sick of you."

He nodded in agreement, dull in response. "I'm not surprised. *I'm* sick of me. I just don't know what to do. So I don't do anything really." He took a deep, shuddering breath.

If he chose this moment to cry, Sarah thought she might hit him. He did not cry; she waited.

"I go and look at paintings of patriarchs and father figures. Wishing I'd ever had one. Wishing I could be one. A man who was able to look after his own." He shoved his hands into his pockets. Even in the cold open air, the coat still smelled. "I thought I might just disappear. It would be better for everyone. Better for Julie in the long run. None of this had any point. Johnnyboy's always known where I was. He's been up to the attic. He's been to William's place. I saw him. He'll get to you next."

Oh, nonsense. She did not say it, thought it. What had William to do with anything? William had been protected from knowledge. She didn't believe in unconscious communication. Nobody would have been to Cannon's dwelling-place: it was an almost perfect hiding-place. She was sick of pandering to fantasy. Then she thought of the torn-up drawings in the garret. *Oh no, I'm never angry enough to do that. Paper costs money.* The cold from the bench struck through into her back, chilling her spine.

"I suppose the *other* thing I could do," Cannon was saying, "is simply go back there and wait. He'll be along, sooner or later." His hopelessness had a quiet intensity she had never seen before. She did not know quite how to rouse him. It grew colder with the darkness; the lights of the grand buildings surrounding the square began to glow. She did not know if she wanted to humour him or believe him.

"Pauline thinks Julie may be pregnant," she said. No forethought to the statement. It simply emerged as the only positive thing she could think of to say.

"What?"

"Your wife. Having a baby. *Maybe.* I don't suppose you take condoms on your nocturnal visits, do you?"

She looked straight ahead, not quite wanting to see the effect of her statement, guilty for making it on such shaky information. Pauline might have said it for effect; it might not be the truth. They were none of them masters of truth: they all made guesses and stuck to them. She could sense him uncurling beside her. Moving from his slump with head in hands. Standing with his hands in his pockets. Then, with his arms above his head, locked into a stretch. Then one hand on hip, the other raised as he performed a jig, like a drunken Scottish dancer ignorant of the steps but feeling the tune, hopping from one foot to the other, singing tunelessly, louder and louder as he moved until he stopped, breathless, punched the air and yelled, "Yeah!" in a voice loud enough to slice across the sound of the traffic and the water. The pigeons, which had begun to approach their feet with the constant optimism of pigeons, flew upwards in an untidy arc. Cannon was transformed.

"Oh, yodleodle*deeeeeee*," he sang, pirouetting with his hands on his head, changing the steps into a kind of hopscotch over the paving-stones, not touching the cracks, as far as the brink of the fountain. She thought he might climb into it, but he put his hands into the cold water, splashed it into his face, hopscotched back, jumped up and down. YES! YES! YES! Sarah leaned forward on the bench and laughed long and loud because he was comical, and out of sheer relief to see him thus: the other Cannon, reminding her of why she had fallen into devotion to him, for all his intensity, his absurdities, his intolerance, his moods, his talent for outlandish joy, latent in his paintings, patent now. She would always love creatures of extremes; the ones impossible for cohabitation; those who saw what she never could. He would weep for a fallen leaf and shout for joy at the colours of a tree. He could make a bomb or paint the soul in a face. She grabbed him and pulled him down.

"Cannon, I said *might* be . . . And it hardly improves the situation, does it?"

She hated to rain on his parade; he had the knack of making her feel cruel for the slightest attempt to restrain him—and how would this man ever stay alive without Julie to direct the dreams?

He sat so abruptly that the solid bench creaked. He was suddenly sober, but his face was still split by his widest grin, which made his mouth look like a cave. A passer-by glanced at him curiously; he glanced back, then pulled his hand down from forehead to chin, as if wiping off the smile with a cloth, pretending to be solemn. It reappeared immediately. Sarah adopted her dictatorial voice, uncomfortably aware that she could sound a younger facsimile of her aunt. Bossyboots.

"Look, Cannon, whether she is or she isn't, this whole charade is at crisis point. We don't just *wait* any more. I'm going to see Julie *now*. You're going to come with me. You're going to march in there without thinking of who might be watching. The hell with it. Why should anyone be watching? Then we sit down and talk about plans, four of us, like civilized human beings capable of making them. Then we either take Julie home or arrange to take her another time."

"Home?" he echoed. "*Home?*"

She shook him impatiently. "Another apartment. I've got one lined up. My home if you want. Anywhere'll do."

"No," he said. "Johnny'll find us."

"If I hear that *one more time* . . . So you say. So you've always said. And what if he does? You barricade the doors. You call the police—"

"Who won't believe a single thing I say. I'm a con, a liar, a thief who cheated my own brother . . . The police were never an option."

"Of course they are. For Christ's sake, if they didn't weigh in for liars and thieves, they'd be out of a job." She paused. "Are you a liar, Cannon?"

"No." Without hesitation. He was sober without being depressed, sitting still and thinking, a rare state of stability for him.

"Good, just checking." *You lied at your trial; I helped you.* "Shall we go, then?"

"Wait a minute, let me think . . ."

"Don't think, Cannon. You either don't think at all or too much, without any good results either way. Come *on,* Cannon."

"I'm not sure . . ."

"Well, I am."

The crowds *en route* to somewhere else had gathered momentum; the traffic growl increased; they were leaning close together, heads almost touching to hear themselves speak.

"This flat . . . How will Julie manage?"

"A bit of rudimentary furniture, enough. More than you're used to."

"Only I don't want her lifting things."

Cannon stood decisively, brushing himself down as if what he did would make any difference to the state of his dreadful coat. "I'll have to go back to the attic. Get some money. Come with me?"

She hesitated, furious at his assumption that she should. She did not want to go back there; shuddered at the thought of the place; wanting to keep a strong hand on his arm, but gripped with repugnance for that grim place and the torn drawings. She wanted to say, "Never mind about the money," but she had little enough to give him, twenty maybe, sufficient for the taxis, not more than that from a bank account looking a little leery at the minute. Surely he could go alone; no sense in duplicating tasks. And what was it he'd said about William? No time to ask. She fished in her bag for cash. "No, thanks. You go, quick. I half promised Pauline I'd be there at half five. The nuns are out, more space. Meet you there, OK?"

He nodded. She watched him lope across the square, scattering more of the pigeons. He gave a hop, skip and a jump, twice, took chocolate from that everlasting pocket, threw it. Optimism rewarded.

Perhaps her own would be rewarded, too. Sarah did not want to move; she stretched inside her coat and closed her eyes. There was nothing but the roar of the traffic and the insistent splashing of the water. She calculated the differing time it would take at this crowded hour to reach the convent. Taxi or tube? She thought of economy as much as speed, rose stiffly, listened to the raucous music of a cacophony of horns and descended, like a thousand others, down to the trains.

He was absurdly happy and he was not going to be afraid ever again. He opened the window of the taxi and let in the cold air and the noise. He wasn't going to be afraid any longer because *this* settled it. New life settled it, redefined everything, because there was going to be a child with *his* blood and his bones, and that made all the difference. Because a man could love his wife with his body and his mind, which he did, and more, but his soul would enter his child. The child would be the ally to make him strong. A male, surely; a little man. He would hold the child like a shield against Johnnyboy; the child would be the final *proof* that he was gone from Johnny for ever. Gone from being buggered, gone from the intimacy, living on a different planet from the one they had shared. The child would be proof that he had become not merely a defector but a different species, a new kind of animal altogether; no longer, in Johnny's eyes, simply an experimental lover, indulging himself in an affair that Johnny would find unspeakably repellent and thought he could squash to death like a bug; Johnny would see what he was. *Look what I've made, Johnny. Look what I've made. Now do you see I can't come back?*"

There was a pause for self-recrimination in the back of the cab. Was he so little and so cowardly in himself that he had needed this promise of new, innocent life to confirm his own certain footsteps? Was he as feeble as that? Was his passion for his wife not sufficient all on its own? He chewed his nail and watched the blurred passage of the world outside; someone ran across the front of the taxi as it slowed for lights; the driver swore. Oh, yes, love for Julie was enough; it was everything, but perhaps not quite enough to quell that greatest fear of all. The fear that, one day, Johnnyboy would be diabolically clever and try the simple expedient of seeking a reconciliation through charm and guile without any threat of force. He hadn't learned a thing, Johnnyboy: his cruelty was powerful, his need insatiable, his kidney punch the worst on earth, but the power of his affection and his tears and his longing, if ever he admitted it, well, that put any kind of threat into the shade.

The taxi lurched round a corner. He was thrown back against the seat. Remembered Johnny with a hand pressed over his mouth, both of them hiding; the fear all the time that Johnny would *beg* him back, plead with him. That he would forget to hunt and bully, that he would crook his little finger in some awful act of kindness and tap into the common sap that made them. That was the real fear.

But not now, not any more: now this had happened, and Johnny had left the ultimate threat of sweet persuasion too late. He would never win now, because there was so much more to lose. *Yes!* He bounded up the steps and into the shabby house, which hid its dereliction rather well, careless for all his thinking. The office workers of the street were in full, colourful exodus, hats and scarves donned, the girls with silly shoes incapable of keeping out cold or wet; he had a fleeting memory of kissing Julie's feet in her practical slippers, feeling the thin skin of an ankle. He ignored the faint scent of Johnny inside this house, because it was impossible to explain and he wanted to concentrate on things he could explain, but it was there all the same. Definable only to someone who had slept with the brute for all those many years, knowing every smell of his body from the peculiar stench of his sweat to the gentle aroma of a freshly soaped chest. No, he had not been forced to love Johnny; not at first. It had been as natural as breathing . . .

He could hear Johnny breathing in here, the pulse of the house; ignored that, too. Crashed through the door to the attic, wishing he had asked the taxi to wait. More haste, less speed, Cannon, my lad.

His stash of cash was under the beam, above the portrait of Sarah without her clothes. Sarah, another convenience, how generous she was; wouldn't he love to do without her, like *they* wanted to do, shedding Granny when she tried, in vain, to keep them in order? And, Christ, how was he going to earn enough to keep a wife and a child? Haste made him clumsy; the boards creaked. He glanced at the painting of Sarah: it was good, very good, provided he did not compare it to Bonnard, and that way lay the death of all endeavour. He had talent; he had to believe it; there was a child to consider and the child had talent to be nurtured, too. He yanked at the beam, fingers exploring impatiently for the plastic bag secreted up there with the survival money inside. Didn't trust banks: you couldn't when the State said you owed it money. He fetched a chair to stand and reach better.

There was only the one wooden chair, a spindly thing suitable for a bedroom. He stood on it regardless, reached again, heard the leg of it snap, clutched at the beam and hung there for a moment, thinking, This is funny. Then the beam cracked, broke, fell, hit him a sneaking, soundless blow on the back of the head as he landed; sent him crashing forward, colliding with the makeshift easel, both of them spinning down noisily. Then he was lying on the floor with a dead weight across his shoulders, plaster and dust cascading into his hair like hailstones. He tried to lift himself up; could not; tried to breathe; could; lay where he was with the cold imagination of having been hit by an explosion. Stay still, think about it; no pain yet; blurred vision, his heart pounding. Remembered, quite inconsequentially, a remark Sarah had made about this room. It's rotten, she had said, but not that bad. And there's not a single beam high enough for a man to hang himself. Such faith she had in him. He felt delirious, ridiculous, with some half-remembered sense of happiness and optimism. He closed his eyes against the grit, reached forward, exploring with his fingers, finding, to one side, particles of plaster and dust, pieces of torn paper, which were oddly unexpected, and then straight ahead, the canvas of the portrait.

The last thing he remembered for a while was that the surface of it was still slightly soft and sticky. Oil paint took a long time to dry.

Sarah rang the bell at the door of the convent and wondered idly how many times she had done this—dutiful visits to her aunt, when she was a child and Pauline in some other institution, nearer what was then home and a long way from London, a place with a similar door, but attached to a school. The convents she had known, her own school included, melded into one another in a single sensation of smells, lack of comfort and a deceptive façade of gloom to hide what was behind: laughter and warmth often enough, charity, devotion, talents and tensions, a code of conduct that kept everything in place.

She noticed the dearth of lights in windows; two, far left, for the two sisters currently bedridden, the rest in darkness, sure sign that most of them were out. Off to the Cathedral, Pauline said, to hear the Cardinal in the afternoon, busloads of them from all over the place, but I've heard enough from priests so I'll keep the home fires burning. In virtual darkness, it seemed. No one here would ever leave a room empty with a light burning: they had a second sense for a switch. They closed doors quietly and turned off the light behind them, like polite guests in someone else's house, ever aware of cost. Sarah had lost almost every aspect of her convent training; all she could remember was the habit of quiet movement, so ingrained that it was natural unless she made herself stop, or some mood of hilarity prevailed with the housework, some excitement overcame the well-absorbed reserve. It was not much to have taken from a moral education; a small souvenir out of otherwise comprehensive rejection. She had not lost it all. There was still that belief in redemption . . . for others.

She remembered, also, the slight and controllable sense of claustrophobia that preceded her like a high-noon shadow as soon as she came here, some memory of small rooms and scoldings, *Sarah Fortune, you are beyond hope* . . . a feeling of inadequacy because she could never, ever get it quite right. Could manage the decorum, but not the obedience; found the rude books about sex and made sure the other girls read them. *Stop sniggering, will you?* She rang the bell again, turned to survey the off-road parking space and the road beyond while she waited for someone to come from the back of the house to the front. A car moved slowly down the quiet road, pausing, as if looking through the trees for a number on one of the great big houses that flanked either side. The door opened. Pauline made a mock bow and ushered her in with a flourish.

"Cannon shouldn't be long," Sarah said.

"Ah, a double pleasure."

To Sarah's relief she detoured away from the parlour. It was a room that echoed; it was more suitable for a summit conference than a cosy chat; she could see visiting dignitaries snoring in there on the pristine moquette, sleeping out of self-defence against the dizzying patterns of carpet and curtain. She followed to the kitchen, where the warmth hit like a soft blow. Julie was by the industrial oven, her face flushed. There were trays of clingfilm-wrapped food on the table, cold meats and bread and butter, a pan of soup to one side of the hob. "They'll be hungry as horses when they get back," Pauline said cheerfully. "A good sermon from a high-ranking cleric always does that for them. Say hallo, Julie."

She isn't a child, Sarah wanted to shout. Let her speak for herself.

Julie smiled a greeting, which lit her face, turning it from interesting to beautiful, despite the fatigue. Sarah turned to Pauline. "You're a tyrant. Julie's a paying guest, remember?" She did not add, *paid for by me.* "You make her work too hard."

"I do *not. You* try and prevent her. I can't."

"Stops me thinking," Julie said. "I'd rather not think." She tucked her hair behind her ears; it was damp. "Can we go somewhere else for a minute? It's so hot in here." It was warm, certainly, without being uncomfortable, but then Sarah had not been labouring over a hot stove. Hers was the easy life: she could see it in Pauline's eyes.

"We'll say a prayer in the chapel, shall we?" Pauline suggested brightly. Julie nodded and moved ahead of them. Pauline and Sarah followed. "She *likes* the chapel," Pauline whispered to Sarah, irritating her with the assumption that Julie might not mind being talked about within earshot, like a deaf old relative. "She feels at home in it, these days." Was this new, or a piece of invention? "Cannon likes the chapel, too," Pauline added.

It was chill enough in here to reduce a fever. Sarah had left her coat and regretted it; the other two, a unit, did not seem to notice. It struck her for the first time that there was a purpose to Pauline's voluminous clothing: it was the equivalent of wearing an adaptable blanket at any time. She herself was dressed for an overheated office, skirt and blouse inadequate for these more Spartan conditions, and there were further advantages in being a holy nun like Pauline, such as never having to worry about co-ordination, whether the shoes would go with the skirt, the skirt with the blouse: she could simply stick to the shroud and put the equivalent of the handbag in the pockets, without vanity as if she had none of that commodity. Which she did have, the darling, in plenty, but vanity of a heavily disguised kind properly belonging to a producer of a play who might dress with deliberate insignificance in the knowledge that it was he who was pulling the strings and creating the scenes. Sarah tried to suppress the suspicion with which she regarded both Pauline's inscrutable face with the marble skin and Julie's guileless exhaustion. How melodramatic to insist on the chapel, as if it were a lay-by on the road to Damascus and Pauline, if not the embodiment of Paul's vision, at least the official breakdown van who collected him for the next leg of the journey.

"There, now," Pauline said, making sure they were all uncomfortable. "Julie and I have had such a lovely quiet day together, haven't we?"

Why this dreadful condescension? Was it saint to sinner? Or was it Pauline, mother appointee, becoming overprotective on the discovery that her darling little flower was in a delicate condition? Sarah looked at the statue of St George around which they seemed to be marshalled, wondered what the pursed-lip princeling thought he was doing waving that stick.

"I told you Cannon'll be here any minute," she said. "Can you hear the doorbell from here?"

"Oh, yes. There's a pager on the wall, a quiet one . . ." That was Julie, confident in these surroundings. A waitress with slightly buck teeth, marvellous eyes and enormous dignity. Sarah felt foolish. There was no disingenuity in either of them; there was only her intense irritation at feeling so much at a loss, that convent feeling of guilt and powerlessness. She had her arms crossed over her chest, defensively, less against the cold than the sensation of their innate superiority, married woman and professional celibate. Maybe all *tarts* felt like this in such a place. Maybe it was Pauline being so condescendingly motherly to her new charge. *You always were an attention-seeking child, Sarah. Still jealous at thirty-five, are we?*

"Look," Pauline said, "you've got us wrong." The *us* hurt. "We like the chapel because we like the chapel, right? And it's perfectly fair to sit here if we're waiting for Cannon to join the discussion, isn't it? He's far more likely to come in the back way than he is the front, if he follows established custom. Never quite took to the parlour, did he, Julie? Prefers the clandestine." Julie nodded. "If he can't get in the front, he'll get in the back. So don't worry about Cannon. You didn't say you were bringing him anyway; the later he is the better. Gives us more time to sort things out."

"Are you pregnant for sure?" Sarah asked, avoiding Pauline's eyes and staring straight into Julie's tired face, fascinated by the changing expressions that altered it so much it could have been a different face; she would be similarly and dramatically altered by different clothes, another chameleon. They had something in common then. It was difficult to describe the change of mood: a sad face in repose; utterly attractive in laughter; the huge eyes of a madonna, mirroring the amazement of discovery. She would be divinely patient with child and husband, given her chance. How they would all grow together, like a twisted and fruitful apple tree.

"Pretty sure. Sure as I can be, short of an announcement from the Archangel Gabriel. And Cannon won't have any reason to think the thing a supernatural object rather than his own, his very own."

There was a note of irony, foreign to her, a new tough self-assertiveness. Perhaps the result of a day with Pauline, to whom ironic understatement was second nature. Sarah could not see Julie being ironic with Cannon: he would not comprehend it. With Cannon she was sweetness and light, not sickly sweet, but firmly indulgent of his primary status and her integral part of his life as the decoder of his language and his needs; his passport to reality. There was pride in the symbiosis, the being the other half; she made it admirable. Feminist claptrap about finding oneself would find as much house room in Julie's repertoire as it would in that of any of the sisters here. Her kind of love made its own ultimate demands and she would obey them completely. Seen in the context of Julie's generously self-sacrificing soul, perhaps a temptation to include love of God into the equation was not so surprising. Pauline had said it once: if you love completely, the heart expands, and calcifies. She always made it sound like a disease.

They may have been right, Julie and Pauline. The coolness and sense of space in the chapel refined thought, gave an instant access to perception in a place where the distraction of movement was minimal and concentration on the non-peripheral was ordered. Personally, Sarah thought being locked in a cold cellar with a few crates of wine might have the same effect. Why had she never noticed before the strength in Julie's arms? Born to hug a man and cradle a baby, quite clear about it. She felt a moment of envy so intense it was painful, followed by a wave of protective feeling that was equally intense. Nothing should harm her; nothing. Beneath that currently calm, strong face, she had all of Cannon's fragility. It was only the combination that gave them the strength. Didn't matter if they bankrupted her. Someone would. Perhaps she could be godmother to the child.

"Some women put on weight very quickly, don't they?" Pauline murmured. "Not that Julie is yet." Still talking about her in the third person, as if impending motherhood made her a subject for discussion rather than a presence. "Can't be more than a few weeks, can it? But all the same, if she stays here it's going to be a little difficult to explain. Nothing insurmountable, provided I don't have to confess to carnal goings-on in the sacristy, but tricky."

"She isn't staying. Are you, Julie? We can go straight away."

Julie gazed up at St George, then at Sarah, then down at the floor, frowning. "*He's* still there, Sarah. Still there. Cannon would never leave me now, not if he knew. But he's still there." Sarah thought for a minute that this was an oblique reference to a saint. There were a lot of them around.

"Who?"

"Johnny. And, child or no child, I'll come apart at the seams if he ever comes near me again. Especially now." Her voice rose. Pauline patted her hand. The wedding ring gleamed a dull gold, insignificant in all the protection it promised. Pauline's rosary beads were more effective, weightier and at least potentially useful for something. They looked ten times more likely to ward off the evil eye. They clicked with the smooth *click* of polished bone as Pauline moved.

"But *why*, Julie? He's only a man. A bad man, but only a man."

"He's much more than a man. He's the dragon in the story," Julie said. She was attempting to smile, but it did not mask the weakness of the fear.

"And a man is nothing compared to God the Father who created him," Pauline interrupted, impatient with it. "What a shame none of you ever once thought of asking *Him* to intervene. Still, better late than not. And you've had the benefit of *my* intercession for months now. Go with God, child, and if you don't believe in your own prayers, believe in mine."

She rose with a shushing of robes, ever the leader. "Come, it's cold in here. Where the devil is that husband of yours? You'd best have something to eat before you leave. The gannets aren't due home for an hour or more yet."

They moved in a slow trio towards the door, Pauline standing back for the youngsters to go through first in case either of them should forget the golden rule to turn off the light. How strange this place was, Sarah thought, that it should exert such an effect, creating as it did an aversion to going inside, followed by a reluctance to leave. Bye-bye, chapel. You can't get at me, God, but sometimes I wish you could. She stroked the gnarled foot of St George's dragon as she moved round it. There was, predictably, no response, but her hand felt warmer for the contact. Poor old dragon. Then Julie clutched her arm, her mouth forming into a scream.

The swing door was shoved by a heavy hand and hit Pauline squarely in the face—contrast to the way in which it was used for sidling through. She fell backwards against the final pew, scrabbling for balance, and hung on, uttering a sharp scream, which sounded oddly girlish. Then she moaned. In the ensuing split second of silence, blood began to pour from her nose. In the same tiny interval of time, Sarah had the absurd notion of a divine punishment, about to be inflicted upon them all for the temerity of leaving the chapel without a genuflection. Pauline's hands moved, clumsily, as if searching for something lost; and Sarah realized, with an unbearable stab of pathos, that she was trying to make the sign of the Cross. A gesture of futile courage.

Oh, Lord, that fool Cannon, coming to find them with all the speed and tact of a raging bull.

"Cannon?" she mouthed, starting forward. "Cannon?"

The door swung on its hinge, a door bidden to silence. All three backed away from it, Sarah and Julie clutching Pauline, dragging her back with them towards the altar. She seemed reluctant to relinquish the knob of the pew, clawing at it with bony fingers white in the light, the other hand splashed with red.

It was not Cannon; there was no apologetic voice. Only a cough, like someone preparing for an entrance while adjusting a costume. Then the door opened and two men came inside. One was grossly stout, a caricature of a man built out of rubber tyres arranged in sequence from his neck to his knees and a rolling step to accommodate the thickness of his thighs, the other slight by comparison. A thickset man all the same, with a breadth of shoulder and enough height to tower over them. A whimper came from Julie's throat, muted by the knuckle she placed in her mouth. The larger man held the kitten by the scruff of the neck; it seemed smaller than a piece of fluff and made no protest. He placed it gently on a pew, where it sat and began to lick itself. Sarah felt a moment of pure terror for the kitten. Wanted to tell it to run and hide.

She knew exactly who it was. He did not look quite so foolish now, Johnnyboy. He looked like Cannon on a good day, with his grey jacket and brilliant white shirt and hooded eyes, which darted glances round the room, uneasily guarded against coming to rest. He looked a useful kind of man in here, where he was not swimming like a porpoise and his strange proportions were hidden by his suit. She knew who he was, and she knew in the same instant of sadness that Cannon had been right. The chapel did not affect him; the presence of a nun of senior years with blood gushing out of her nose did not affect him. There was no conscience of any kind to influence. None.

He paused in his progress towards them, shielded his eyes with a cap, as if their presence blinded him. Julie began a slow keening.

"Stop that," he said mildly. "Whoever you are." Then louder, a trace of nervousness in the voice. "*Stoppit.*"

She stopped, dropped her head and let her hair fall across her face. It had grown long. Pauline came to life. Her voice shook, still held an unmistakable note of authority. "Get out of here. How *dare* you?"

He seemed to consider this clichéd rebuke faintly amusing, came two steps closer. In unison, they took two steps back, like a single animal with six legs. Sarah could smell Julie's fear: it rose with the power of perfume, bringing with it the smell of the kitchen, talcum powder, acrid sweat. Now that he was closer, shortening the distance between them, gaining confidence, she could smell him, too. He extended a hand towards Pauline, let it drop, shook his head.

"My brother's *friends* . . . His powerful *friends* . . . a bunch of *women*. Oh, come now, Sister. Don't worry. What on earth would I want with a woman like you? It's *Julie* I want. My brother's *wife*. She owes me something." Julie began to whimper again. Sarah felt for her hand across Pauline's shoulder, grabbed it. The grasp in return was soft, as if she were already giving up, had known this was going to happen all along and was unable to fight it.

"Look at me," he commanded.

Slowly, all three raised their eyes and stared at him. The larger man was motionless, simply a fat man, standing still, waiting for his cue. Johnnyboy held their gaze until his own faltered and fell away, talked over his shoulder to the companion. Any hint of nervousness had gone. He seemed almost relieved.

"Well, that's easy," he said. "*He's* made it easy. He's a good artist with a likeness, you have to grant him that. We'll just make sure since there's two to choose from." He turned back to them. Crooked his finger at Sarah.

"Come here."

Pauline was grabbing her, putting the crucifix of the rosary into Sarah's hand, begging her to hold it, go no further than that short lead. She detached it gently, squeezed the cold silver into Pauline's palm and moved forward. There was a sweet sense of freedom in moving at all.

"*Mrs.* Julie Smith, as I live and breathe," he murmured. "Well, he certainly captured the likeness, didn't he? I could almost be proud of him for that." He was close enough for the spittle to reach her face; it seemed to require an extra act of courage for him to speak with such venom. She remembered the way he spat. A small gob landed on the floor. Imelda would clean it up in the morning, she thought, along with Pauline's blood, her own, too, perhaps. Julie's whimpering intruded. There was a sniffy sound and a *yeugggh* noise of anguish from Pauline.

Sarah sensed she could scarcely stand or speak. The thought of her helpless like that was shocking. She wanted the power to usher the two men out ahead of her like a flock of sheep, letting the door close on safety.

"My, my. I can see his point, I suppose. Pretty enough and Irish enough looking for an older hen, though I did think you were younger. He never described the hair. Magnificent, isn't it?" Again, the over-the-shoulder remark to the silent companion, met by an indifferent nod. "Couldn't bear to look at you, could I? Covered your face and only saw you in the dark that time. No, *he*," jerking his thumb backwards towards the fat shadow, "was *him* covered your face, right from the start. Hurt you. I didn't want to touch you, you disgusting piece of . . . but I did, didn't I? Not much. Women *like* to be touched. *You* did."

Another gob of spittle on the polished floor. She wondered where the kitten was, diverting her eyes and her mind from the spotlight of his hatred. The man behind was wearing big boots—surprising they had not heard him: rubber-soled perhaps; black and dirty, making marks on polished floors.

"You *are* Julie Smith?" Johnny asked, suddenly doubtful all over again.

She said nothing and, out of a perverse instinct, smiled at him. In a reflex action he smiled back, revealing a set of brown, uneven teeth. They looked almost artificial; joke teeth worn by a child to give offence on Hallowe'en; they made him look dead, tingeing his skin with their own appearance of rottenness and giving him the look of a sarcophagus. Lips like Cannon's, but pale and greedy. As soon as he was aware of the smile, he stopped and spoke through the pursed pocket of his mouth. "See if it's her. Make sure. Bound to be her."

There was a muffled sob from behind. The fat man came forward with his waddle of a walk and, with one easy motion, ripped Sarah's blouse from the neck. The buttons held. He yanked again, exposing a lacy bra and a collarbone. It had been a good blouse; she mourned it. There was a strangled gasp of outrage from Pauline; Sarah closed her eyes. Don't, Pauline, don't speak. There is more nudity on a beach, and I have been here before. I've done this kind of thing before. The big man was prodding her, as he would a piece of meat for tenderness, fat fingers tapping her breastbone with a hollow sound, reminiscent of a doctor tapping a bronchitic chest, touching with the same degree of indifference. He was feeling the tiny raised ridges of the white scars. Nodded. His hands rested on her neck; she knew he could have snapped it. There was a minor sense of relief in the understanding that this was not his purpose; it brought her to her senses. The man stepped back, waiting orders.

She remembered the oil painting of herself in Cannon's attic and suddenly understood the nature of the mistaken identity. The fat hands were confirming it.

"Of course I'm Julie Smith," she said. "Who else would I be?"

Part of her wanted to hear an emphatic denial from the two shivering women behind. Longed for the sound of words, saying, "*no*, she isn't, I am; *she* is," in a convincing chorus, but there were no such words. The other part was relieved that they kept their silence. That was what she wanted them to do, however intense the feeling of treachery.

"What do you want?" Pauline's voice was old and querulous.

"Only her. Nothing else."

The foolish kitten went to play around the fat man's boots. He scooped it up and held it aloft. They could all see him, dashing it against the knob of a pew. Or putting it on the ground, under the boot.

"Give me the kitten," Pauline said faintly. He swung his arm, and threw it gently enough in her direction. Sarah could hear the swish of robe and click of beads as she picked it up. The beads were no guard against the devil. She kept her gaze on Johnnyboy, but he could not return it. He clicked his fingers, like a man calling an animal to heel, and moved towards the door. The fat man came back towards Sarah and, with one enormous hand on the back of her neck, propelled her forward. She resisted, but his fingers spanned her scapula; her head was level with his shoulder; there was no choice. Still she waited for the words of denial, which did not come. The fat man seemed to relent slightly at the sight of Pauline's bloodied face as she sprang towards him and he shoved her back with ridiculous ease. Johnny was beyond the door, holding it open.

"We'll bring her back," the fat man whispered. He seemed, temporarily, in awe of the place. "She's only going for . . ." he hesitated ". . . for *treatment*. We'll bring her back. Honest."

The last hint of conscience and then they were gone, the steps they had not heard in advance only audible in retreat. By the time Pauline had stumbled down the corridor after them and looked wildly into the road, the car was long gone.

13

No real pain yet. Only a dull pain like a stiff neck after a night spent in a draught. A pain in the neck; laugh about it. That was what Cannon had been doing when he came up the stairs, laughing, and that was what he remembered when he opened his eyes. There was a trick they had practised as children suffering minor wounds, such as grazed knees or cut fingers. They would concentrate not on something better but something worse. Stare at each other with their almost identical eyes, Johnny and Cannon, saying over and over again, This does *not* hurt, not *really* hurt, does it? Think of something that *really* hurts . . . something *really* scary, like the dentist, and this one will go away.

Cannon tried it now; thought of real pain to put this dull ache into perspective. His fingers touched the stickiness of the canvas; he imagined himself touching the heat of Sarah's neck, feeling for a pulse, finding it. Those little scars of hers must have involved real pain, like the cigarette burn Johnny had once inflicted for fun, sneaking up behind him, stubbing it out on his bare back. That was real pain, like the dentist Johnny so feared and he no longer did. Johnny always lied about what pain was. The worst pain was loss and the worst result he could envisage was remaining as he was, beaten into accidental submission by one of Johnny's dilapidated houses. *Laugh* about it, go on. *Man who plays with fire since age of four dies under falling beam.* Johnny never used to let houses rot. It was loneliness and despair made him do that. Three years of wilful neglect could bring down the beams of a house. Cannon thought of the house he had destroyed on Bonfire Night and what a pointless piece of destruction that had been. As if Johnny would care. All this time he had thought he knew what made Johnny tick, but no knowledge was complete.

The joists in an attic floor, he remembered, often marked the point in the building process when the contractor ran out of the best wood. Rot might have made the broken beam lighter. He could not *stay* like this; it was *ridiculous.* He heaved and, like Prometheus unbound, he was, if not free, free enough to raise his torso and shuffle the weight of the broken rafter down his body and on to his buttocks. Then he lay, twisted to one side, grabbing the portrait with its wooden stretcher to use as a lever, shoved under the beam, raising it a fraction before the fragile frame of the stretcher snapped and he slithered his legs free, like someone curling away from a snake, leaving the skin of his coat. The portion of beam rolled to the floor with a dull thump like a sledge-hammer, bounced and landed on Sarah's portrait. He stood uncertainly and gazed at it briefly, looked at the hole in the roof and then back to her. There were notes from the money stash scattered over the floor, one or two directly across her face. Sarah with ten pounds sterling over her lips, more on her bosom.

No real pain yet, but he hurt. His shoulders were stiff, his left arm curiously reluctant to move as he tried to use it to hail the cab. He wanted a drink. The darkness had come down like a curtain at the end of Act Two. Not final, but determined. A taxi stopped; he flung himself inside.

"Aren't you a bit cold, mate?"

Cannon looked at his torn sweater and dusty trousers. The temperature was irrelevant, the question perfectly stupid. "What time is it?"

"Seven o'clock, near enough. Where to?"

It felt like the middle of the night; still early and the roads full. He felt he had escaped lightly from a stupid accident and the omens were therefore good; he was smugly pleased with himself, bordering on the euphoric, apart from a monstrous headache, into which there nudged that memory of happiness. Julie and a baby; the end of rotten houses and the old identity. Singing to himself softly and tunelessly as the cab rolled along. "'Rock-a-bye, baby boy, Go to sleep, son.'"

The door to the convent was open. The ground floor blazed with light so that he was almost shy to go in, used as he was to its cautious darkness and the single light from Julie beckoning him inside. He should have been here at least an hour ago and he waited, humbly, for the chastisement of women, only mildly suspicious of the frenzied activity inside. Into that suspicion there crept the other fear about Julie and how she had come to belong where she did not belong; a little nag of doubt about her. Sarah would dictate and they would obey. Sarah with the ten-pound note stuck over her mouth and all the good ideas.

There were flitting figures, like a nest of moths disturbed. He pushed past a sister who seemed so pleased to see him she must have mistaken him for someone else, apologized automatically and crossed into the parlour. There, more of them were huddled in a posse, clucking like quiet hens, Pauline resisting the attempts of Imelda to hold her hand; Julie curled in a tight, cold ball into one of the chairs, uncurling and racing towards him with a cry, flinging her arms around him, grabbing at him and holding on like a limpet. For a full moment, he enjoyed the sensation of public embrace. It seemed years since they had ever hugged openly with other people watching, but the pleasure and the pride were fleeting. Pauline's voice cut through like a whip. Her face showed the presence of tears, as did the face of his wife, but in Pauline's case, the weeping and the shock were under control. Her face was altered and aged, the sight of her iron grey crop as startling as if he had seen her naked, the voice unmistakable.

"Your brother and his minder took Sarah away. Because they thought she was Julie. There's no comparison, is there? Why would he do that?" The voice rose in anxiety. The crucifix on her rosary beads was curled inside her palm as she shook her head. "And . . . *we* . . . *we* let him do it. God help us."

Her head was bowed. Imelda murmured to her. She sat back obediently, neck stretched, contemplating the ceiling. There was a red handkerchief in her lap. He was slow to smell the blood. "I am so sick of kindness," she said.

"He's going to come back, the man said they were going to come back. Cannon, we've got to go before they come back. Before he realizes—oh, Cannon, we've got to go—now." Julie's voice was high with hysteria, shrill, demanding, insistent. "NOW."

"Shut up," Imelda said.

To think, all this time, he had been waiting for this. Waiting to find that Johnny had taken his Julie away; waiting and hoping not, while those who had once believed him had ceased to believe him, so that he himself had grown careless and hopeless, and all he could feel now was relief, because *something* had happened to show he was right and because Johnny had kidnapped the wrong one. He wanted to snigger at the mistake because it was all Johnny's fault for refusing to look at Julie's picture in the first place, refusing ever to meet her, couldn't look at her face even when he had had her beaten, serve him right. But after the relief, there was speechless rage, and outside that he was only aware of Julie's hand clawing at his arm, pulling him towards the door and the outside world.

"The police are coming," Imelda ventured comfortingly, as if that would be the answer to everything. "I don't know why you didn't call them at once."

"Because we were waiting for this gentleman," Pauline murmured. "Well, Cannon? Are you going to go and leave us to explain to them? What shall we say to the officers? We don't even know where he lives."

"He wouldn't take her there," Cannon said quickly. He shuffled his feet. He never did want the police near Johnnyboy; always tried to save him from that. Besides, he would never take her home; never. "I don't suppose they said where they were taking her? Or why?" A foolish question. He wanted to be gone, out there, anywhere with Julie, even if it was nowhere, running in the dark, and he was finding it difficult to consider anything else while she still pulled at him in panic, even though he knew there was something wrong with his reaction; something abominably selfish.

"She'll be *all right*," Julie was screaming. "They said they'd bring her back. He *promised*. Sarah's always *all right*—she's a survivor. Don't think about Sarah, think about *me*. Get me away before he comes back for *me*. She did it for us."

There was a moment's silence and her hand dropped from his arm.

"They're only taking her for *treatment,*" she gabbled. "He won't hurt her as soon as he knows she isn't *yours,* why should he? And that's why she let it happen. To give us time to get away, don't you see? Come on, Cannon. *Come on.*"

There were echoes of similar, brisker orders from Sarah. "Come *on,* Cannon." Julie was in a rage of cowardice and he could not blame her for it. *Treatment; taken away for treatment.* Giving us time to escape. He tried to justify it. They won't hurt her, not *really* hurt. And if Johnny were to wreak his revenge on Sarah, surely that would spend his forces and be the end of it. There was always a limit to his energies. He wouldn't do it twice; it was over; the loss of face, the wasted malice would exhaust him; they were free; he knew it; they should go, now, anywhere, and never hear of him again. He thought of his own cowardice and what it had created: Sarah's portrait, prominently displayed, part of him wanting to say, I told you so, don't say I didn't warn you. I *told* you and you stopped believing me. Let her take the brunt. She would outwit Johnnyboy, with her hands tied behind her back, a woman like that; she was clever with men, a *tart.* She knew loads of men.

Not men like Johnny. She couldn't imagine a soul like that any more than sweet, gentle-fingered William could. No one could. He could feel Pauline's eyes, gazing at him; her pale face glowing with pain, the voluminous handkerchief red with blood; the fine nose, bloated. What was the worst pain Johnnyboy could envisage to inflict on the woman he perceived as enemy and thief and rival? Going for *treatment.* He knew where they had taken her and knew in the same breath that no policeman would believe it or act on it soon enough. Julie was clutching him again. Freedom had a price. Somebody else was paying. He kissed her and ran from the room, followed by the sound of her screams. "I've done everything for you. *Everything.*"

It was not a special kind of car, Sarah noticed, as they drove away through the dark streets. Nothing about it designed for the conveyance of prisoners, no extra locks on the doors of a middle-range saloon. She could never remember the makes of cars—disinterest foxed the memory—but she tried to remember details in case she was asked and because it helped her to avoid the present. Blue: the inside of it was blue and the back of Johnnyboy's head was blackish grey as he drove with quiet precision. Perhaps she could get out if they slowed for a light; he was a careful driver, never exceeding the speed limit. Perhaps she should open her mouth and speak, but all she could have uttered was an instruction to go back and collect the right woman because that was all there was in her mind to say and she did not want to say it, not yet. Not until the convent was full and Julie was protected. Give them an hour. She felt for the handle of the door.

No need for locks. Only the big man, holding her hand like a father in the back seat of the limo taking the bride to church, proud and protective and possessive, his hand large enough to crush the bones of her wrist, the way he could have crushed the kitten. He had spared the kitten; she took some comfort from that and hung on to his final, hurried, whispered words and their suggestion of conscience. Don't worry, we'll bring her back, he'd said. She felt the loneliness of the condemned, the fear of the sacrificial victim led towards some altar in the presence of a crowd who applauded the ritual and would not let anyone spoil it. She had never quite understood the existence of evil. The blue upholstery stank of newness.

She could see where she was going: there was no subterfuge about it, no blindfold; no twists and turns. They were soon in the familiar territory of the West End with shoppers still streaming home, and hope rose like a bubble. It was all so ordinary; in a moment, she could step out and join the throng, run across this road and down the next and slip into the side-door of Selfridges to meet Mrs. Matthewson, or plunge into the stuffiness of the tube. They had cruised beyond Piccadilly, across Bond Street, pausing at the corner where the Mole lived. Past the house of another lover; there would never be any rescue provided by lovers; there never had been. Lovers were solace, not power; the strongest of emotions, the weakest links. Then they were in William's territory, the district of doctors: civilized, handsome, full of the promise of a cure. If they passed his house, she could wave at him, scream for help if she had such a thing as a voice left. An hour, and the convent would be safe. Cannon would have got there. Useless in a crisis; better than nothing. Take Julie away, you fool. Take her away. From inside the self-contained vacuum of her life she thought of the people she loved and doubted if any of them would try to help her even if they knew the danger. She doubted it without bitterness. Each to his own life. She had never expected much and she was not sure of what the danger was. Only that it was immense. She made herself small and silent and unobjectionable.

Not only William's territory but William's street. She recalled his kindly face with a desperate surge of affection, wanted to see him running along beside the car, tapping on the window, saying, "Stop, stop, stop. You've made a mistake."

They stopped.

Early evening, and the city, as far as he could sense, was lingering at the breakpoint between day and night. William would have liked a town crier to patrol this street, telling the hour, every hour, and confirming that all was well. Not that he doubted it as he surveyed the surgery with no more than the usual anxiety, checking the cleanliness, the detail, taking it in with a pride that no one else shared. He had dusted the reception area as if it had not been done early in the day and would not be done again, first thing in the morning, by the cleaner. He liked the way he had designed it, so that when one moved from the reception to the surgery there was only another pleasant vista towards the window when the door was open. William mourned the necessity for closed doors. He crossed and looked out. Traffic subdued by double glazing into no more than a distant buzz; lights catching empty windows. In the waiting room, the paintings glowed with their own life.

He always liked the building best when it was empty. Felt like a king in a castle, forgetting he was the mere tenant of a few rooms with his throne undermined by debt.

It was perverse of him to want the place to look comforting for tomorrow's patient, especially since the patient was not due to arrive until the afternoon, and heaven knows what disturbance there might be in the morning. Nothing arduous; he had checked. This evening would be alone with the journals, thinking time. The elaboration of his preparations for John Smith could mean nothing more than the fact that he was afraid of the man, and he decided that that was not the prime motivation for all this fussiness. The fear was of failure. Not being good enough even to inspire faith.

This is silly talk, William, and you were never any good at communication, he told himself, as he went down to the basement, finding no comfort in the chaos the way he usually did. There was an atmosphere here that he did not trust; the cold from the window, which since last week would not shut, warped by the wet. The place did not feel as if it belonged to him any more, but then, looking at his life, he did not think anything belonged to him. Back upstairs, checking again, suddenly a little bit lonely and wanting to talk, having a chat with the paintings, the way he did sometimes, although he was not usually quite so sober when he resorted to such inanimate company. Wanting Sarah, because Sarah would understand this, but pushing the thought from his mind. Good athletes and, possibly, good dentists should put such feeble need for womankind from mind on the eve of combat. But it wasn't combat: it was nothing more or less than *treatment*. They might do *nothing* tomorrow. No one was going to give him a medal for this. He wasn't even sure he was going to get any money.

The phone rang at the desk as he tidied things round it. He interrupted it, reluctant to hear the sound of his pre-recorded voice. "Yes?" he barked.

There was the sound of shuffling and adjustment, a gasp, as if the person phoning expected the anonymity of his recorded voice rather than this distinctly personal, impatient reply. Followed by a sniffing sound, a hawking into a handkerchief, a tremulous sigh and a sob. A patient with a post-operative problem—bound to be one of those. He softened his voice. "Yes," he murmured, "how can I help?" professional solicitude creeping into his tone like a wheeze.

"William? Is that you?" Isabella's sobbing grew earnest. He could feel himself melting, slightly. Who was it said, "Let me not go to death surrounded by wailing women"? Some king who was spoiled for choice. It didn't strike William as a bad way to go if one had to shuffle off the mortal coil in any kind of company at all; women rather than men, any time. A wailing woman was one in need and William liked to be needed.

"Isabella? What's the matter?" *There, there, there,* he wanted to say, but it might sound condescending. He took refuge in a cough, the way he sometimes did when searching for a patient's name, hoping the spasm would jerk it into memory.

"Nothing," she said. "Nothing, nothing, nothing." The voice trailed away, leaving behind it William's unsteady breathing. He flattered himself that her occasional calls to the answer-machine might have been something to do with concern for his health, but this was the first time she had taken the risk of communicating unhappiness. The sound of her distress provoked a series of responses: irritation, grief, concern, foolishness, guilt, and that shameful pitter-patter of the heart which had become his neurotic condition as soon as he heard her voice. Nightmares about Isabella and the children; day-dreams that she would come back through the door and beg his forgiveness.

"I made a mistake, Will, a bad mistake. I misjudged you."

He had once longed to hear such sentiments, but now they left him disconsolate and strangely annoyed. Why was she the only one who ever diminished him by calling him *Will*, and why say this *now*, when he had other things to think about, choosing a time when there was no possibility of his indulging the slightest sense of triumph?

"Do you think we could try again? I miss you so much."

Missed him? Such as, shacking up with someone richer while receiving maintenance without gratitude? That was *missing* someone? All the same, he felt a flush creep up from his neck and over his face and, if it wasn't quite pleasure he felt, it was a close relation, which he managed to control, as well as the silly smile on his face that made him vaguely embarrassed as if she was there, watching. The pause stretched into half a minute.

"Will . . . there's no one else, is there? No one special, I mean . . ."

No one. Just Sarah. Mysterious, adorable, dependable Sarah. A tart with heart and morals.

"Perhaps we should meet and talk about it."

"Can we do that soon?"

"Well, yes. Soon."

He was staring at the door, not even half listening to her. A crucial conversation in the history of his life, and he could not pay attention, because there was someone outside, knocking against the door so hard it vibrated. He had the ridiculous thought that it was her on the other side, only pretending to talk from a distance.

"Like now?" Isabella was saying plaintively. "Oh, darling, I'm so unhappy . . ."

"Soon."

He was slamming down the receiver, not quite believing that he had actually done that and choked her off. He watched, with his fingers still touching the lifeline of the phone, as the door opened abruptly.

John Smith first, smart and unsmiling, Sarah next, and the fat man who had gone through the records bringing up the rear. John took the key from behind the desk, locked the door behind himself and gave the key to the fat man. It was a heavy door, like the separate door to the surgery, guarding against crazies in a misguided search for drugs even in these respectable quarters. The presence of all three in the small area by the desk was at first astounding then immediately claustrophobic. John's aftershave was oppressive and the silence was overwhelming. William gave his indecisive, nervous cough before he spoke, sounding officious. "Mr. Smith, you've got the time wrong. You're due here tomorrow. Not today. Tomorrow."

John Smith sighed, spoke softly, shaking his head at the error of such blithe assumptions. "Oh, no, it was always going to be today. Tomorrow's too close to Christmas." He ushered Sarah forward, without touching her. She was held by the fat man's meaty paw on her neck, making her stoop under his weight, preventing her eyes from meeting his. "And *this*," he was still murmuring, "is the patient. Bring her in."

"Sarah . . . what are you doing?"

"Julie," she said. "My name is Julie Smith."

She was propelled past William's stupefied face into the surgery. The fat man hesitated on the threshold for a second, disoriented by the absence of the chair in his immediate line of vision, then saw it round the corner. It was low to the ground in this resting state, easy to shove her into it, but following, watching with increasing agitation, making small, inarticulate squawks of protest, what puzzled William most was her calm lack of resistance, as if she had already learned the futility of it. She was not easily coerced—that much he knew; she was as stubborn as a mule, and it followed that there was some form of conspiracy between them. A joke, a trick, a mystery designed to make him look a fool, like a strippergram victim at a party, all of them knowing about it except himself. Then the fat man, with the efficiency of a policeman in a second-rate film, produced a piece of tape and attached her wrists to the supports at the side of the chair, so unlikely and deft a set of movements that William could not believe it, even though he was beginning to perceive the sickness of the joke. The fat man found a scalpel out of a drawer to cut the tape. They had been here before. She lay as still and uncomfortably posed as a plastic mannequin in a shop window. Only the abundance of curling red hair, spilling over the back of the chair, showed her to be real.

"A woman's crowning glory," John Smith was saying dreamily. "Her hair. They can seduce a man with hair like that. The smile's more important, don't you think?" He was locking the surgery door, putting the key in his top pocket. "Cannon was always a sucker for a smile," he went on, "because of the reaction to his own. Must have dreamed of a smile like hers." He paused, remembering something, his face sad. The figure in the chair remained immobile; William could see that only her fingers moved restlessly, as if trying to signal, looking for something to clasp. John Smith seemed to remember where he was and his purpose, looked at William directly and spoke with the authoritative patience of a teacher to a recalcitrant child.

"And it was that smile which hooked him," he went on, "*stole* him from me. *My* lover, *my* heart, *my* flesh and blood, *my* soul, *my* reason for anything. And then *you*, Mr. Dentist, *you* did the rest. You gave him his film-star teeth, so that when he looked in the mirror he didn't see *me* any more. Made him think he was different from *me*. Kid himself he was no longer part of *us*. And how can I live without him? Answer me that, will you? I rot inside, is what happens. I rot away, like my houses." He was shouting by now, wagging his finger, coming closer, so the spittle landed on William's face. Then he controlled himself, became calmer. "No, I can't blame you for *that*. Such a conscientious fellow you are. But it does seem fair you should share the punishment. Don't get me wrong . . . I'm not asking much . . ."

He perched on the ledge to the far left of the chair, still not looking at her, legs crossed, relatively relaxed, the sweet soul of reason. "I don't want you to *kill* her," he added conversationally, as if they were simply man to man in a bar, discussing a friendly proposition of mutual interest. "It would be *dreadful* if you did. What *you* have to do is wreck that smile, tooth by tooth. I mean, there must be a way of poisoning them at the root, just like someone did with mine. Murder them and that fucking smile. No anaesthetics, of course." He looked at his watch, businesslike. "How long do you think it will take?"

"I thought it was *you* who wanted treatment," William said. "I want to treat *you*."

"No. How long will this take?"

The obscenity and seriousness of the revolting suggestions finally penetrated William's shocked and sluggish mind. He punched John Smith on the jaw. The blow jarred his wrist, seemed to recoil like a heavy gun, thumping into his shoulder as if he had missed contact with flesh and hit the wall instead. He was as fragile as paper, all height, no density, no skill for a fight. John Smith returned with a punch to the abdomen and a series of kicks to the legs. The room swam; he was on his back with John and the fat man leaning over him solicitously, so easy they were scarcely short of breath.

"You forgot to tell him something, Mr. Smith, sir," the fat man whispered. Their expressionless faces mesmerized him, and out of the corner of his eye he could see the fat man's enormous boot, pinning his forearm to the ground with enough pressure to hurt extremely.

"Oh, that," John Smith said carelessly. "I forgot to mention that. Silly me. If you don't do what I say, my friend here is going to stamp on your hands. *Pulp* them. Your precious hands . . . and you do *love* your hands, don't you? You even have fucking *drawings* of your own hands about the place, like other stupid idiots have portraits. *Pulp*. Not a whole bone left, even the little ones. I hold, he *stamps*." William swallowed the scream. The foot pressed against his arm relentlessly; the pain increased. Then the fat man held his right hand lovingly, tut-tutting under his breath, bent the fingers back until William gasped. He could picture his hand dismembered, all those complex bones rearranged in a pattern of red on the clean white floor.

Sarah's voice, sounding resigned: "Better do as you're told, William. You need your hands."

"Why?" William screamed. "*Why?*"

"Because she's a thief," John roared. "A fucking *thief.*"

"You aren't a thief, are you, Sarah?" The body on the chair seemed to wilt and remained utterly silent. It perturbed him almost more than anything else. Smith's smell was a disgusting mixture of adrenalin and scent. William hated him.

"And it's not called Sarah, it's called Julie," the fat man stated, then clamped his mouth shut, aware of speaking out of turn. William looked at him. Of the two, he might be the one with conscience.

"She's—"

"Shut up, William. If you don't do what they want, they'll do it themselves."

Yes, they would.

They seemed impervious to the sound of her voice, both of them jittery now, anxious for something to begin, as volatile as crazed insects, mad with captivity. William was on his feet, hoisted without effort in arms that felt like girders, standing upright, clasping his hands and gnawing on a knuckle as if he were a baby instead of the puppet he felt. The fat man was handing him the white coat. The door was locked, the building was empty, and that mystery person in the chair, his lover, his best friend, seemed to encourage them by her very compliance. And his hands, his trembling hands. He could not live without his dextrous, sensitive hands. His mind went back to the bonfire, the last time he had worried about his hands, wondering then if he would risk them, for love, for rescue, for his living, for his pride, for anything. The fat man was holding out his white coat. It reminded him now of the uniform of a butcher: high-necked, double-breasted stiff white cotton, the better to absorb the stains. *If I don't do it they will; better me than them; what will they do if I renege?* He imagined an amateur let loose with a high-speed drill. Mind in overdrive, brain going tick, tick, tick, like a bomb, making his voice sound as clear as a voice that belonged to some other person entirely, another kind of man. The Inquisition's torturer, paid by the hour, with an agenda all of his own.

His hands were stinging as he pulled on the gloves that would make the allergies worse; his hands remembered pain in the way he hoped the mouth did not; hands were impossible to mend. Why did Sarah fail to deny she was a thief, and a thief of what? Affection? Lust and trust? For the slow passage of time expended on putting on the gloves, he hated her, too. For all the trouble and the disquiet she brought along with her reassurance; for never letting him know her. Never letting him be needed or letting him near. The resentment was temporary, gave him that distance he needed to *think*.

"There's one thing I need to establish," he found himself saying. "I mean about your priorities, Mr. Smith. I presume you aren't coming in for treatment tomorrow, even though I have blocked out the time, so I'd like to be paid, please. And for this. Two thousand, minimum. Be fair. I can't keep myself on less." He needed them to believe he was a torturer paid by the hour; he needed, in one way, to think that himself. There was a nod in response, a glint in the eye suggesting admiration, a hint of true minds meeting. The hatred burned like a furnace beneath his skin. "And there's another thing," he continued, "which I need to know before I start. Priorities. I can't do two things at once. Sure, I can disfigure her, but simply pulling teeth will take two minutes. What is it you want? A wrecked mouth and pain? Or do you just want me to take out her teeth?"

"Pain," said John Smith. "Pain and all the rest. But pain."

"I can, as you suggest, poison at the root, so they drop out later. Very painful too. Will that do?"

"Yes. That's what I told you. Drill in the poison. *Do it.*"

He prevaricated. He tried to say that the injection he proposed was disinfectant saline—they didn't want her dead, did they? No syringes, John Smith said, not unless I say so. Only needles for stitching. They would ration what he could use: scalpels and drills, the elevator for extraction, the clamp he used to keep the mouth open. It seemed that John Smith had made an inventory of the equipment and was not going to let him use a syringe. John Smith wanted him to use the drill without the water coolant. He liked the idea of a tooth glowing hot. Impossible, William said. This one works with the water or not at all.

One lie, another lie. They let him give her an antibiotic; dries the saliva, he said. They all seemed to be getting along fine, even cheerfully. William popped the pill into her mouth, watched her swallow obediently while he tried to communicate with her eyes, pretending he was talking to them, but talking to her.

"Reminds me of the Inquisition," he remarked. "Or any era when the professional torturer was employed. They were never paid enough. Needed a union."

The fat man laughed uncomfortably; John Smith didn't. *Remember what we talked about, Sarah? Remember walking in the park? Remember what I said a good dentist would do? Put on a show . . . a performance. Avoid destruction. Trust me.*

"Stop talking."

By now the identity of the patient was totally irrelevant. She was just a thing. John Smith could look at her now, arranged himself to watch. Fascinated and disgusted and determined. The aspirator in her mouth made its liquid slushing sound and, unable to delay further, William found his scalpel.

They wanted blood; they should have blood. Apicectomy of the lower central and lateral incisors. He found himself lecturing under his breath: this is the second line of treatment after root-canal surgery has failed. And why does it fail? Because it is impossible to prepare and fill the apical third of the root, for whatever reason: because it is persistently infected; because there's a broken instrument blocking the canal, so you can't reach it from the occlusal surface, so you have to get in there, through the gum. As if poisoning the roots.

He would concentrate on the lower front teeth. They were so much less visible; it was the upper buccal surfaces that were the aesthetic hallmark of the mouth, but John Smith would not think of that once distracted by blood. William pulled down the lower lip, held it with a lightly weighted clamp. A clamp holding the mouth open and an uncontrolled, hanging lip made a person look subnormally stupid; Smith would like that. He fussed with the equipment as long as he dared, mincing round it, delaying until he could not delay. Apicectomy was safest on the incisors and canines. He cut an incision across the gum level with the emerging teeth. Perfect gingiva; perfect teeth; he winced as he did it. Then he began to cut down behind his incision in a chiselling motion, keeping his hand steady and his eyes focused on the task. He released the gum and the periodontal ligaments, revealing the root of the tooth and the alveolar bone. He could never do this without being reminded of a precise butcher, shaving meat from the spine of a carcass. Such central teeth; such a lot of blood. Maybe the blood alone would satisfy. He had the horrible thought that he had overdone it and maybe it would have sufficed to cut a single flap for a single tooth rather than four. He peeled back the section of gum and ligament neatly. The gum flapped over the lower lip; the effect was garishly hideous. Stay still, Sarah; stay as still as you can so I don't make mistakes.

The movement of her head was limited by the chair; she was rigid with pain but braced against it. The aspirator slushed at blood; he kept on adjusting it. Keep still: this is difficult enough without an assistant, especially under such watchful eyes. Her head seemed fixed to the back of the chair, heavy and immovable; there was, so far, an appalling control in her, co-operating with him, understanding, he hoped—oh, God, he hoped she understood. She was staring, fixedly, at the light, as if it could save her. Staring, but she could not keep her tongue still: it moved incessantly, poking over her lower teeth in her open mouth, interfering and insulting.

"Make her stop that," John said, his only words in minutes. "Make her bloody stop."

"She can't stop it. No one can."

"Cut it, then."

"No, there's a better way."

William had never done this before, but he had seen it done. He took a long, curved needle with silken suturing thread, stuck it straight though the forward flesh of the tip of the tongue, doubled it back and tied it round the prominent third molar to the left. The wisdom tooth was gone: he could secure the thread without much difficulty. There—did that look savage enough? The gurgling, gagging sound in the back of her throat had all the makings of a scream. He adjusted the aspirator again. That was what it meant to be tongue-tied.

He continued to chisel, revealing more bone. More blood. John was restless, waiting for the drill, shouting for it. William could no longer avoid the drill. Bloodlust was not enough.

The appalling thing was that he was proud of his technique. He could not do this without being absorbed.

Cannon crawled through the basement window and crept up the stairs. There was something wrong with his left arm: it functioned, but badly—

no force in the grip. Outside the surgery door he listened and heard, briefly, the high-pitched whine of the drill. There was a strange, distorted, semi-human sound in the wake of it; a pause for either discussion or argument; the unmistakable sound of Johnny's guttural laughter; the sucking noise of the aspirator, louder than anything else, and, again, that deep-throated moaning like someone mimicking an animal. Would they kill her? Would Johnnyboy watch as William's hands were smashed to pieces? It would hardly bother what passed for his conscience to do that to a dentist. Was it Johnny himself who wielded the tools of torture? No, he would always delegate under threat; no one understood that about him. And what, from the other side of a heavy locked door, could he do about it? They would hear if he called the police. There was no time to call the police—it was too late for that and this was his task, not theirs. It had nothing to do with anyone else. It had to do with Johnny suborning everything Cannon had and everything he was, maiming and corrupting his friends in the process. If only he could make the anger so cold. Then there was the drill again, followed by that same unbearable, inhuman sound.

Cannon was back in the basement. Almost a second home, he knew it so well, knew what an arsenal it was. He was calmer now, cool even, aware of the left arm throbbing. Let's play a game, Johnny, the way we used to, remember? One of those boyhood games. We did it before; I can do it again, even though I promised I wouldn't. He would have to remember his instinct to get the mixture right. Potassium permanganate crystals; throatwash. The sugar, in a well-handled, sticky packet left ready for someone's tea. The malfunctioning sterilizing kettle for dental instruments, which would contain it. Fate provided the tools. William never threw anything away. It was insane. He could destroy them all, but anything seemed preferable to the sounds Sarah made.

The purpose of the apicectomy is to sustain an apical seal at the end of the root, to prevent the invasion of bacteria . . . Once the apex of the tooth is exposed, excise. They would have the smell of burning, which was not burning but dentine dust. The apex of the first incisor was easy to find, marked by a bulge. "I've isolated the roots," William said. "Now I'll poison them." The bleeding was still copious. He thought only of the technique; ignored the tongue that strained against the knot; the hands in the shackles turning bruised and blue, the wrists raw with burns. It was a final cruelty that she could neither clench her fists or scream. Her eyes had the vacancy of a dying dog he had once moved to the side of the road, careful of the bite. Tears flowed quietly from her eyes into her hair. The lead X-ray apron he had laid across her chest as extra ballast to steady her was littered with debris. He pushed away the high-speed drill.

"Why are you doing that?"

"Slower drill. Hurts more." Slower drill because the high-speed would lock itself in the bone. The slower drill did less damage: John Smith would be more familiar with its vibrating sound. Choosing the site carefully, he began to drill not the root but the bone. Denser, harder; marginally less painful. Look out for the mental nerve; damage that and . . . The drill had a different, vibrating, droning, louder but less sibilant sound. It echoed in his ears; he could feel it in his own bones.

They needed more blood and he needed an excuse to stop. He let the burr of the drill catch the inside of her cheek, watched as all that copious blood supply responded to the wound. It would take him a while to mop up. Perhaps, by then, John would have tired of this, but he looked on with the rapt attention of a keen student. The fat man huddled in a corner with a handkerchief held against his mouth, but still warily observant of what William did rather than what the patient suffered. The flaps of the gum still hung over her lower lip. Unless John tired, he would have to move on. Drill further holes in the bone, big enough to see through. Windows into the mouth; the drill again; the fine spray of healthy bone.

"There," he said. "That's enough for now."

"No," said John, standing over him. "It isn't enough."

William took the elevator he used to raise a tooth for extraction, deftly punched a hole in the atrium of her mouth. Blood poured out of her nose.

There was a bucket for the mix, crystals and sugar, treated with respect, but hurriedly. Three parts to one, and he was filling up the spare space with lumps of plaster. No detonator; this little mix required none. Cannon was hurrying up the steps, like an anxious cook with a meal for the master, the sterilizer kettle upturned, his finger blocking the aperture in the lid. A fire—he could simply start a fire with this. Why not? But he had to get through the door and get *her* out. William, too. And he would have the advantage, because no one but he would be expecting the bang, if it worked. They would be dazed. He was visualizing the layout of the surgery; he had been in that chair often enough to know it by heart, always conscious of his surroundings, always trying to catch sight of something new to avoid the Siemens letters on the overhead light. You should decorate this ceiling with wild colours, he had suggested; make a distraction. Or I could paint my face, William had said. But there was nothing wrong with William's face. It was a kind and gentle face, worried and infinitely reassuring. Sarah's, too, if it was still recognizable by now.

Cannon remembered the layout: the chair round the corner not in line with the door; the little seating area; the window further beyond. He let a little of the mixture trickle out of the sterilizer as he walked backwards, slowly, leaving a snail-like trail to the basement steps, then skirted round it and placed the upturned container close to the surgery door. It sat unsteadily on a small heap of mix, looking untidy and harmless. Cannon hesitated. A piece of homemade explosive like this was not entirely predictable: it might simply burn; it might do so much more than he intended. All he could think of was the fact that the fragments had no choice but to travel in straight lines and not round corners. Still he hesitated. *Cannon, you always overreact, you stupid creature—you do too much or too little, nothing by halves . . . No judgement of your own responses, indolent or frenetic.* Sarah's voice from the back of his head, scolding with affection. And then, as he hesitated still, that terrible, gurgling sound of agony. He ran to the shelter of the basement stairs and flattened himself against the wall. Hesitated again, watching the flame of his lighter.

The thudding whine of the drill . . . the third hole in the bone. She would not, could not faint away, and all William could wish for her was the mercy of oblivion. He was pausing too much, going too slow, his lack of dedication becoming obvious. John Smith was impatient, beginning to move about, and it occurred to William how pointless was all this deployment of skill. They were still going to tread on his hands, and he had the added, tired fear that at any moment now John would seize the drill himself, that all the careful watching was only for the purpose of establishing how it worked. He would push the dentist out of the way, activate the machine in the way he had learned through his close observation, drill through the incisors, shatter the exposed roots . . . or he would grab the scalpel and lace her face with wounds. That would be true disfigurement; this, so far, was not. John began to prowl, stood behind William, breathing down his neck. William's coat was soaked with perspiration, his hair wet, his hands slippery. From the fat man, now standing at Sarah's feet, there rose a stench of vomit.

"I think we could do with a drink," John Smith said, and moved towards the door. "You're playing games with me, Mr. Dentist. You know that?"

"Games?" William screamed. "*Games?*" He pointed at the hideous mouth. "Look at what you've made me do."

John Smith shook his head, reached towards his top pocket for the key. "You wait until I start. Then *no one* will want her back."

Cannon lit the fuse.

14

The sound of an explosion always brought tears to his eyes: jubilation, of a kind, to a toddling boy; later, in his early teens, they were the tears that mourned anticlimax, a touch of regret, until finally they became tears of horror that it was now too late to stop it. Cannon's forefingers were firmly wedged in his ears, but the blast still shook his feet, his knees, his skinny ribcage, and the tears followed through eyes squeezed shut against the flash. There was always the desire, again as a child on a piece of wasteland, to run towards the sound immediately, until he learned better the wisdom of waiting to see what the first flash did. The flash and the flame were worse on his side of the door, the sound of splintering wood lost in the settling of the debris and that sudden, wonderful silence. There would be fires; he remembered the surgery and its mostly metallic contents and tiled floor. Then he remembered wooden-framed pictures on the reception walls: he had forgotten the vulnerability of those.

The dense smoke was grey white in colour, thicker than the mist of dawn, but penetrable. There was a crackle of flame, the tinkle of glass from a window he could not see. The light-bulb central to the reception area remained intact and burning. Something else was burning, with a sickly, oily smell. Cannon stumbled towards the surgery door.

A huge, squat figure emerged, screaming, tripping into the crater left by the bomb, stumbling ankle deep into the hole, the body falling forward, saved by the hands. Then he was crawling until he was upright, arms thrashing a passage through the smoke so that Cannon could feel the draught of his progress across the room to the outer door, howling as he went, like a drunk baying for the moon. He could hear him shaking the door, the howling turning to sobbing, the door released and the flat footsteps running away. A survivor, then. A ludicrous, unbidden thought crept into Cannon's mind about how Johnnyboy never could keep the hired help. How he might have enjoyed this.

Then he was shouting himself, standing on the threshold, avoiding the hole and the shattered door, screaming, "*William! Sarah! William!*" The far window had gone: there was splintered wood, the lights in here still burning; the intense heat of an oven and the spotlight over the dental chair shining down the blessing of Siemens. The aspirator still gurgled.

Cannon's brother lay at the furthest end of the room, in a straight line from the door, tidily out of the way. Cannon noted the figure on the floor, familiar even in the smoke; familiar from any angle. He looked for William, who stood like a long thin rag doll, hands loose against his side, back against the wall around the corner, his whole body numb. Cannon shook him, the response was nil, shook him again, harder, and then slapped him across the face. William prised himself away from the wall, his eyes beginning to focus on Cannon's face, then on the rest of the room, then on Sarah. Cannon followed his roving glance. Bile rose in his throat. Both of them were covered in blood, Sarah's mouth a wound clamped open, her lap a repository for blood. The bomb—no, the blast did not go round corners. The bomb had not done this. *William* had done this.

"Christ, Jesus . . ." He moved, in some instinctive attempt to block Sarah from William's sight. William came back to life, snarling, screaming at him, "Get out of the way, get out of here," pushing Cannon away, pummelling at his chest even before he recognized him.

Cannon retreated, suddenly shivery; watched. He could not go to Johnnyboy, not yet. It was not Johnnyboy he had been trying to save.

"Get me an icepack, you cretin—*now.*"

"Where?"

"Fridge, behind me—are you blind?"

William was hovering over that dreadful mouth. There was no sound from her, the lip hanging like a foreign object belonging to no known creature. The eyes were closed. He wanted to remove the weighted clamp and the clamp that held the mouth open, close the mouth and let everything rest. No. Scissors; remove suture to free the tongue, no, leave that till last. Bring the flap back up, stitch, and, Christ, in this smoke, the place was rife with infection. Work. Don't go too fast.

Cannon found the icepack and put it down on her lap. He moved towards the figure on the floor. The smoke was clearing efficiently through the broken window; it blurred rather than ruined his sight, and his eyes still stung. There was a distant sound of sirens. Cannon dreaded going closer. Perhaps only part of Johnny had been in line with the door, not all of him.

"See what you've done, Johnny? See what you've done?" Cannon said, kneeling next to him. The eyes were open, the chest heaving for breath, the clothes torn, a gash in the forehead. The tip of a key was sticking out of his bosom below the left nipple, giving the faint illusion that if it were pulled and turned, he would spring to his feet like a mechanical toy. Such a little key would not kill him. "Didn't mean it, Johnny. Didn't quite get the mix right, did I?"

The hand, which had been clawing at the groin, reached out, feeling for his own. There was a huge splinter of wood sticking out of the palm. He did not seem to see it. The sirens had grown closer, deafening in a static whine outside. "At least somebody noticed, didn't they, Johnnyboy?" Cannon said. There was the flicker of a smile.

"We never did get round to the Houses of Parliament, did we, Johnny?" He patted the hand ineffectually. "Now, don't die on me, Johnny. Don't do that. See, no one else knows me like you. See, we didn't care about fuck all, did we, Johnny? I'll be lonely without you. There'll never be another bastard like you . . ."

There was a whispered sound from the pursed mouth. Johnnyboy was still hiding his teeth.

"You won't want her now, will you?"
"No, Johnny. No. No. No. I want you."

Two mattress sutures. Enough to hold it. Stuff the mouth with xylocaine gel . . . No, benzedrine hydrochloride, good, topical anaesthetic and anti-inflammatory. Release the tongue; unclamp the jaw. Let the lip hold everything in place. Hope the bleeding'll stop now. Icepack. Trust the mouth to heal. The ambulanceman coming up the stairs would treat for shock. Do everything in the right order, you fool, don't *rush.* He slit the ropes with the scalpel, reset the chair to bring her upright, chafed her hands. And all to the sound of Cannon's keening. There were shouts from the other room.

He took off his filthied jacket, folded her hands, tucked the jacket under her chin for warmth. The heat had faded fast: a damp chill filled the room, smoke drifting from behind him. He stared at her vacant face, wanting to wipe away the blood. No, not yet; too tender to touch.

Cannon's keening was down to a steady sound, a slow howling of grief.

What to say? He did not know what to say; he never knew what to say. *I have disgraced everything I ever stood for.* Lies would be best for now. William moved to the shattered door and looked beyond. Three masked men in the room, looking like aliens. He noticed how two of them were stamping out small fires. He looked, as he always automatically looked, for Cannon's picture on the wall, looked again. That was the one smouldering on the floor. He knew it by the remnants of the frame.

He carried her through the clearing smoke. It was dark outside: they would mistake him for a rescuer. No one was going to admire his technique. *She was in the middle of treatment when the bomb went off,* that's what he would say. He set her down on the old dental chair by the basement stairs. He kept his hand over her mouth to make sure the lip stayed closed. She breathed raggedly though her blood-filled nose. It looked, even to his own eyes, as if he was deliberately trying to stop her from speaking.

She was never going to love him now.

15

On the feast of the conversion of St Paul, three weeks into the New Year, Pauline sat and bowed her head in prayer. The chapel was warm. No one should be asked to conduct intimate conversations with God in the cold: life was too short for that.

The ability to pray was slow to arrive. It was no use talking to the Creator and expecting Him to direct what she wanted to say into the consciousness of others when more direct communication was required. She could not hold the necessary conversation with God. All she could do was hold imaginary conversations with the human beings she most needed to see and pray for the intervention of the saints to send those people to her door. Her conscience was far from happy. She seemed to have alienated her acquaintance. Sarah, beloved Sarah, who never seemed to know how much she was loved; Julie, who was maintaining the silence peculiar to those who had revealed a little too much of themselves and were ashamed of it. Julie, with her bitter words between the time Cannon had left and the others had arrived, none of them to be believed, because fear and fury made liars of them all. Pauline apologized for her lack of concentration and told the Lord it was just as well He had made her a nun and not a priest. She would never have been able to obey the ultimate strictures of the confessional.

They had been given copious quantities of wine over Christmas. Pauline seemed to have consumed the lion's share and felt relieved that the supply was not endless. So easy to take to that kind of thing, especially if one had an obsessive disposition. In a minute, she was going to sit in the parlour and smoke a cigarette since in the hierarchy of sins it seemed entirely unimportant. She felt the bridge of her nose, still tender to the touch, the black-eyed bruises no longer more than permanent shadows. Her fine proboscis would remain tender for months. As an excuse for bad habits, it was adequate.

Forgive me, Lord, I betrayed my niece into the hands of sinners. I did it for the best of reasons, namely that she was *stronger* than the victim they intended to wound. She knew more about life; she was *less* vulnerable; she was the cleverer. Had there been a chance that they might have taken me instead, I would have gone. You know that, Lord, don't you? But I told a silent lie, and let my own flesh and blood suffer, and I cannot see any justification for that. Or, more to the point, I do not for the life of me see how *she* will ever see the justification for that. I have tried to see her, Lord, and she has evaded me. Can I blame her? But I *need* her, Lord. I cannot carry this burden.

And give me the right words to say to this man. He has even more on his conscience than I.

William sat in the parlour, indifferent to his surroundings. He flexed his hands, extended his arms and held them rigid to see if his fingers still trembled. The tremor was improving, so that he was only noticing what was not visible to anyone else. He doubted it would ever quite go, which would not matter one way or another if the General Medical Council, at the end of their deliberations, should decide he was still fit to practise. Early indications showed a tendency to leniency; there was a shortage of dentists. Sexual misbehaviour alarmed them most, and this particular patient had lived to tell no such tale. Had not only lived but had exonerated him. It was the dentist who had lost his innocence.

Pauline glided into the room at the same time as William began to nudge himself out of his reverie and notice where he was. There were three statues of saints. Perhaps in another life he would collect icons, the better to bless his existence. He thought of the destroyed paintings, drawings and sketches that had occupied the reception-room walls and reflected without regret that the patients had noticed them as little as he had noticed these. Pauline came towards him, looking relieved to see him. Two people, sent to limbo.

"Don't call me the inquisitor's apprentice, will you?" he said. "It's the kind of description which tends to stick."

She shook her head. "I wouldn't dream of it." She inspected him closely, eyes examining for the details of thinning hair, requiring a comb. Longer hair than she remembered, thinner limbs, too, the face gaunt and the hands restless—a man fighting the demons of his own wretchedness. The mere presence of them made her feel stronger. God put her on this earth to *do* things, not to loll around in a self-indulgent mess of recriminations, and nor should he. She was not going to have it.

"Do you smoke, William? No? Well, don't mind if I do. Imelda will bring us some coffee in a minute. Do you know, she doesn't grind her teeth any more? We're all very pleased, I can tell you. You did a good job there."

"I doubt the connection, but thank you. I'm glad someone's better for seeing me."

He was not going to say, Smoking is bad for your teeth. Life was bad for the teeth. The people who smoked managed to stay alive. Cannon's brother had scarcely smoked, William had been told, and he was the one who was dead. William was suddenly unsure of why he was here but, then, there did not need to be a particular purpose, apart from the critical need of each of them to talk to the other.

"Are you *sure* she'll make a full recovery? *They* say she has. They tell me things, you see. I'm her only relative so they have to, even though she doesn't want to see me . . . but are you *sure?*"

"Everything I did was deliberately done to cause minimum long-term damage. The capacity of the mouth for recovery is miraculous. You see, what I did was—"

"Yes, yes," Pauline interrupted. "Quite." She had considered the detail and did not want it rehearsed.

Silence fell for a minute, until they both began talking at once, both wanting to avoid contemplating the pain. Pauline had knelt in prayer, trying to assume that pain to herself, offering her own injury as inadequate compensation. The problem with prayer was the rarity of seeing the result.

"Cannon? What about Cannon?" Her voice prevailed over his, but he had the better information.

"In his brother's house, with Julie, for lack of anywhere else. Unhappy—how could he be otherwise?—even though there are compensations. The child—he thinks of the child. He's on police bail for the explosion, doesn't know what will happen any more than they do themselves until they've done with enquiring. But they found the fat man, you know. Not *found*, as such. He found them."

"Don't tell me what he said."

She drew on the cigarette, looked round for the priest's ashtray. Why them and not her? Imelda whisked into the room with a tray of coffee. Weak and milky, the way William hated it. She dumped it down with a crash, smiled at him warmly, scowled at Pauline and left.

"We're a little bored, that's the truth of it," Pauline said. "After all the excitement. And Cannon, now. He'll be relatively rich, I suppose. The brother's will . . ."

"There wasn't one. He inherits anyway. There's no one else. He offered to pay for the surgery. I said no."

She clicked her tongue, stifling the unworthy thought, *And perhaps he'd like to make a contribution here, too,* a thought that had no place in this conversation but was second nature to anyone like herself, whatever the situation. She had spent her religious life begging shamelessly for things. What she wanted to ask was, Do you think she will *ever* forgive us? and what she asked was, "And your surgery? Is that coming along?"

"Yes. It's workable. Not beautiful, but workable. Buildings can mend very fast. Like the mouth, given money. I don't want to work. I desperately don't want to work. But I have to. I've got faithful patients. I don't want to send them to anyone else and they don't want to go."

"That's entirely right, William. Couldn't be more right. That's exactly what you have to do. Work. And the damage . . . what about the damage?"

"Not as bad as it seemed. As Cannon said, he's good with a bomb."

"Not *so* good. The effect was the last he intended."

"*Was* it?"

There was another lengthy pause, devoted to the sipping of boiling coffee that tasted of nothing, offset, in William's case, by a sweet digestive biscuit that stuck to his teeth. They were failing to comfort one another; a little awkward.

"I wonder if *she* knows how much we love her," Pauline said. "She never felt able to believe that anyone would or could love her, which is probably why she believes in the safety of numbers and being needed. And fun, of course. Never could believe in being loved after that unfaithful husband of hers . . . and that sadist and . . . Never mind. She'll come round and bounce back. She always does. She's got a long memory but a great talent for forgiveness." She seemed to find that reflection infinitely reassuring.

"I didn't know anything much about her history," William said wonderingly. "I didn't know much about her at all."

Pauline glared at him, suddenly changing from the concerned confidante with an equally troubled confessor into a matriarch approached disrespectfully by an unsuitable suitor for the favours of a daughter. "Well, you'd better find out, hadn't you? Go and find her."

Cannon had thrown everything out of the living room into the back garden. Everything. Julie had not tried to stop him. They would not be here if it were not for her condition: he would have stayed anywhere rather than here, but this last of Johnnyboy's houses, the one currently occupied, would be free of rot and awash with creature comforts. He had always done that: gutted the bathroom and installed something new, new kitchen, new carpets, for the pleasure of becoming bored with them and moving on to install the same kind of thing all over again. Cannon hated the stultifying warmth of it: he could feel the smell of Johnny in his nostrils, oozing from the pores of his skin; he did not know if he wanted to eradicate it or preserve it. Windows open, both of them used to the cold. Not a stick of furniture left in the room and not a picture either. Julie remained quiet throughout this exercise, helping as help was requested whenever he forgot his constant instructions to her not to exert herself. He would regret this later. Perhaps.

She had the strange recurring desire to *pray.* Found that she crossed herself when he wept, warding off the devil. Saying thank you for salvation. Wanting to *pray* when she crossed the road.

He had whooped with glee as he levered the desk over the window-ledge and watched it fall, crashing through the branches of the tree. He had screamed with delight as he tossed out the ghastly painted-to-order battle scene with its garish reds and postured figures. He had yelled with rage as he slung the huge silver bird of prey to follow the painting. Then he had sat and wept. He wept often, at the slightest stimulus. Wept in her arms and huddled in corners; wept in the lavatory beyond what he thought was her hearing, when he thought he had wept too much. Now he laughed. He did both in turns.

She was trying to be patient with him. Filled with lassitude, a strange reaction to promised safety, she was passive rather than patient. The realization that Cannon was the inheritor of a dozen decaying houses was slow to arrive. They had never occupied more than a corner of anyone else's abode. This felt dispiriting, palatial in a way she disliked—another reason why she was not going to stop him turning it into a barn. The thought of sleeping in sheets Johnnyboy might have used gave her nightmares. She chose the ones still wrapped in their brand new packets; there were many of these from which to choose, as well as brand new towels, bath mats, napkins, cutlery. He had been a man fastidious to the point of mania; there were goods newly wrapped beyond the point of contamination, but when she imagined his fingers touching them, if only in the process of purchase, she shuddered.

"It's stuck," Cannon was muttering. "The fucking thing's stuck. Think I'll go downstairs and shake that tree."

"And then it'll fall on top of you."

"No, it won't."

"Leave it. It'll fall one of these days."

Such a robust tree, with big careful branches that looked, in their winter state, like a series of frosted feathers fit to make a nest. They did not sleep in Johnny's bed. That was gone on Christmas Eve. There was another bathroom, too, unused like the room beside it, virtually shrink-wrapped, waiting for the visitor who had never arrived.

"Both of them stuck."

"Let me look . . ."

"That silver eagle. And that painting of the mouth. How could he buy that?"

The silver eagle swayed in the branches like an anxious predator devoted less to hunting than fear of flying. She could almost feel sorry for it. Almost. The torn-up carpet revealed a fine wooden floor. She was hungry; always hungry. Today's rage of destruction was almost spent. Julie wondered, with a brief moment of dread, swallowed by inertia, how often this might happen, and what, if anything, might provoke it. The question seemed best answered as the occasion arose. She did not want him to cry. She wanted him to look at her without his glance ever sliding away. She wanted him to adopt this glorious south-facing room as his studio and paint her again and again, like Bonnard with his wife. She mourned the Bonnard sketch.

He sat back in one of the two remaining innocuous armchairs. They had muted rose-coloured fabric, which did not seem to offend him.

"Houses. I might have to go back to being a builder. When they've decided if they're going to charge me."

"No," she said. "No, no and no. You're a painter. An artist."

"A good builder's an artist, too."

"We'll just wait a while, shall we? We've g-g-g-g-got to this by a series of miracles, lovely. You can wait for another."

He had found Johnny's stash of booze and cigarettes—odd that he should keep it. He had never had much time for either, so Cannon said. Unlike his brother, who was not an alcoholic in the making but not a temperate being either, prone to binges. She had lived with those; she could handle them; she loved him; it was simple, if not for the fact that this house had been waiting for him, not for her, stuffed to the gunwales with things they did not need. Fully equipped for the advent of a baby. She was used to her tiny room in a silent place. When her energy returned they would not live here. Let him wreck it.

"I'm doing all this," Cannon said, "and then I suppose I'll wish I had something of him left. Something to remember him by."

She was very quiet. It was a knack to know when he wanted her to be quiet and when he wanted the intervention of speech. She was grateful for the lassitude. It made her slow and diplomatic. If in doubt say nothing, or go to sleep.

"I should go and see Sarah."

"Not yet, lovely. You saved her, you know. You don't *have* to go. Not yet. Besides, I went. I told you I went. I went for both of us. She's fine, she's moving house. You went to see William, I went to see Sarah. I told you she sent her love."

"Love? Are you sure?"

"Sure I'm sure."

"We'll get her and William to visit when we settle," he announced.

"Yes, yes. Of course we shall."

Crossing her fingers and saying to herself, *Of course we shan't. We begin* here. *We begin as if we really began* here, *at this point in our lives.* Our friendships are going to depend on exactly what we create from *now* onwards. Our lives are going to exclude *anyone* and *everyone* who knew us before now. *Every single one.* Clean slate, fresh set of canvases. She wanted the stink of white spirit, ink and oil, and the smell of his righteous rage when the work was not going right. She would sneak inside his studio and preserve what he did. Someone must. She loved him. If he went back to prison, it would surely not be for long and the child would tie him to her. She had earned her spurs. Who would believe the fat man?

He crossed to the window, looked down, cigarette burning with its comforting drift of smoke. She would always see him thus, free of grief for a moment, letting the laughter light his face, smiling into the dark as she heard the warmth surge into the radiators with a teeny *click, whoomph.* He began to close the enormous sash window and shut out the dark, looking down as he did so at that stupid silver eagle caught in the tree, clutching at the branches like a last survivor against the stiffening wind.

"The lawyers want me to help organize their art collection, did I tell you? Strange people, they are. At least half human."

"Come inside," she said, "you'll get cold. And don't worry about the charges. It'll come to nothing. You've the best legal help. Andrew Whatsit and Matthewsomething. The best."

"I'd rather Sarah."

"She's a witness, lovey. She can't do both. And . . . well, she wasn't the best lawyer, was she? An amateur compared to these. They're the *real* experts."

The wind shook the branches and the silver eagle crashed to earth with all the aplomb of a sparrow. They watched it land on the barren January grass, alongside the painting of the mouth.

"Got a message from William. He says come and see him. You've got to take special care of your teeth when you're having a baby. So I said you'd go, all right?"

No. No one who knew us in another life is going to know us now. He would not believe it, but that was exactly what was going to happen. She had absolutely no doubt about it. There were other dentists.

But that was only one husband, who would never know how much he was loved, and only one baby. She would do anything to preserve them from the past. There was only the future.

"Perhaps I wouldn't mind so much if I hadn't just painted it," William quipped to the patient, a man who expressed only the mildest curiosity concerning the changed décor of the premises of his dental surgeon. The patient accepted without demur the explanation of a minor gas explosion of a purely domestic nature, ignoring any coincidence between this and a story he might have read in a newspaper, because it suited him to do so. The dentist's problems were peripheral to his own toothache and quiet dread of the drill. Conversation was not what he wanted. William could answer questions about the changed state of his rooms quite casually once he had decided that a minor gas explosion was really what everyone wanted it to be, marvelling at the speed of the repairs and blessing his insurance company. There was only the memory of blood on the floor, and the consequent need for the place to be reconsecrated, as if it were a church.

Cannon's bomb had avoided the essentials, a straight line of damage removing the window, making the hole in the floor, then leaving the souvenir fires, which did the greatest harm. A decorative disaster. William was surprised to find that he did not mourn the destruction of the pictures in the way he had always imagined he might when he visualized theft or vandalism. Perhaps possessions really did not matter; perhaps the life in the lost paintings, even Cannon's piece of beauty, were pieces of borrowed life and never owned by anyone at all. The bareness of the walls was an excuse to start again, take a different direction; think anew. The drawing of his hands still occupied the prime position opposite the chair. He hated it there: it was a reminder of what he had done, and that was why it would remain.

Nightmares jumbled into long, weird narratives and recriminations. What *else* could he have done? The girl-child with the missing teeth, the boy with the amalgam stuck in his lungs frolicked into his dreams along with John Smith, smiling with an empty mouth, and Sarah, who had never told him anything. If *only* she had told him about Cannon's twin none of this would have happened. But, then, why should she infect him with dangerous knowledge? Guilt was so much worse when there was no one to blame.

"Right, all finished. Don't eat anything hot or solid for the rest of the day." The patient scuttled away; a face forgotten.

He was trying to remember if he had actually received a message from Sarah not to contact her, or whether it had simply been a friendly directive from a police officer that it was better they should not for fear of each contaminating the story of the other, he supposed. No collusion. The yearning to see her, numbed in the beginning by the appalling knowledge of the exquisite pain he had caused, however careful he had been in its infliction, grew in intensity, not only every day but every minute of every day. Seeing Pauline had been a pale substitute.

There was so *much* requiring explanation, irking him, the relevant nudging at the irrelevant, elusive memory getting in the way. Such as Cannon's Diconal murmurs. Remembering the day he had asked conversationally in a line of chat during that one-minute interval between the needle in the arm and the onset of oblivion, not really expecting a reply, *Do you have any children, Mr. Smith?*

The ramblings that had followed in his sleep. *No kids, not yet. Tried for a year. Think I'm firing blanks.* William thought of Cannon with intense affection and not a little envy, tinged with regret for a bizarre friendship suspended into a dim, fading promise.

He sat in the reception room on one of two borrowed chairs, looking at the fresh plaster of the walls waiting for paint. God was good all the same, Pauline had said. If Cannon had not known there was a beloved child on the way, he might have died of grief for Johnnyboy. He quite understood that Cannon would not come back.

A patient had cancelled. The afternoon was young, the decorators due tomorrow, and he was profoundly tired. He was never going to bother locking his doors again; there was no point. He would open his practice to the street.

Isabella crossed the room, heels loud on the paper temporarily covering the floor, sat next to him, waiting with the impatience of one arriving for an appointment promised twice, postponed and now arrived. She had been sympathetic to an annotated version of his disasters learned from a headline, which had been swallowed the next day by a greater headline about a different kind of bomb in the City and a suspected resurgence of Islamic terrorism, William's face and his name easily forgotten. He had refused offers of solace and help, but now, finally, here she was, looking at the bare walls like a person hungry to weave a spell on it with wallpaper and swagged curtains to cover the cracks, beautifully, informally dressed, not quite in command of her agitation, but trying. They did not even greet one another.

She came straight to the point. "William, you look awful. You need someone to take care of you. I told you I was wrong about everything. Can I come back? *Please.*"

Visions of a comfortable nest, food on the table, sofas long enough for lounging. A flat somewhere replete with tasteful design. Wonderful coffee in the morning, beef cooked to perfection, Sunday lunches with friends. Clean sheets, no domestic decisions; the hum of an efficient washing-machine, fine china and fragrant flowers. A dozen irritating tasks per day, supermarket included, abdicated to her efficiency. An organized life. Always a sufficiency of bread, eggs, milk; the daily newspaper of choice.

A brittle body to hold in bed. Magazines, not books. No pictures; no nakedness as they grow older. Conversation of *absolutely mind-numbing banality.*

"Have your gums been bleeding?"

She gasped, looked on the verge of outrage, then lowered her fine eyes to the hands clasped in her lap. "Yes. Nothing odd about that, is there? I mean, what has it got to do with—?"

"Everything," he said. "You must go to a dentist as soon as you can."

"*William!* Did you hear me? I want to come back. I've been so unhappy . . . I know I could make you happy. I did before, didn't I?"

There was no answer to that. Except to say, *yes,* you did, and *no,* you didn't. She would cling to the power he had given her. Given her willingly, foolishly, completely, so that he could not even blame her for wielding it. Or failing to believe it had ended. It was never a question of her releasing him from the spell; it was he who had to dispel his own illusions.

"You can't come back," he said loudly. "Because I love someone else. I've loved her for a long time."

There was a new kind of silence after Isabella had left and he remained where he was, sitting in the chair and looking at the empty wall. Not crossing to the window to watch her go across the street. A free, uncluttered silence, as if there was one less thing buzzing round in his head and the traffic outside had ceased out of sheer respect for his sudden clarity of mind. All he could feel was relief. At least now he knew, and even if the knowledge came too late, it was still of a joyful kind. He closed his eyes, and thought briefly of what colour he should have for the walls. Remembered he had chosen the total anonymity of white and thought, I can do better than that. The outer door creaked again. Someone stood by the desk, just out of sight. He thought, with mild frustration, She's come back . . . I'll have to say it all again. Leave me alone. He squeezed his eyes shut, clenched his fists, felt tired.

"Mr. Dalrymple? You haven't changed. Remember us?"

He opened his eyes. A trio. One large mother and two golden teenagers, all smiling as if posed for a camera.

"Mr. Dalrymple . . . we've been looking for you for years. Moved away, you know how it is? Couldn't find you, lost your card. Then I saw your name in the paper, and thought, *There* he is. So I brought them back to re-enlist. You remember my children, don't you? Are you all right, Mr. Dalrymple?"

The girl, flashing fine symmetrical teeth, no gaps, her face as pretty as her early promise had suggested; the boy, bored, tall, healthy, with the build of an athlete and cheeks like rosy apples, looking like a youth who might have accidents, but never illnesses.

"Never had a single problem since you sorted them out," the mother said proudly, as if this was solely his achievement and nothing to do with their inheritance. "So we came back."

I took out the *right* teeth for that pretty little girl. If that boy Adrian had ever swallowed amalgam, it did not hurt him.

He recognized a moment of profound happiness, which was similar to standing under a hot shower and sluicing off the stickiness of the day. He struggled to his feet, hand outstretched with not a tremor in it. "I'm very pleased to see you. Of course I remember you. Very well indeed. Shall we make an appointment?"

The second dentist, a professor organized by the investigators, had told her that there would be no long-term damage. He must be a man with steady hands, he told her, able to think as he worked; an excellent and creative surgeon. Sarah tried to distract herself with the reflection that this was the only time she would be examined by a professor without paying for it. Holes in bones are nothing more than holes in bones; they heal, he said. Everything in the mouth heals, even with infection, and you have none of that. Tell me, what did he use? How long did this *procedure* take? Purely scientific interest, you understand. What happened to you is of far less importance than *how* it was done.

That was the way it was: they all had the mindset of engineers exploring either a problem or the history of it. She found it difficult to be pleased that someone so admired dear William's skill. Then, with the looming of the terrible empty week between Christmas and New Year, a time when in previous years she would have lain deliciously low with a crate of wine, she hated his skill; forgot she had encouraged him to use it; forgot she had, in one sense, volunteered, and that *yes*, she had understood what he was doing and why, forgot everything but dull, residual pain, a sense of violation, night sweats and nightmares. The knowledge of being nothing but an *it*. A piece of flesh vandalized for a purpose. She had hated him then.

When the second dentist asked her to open her mouth, she could not do it at first. Whimpered and refused, her tongue pushing at clenched teeth. The touch of his instruments and the closeness of his scrutiny were little kisses of horror. Even his hand, powerful, broad and dry, shaking her own on leaving, had felt like a claw. Better the devil you know, with hands like a pianist.

On the fifth or sixth of January, she could not recall which, since the days were blurred, punctuated by nothing more than darkness and light and the obliteration of messages on the answer-machine, she walked down the road in the early-morning dark and put the remainder of the Valium prescription into a rubbish bin. Shoved some noxious household rubbish on top, so that she would not be tempted to return and fish through it later, wiped her hands on her trousers and went home and washed her hair. Took every single picture off the walls, dusted them and propped them in layers in doorways, according to size. It took brute strength and hammer blows to dislodge the nails supporting the lifelong friends. Then she sorted out the contents of her wardrobe, preserving only what she loved best and putting the rest into sacks. Her labelling of these was precise, laborious and clear. There were good clothes, not so good clothes, and clothes so mistaken, so shrunken, so far too well worn no one would benefit from their existence, kept out of sentiment or laziness. She piled the last category on the kitchen floor and systematically cut them into very small pieces with a pair of sharp scissors. Then she threw the kitchen plates she had always disliked out of the window at the back, listened to them break in the back garden. *Good.*

Tomorrow she would go and see if she could find that red dress in the sale. She knew it would be there. Opened the wine; wrote notes in a small, crabbed hand.

William is one of the nicest men you could ever meet. You can't stand the fact that he hurt you, even though it was a situation where you knew, and he knew, that there was no choice.

He couldn't love me and do what he did. Yes, he could. He saved you from worse. What do you think you've done to him? What does it feel like to be a torturer? Is it worse than being tortured?

It achieved something . . . didn't it? YES. The survival of a partnership; the possible survival of a child.

No matter which child.

Earlier in the afternoon she had taken the painting Cannon had lifted from the exhibition to the post office. Sent it, carefully overwrapped, to the dealers described on the label on the back.

That was the day before Julie came round, cool on the heels of the policeman who wanted to check with her what the fat man had said and then retracted. Spoke a whole lot of rubbish and then took it back, troubled first by conscience, then by fear of the consequences. Julie, sitting in the corner of the barren living room, looking at the ragged holes in the walls where the pictures had been. Julie, hell-bent on the survival of what was hers and knowing beyond doubt that the pursuit of love justified everything and anything, wanting co-operation, looking at Sarah as if she was an *it*. Thanking her as if she was a stranger, relieved to see she looked *normal*. Asking odd, airy questions about inheritance between brothers, DNA between twins and a mixed bag of queries that showed an overburdened mind in an anxiously pregnant body and making her final announcement on leaving. They were the same height when they stood up to say goodbye, like actresses paired for a part. Julia made the final announcement.

Cannon says William loves you. He'll never stop, Cannon says. You mustn't let Johnnyboy win with him too, you know.

In the silence, Sarah lit another of the cigarettes which were bad for her teeth, blew a defiant smoke ring into an empty room.

If William thought he loved her, he had better fight for it. She could not quite stop crying and she was not going to try any more. If he could not recognize her from closer than three paces, no one could. And in the absence of that close scrutiny of love, liking would suffice. It was recognition that mattered.

Yes, it was worth it. Even with the lies.

They were all safe. If there were any thanks, she had not asked for them anyway. She would keep the secrets. Begin all over again, with an empty slate.

Julie found a church on the way home. A silent place, empty of people. She needed to pray.

Listen, Lord, forget it. He raped me, right? Got that? He came round with his fat mate and his pillow-case, put that over my head, no lie about that, told me to get lost and I told him get lost too. Stood three yards away and told me Cannon would never be able to get a kid, said he tried hard enough with all those other girls when he was younger, never stopped trying, if you get my meaning. Obsessed with babies. Nothing happened. That's what Johnny said. You want one, better be mine, be mine, be mine . . . that's what he would want . . . you aren't enough to keep him. Who do you think you are?

And I believed him, Lord, for a minute. Let him take me from behind so he didn't have to look. Then he went mad with disgust and I went mad too, because I must have been insane to think Cannon would never stay with me without a baby. Or think there had been other girls. Anyone with Cannon for a second would know there were never any other girls. I dived over the stairs; I threw myself against walls; I clawed at my skin, long after they hit me. I screamed at him and he laughed. I know whose baby this is. Does it matter, Lord? Blood tests wouldn't tell, because the blood will be the same, and even You don't know, do you? Fine God you are. Cannon wanted something to remember him by. Now he has it. And I love him.

Is that all right, Lord?

The bubble of happiness blew as large as a balloon and drifted away. She does not want to see me, or maybe she does. She forgives me, or maybe she doesn't. The decorators come tomorrow and I shall not have the walls painted white. I am still wearing my gloves.

William reached the green across the road from her flat, sprinted across, rang the bell. No preliminary phone call, like other men, he was simply *here*. Muttering under his breath the opening line, "Anything you want fixing, lady?"

Empty. SOLD written on the board outside. He was always slow.

She had said she was moving. She had said she had fallen in love with that new place, lovingly described. Street name? He could not recall. Description, rough location . . . *YES*. He had nodded when she told him about it, got the idea. There were highly distinctive railings outside; he had a rough idea where he had seen them.

He hailed a taxi to take him back to his own front door. After that, he had to stroll in a way which was precise and casual, because if he was to see her in the headlights of a car, she might be running. He began to walk in slow concentric circles.

Looking for the other sign that said, *SOLD*.